I0672671

The Swedish Bodyguard

Ashley Maureena

Copyright © 2018 by Ashley Maureena

All rights reserved. No part of this publication may be reproduced, distributed, or transmitted in any form or by any means, including photocopying, recording, digital scanning, or other methods without the prior written permission of the publisher, except in the case of brief quotations embodied in critical reviews and certain other noncommercial uses permitted by copy law.

Published 2018
Printed in the United States of America
ISBN: 978-1-7328725-2-3
E-ISBN: 978-1-7328725-3-0
Library of Congress Control Number: 2018965341

Cover design by Ashley Maureena

For information, please write:
PhoenixCrossFire Press
PO Box 962
Frisco, TX 75034

www.ashleymaureena.com

in memory of my Aunt Mary

and all those who have fought and are still fighting cancer

Table of Contents

Part One: America

Chapter One

Laughter and merriment filled the atrium of the South Hills Cancer Center. The sound, rare for such an establishment, frequented this location as children learned to face the ailment which plagued them or a loved one. Today, they found hope in the form of a puppet stage where a skit involving a donkey and pig carried on.

Surrounded by nurses and bodyguards, a family of five walked past the scene. The mother of the family, graceful but aged with apprehension, sat in a wheelchair pushed by her husband. Worry plagued the lines of his eyes as well, and his laugh-lines now faded to dread. Their youngest children noted the excitement of the audience, and, in curiosity, pushed past the stoic bodyguards to peek at the entertainment.

They glanced back at their mother, expectantly.

"Please, stop," she told her husband and the entourage surrounding them. Her thick-Scandinavian accent was still hard for the treatment center staff to process, but those from her native land quickly did as beckoned. "What is this, doctor?"

The doctor who accompanied the family stood on his toes to see the puppet stage. "This looks like the exploits of the pig, Frauline Hamburg, and her donkey friend, Senorita Burrita." He chuckled and turned to the family. "We have a volunteer who comes a few times a week to cheer up the children. She puts on puppet shows, does some crafts and magic tricks, and she even talks to the kids one-on-one when they need a pep-talk from someone they see as a friend."

"And it helps the children?" The woman and her husband attempted to see past the crowd of children.

"It does. There is truth to the saying 'laughter is the best medicine'."

The youngest child of the family, a boy no more than six years of age, turned to one of the suited men nearby. He tugged the tall gentleman's jacket, causing the giant to kneel down and listen to the child. The boy whispered in his ear shyly. The man nodded and lifted the child onto his shoulders, allowing him to see the show without obstruction.

Inspired by her little brother, the daughter turned to her father who obliged and held her aloft to watch the show. She hugged his neck as she watched Senorita Burrita hand a bouquet of flowers to Frauline Hamburg. The pig ate the flowers. The children in the audience were delighted. The show ended, and the puppets disappeared behind the curtain. A moment later, a woman appeared from behind the stage to the applause of all viewing. She bowed, clapped her hands, and caused confetti to magically appear in her hands. The children roared in amazement.

The mother began coughing, distracting her family and medical entourage from the show. "I am okay," she protested their concern. They ignored her objection and continued past the crowd to the hallway for her diagnosis meeting.

"In here, please." The doctor held a door open. "There's not room for everyone, I'm afraid."

"That is okay," the father responded. "They can stay outside," he indicated the bodyguards. "Gunnar, come with us."

The tall man whose shoulders carried the young boy moments before nodded and entered the cozy meeting room with the family.

"I've received the results of your test, Your Majesty," the doctor told the woman.

She reached out for her husband's hand. Their eldest, a teenage son, stood quietly behind them, visibly upset about the situation. He had found no joy in the puppets or magic of the show. The youngest children clung to Gunnar, uncertain of everything happening.

"How bad is it?" The husband asked the firm words, but his voice trembled in fear.

The doctor held up his tablet to the couple. "The cancer has progressed significantly in the body." He used a stylus to indicate the areas of the body touched by the disease. "We call this stage four, and it takes an intensive, varied treatment to fight this level of progression. A change to a nutrient-rich diet that focuses on Vitamin-C and K, and a hormone-injection we give, makes chemotherapy more successful in many of our patients."

He continued listing the treatment options, but husband and wife already exchanged knowing-glances. There was a slim chance she would live.

"How long do I have, doctor?" she interrupted him.

"We will do everything in our power to prolong your life and ensure you a high quality of living..."

"How long?" she repeated firmly.

The doctor sighed. "Only a few months if left untreated."

The reality of the doctor's statement caused the husband to cover his mouth and pace the room. He did everything in his power to stop the tears that wished to overwhelm him. Gunnar hung his head and held the children close.

"But with treatment, we can target these cells, slow the spreading," the doctor continued.

"Slow it, not eradicate it," she clarified.

"I cannot promise eradication, but it has happened before."

"And would I have to live here to receive such treatments?"

"For our most intensive treatments, as this would require for success, yes." The doctor nodded. "We would need to have you here almost daily."

The woman studied her family, slowly processing the news and their reactions. "You understand why I cannot do that. I cannot abandon Sweden."

Her husband knelt at her side and began speaking urgently in Swedish.

The doctor shifted uncomfortably. Of all the bad news he had to give, he never had to do so to royalty. The spread of the cancer would be far more than the Queen's body – it would be spreading through a pillar of an entire country.

The queen kissed her husband's cheek but shook her head. "I can follow this diet at home, surely?" she asked the doctor.

"Yes. We can send you home with information, recipes, whatever your cooks will need to prepare. I highly recommend you hire a nutritionist if you do not have one already. I will make calls to colleagues and see what we can do to set you up with treatments in Sweden and Norway. But I do recommend a monthly visit to our facility here, if possible."

"Yes," the king responded. "Yes, we will do that."

"Let me see what I can find out from Sweden, and I will return shortly." The doctor left the room, offering a sorrowful smile to the children as he did so.

The Queen instructed her oldest son in their native language, "Niklas, take your brother and sister out into the hall. I need to speak with your father and Gunnar alone."

He began to protest, but opted instead to do his mother's bidding.

Once alone with his wife and bodyguard, the king began to cry. Gunnar, on the verge of tears himself, found a box of tissues and handed it to the man. He took the seat the doctor had used, unsure what to say to comfort the man and woman he had protected for his entire career.

"We cannot fool ourselves," the queen told them. "Short of a divine miracle, I will die. We must prepare for this."

"We are going to fight this, my love." The king sat beside her, taking her hand once more. "I would move the family here, if you would not be so stubborn."

"Roffe, we cannot leave Sweden. Niklas cannot leave. Royalty may not carry the same responsibilities as before, but there are still responsibilities. We cannot ignore those. We serve Sweden."

"I would abdicate the throne to save you Jonna." He pressed her hand to his lips; tears glided down his cheeks.

"I know you would, but it would not save me." She gently used her thumb to caress the subtle dimple in his chin. "We must think of you, and the children. You know how the press will hound them. The paparazzi know no sympathy."

"I'll increase the security detail on them," Gunnar offered.

"They need more than armed guards." She leaned her head back against the wheelchair, inhaling deep breaths slowly as she pondered. *"That woman with the puppets. What about her,* Roffe?"

"You want her to speak to the children?" he attempted to clarify her question.

"I want her to be their nanny."

11

Roffe stared at her in disbelief. *"You hate the idea of a nanny."*

"I must face reality. Imagine, a nanny that already has experience in helping children whose parents are battling cancer."

"But an American? We know nothing about her except what we saw a moment ago."

She nodded her head toward Gunnar. *"That is why we have Gunnar."*

A knock on the door interrupted their conversation. The doctor entered, followed by the nurse. "I'm waiting to hear from my colleagues. In the meantime, we want to set you up in a room and make sure you are as comfortable as possible during your stay. This is Julia – one of our most dependable and experienced nurses." He indicated a cheery woman in pink scrubs next to him. "She will take you to your room and help you with anything you need."

"Thank you, doctor," Roffe told him, shaking the man's hand.

"Of course. We are going to do everything we can to save your wife." He patted the king's shoulder and left the room.

"I was told you prefer to navigate," Julia said to Roffe with a slight indication toward Jonna's wheelchair. "So, if you could, please follow me."

The group, including the children and staff that had waited in the hall, followed Julia down several twists and turns of the center's corridors. "We have a private wing that is currently unoccupied, and Doctor Richards has ensured that you will be the only occupants there during your stay with us."

"Thank you, Nurse Julia," Roffe gratefully accepted the privacy. His family needed privacy more than ever.

"Miss Julia, what can you tell me of the lady who does the puppet show?" the queen asked.

"Brodie Mayer? Oh, she's a sweet girl, and a riot. Comes in whenever she can to help with the kids, completely voluntary too. When she first came, the director told her we couldn't afford her. All the money had to go toward research and treatments." Julia smiled and her rosy cheeks wrinkled. "She understood, but insisted the kids needed more than medicine. She volunteered herself. I think it's because of her we started building up our psychological and spiritual needs department. She made everyone realize there's more to people to heal than what can be read on charts."

"She sounds like a very wise woman," Roffe agreed. "And she is still a volunteer?"

"We push for her to be hired on as a full-time staffer. The board still hasn't bought-in. They can understand a clinical psychologist and a chaplain, but they can't see the power in a magic trick or a puppet show. They don't realize she talks with the kids too, when they refuse to see our psychologist or chaplain, which is quite often." They walked through double doors. "This is the entrance to the private hall. Everything from these double doors down to the emergency exit at the end of the hall is yours. We'll put you in this room, but there are also restrooms down the hall for your group to use and a lounge area with televisions, coffee, and vending machines."

She opened the door to the room for Roffe to wheel Jonna in. The room was spacious, with a large window overlooking the gardens below. Plush armchairs sat at the window near a hospital bed with a thicker mattress than most. Marble counters held a serving tray with glasses and a metal ice bucket. A television was mounted on the wall and beneath it sat a marble-topped desk with electrical sockets and internet connection at the ready.

The younger two children hurried to the window, ogling over the garden and its fountain.

"We have a gown for you to change into..." Julia stated.

"Thank you, Miss Julia. But I must speak with someone first." She indicated the chairs. "I will sit in these until then." Roffe helped her to her feet and guided her to the chairs.

Julia hurried about the room, letting them know where extra linens, pillows, and blankets could be found, the restroom's conveniences, how the television control worked, and any other amenity she could think of. "I will give you some time alone. Press the red button if you need me. My station is across the hall from the lounge I pointed out earlier."

The family offered their thanks.

"*I wish to speak with* Brodie Mayer," the queen told Gunnar after Julia's departure. Roffe's brow furrowed in concern.

"You don't want me to run a background check first?" the bodyguard asked.

"You may do that later. While I'm here, I wish to speak with her."

He bowed slightly and left the room.

"Look at the fountain father!" The daughter pointed at the water feature and smiled at her father. "It's like ours at home. And look over there, they have a castle!"

Her father laughed. "You live in a castle, Kjerstin. One that is a bit bigger than their castle."

"Can we go play in it father. Please?" she implored.

Roffe regarded his wife. She nodded. "I wish to speak to her alone. Take the children and tour. I saw a mural in the atrium as well."

14

He kissed her cheek and rounded up his children, leading them out of the room. Two of the security detail in the hall followed them.

The queen, finally alone in her room, began to weep.

Brodie Mayer sat at a child-sized table in one of the treatment center's "Kid zones". Several children sat with her, coloring paper crowns supplied for them. "What country are you going to be the prince of?" she asked one young boy who vigorously colored his crown gray and red.

"Russia!" he shouted. "And I'm going to ride around on a bear."

She chuckled. "A bear? That sounds fierce!"

Another girl, her hair long gone from chemotherapy, chimed in. "Well, I'm going to be princess of Australia and lead an army of kangaroos."

"I want a unicorn!" another girl exclaimed.

Brodie finished coloring her seafoam green and purple crown. "I am going to be a princess of Atlantis and ride around on a giant stingray, like a surfboard. What do you think?"

"Are you going to be a mermaid?" the Princess of Australia asked.

"What if I said that I grow a mermaid tail when I enter the water?"

The Prince of Russia gave her a skeptical look. "If you are a mermaid, then you can speak dolphin, right?"

A staff member walked toward the table with Gunnar. He motioned for the bodyguard to wait and let Brodie finish. To answer the Prince of Russia's question, she squeaked out the high-pitch shrieks dolphins were known for, ending in a flutter. The kids nearly fell out of their chairs from their mirth.

"She is a mermaid!" exclaimed a boy who had until then been silent.

"I am!" Brodie responded. "And look what I found last time I was out at sea." From her oversized tote bag, she revealed a miniature treasure chest. The children stopped coloring in order to watch her in wonder. "Inside is an empty, purple pouch." She opened the chest and took out the velvet pouch, showing all the children that the bag was indeed empty. The skeptical Prince of Russia reached into the bag for confirmation. "But when I put the pouch back in the chest, and hold it above my head..." she performed the actions as she spoke, "... then blink one time, a jewel will appear in the bag. However, if we all blink ten times many jewels will appear. Are you ready to blink with me?" The kids joined her in blinking and counting to ten. "Alright! Let's get those jewels for our crowns!"

She set the treasure chest down on the table and opened it all for all the children to see its contents. The purple, velvet pouch bulged with visible proof of its contents. "Wow!" the children shouted.

Brodie poured the jewels onto the center of the table. "Now, these are special crown-making jewels. The back is flat and if you pull the white cover off, it's sticky so you can plop it right on your crown." She used a few of the craft-store gems on her crown to demonstrate. "Let's see if you can finish your crowns with gems!"

The youngsters eagerly followed her lead.

"Excuse me Brodie," the staff member with Gunnar called to her. "This guy wants to talk with you."

She took her flat paper crown and handed it to the man. "Alright everyone. I have to return to the sea, but Erik here is going to show you how to finish your crowns."

They hugged her and lamented her departure.

"How can I help you?" she asked Gunnar, shouldering her giant tote bag and treasure chest.

"One of the patients at this facility is Jonna af Victorsson, Queen of Sweden. She wishes an audience with you."

"Um... is this a joke?" Brodie could not comprehend royalty being in her town's cancer treatment center, let alone a queen wishing an audience with her. "I can't speak a word of Swedish; not sure I can help."

Gunnar folded his arms across his chest. "I do not joke."

She took a cautious step back. "Do you smile?"

"The Royal Family was recommended to this center for Doctor Clark Richards who is considered the best oncologist in the world. While walking through a moment ago with the doctor, she witnessed your puppet show with the donkey and pig. Staff members spoke highly of you to the queen; now she wishes to speak with you."

Brodie stood motionless, letting the wave of shock spread over her. "What about?"

"That is between you and her. Come with me."

Brodie followed the tall Swede down the hall of the center. She had to slightly jog to keep pace with his long, purposeful strides. He wore a sports coat and jeans, and, from her vantage point behind him, Brodie could discern the leather harness of gun holsters. Either he was some version of the Swedish Secret Service, or he was a hit man luring her away. She could not imagine anyone paying to kill her. It was almost as unlikely as the Queen of Sweden wanting an audience with her.

17

"You are nervous."

"What?" She fretfully chuckled. "Why would you say that?"

"Your breathing has tensed. You are hugging your bag closer." He stopped walking and looked down at her. "Either you are nervous about meeting Her Majesty, or you noticed I am armed."

"Um… both?"

He grinned. "Heh. Of course, I am armed." From his inner coat pocket, he pulled out an ID and badge. "Gunnar Nyström, Säpo, Swedish Security Service. I am in charge of the royals' personal bodyguards. Does that put your mind at ease?"

Brodie shrugged. "Only partially."

"Do not worry about Her Majesty. She is," his voice slightly broke, "far too kind for what has befallen her. Come."

He led her around the corner where closed doors were guarded by two men. They acknowledged Gunnar with a nod of the head. The hall on the other side of the door was almost completely silent compared to the normal hustle and bustle of the treatment center. Brodie could feel the depression clinging to the air. She hoped none of the props in her bag would squeak while they walked.

"The Queen will be inside, alone, to speak to you privately." Gunnar stopped at the door. "I will be here on the other side."

Brodie felt that the words were one-part reassurance, and another part subtle threat. She swallowed hard and walked in.

In an arm chair by the window sat Queen Jonna af Victorsson. Her petite frame wore a pale pink designer dress, and a, most likely, heirloom necklace. Her blonde hair was carefully styled, held in place with bobbie pins. Brodie was

18

reminded of pictures of Jacqueline Kennedy as the First Lady. In comparison to such grace, Brodie felt frumpy.

"Miss Mayer," the queen frailly stood. "Thank you for your kindness by obliging my request."

Brodie offered an awkward curtsey. "The pleasure is mine, Your Majesty."

Queen Jonna smiled and held out her hand. "Please, just Jonna. We are alone, two women who can put such formalities aside."

"Yes. Please, just Brodie then." She delicately shook Jonna's hand.

"I am certain you are curious as to why I called you here." The queen indicated the arm chairs with a wave of her hand. "Please sit. May I get you a refreshment?"

"No, thank you, I'm okay." Brodie sat in a chair, placing her bag on her lap with a loud squeak. She blushed.

Jonna chuckled and returned to her seat. "I was fortunate to catch one of your shows earlier with the children. It is an incredible thing which you do, helping the innocent to overcome the fear that accompanies loss."

Brodie, unsure how to respond to the compliment, simply smiled.

"I have been told by the staff you do more than the puppets and comedy. You meet with the children. Connect with them. They say you are exceptionally talented. And they say you do it all for free, a volunteer." She smiled and shook her head. "In these materialistic days, I cannot deny that such altruism impresses me. You are an admirable woman."

Red-faced from embarrassment, Brodie managed to mumble a "thank you".

"Tell me, Brodie, how do you pay the bills, if I may be so bold to ask?"

"I, um, work as a teacher's assistant and cut a lot of coupons. But the staff members here are very kind and buy many of my meals, so that helps too."

"And in the summer? If I'm not mistaken, your public-school semester is coming to an end."

Brodie bobbed her head. "I've put in applications at local stores, but the economy hasn't been favorable the last few years."

"I understand. I ask this because I am in need of your talents." The queen offered Brodie a half-hearted smile. "I have been diagnosed with Stage 4."

"I am so sorry," Brodie gasped. Without thought, she reached forward and took the queen's hand in hers. The queen, although surprised by the motion, did not move away.

"Foolish me. I believed I suffered from digestive distress, perhaps a stress-induced ulcer, and kept silent about my pains. I did not want to disturb anyone. Now they say it is too late. Six months if I am lucky. A year if a miracle happens. Of course, they say we will fight. But how often can I travel to America to visit this center? I certainly cannot live here. Thus, if I am lucky, six months. Not long enough to see my Niklas attend a university. Or prepare my Kjerstin for her first date. Or see my Mikkel's first day of school." Tears filled the queen's eyes; Brodie turned her face away to keep herself from crying. "You see, Miss Brodie, we have staff, but I raised my children, not a nurse or an au pair. There is no one to aid me as I wither away, and no one to replace me. Who will be there for my children? Who will give them hope in spite of their fears?" A tissue attempted to stop the eminent tears from spilling over past the rim of her eyes.

Brodie placed her hand over her mouth, doing all she could not to join the queen in crying. "How can I help?" she choked out.

"Please. Return with us to Drottningholm. Live with my family. Help my children as they see their mother dying. This is a burden no child should bear, but harder so for young royals with paparazzi constantly swarming about."

"Move to Sweden?" She understood the queen's love of her children, as well as her fear. England, 1997, proved how harsh the paparazzi could be to young royals who lost their mother.

"I know I ask much of you. You will be well compensated, of course, and room and board will be provided. I will even direct Gunnar to be your guard."

"Gunnar? But isn't he… over everything?"

Jonna wiped the straggler tears that had achieved in reaching her cheeks. "He is. His work is his life. But Niklas is the future king of Sweden. He will need you, and Gunnar, to see him through this."

"A future king? Whoa." Brodie felt her chest tighten with the magnitude of the queen's request. "I am honored, Jonna, but I don't know."

"Oh, of course. You have family to consider. A relationship."

Brodie shook her head. "My sister has her own life, and I don't know what a relationship is." She stood, bowing slightly. "But I love what I do. Here. I need time to consider."

The queen nodded. "We leave tomorrow. But I will have Gunnar remain until you have reached a decision. He will answer any questions you may have." She slowly reached for a nearby phone and pressed a button.

Nearly instantly, the door of the room opened and Gunnar walked in. "Your Majesty?"

"I wish for you to remain behind while we depart to Drottningholm. Stay with Miss Mayer until she has reached a decision about employment. She is to be afforded the protection of the Royal Family until then."

He frowned, and the scar that covered the right-side of his lip was highlighted. In a low rumble, he rapidly began speaking to the queen in Swedish. The only word Brodie could make out was "Strand" as it was repeatedly frequently, and angrily, by the man. He was not happy with the queen's decision.

Queen Jonna's response was short and calm. Gunnar quietly seethed in reaction.

"You know, I'm sure I will be fine. I can just call when I've reached my decision," Brodie offered.

"There is no need," the queen replied. "Gunnar will be happy to accompany you."

"Are you sure?" Brodie asked, looking at the angry giant.

"This is my happy face," he growled.

Brodie raised her eyebrows cynically.

"Thank you for the visit, Miss Mayer. I look forward to hearing of your decision." Queen Jonna offered her a parting smile and nod of the head, and Brodie realized this was a dismissal.

"Thank you, Your Majesty." She bobbed her head in return and exited to the hallway with Gunnar behind her.

"How long will it take you to decide?" he asked gruffly.

"I'm not sure. If I knew that, I probably would have known the answer," she sarcastically answered. She held her bag

22

close, hurrying to the double doors at the end of the hallway. This was too much to compute without at least a cup of coffee – and she was not a coffee-drinker.

"Ouch. Sharp tongue for a girl who works with children."

The hallway doors opened before they could reach them, and Gunnar raised a hand to stop her. Roffe and his children entered, and Roffe stopped to speak with Gunnar.

Brodie eyed the children, and suddenly she realized who the man was. It was the king, and these were the three children the queen spoke of. Little Mikkel held on to his father's leg, afraid of all the new, scary places and people around him. Kjerstin's eyes were red and puffy; the only daughter of the family had resorted to crying out her fear. Then there was the teenage boy, Niklas. He said nothing. His eyes were filled with resentment. Brodie had seen this look before in teenagers going through this life crises; she knew the feeling intimately.

Kneeling down, she smiled at Kjerstin, unsure if the children spoke English as their mother had. The young girl offered a quick smile in return. From her bag, Brodie retrieved a sickly, dying rose that seemed ready to fall apart at the slightest touch. The girl frowned at seeing the flower in such a sad state. Brodie covered the flower with a silk handkerchief and wiggled her fingers above the hidden flower. She snapped, and the young princess jumped slightly.

Gunnar and the king stopped speaking in order to watch Brodie.

She removed the handkerchief slowly, revealing a healthy pink rose in full bloom. Kjerstin smiled and clapped her hands in excitement. Brodie handed the child the flower.

"Thank you," Kjerstin smiled, accepting the flower.

"You are welcome. I am Brodie. What's your name?"

23

"I am Kjerstin." She pointed to her younger brother. "This is Mikkel. He is only six. His English is not good."

"Hi Mikkel," Brodie said to the boy.

Embarrassed, he buried his face against his father's leg.

Brodie held out her empty hand to him, palm face up. He chanced a peek while she concealed her hand with the handkerchief. Her free hand waved over the hidden hand, and then smashed them together. He gasped at the sound. Brodie lifted her free hand and handkerchief simultaneously to reveal a fist-sized bouncy ball in her palm.

"Wow!" he exclaimed. Brodie handed him the ball.

"Are you a magician?" Kjerstin asked.

"Sometimes."

Niklas snorted. "Anyone can be a magician if they buy a cheap book of tricks," he told his little sister derisively.

His father made to reprimand his son, but Brodie interjected. "You're right," she agreed. "But it's a nice book to own. It's a skill that can cheer up a sad child, or impress your friends with. Everyone needs a hobby."

The Crown Prince rolled his eyes and continued down the hall.

"Thank you, Miss Mayer. I understand why my wife felt compelled to speak with you."

She bowed. "Thank you, Your Majesty."

He eyed Gunnar who stood rigidly with his arms folded. "I am certain Gunnar will ensure you are comfortable and protected until you have reached your decision."

"Yes, Your Majesty," the man responded.

24

The king took the hands of his youngest children and ushered them to their mother's room. Brodie watched them disappear from view.

Chapter Two

"Fancy tricks you have," Gunnar told her. Despite his rough features and occasional scars, he looked genuinely impressed with her.

"Once, I thought about running away to Vegas."

They left the hall to the bustle of the main treatment center once more. "I always wanted to go there. Watch those guys with the tigers."

She was surprised the gruff man was opening up to her. "I've never been, but I wanted to watch those guys too. I like tigers."

He smirked. "You probably think they are cute, but they can kill you with one swipe."

Brodie turned to Gunnar with a matching grin. "Just because something is deadly doesn't mean it can't be cute."

Her comment caused him to clear his throat. "That is the problem with you women. You think 'oh it's still cute', and can't comprehend how you got hurt." He shook his head. "Foolish women."

She giggled at his gruffness. "I need coffee. Should I expect to have you following me around?"

"That's my orders." He followed her out of the treatment center to the bus stop outside. "We're taking the bus?" Gunnar asked in surprise.

"I don't have a car. For that matter, I only have a bus pass for one." Brodie pulled the pass out of her bag and waved it at Gunnar. "We can get you a day pass down at the machines…"

"I don't ride buses."

His bluntness made her frown. "That's not friendly to the environment."

He pulled keys and sunglasses out of his coat pocket. "Buses are filled with an assortment of people. You don't know who they are, what they are thinking, or how bad their day was. What if they leave a suspicious package on board? What if they decide they've had enough with their boss or spouse or whomever is upsetting them, and they open fire to take it out on innocent bystanders? What if they're a terrorist hoping to make the biggest bang they can? It's a security risk." The man put his sunglasses on to counteract the strong north Texas sun. "Come on."

"What's it like to live in paranoia?" she asked, once again jogging to match the pace of his long strides.

"It's great!" he replied in a happy-sarcasm. "I've been in security for twenty-two years, and I'm still alive, despite everything."

Brodie grinned at his response; she had not expected such a reaction. "Wait, am I supposed to allow you to drive? Do you even drive on the right side of the road?"

"I'm Swedish, not English." They passed a few cars with Swedish flags and diplomatic plates. Brodie slowed her walked, expecting one of these vehicles to be the one Gunnar held the keys for. "What are you doing?"

She pointed at the blue-and-yellow-flags. "Swedish cars?"

"No." He pressed a button on the key-fab and a black, American muscle car beeped in response. "No flags. No special plates. Just a powerful engine in a non-conspicuous vehicle. Plus, it has auto-start." He started the car using another button on the key-fab. "I love auto-start." He circled the vehicle, inspecting it from various angles.

"I'm sorry, but, does the Swedish royalty get a lot of death threats? I didn't know it was like some action movie. The president? Sure, I can see our president getting a heck of a lot of death threats daily, but Swedish royalty?"

"They're royalty, sweetheart. There are psychos out there obsessed with royalty." He knelt down, glancing under his car. "And some become obsessed with those protecting them." Satisfied with his vehicle inspection, he opened the passenger door for Brodie.

"This isn't selling the job on me," she responded flatly as he slipped into the driver's seat.

"There is nothing for you to fear, as long as I'm in charge." He offered a wink and grin as he restarted the ignition with his key.

"What if something happens to you?"

"That's why I'm paranoid, so nothing does." He pulled his phone out of a coat pocket. "That's why the quicker you make your decision, the faster I can return to Sweden so I can protect the family."

"I will try to be swift. But it's a big life-altering decision."

He handed her his phone. "Tell it where I'm going." As she typed in the address of her favorite coffeeshop, the Swede asked, "Do you have a boyfriend or something holding you back?"

"No boyfriend."

"...girlfriend?" he asked hesitantly.

"Girls really aren't my type, Gunnar." She handed him his phone with the GPS ready. "I have a job, though the semester does end Friday, and in the education-world, the summer is the time to change positions or locations. But even then, I have the treatment center. I've made friends there. I help people there. I really, really like volunteering there."

He pulled out of the parking space. "You'll be helping the entire country of Sweden if you take the job."

Her chest tightened. "A whole country?"

"Don't sound so scared. Technically, I do it every day. You don't think about how big of a reach you have, you just focus on the job at hand. But those who serve the Royal Family, serve all of Sweden."

"That's very inspiring."

He nodded. "It's from a SÄPO recruitment brochure," he joked.

"That's less inspiring."

Gunnar grinned mischievously. "Mind if we swing by the hotel after coffee so I can grab my bag?"

"Why do you need your bag?" Before he could respond, Brodie frowned as realization dawned upon her. "Wait, no, you're going to live with me?"

"It would be very hard to protect you from my hotel room," he sarcastically answered her.

"I don't *need* protection," she protested.

"Queen's orders."

"Yeah, well, if I knew this is what she meant, I certainly would not have agreed. It's ridiculous. I'm an American; I like my privacy."

"Judging by the amount of selfies and tweets posted by American women, I would suggest that's a horrible defense."

"I'm not one of those women," she huffed. "I mean, what if I wanted to walk around in my underwear in my own home? I don't need you around."

He shrugged and grinned. "Hey, if you want to walk around in your underwear, I won't stop you."

"Creep," she responded with a snort. Her arms folded over her chest to emphasize her desire for privacy. He was a stranger, after all, even if he carried a gun and a badge and worked for the Royal Family of Sweden.

"Listen, normally, I'd rent the place next door or something. But I don't plan on being here long, and I'm not sure if that's even possible. I'm just asking for the couch or floor, and while I'm there, the Crown will cover your expenses."

Rent and utilities were due before she would receive her paycheck from the school, and her pantry and refrigerator both sat nearly empty. She knew her finances would be unable to cover the bills; teacher's assistants made very little. "Fine," she grumbled her consent.

"Good. I promise I'm housebroken." He slipped the car into an angled-parking space off of South Hills' Main Street in front of a turquoise-faced coffeeshop at the behest of his GPS. A group of young people exited the 50's-diner-styled doors, and Gunnar noted the sharp contrast between the style of the doors and the old west look of the building. "This the place?"

"This is it. Our neighborhood's charming, locally-owned and operated coffeeshop." She slowly exhaled, hoping to release the tension growing in the back of her neck and pit of her stomach. Her mind raced with a million questions, pros and cons, and scenarios. The idea of the man living with her, even on her couch, formed a headache-inducing mental storm. She quickly stepped out of the car, eager to see a friendly-face and the rare-treat of a cappuccino.

The Swede looked down the historical street. All the shops appeared to be from the late 19th-century in their form, but each were whimsically painted and decorated to provide a unique, eclectic feel to the street. "Our neighborhood? You live here?"

She stepped next to him and pointed at the brick apartment building that sat at the far-end of the nearby park. The bottom story of the building held more commercial spaces and the building's rental office. "That's my building. It's older, but it's a great view, walking distance to all of these stores and the bus stop. And the rent hasn't shot up to four-digits like so many other apartments have with this South Hills' boom we've having. Everyone is moving here to get away from the big city, but all it's doing is turning our small town into the next big city."

"You don't like big cities? Or you just don't like change?"

"They both have their place. Some things about the big city are good; some things are bad. It's like how sometimes change is good, and sometimes change turns a once beautiful ranch into an atrocious, cookie-cutter housing development." The disdain in her last few words indicated to Gunnar that Brodie did not enjoy the rapid-suburban sprawl happening to her community. "I moved here because I liked the quaint, historical downtown, and the surrounding houses built at the turn of the century by prominent ranching families who wanted an in-town residence. I liked the rolling ranch land, and the peace and beauty it afforded. Seclusion, but still close enough to the city for all of its amenities too."

"I can understand."

"The apartment building I live in used to be an old-west bordello." She laughed. "It has gone through many, many upgrades in the last one-hundred-and-something years. Remaking a bordello into an apartment building is change I can believe in."

31

He joined her laughter, and Brodie noted it was the first time the man had sincerely laughed since she had met him. It was understandable, given the circumstance, but she greatly enjoyed the deep baritone of his hardy laugh. Lines formed around his lips and at the corner of his eyes in his merriment. "I can finally cross old-west bordello off my bucket list of places to visit."

"You have an incredibly strange bucket list compared to mine."

He opened the door to the coffeeshop for her. "Old-west bordello, haunted mine shaft, Snake Island... these things are not on your bucket list?"

"No," she giggled. "Mine is more like, go to Paris, London, and Rome. Take a gondola in Venice. Normal bucket list items."

"Depends on your definition of normal," he winked. His attention quickly turned to the pastry display at the counter.

"Good afternoon Evelyn!" Brodie greeted the red-haired woman behind the counter. "How are ya today?"

"Hey there Brodie!" They attempted a half-hug over the cash register before the shop proprietor raised an eyebrow at the presence of Gunnar. "Who's your friend here?"

"Funny story that," Brodie replied, unsure how to answer.

"I'm her mail-order Swedish boyfriend," Gunnar replied, standing back up from his thorough examination of the pastries. He remained in his jovial, teasing mood and grinned at Brodie to let her know it.

Evelyn shot Brodie an inquisitive, and shocked, look.

"I'm joking. Gunnar Nyström, SÄPO, Swedish Security Service." He shook the woman's hand. "Brodie has just been offered a job in Sweden, and I'm checking out her connections stateside to ensure she is not a security risk for my country."

"Brodie? A security risk? I don't think Brodie would hurt a fly, let alone the country of Sweden," Evelyn responded. "She's a vegan."

Gunnar shot a surprised look at Brodie. "Vegan? You don't eat meat?"

"Actually, I'm a vegetarian," she corrected them, "but no, I don't eat meat."

"What's the difference?"

"Vegans are stricter, and I love milk too much to be a vegan." She turned to Evelyn. "Speaking of which, my usual, but with a cappuccino instead."

"Coming right up. Officer Nyström, anything for you?"

"Please, just call me Gunnar. And I'll take the biggest size of black coffee you have. And that giant blueberry muffin."

"Sure thing." She pressed her screen to take the order. "Is this separate or together?"

"Separate," Brodie responded as Gunnar answered, "Together."

"Okay..." Evelyn eyed Brodie whose face once again turned red. "That will be $18.76."

Gunnar handed her a card from his wallet. "I promise it's good in America." He turned to Brodie and noted her red face. He knew what he had done was a faux pas in Sweden, but not in America. Swedish women preferred to pay their own way at meals, even on dates. The American women he knew were often the opposite, and even expected the man to pay. "Think of it as a business meal," he offered, hoping that the thought of the Crown paying for their coffee would ease any wrongdoing on his part.

Evelyn handed Gunnar his credit card and receipt before turning to make their coffee.

Brodie walked away to a small table next to the window, not responding to his comment. She felt relief that her drink and snack were being paid for by another, but also embarrassment that she could not truly afford a simple coffee and pastry.

"Not the window," he whispered to her. He motioned to a booth on the side of the shop. "Snipers love windows."

"There is no sniper following us," she stated. "There are people walking their dogs. There is a woman with a baby stroller. There's a businessman on his cellphone. No snipers."

Gunnar checked the street and the buildings across the way. Satisfied, he sat down at the table with Brodie.

"I think you watch too many action movies. Your entire movie library is probably full of titles only a word or two long with a serious guy on the cover and a large explosion behind him."

He shrugged. "That may be so, but it's not just in the movies. Snipers, explosions, I've seen it all." He opened his jacket and tugged at the collar of his shirt to reveal a scar over his left shoulder. "Helsinki, 2008. Sniper missed because I sneezed." He motioned forward like a sneeze and traced the trajectory of the sniper's bullet at the same time. It proved had he not jerked forward in his sneeze, the bullet would have pierced his heart. "Overall, was a good day. Helsinki is lovely this time of year."

"That's incredible, and scary." She glanced at Evelyn walking to them with their order. "Wait, isn't Helsinki the capital of Finland?"

"You know your geography. It is. But it used to be Sweden. Finland, that is."

"Right, until the Russians invaded," she replied.

"You also know your history. I'm impressed." Evelyn placed their drinks and food on the table, throwing a smile to Gunnar. He responded with a smile in kind. "Thank you, Miss Evelyn."

"You're welcome, Mister Gunnar." She pushed her red-hair out of her face. "I'm happy for you Brodie, getting a new job and getting out of here. I've been thinking about it myself."

"Getting out of South Hills?" Brodie asked in surprise.

"This population boom is making rent expensive, bringing more competition from international chains," she sighed and slumped her shoulders. "Lots to think about."

"I'll be praying for you," Brodie reassured her friend, patting her on the hand. "No matter what, you stay in touch."

"Thank you." Evelyn returned to her counter; Brodie silently lifted her fork to enjoy the delicious goods her friend always baked.

Gunnar pointed at Brodie's plate. "What is that?"

"Cranberry and chia crumble."

"Chia? Like those green pet things?"

She rolled her eyes. "Chia is a seed that's full of Omega-3's. I would think that a bodybuilding-looking-guy like yourself would know about eating healthy."

"I do. That's why I eat meat." He pulled down the wrapper of the muffin and began eating the bottom half of the muffin first.

Brodie sat back in her seat, drinking her cappuccino as she watched him. His eyes constantly darted to his surroundings, observing everyone. She could tell he analyzed every person and their every action. He probably thought ten steps ahead of where he was at, and still managed to hold a conversation in the present. His years of experience shined in his every action, but while eating the muffin he acted like a young boy. She smiled.

"What? You don't eat your muffins bottom up?"

"No. I've never met anyone who has."

"You know how to properly eat a cupcake at least, right?"

She shook her head. "I was not aware there was a right way."

He used his muffin to demonstrate. "You tear off the bottom half, and then put it on top of the icing. It makes a cupcake sandwich."

"You certainly know about eating healthy."

His smile curved the scar on his lip. "I earn my cupcakes, and all my *fikabröd*."

"I'm sorry. Fee-ka what-a?"

He scratched his chin to think of a translation. "Pastries? Fika bread. What we eat with coffee." He indicated the coffeeshop and where they sat. "Fika is a tradition in Sweden. We drink coffee, black by the way, and eat delicious sweetbreads, and gather with our friends. It's like..." he snapped his fingers as he attempted to think of a comparison she would likely know, "it's like afternoon tea in England. But with coffee. We love our coffee."

"I'm actually not a big coffee drinker," Brodie confessed.

Mockingly, he held a hand to his heart. "What? Don't say such words to a Swede!"

36

She laughed. "And if I told you I don't have any coffee at my apartment, just various teas, would that change your mind about staying there?"

His mouth dropped open. "You don't have... coffee?"

"Not even a coffeemaker."

"I've never seen a home without coffee and a coffeemaker." He shook his head. "I'll have to remedy that with some instant coffee." He blanched at the notion of instant coffee. "It's not the same, but it will have to make due."

"I don't have meat, either." She wanted to dissuade his intent from living on her couch, but could not find it in her to refuse the financial offer.

"That's okay. I'm taking you out to eat. I need meat."

She raised an eyebrow. "You're taking me out?"

"I'm not just here to protect you, Brodie Mayer. I'm here to sell the job to you." He popped the rest of the muffin in his mouth. "Which is why I need my bag," he said with a full mouth.

"Then I guess we should go to your hotel." She took the final bite of her crumble.

"It's not every day a woman says that to me." He picked up his coffee and lead Brodie out to the sidewalk.

"Hey!" A man greeted them with the waving of a flyer. He wore thick-rimmed, square-framed glasses, short hair gelled to one side, and a thick beard. His button-down shirt's sleeves were rolled up to his elbow, revealing multiple tattoos on each arm.

"Friend of yours?" Gunnar asked quizzically.

"Not really, but I've seen him in Evelyn's before." Brodie greeted the man with a smile. "Hi! What's up?" She nodded at the flyer.

"We're having a concert tomorrow at the Farmer's Market." He handed her the brightly colored flyer. Printed in bold letters were the words 'BENEFIT CONCERT FOR SOUTH HILLS COMMUNITY GARDEN'. "Would love to see you out there."

"Wait, when did South Hills get a community garden?" Brodie asked him as she read the flyer. "I would have been all over that."

"We don't yet!" the man cheerfully responded. The fact Brodie was a fan of the community garden idea obviously delighted him. "We've created a non-profit to buy the empty field on the corner of Lamar and Bowie so we can create one. Trying to raise funds for the sale."

"That's a brilliant idea," Brodie agreed. "I like that it will be owned by a non-profit instead of government-run. That way a lobbyist can't sway some officials to change their mind." She winked. "Let's just hope a certain football team owner doesn't set his eyes on the property."

The man laughed. "I laugh only to keep from weeping at that injustice."

Gunnar eyed the stance of the man and wondered if Brodie realized the man was flirting with her via his body language. Whether or not she did, she did not reciprocate.

Brodie held up the flyer. "I'll be there. Going to the Farmer's Market anyway for groceries."

He grinned. "Awesome! Look forward to seeing you there."

She gently turned to Gunnar's car, reviewing the flyer once more.

"Community garden, huh?" the bodyguard asked her as he entered the vehicle.

"I always wanted a garden, so I think a community garden would be a great idea." She smiled. "Not that I would get to enjoy it, should I take the job. I'm putting it on the table as something you have to overcome."

"Won't be a problem. Once you see the grounds at the palace, you'll understand." He grinned at her roguishly. "Plus, I know a place in Stockholm you will absolutely love. They scream vegetarian-hipster."

"I'm not a hipster!" she protested. He snickered a response and continued to his hotel.

Chapter Three

Gunnar sat on the couch of Brodie's small apartment while she prepared for their dinner. The entryway of the abode was too tiny for any adornment as immediately a wall separating it from the petite kitchen greeted the visitor. He could not imagine how she maneuvered her couch or bed around such a tight corner. The wall of the kitchen lowered into a half-wall with a bartop-counter serving as her dining room. Two hand-me-down stools sat pressed under the bar, making the space between the entryway and the living room even more narrow.

The galley kitchen had counters on both sides, the sink on the side with the bar and the refrigerator and stove opposite of it. It was without a coffeemaker, as she had previously confessed, though a worn teapot sat on the counter. An archway sat at the end of the galley kitchen, opening to a pseudo-laundry room. On the left was a stackable washer/dryer unit, and on the right were wired shelves serving as both pantry and laundry racks for her. A mini hallway led from where the living room met the kitchen and led to the door of her bedroom. The entrance to the bathroom was inside her bedroom, as well as a small closet with a sliding-door.

All were tiny, sparing barely enough room for her twin bed, nightstand, and makeshift short bookcase full of used bookstore paperbacks. An antique sewing machine set on her nightstand, and when Gunnar questioned her about its use, Brodie admitted she used it to sew her own dresses. He was surprised at the confession, not because of the frugality of making her own clothes, but the skill required to do so. Never would he have guessed the dress she wore was handmade; it looked professional.

His eyes landed on the small, framed print that rested above her 13-inch, leftover-from-the-nineties tube television set. It was one of Edgar Degas' ballerina paintings, though Gunnar could not recall the name. He had seen it before at the museum in Stockholm, but the graceful paintings of the dancers never held his interest. No other pictures existed in the entire living room. A large bulletin board full of index cards with names on it hung on her bedroom wall over the bookshelf. Aside from the Degas and the bulletin board, her walls were bare.

The woman lived on the bare minimum; there should be no debate about taking the job. Why delay in her answer?

He glanced at his phone, noting the nearby five-star restaurants. Given her meager quality of living, he suspected she had never had a fine-dining experience. Despite his concerns about the safety of the Royal Family, the Queen had given him orders to persuade the girl at any expense. The Queen was on her death bed, and she was desperate. He could not deny her anything, given the situation.

"Vegetarian..." he mumbled, checking the menus of the restaurants that caught his eye. He wanted steak. She wanted rabbit food. One restaurant finally caught his eye: steak, seafood, chicken, and a large vegetarian menu for herbivores. He clicked on the reservation button and entered his name and time. Reservations were set. Now he only had to work on his appeal to the young woman. That was beyond him. He was a 44-year-old man who only knew guns, hand-to-hand combat, and how to manage men who needed discipline. He was never suave with the ladies except for the occasional fling, and his title often filled in the gaps of his charismatic abilities. Even then, he had been long-out of the dating game.

Brodie was neither impressed with his job title nor a simple fling. He could tell she was deeply principled, and therefore deeply stubborn. And she was young, attractive, and everything else that had barely glanced his way in his lifetime.

41

He stood and tapped on the closed bedroom door. "Brodie, I made reservations for us. Are you almost ready?"

"Reservations?" Her voice squeaked, confirming his suspicion about her experience in fine-dining. "How... how fancy do I have to dress? I'm not that fancy of a person Gunnar."

"You can wear whatever you want kiddo." He glanced down at his suit and wondered if he had overdressed. He did not want her to feel out of place.

"Okay, just, tell me how this looks." She opened the door, and Gunnar caught his breath. She wore a nautical-style pencil dress with a white top and navy bottom. Across the collar sat a red bow, matching the red heels she wore. Her hair, up all day in a ponytail, now flowed long, resting in gentle ringlets at the bottom. "What? Is something wrong? Too casual? Should I put my hair up?"

"No," he rapidly responded. "You look great. This is great." He caught himself before he kept repeating the word 'great'. "Come on, let's get going."

"Hold on. I haven't put any makeup on."

"What?" He could not believe her. Her skin looked flawless. "I didn't know you weren't wearing any, so you obviously don't need makeup."

She turned her face away to keep Gunnar from seeing her blush. "I don't wear it often. But I don't get taken out often either. I'll be finished quickly." She hurried back into the bathroom, but left the door open.

"Did you make the dress you're wearing?"

"No. My talent isn't at this level. I got it from... a store around the corner."

He noted the pause in her voice and assumed the dress came from the resale thrift store on Main Street. Gunnar could tell her monetary situation embarrassed her.

"So, tell me Gunnar, will I need to learn Swedish, if I take the job?"

The Swede leaned in the bedroom doorway, watching her wrap a towel over the top of her dress. "Most of the staff speaks English. The only one you'll talk to that's not fluent is Mikkel. But he's learning. It's probably best if you speak English-only to him anyway. Will help him learn the language."

"But say I did want to learn. You know, in case, in case of emergency?"

He laughed. "You mean so you can understand what people are saying behind your back?"

Her foundation brush paused above her cheek. "Well, yes."

"Don't worry about that. If anyone talks behind your back, I will translate, and administer punishment if necessary."

"That seems, I don't know, harsh?"

"You're going to be the special guest of the queen, under my protection. Anyone causing you problems will understand their fate."

She remained silent as she applied her eye makeup. Gunnar watched her quietly, keeping within the doorway and out of sight of her mirror's reflection. "Do you think... will there be problems?" she finally asked as she finished her mascara.

"Not with anyone at Drottningholm," he responded. "Just the lurchers." He noted her putting away her makeup, and therefore walked back toward the couch.

"Who are the lurchers?" she asked, walking out of her room with jacket and purse in hand.

He paused, noting the simple affect her makeup had on highlighting her facial features. "The women who will want to marry the king while his wife is not even cold in the ground."

"Would they really be so vile?"

Gunnar helped her into her jacket. "He's a king. So, yes. There are noblewomen from multiple Swedish houses, and even other countries, who will be desperate to marry a king, no matter how young they are."

She faced him. "What does age matter?"

"Well…" Brodie noted his Adam's apple bobbing hard as he swallowed. "Younger women can by starry-eyed. They don't understand that men in their forties, like the king, are set in their ways. Plus, they want to start a family of their own. Where does that leave the current children?"

"It is my understanding that Niklas is the Crown Prince, whether the king remarries or not."

"If he decides to take the crown. He can abdicate." Gunnar opened the front door, cautiously checking the building's hallway before allowing Brodie to exit. "And I am certain that a new bride would love to undermine the current queen's children so that they do decide to abdicate, and allow her child to wear the crown."

"That's wretched."

"That's royal politics. In Sweden, nobility means nothing. There are no perks for being a noble except you have a few bragging rights about your ancestors, and a fancy title to be used at dinner parties. The royalty, however, still retain special privileges. It increases the desire for the crown even more, in my opinion."

She locked the apartment door. "Huh, undermining the children, they would try to get to me? Right? The Queen wants me in place to keep that from happening. That's why she wants me there."

"Your talents will be needed to strengthen them, especially Niklas. I'm sure you could tell how this is affecting him." Her hand shook, and she dropped her keys. Gunnar knelt down to pick them up for her. "Are you okay?"

"Um... yes. Maybe just hungry. Let's not miss those reservations you made." She marched toward the building's staircase.

"This is why you should eat meat. Protein helps you from getting faint like that."

She smiled at him. "You're like a preacher for meat."

"Missionary. I came to a whole new country, just to spread the glory of meat." He returned her smile.

"How tall are you? I'm 5'7" but in these heels, I am barely eye level with your shoulder."

"198 centimeters." He calculated mentally for a moment. "That's six and a half feet in your American system."

"Wow." She sighed. "I would stick out like a sore thumb in your country."

"Sweden is a diverse country. We're not all tall blondes."

"I forget; you have tall brunettes too."

They reached the bottom of the stairs, and Gunnar opened the building door, stepping out in surveillance-mode. "That just means we should import more short brunettes."

"Clever."

He winked and led her to the car.

45

The car ride to the restaurant was silent save for the local classic rock station softly playing on the radio. When Brodie spotted the valet parking sign outside the restaurant she excitedly wiggled in her seat. "Oh, look how fancy," Brodie stated.

"I don't valet."

"Right. Security breach." She nodded her head seriously. "Can't live on the wild side. That can get you killed."

"It can. That's why people die when they do wild and crazy things." He pulled into the parking lot. "Look at all the empty spaces. We don't even need a valet."

"You're not the one wearing heels," she mumbled with a roll of her eyes.

"I never suggested the heels. Heels are horrible for shoe-choice. You can't run in heels, and those women who do it on television and in movies are liars."

"I don't expect to run tonight."

He turned off the ignition and turned to her. "You can't assume such things."

She responded with a tilt of the head. "I assumed if I were in danger you would just shoot the guy after me."

"I will," he acknowledged with a nod of the head. "But I would prefer to avoid any international incidents, like using my firearm on American soil."

Brodie smiled. "If I need to run, I will simply kick the shoes off and run barefoot. You can buy me a new pair. How does that sound?"

"I will drive you to the shoe store personally." He stepped out of the car and opened the passenger door as Brodie glanced in the mirror a final time. "You look great. Stop worrying."

"I have never been to a nice restaurant before. I don't want to embarrass myself." She accepted his hand as he pulled her to her feet.

"The only reason for that is because men around here must be blind." He slammed the car door shut.

"Gunnar Nyström, was that a compliment?" she asked teasingly, bumping her hip into his leg.

He grinned. "I don't do compliments. I do facts. Now watch how to get amazing service at this place." He wrapped his arm around her shoulders as they entered the restaurant. "Reservation for Gunnar Nyström," he said to the maître d'. His accent sounded thicker than normal. "And I am here on rather delicate business from Stockholm." He nodded toward Brodie. "Give us someplace discreet." His request was amplified with the exchanging of a handsome cash tip.

The maître d' smiled. "Of course, Mr. Nyström. Follow me." The man grabbed two menus and led them to a table set away from the others with a privacy screen. "Do you find this table pleasing, sir?"

Gunnar eyed the room, analyzing each patron, the waiters, the busboys, the location of the bar, the restrooms, and the entrance from the kitchen. "Yes, this will do. Thank you."

They were seated and handed menus. "Might I recommend our house wine? It is a fine Cabernet Sauvignon from Bordeaux."

"I do not drink," Gunnar responded. He turned to Brodie. "Would you like some, sweetheart?"

Brodie shook her head. "None for me, thank you."

"As you wish. Your waiter will be here shortly with water."

Upon his departure, Brodie glared at Gunnar.

"What?" he asked innocently.

"The thick accent. The indication I was your mistress. The no-wine?"

He shrugged. "I wanted to ensure a private table so we can speak openly. And I don't drink. I'm on the job 24/7. You were more than welcome to order a glass."

"I don't drink. I don't even know what a," she attempted a French accent, "Cabernet Sauvignon from Bordeaux is."

"A fairly common red wine. He just made it sound special with his fake, melodramatic accent." He turned her menu to the third page. "They have a vegetarian menu, just for you."

"Awww. How thoughtful of you Gunnar." She perused the menu silently.

Gunnar attempted to do the same, but the words seemed slightly blurry. With a sigh, he pulled his reading glasses out of his pocket and put them on. A quick glance at Brodie caught her smiling at him. "Yes. I'm old and blind," he responded. "I only need them to read small print though." He quantified hastily, afraid that she would find him *too* old.

"I thought they made you look smart and dashing."

"Two words never used to describe me." He held the menu up, reviewing the contents clearly now with the glasses on.

"So... women around Sweden must be blind?" She used his own compliment against him before turning her attention back to the menu.

He refrained from responding, but smirked behind his menu. "Tell me about yourself, Brodie Mayer."

"I am a twenty-nine-year-old late bloomer who worked her way through college to graduate a couple of years ago with a bachelor's in early childhood development and adolescent psychology. My parents died when I was young. My sister and I were raised by my aunt, who has also since departed. Sister lives two states away with her husband and daughter. I've never been married and tend to avoid serious romantic relationships since Barry Ferguson broke up with me via post-it note on my locker in the twelfth grade. What about you, Gunnar Nyström?"

"I am a forty-four-year-old early bloomer who grew up with Roffe Victorsson as his best friend. My father served his father like I serve him now, though SÄPO had not been formed at that time. The king was gracious to my family, and I attended school alongside Roffe, friend and bodyguard, even as children. Once I was older, my father and the king sent me to America to train with the Secret Service. I returned, bringing my new knowledge for the Royal Family's own bodyguards. My entire life has been such. My father has since passed away, my mother still lives, and I have no siblings. Never been married, and, might I say, Barry Ferguson is an idiot."

"I cannot deny such an observation about Barry Ferguson. Though I hear he's a dentist now and very successful." She scowled. "I know it's been over a decade, but I was hoping he'd fall flat on his face in the real world. Guess that was me instead."

"You have not." He put down the menu and looked her steadily in the eyes. "You have a career in education. You help kids freely. You've made a difference in countless lives. Just because you are not rich, does not mean you have fallen flat on your face."

"Then you understand why I was unable to accept the queen's offer so quickly. If I leave for Sweden, who will look after the children left behind?"

Gunnar had no answer for her question, but was saved by the arrival of the waiter with their water glasses. "I apologize for my tardiness, Mister Nyström," he apologized. "My name is Joe, and I will be your waiter tonight. Are you sure we cannot offer you a complimentary bottle of wine?"

"No worries, Joe," Gunnar responded. "The wine is not necessary. But I am ready to order. Brodie?"

"Yes, I'm ready."

They placed their orders, and Joe the waiter hurried away.

"No pets?" Gunnar asked, hoping to return the conversation to a more casual topic. In her desperation, the Queen wished for Brodie to accept the job. But in Gunnar's cautiousness, he wished to learn all he could about Brodie before entrusting her to the children of the Royal Family.

"I never felt I was at a place in life where I could be responsible for another living creature." She smiled. "I have a rock who cuddles with me at night though. I named him Alfred."

"A rock? I'm sure he's a wonderful cuddle-buddy. I imagined you as a cat person; clearly, I'm mistaken."

"I do like cats. And dogs. But rocks are really where it's at. They have impeccable taste in music."

"Rock n' roll?" he asked with a sip of his water.

"Swing actually. I don't understand it either."

Gunnar laughed, nearly choking on his water. "Not even rockabilly? This Alfred sounds precocious."

"That's absolutely atrocious," she joked, joining his laughter. "And what music do you like, Gunnar? Classic rock? That's what you play in the car."

"I'm partial to classic rock, hard rock, anything rock. When Roffe and I were younger, we used to smuggle in records to play on our contraband record player at the boarding school. Rebellious youth. The staff hated it, but when those guitars wailed, we became the heroes of Sigtuna." His chest puffed slightly at the memories. "Now I just listen to the music to get my blood pumping during a workout."

"Sounds like you had a good time in school."

"Didn't you?"

She shrugged. "High school was pretty fun, for the most part. Was the beginning of a new decade, a new century, and a new millennium. The world was my oyster, right?"

"New millennium," he shook his head. "You're so young."

"I'm almost thirty. I certainly don't feel young, and my high school friends have accomplished so much. There's a good chance I peaked in high school."

"Working for a royal family would certainly be considered a peak, in my opinion."

Her finger traced the edge of her water glass, and she nodded her head slowly. "That is true, it would be."

A short silence passed between them before Gunnar cleared his throat. "And what music do you like, Miss Mayer? I don't see you as the hard rock type."

"Indeed. That's why Alfred is a cuddly-rock." She grinned, allowing the sad silence to depart from her. "I suppose I like indie rock and pop, folk, some country, some alternative. Most of the music I like isn't played on the radio. Lots of local artists, lots of groups that are desperately trying to be noticed

51

by a record label so they put everything they have out on the internet. Probably like the group that will be playing tomorrow at the Farmer's Market. He seemed the sort, though I may be judging the book by its cover."

"He was interested in you, you know."

Her mouth opened partially in surprise. "No, I didn't know. How do you know?"

"Body language. I'm very good at reading body language."

The statement made Brodie feel self-conscious, and she fidgeted with her hair, her dress's bow, and the tablecloth.

"You can relax Brodie. I'm not examining your every small movement. We're simply having a nice dinner so I can get some Texas steak." He leaned back and crossed his arms casually. "How did you get into magic and puppets and all of that?"

"Church youth group, when I was still in high school. We were like a missionary group, but not the kind that goes to Africa or South America, or wherever. We simply went to local hospitals and schools, and even homeless shelters, whoever had a need and would allow us. The group put on shows for the kids. Singing, playing music, puppet skits, and magic illustrations. When I was freshman, a senior by the name of Daniel Bell taught me some magic tricks so the act could stay in the show. He told me I was smart, a quick study, and had dexterous fingers, so I was perfect for either magic or a life of pick-pocketing. I agreed that magic would be a safer path in life."

Mockingly, Gunnar began patting his coat and pant jackets. "Is that where my wallet's gone to?"

She giggled. "I'd say 'I wish' but that sounds fairly nefarious, and you're a cop, so... I plead the fifth." Upon Gunnar's quizzical glance, she quickly added. "Plead the fifth, amendment? It's an American thing. Sorry." Her hand went to her head. "I'm going to be a fish out of water in Sweden, won't I?"

"*Låt inte gräset gro under fötterna*, as my mother says."

"What?"

"I'm sorry; I was trying to confuse you with a Swedish saying to counteract your American one. But it roughly translates to, 'don't let the grass grow on your feet'. You can't stay idle in one comfortable place. You have to get out and try new things."

"So, does that mean you try new things?"

He tapped his finger on his chin. "Touché. It has been some time since I've tried new things. My feet may have taken root. But then again, I've never lived on the couch of an American girl. There's that."

"And I've never had any gentleman, from any country, live on my couch. So, see? I'm trying new things. Baby steps." She tapped her nails on the table. "What are sports like in Sweden? Besides cross-country skiing, because, you know, I watch the Olympics and know who kicks our butts in those events, you saucy Scandinavians."

They shared a laugh, allowing their conversation to meander from sports, to books, to politics, to food, and to a comparison of Swedish and American culture. Gunnar allowed himself to relax, focusing on Brodie as a person and not an object to analyze and protect. And for the first time in a decade, he enjoyed an evening out with a friend.

Chapter Four

"I hope I didn't make you deaf," Gunnar told Brodie as they enjoyed a post-church brunch at a busy café a block away from her home. It roared with life as the after-church Sunday crowd filled every available space. The two were huddled together at a small patio table in the corner. He tapped on the rod-iron base with his knee nervously. Perhaps he should have merely mouthed the words instead of actually attempting to sing along with the praise and worship.

Brodie smiled but her mouth was full of French toast. He noted the slight hint of powdered sugar on her upper lip and grinned. The imperfection made him feel more at ease in her presence after his dismal performance during the service. Reaching out with his thumb, he wiped away the sugar. The intimate gesture made Brodie pull back slightly.

"Sorry. You had a little sugar trying to form a moustache," he explained. "Unless powdered sugar moustaches are the new trend in America. Then by all means, I can replace it for you." He reached down to the powdered sugar on her plate.

"No, no, that's quite alright. Thank you." She scooted her plate playfully away from him. "And your singing was alright, Gunnar. You don't have to be self-conscious about it. That's the best part about singing in church; you don't have to be talented, just joyous."

"Except that you're remarkably talented."

"What?"

"Your singing. It was good. You're talented."

Her cheeks tinted pink as she blushed. "I'm not that talented. Did you hear the singers at my church? They're very talented."

"Sweetheart, I'm from Sweden. We take our music very, very, very, very seriously. Your American reality talent shows pale in comparison to our more grandeur version, trust me. Therefore, when I say you're talented, you're talented."

"More things to learn about Sweden," Brodie confessed, ignoring his compliment.

"If you take the job," he reminded her.

"Right." She shook her head and turned back to her French toast. "If I take the job."

He drank his extra-large black coffee slowly before asking, "What did you think of that sermon?"

"I thought it was a good sermon."

"No, I mean, sure, but, that part about the bitter resentment," he stumbled over his words. "What did you think about that? He said something about forgiving those who do wrong to you so you don't return their sin with the sin of resentment. I'm not sure how I feel about it."

"Anger and bitterness aren't good things to hold on to, so I thought it was a very wise message. The comparison to Moses and the Ten Commandments were very spot-on." She thoughtfully tapped her plate with the tines of her fork. "The Israelites sinned, greatly, and he became angered. I can't blame Moses. I get angry every time I watch that scene on the movie. Anger is human nature I suppose. But what he did, throwing the tablets and shattering them like he did – that's when he took it to the level of sin. I wonder if that's what grew in him – the rage, the bitterness – I wonder if it led him to striking the rock and keeping him out of the Promised Land?"

"But it's human nature, like you said."

"Anger is, but I think rage is where we go beyond the anger. I would have yelled at the idiots for building an idol and worshipping some innate object, but destroy tablets God wrote with his own hands in a fit of rage? That's fool-hardy. That's like, throwing a trophy I earned at Barry Ferguson's head because he was a good-for-nothing-scoundrel."

Gunnar let out a short laugh. "Did you really?"

"No, but it crossed my mind. Then I thought, why would I let his actions destroy this trophy I valued so much? We can't let someone else's actions take away what we hold dear. Fear, sadness, anger, all those things make it so easy for us to let that very thing happen, but wallowing in those emotions only make it worse. The enemy wins when we give up the things we love." The Swede did not respond, so Brodie continued. "Kind of like, after 9/11, so many changes were made in America, especially our security, but at the same time, there was a wave of national pride, even cultural pride. We refused to let the terrorists and their sin change who we were. Paris was the same way after the bombings. They refused to let another's sin take away their wine and art and everything else Parisians hold dear."

"But neither Americans nor Parisians have forgiven the terrorists," Gunnar reminded her. "Your pastor said forgiveness of the other person, the one who committed the sin, was the best way to combat resentment."

Brodie nodded. "Maybe those were bad examples then. After all, we've been in a war for more than a decade in response to the attacks. Not to be in a political discussion, but I think a war that's lasted over a decade does speak a bit of resentment." She cut a strawberry with her fork. "Then again, they haven't asked for forgiveness, nor have they stopped doing said sin. They keep repeating it over and over. I guess there's a lesson in that for us. Repeating sin over and over, and expecting God to forgive us. But I digress."

He stared at Brodie as she ate her strawberry. The woman stared off at the nearby window, watching midday shoppers stroll by. Her mind was obviously not with the shoppers, but far away, considering all she had said and what the pastor had said. Her thoughtfulness and wisdom caused him to smile. She was certainly different than the women he had become accustomed to.

"I think it's a balance. We must forgive, but not foolishly. We cannot be blind to evil, but we must not let that evil consume us to the point that we seek vengeance and dwell on that vengeance daily. I think that's where our sin comes in. We become so hurt and constantly look inward in self-pity, that we forget to look up and ask God for peace. Christ said: 'those who mourn are comforted'. We can mourn, but we must allow Him to comfort us." She nodded. "Yes, maybe that's it. We can wage our war with terrorists, but we can't let the resentment of the act consume us. And for many, it has consumed them. Think about how their anger and resentment of the terrorists has turned to hatred. We're not supposed to hate people. We're supposed to pray for their salvation."

"You're speaking to a SÄPO agent, Brodie. It's not easy to pray for a terrorist's salvation, trust me. And some don't deserve salvation." His words were cold, and they sent a chill through Brodie. This was not a man speaking of a random terrorist. This was a man speaking of a specific terrorist he held the upmost contempt for. She wished to reprimand his statement and tell him it was not his place to judge, but the dark glare in his eyes caused her to remain silent.

"So, are you ready for some shopping?" she attempted to change the conversation to something more light-hearted.

"My heart be still. How I do love shopping," he responded with mock melodrama. She noted his words were not as cold as before. "What painful torture do you have in store for me?"

"I go get my groceries for the week from the Farmer's Market." She pulled the previous day's flyer from her bag. "And we have a concert to attend to help get a community garden up and running. I think it's a very good idea for this area. Those who still treasure the small town of South Hills, and not the growing suburb, will embrace it, and the garden can counter-balance all of the urban sprawl."

Gunnar laughed and waived down the check. "I've never met a hippie Christian."

"I'm not a hippie," she argued, though she smiled in spite of herself. "Being a good steward of the earth is one of the earliest commissions God gave man. I'm just doing what he told us, you know."

"Your knowledge of the scripture is far better than mine, so I consent." He noted her writing a shopping list on the back of the flyer. "I appreciate the list. Hopefully that means less roaming around shops, and more get-in-and-get-out."

"What? Roaming is the whole fun of it."

He placed her empty plate on top of his. "We may have differing opinions on what fun is."

"Hey!" She gently nudged his arm with her elbow. "Consider this part of my background check or whatever it is that I know you're secretly doing. I'm certain the assignment isn't just 'protect her and sell her on the job'. You're too high up in rank for that, right?"

"Maybe I'm the most charming member of the team so I was chosen to overwhelm you with my personality. Muscles, brains, and beauty. I'm the total package, *sötis*."

Brodie nearly choked on her tea from laughter as the waitress handed Gunnar the check. "Yes, I am going to need shopping therapy after that statement."

He slipped the waitress cash. "Keep the change. Thank you."

"Thank you," the waitress responded gleefully for her handsome tip.

"The list is the essentials that I don't forget. I plan on dragging you through so much shopping today. I need to know how strong of a warrior you are. Give you time to do that sales pitch." She patted his leg. "Come on, Ragnar."

He followed her out of the café and down the winding streets of South Hills' downtown district. The center of the district, where Evelyn's coffeeshop was located, was the original historic downtown from the late 1800's. Each population boom of the north Texas suburb left its mark on the area, creating a ring of new stores around the old. Each ring bore its own architectural mark. The old west main street was encircled by art deco building of the twenties and the mid-century style of the fifties. The final ring was from the eighties. No newer buildings existed. Gunnar suspected no newer buildings ever would exist if the locals succeeded in preserving the small town feel they adored.

Brodie mainly remained with window-shopping, well aware that she could not afford those items which peaked her interest. A jeweler's window caused her to linger as she eyed a necklace on display. It was a simple silver chain with a pendant made of four hearts that formed a cross as they wrapped around one another.

"Do you like it?" he asked her, pointing to the necklace.

She chuckled. "Of course, I like it. I like many things." Her hand drifted to her neck for a brief moment. "But I would hate to see the price tag on such a beautiful piece, especially given that robin's egg blue box behind it. There are more important things in life, right?" She pointed to a boutique clothing store

59

with a bright yellow door. "That is the thrift store. See those dresses in the window? Same style as the department store, but instead of one-hundred dollars for a dress, they cost maybe fifteen or twenty." Gunnar watched as Brodie swallowed her embarrassment about her finances. "Like the dress I wore last night. You asked me where I purchased it, and it, it was from there. I purchased it for ten dollars and change. I try to shop smart when I must shop."

"Being frugal is a positive trait to have, Brodie," Gunnar tentatively stated. He could see shame fight with the harshness of reality upon her face. "And there is no shame in your situation. You work hard, understand the limits of your finances, and budget accordingly. Correct me if I'm wrong, but those are qualities Texans admire."

"That is true, I suppose."

"I know they are qualities I admire."

She blushed and bowed her head. "I wonder if I should shop for clothes, I mean, should I take the job, as a royal nanny, I can't possibly imagine these clothes I wear would be okay." Her hands lowered to the floral apron dress she wore. "They are, I guess, immature?"

He held up his hands innocently. "I am not one to ask about fashion." Brodie made to walk to the store. "No, please, don't make me shop for clothes."

"Not today. But if I take that job," she warned him, "I will drag you back here and force you to go through every outfit on every rack in that store."

"I see what you've done. Place my fear of shopping for clothes against my honor and duty to convince you to take the job." He took her by the elbow and pulled her in the opposite direction of the store. "I've taken several bullets for my King and Queen, but this may be the cannonball that I can't handle."

"Is it really so bad?"

"Brodie, I've been in a jungle fighting knife-to-knife with guerilla warriors, and that was favorable to shopping for clothes with any woman." He grinned as he slowly walked down the sidewalk alongside his charge. "I must admit those chick-flicks are far worse. Shopping for clothes is painful, but romance movies are torture."

"Depends on the movie. I'm not a fan of the vulgar ones myself." She leaned against him in a teasing manner. "But those Regency-period romances are to die for."

"What?" he snickered. "Those British movies of hormonal women who cry all the time and can't decide on a man?"

"As I recall, most of those movies have the men playing with the women's hearts which keeps them from deciding on a man, and which makes them cry." She lifted her hand and poked Gunnar's shoulder. "Mostly because the men keep secrets from the women and don't share their emotions."

"They're English. That's what they do."

"From what I've seen, it's a universal truth."

"Just like hormonal, crying women is a universal truth?" he jested.

"Gunnar!" She laughed. "That's so cruel and inaccurate."

"You don't get hormonal and cry?"

"Not in public."

"Point proven."

She laughed again, and they continued their stroll down the block, enjoying the warm sun and the sounds of music from the ever-closer Farmer's Market. Gunnar, hands in pocket, enjoyed the casual nature of the outing. Within the day he had managed to refrain from his constant paranoia, admitting that

61

no one knew his presence in the states, let alone the small town of South Hills, Texas. Brodie, on the contrary, wrapped her arms around her waist, staring at the ground directly before her as she walked. Her mind quarreled with itself about the decision she had to make, and needed to make soon. He noted the turmoil on his companion's face, but could not find words to say to ease her burden.

"Welcome to the South Hills Farmer's Market!" they were greeted as they reached the ample park in front of Brodie's apartment building. The sizable field had been transformed into a lively bazaar full of families, pets, street entertainers, craftsmen, bakers, and farmers. A bandstand in the middle housed the ensemble performing their acoustic concert as promised. Banners announcing the community garden fundraiser surrounded the stage.

"Thank you," Brodie responded to the greeting. She reached into her tote-purse and pulled out several rolled up reusable bags. She began pointing out various stalls to Gunnar. "That farmer over there, always, always has the freshest fruit. And so juicy too."

"Fruit must be juicy," Gunnar agreed. "Does he have berries?"

"Absolutely. He has fresh strawberries, blueberries, and blackberries every time. I've made many a fresh parfait using his berries." They walked over to the man's stall, gazing over the baskets brimming with fresh produce.

"Sweden is the berry capital of the world. We have every kind of berry, and they grow wild there." He picked up a cardboard box holding blueberries. "My father and I used to hunt for the wild bushes on our land and bring baskets and baskets back to my mother. She made jams out of the ones we didn't eat fresh."

"That sounds lovely. Is that a tradition you hope to pass on?"

He scowled and shook his head. "I would have to find a woman that knows how to make jam first."

"I think she's over there," Brodie joked, lifting a box of strawberries to point toward a tent-covered booth. "Maybe in her seventies, but I've no complaints about the quality of her work. Wouldn't mind learning how to make jam myself. Every time I see mason jars in the store I think about it."

"Do you really?" he asked with a slight grin. "Let me see, you garden, make your own clothes, and now want to make your own jam?"

"I dream big. I also want to get my doctorate and write a book or two. Have a couple of kids. Travel." She sighed. "A girl can dream, right?"

"She can." Gunnar held the burlap bag open for her as she lowered produce into it. "Brodie, I really think you would be good for this job with the family, and I think the job would be good for you. You'll be helping those in need, and it can open many doors for you. Open doors you deserve."

"I... um..." Brodie stopped herself from responding. She prayed for clarity, but no clarity had come yet. Patience and trust in the Lord dictated she should refrain from giving the Swede an answer.

The duo filled their bags with fruits, vegetables, baked goods, and fresh preserves. One local seamstress lured Brodie to her stall with colorful scarves, handstitched with designs and beadwork. Gunnar enjoyed watching the young woman lose herself in the beauty of the craftsmanship, and purchased one of the pashminas for her.

"It will be colder in Sweden than here. You may need something to keep warm."

Brodie did not contest the implications in his statement. "It's gorgeous. Thank you. It's something I never would have been able to get myself. I mean the price is fair due to the quality, but..." she blushed. "Thank you, Gunnar."

He smiled. "Play your cards right, and I'll get you a face painting."

"There was a gentleman doing balloon animals too. I can get you one of those. Make things even."

"I saw. He even uses a marker on them and did an excellent tiger a moment ago."

They continued to make their way around the circuit of stalls and performers, even pausing to enjoy a few songs from the band. Friends of the band walked through the gathered crowd, offering brochures about the community garden and associated non-profit. They held metal buckets to collect donations to reach their lofty fundraising goal.

"I hope they can reach their goal," Brodie stated as she opened her wallet to find only a few dollars in cash. "It's amazing how expensive land is in this town anymore. The growing development of the last few years has made property value skyrocket. I guess it's good, for the city budget or something. But not good for the people who can't afford it." She frowned at the little she could offer.

Gunnar opened his wallet and retrieved two large bills from his personal cash. "Consider this a token of appreciation," he told the fundraiser volunteer, "for gardening - from Sweden, with love."

Brodie smiled at him. "That was kind of you to do."

"If you don't take the job, then I want you to have a place to garden."

The sentiment of his statement forced Brodie to turn away and set her sights on the band. Couples began waltzing to the music, and Brodie enjoyed their graceful movements with a smile on her lips.

"Do you dance?" he asked her.

"That's one hidden talent I do not possess."

He nodded. "The King persuaded me to take dance lessons for his wedding. The instructor resigned after one day."

She giggled. "I thought warriors were supposed to have grace?"

"I'm a Viking, *sötis*, not a ninja." They left the dancing to the romantics and strolled to her apartment building's entrance. Brodie did not point out that Gunnar had failed to retrieve any meat from the market, but she suspected he had done so on purpose to satisfy her.

Chapter Five

All the lights in the apartment were off save the glow from the laptop screen sitting on Brodie's kitchen bar. Gunnar sat on a stool, staring at the multiple internet pages opened. Brodie Mayer remained the topic on all of them as he performed a comprehensive background search on the woman. She had a limited social media presence: a profile on an education forum, another on a magic forum, and a blog about crisis-coping mechanisms for children. Her background from her childhood was another matter, finding local news stories about her high school achievements, the death of her parents and aunt, and other odds and ends that Gunnar pieced together to give a complete biography of the woman for Queen Jonna.

The door to the bedroom opened, and Brodie drearily stepped out to her kitchen. "I thought I saw a light. What are you doing awake, Gunnar?"

He quickly saved the files and exited his search. "Sorry. I did not mean to wake you. Jet lag, insomnia, or maybe a mix of the two."

She wore a long button-down shirt that engulfed her petite figure. "That's never fun." Brodie opened the refrigerator and grabbed a jug of water. "Water?" she offered.

"Sure, thanks." He took off his reading glasses and rubbed his face with his hands. "I'm used to working long nights and living off of coffee."

"Sleep is vital; I wish it wouldn't elude me tonight." She pulled two cups from her cabinet and set them on the bar. Her eyes drifted to the man's bare chest. It caused her to gasp.

"What's wrong?"

"Your chest." Gunnar feared that he offended her by wearing only pajama pants. "It's all scarred up," she continued.

"Oh that." He glanced down, touching a few of the scars on his chest. "It comes with the job, I guess."

Brodie handed him a cup of water. Thoughtfully, she leaned on the bar, staring at the multiple scars. "You know, they have a cream you can put on scars, and they go away."

"They go away on the surface, but not in the memory," he replied.

"You remember where each one comes from?" She reached out, mesmerized by the biggest scar that crossed his chest and stomach. The cut which caused the scar must have been the deepest and widest.

"They all came from the same place." He flinched as she touched the scar. No one had touched the scars since the doctors who had tended his wounds.

"I'm sorry," she whispered, jerking her hand back in reaction to his flinch. "Does it hurt?"

"No, it doesn't hurt. I'm just not used to... someone like you." Her confused expression caused him to shake his head. "I mean, someone nice, like you. You know, someone who does all these good things for kids. A church girl. A friggin' vegetarian. You're not supposed to exist in reality. You know that Brodie?"

"Says the guy who looks like he's starred in million-dollar action movies."

"Heh. That's flattery." He took her hand and placed it back on his scars. "These aren't made by Hollywood makeup artists. These were caused by a psychotic madman who wanted to kill me. That's who I am. That's all I'll ever be."

She stared at him, wide-eyed at the realization of his scars. "Strand?"

His hand tightened around hers. "How do you know that name?"

"You were arguing with the queen, and you kept repeating the word 'Strand' over and over. It was the only word I recognized because it's an English word too. I checked to see what it meant in Swedish: a beach or coast. I decided you couldn't possibly be upset by a beach or coast, but it was also a surname. It has to be the guy who gave you the scars, isn't it?"

"Yes." He dropped his hand from hers. "Anders Strand. I attended school with him."

"So, he went to school with the king too?" Brodie slipped onto her other stool, lifting her feet up to the seat and causing her legs to be pressed in a V-shape against the bar.

"He did. They did not get along." Attempting to ignore the sight of her legs, Gunnar shifted toward his laptop. "Anders had a following at the school: boys who had a disdain for nobility and royalty, mostly sons of business owners and other non-noble wealthy families. They would attempt to ambush Roffe in the halls, or cause him problems with teachers."

"Why? You said nobility carries no special privileges in Sweden. It's just an empty title with ancestral bragging rights. Why would they care?"

"It's extremism. They're not satisfied that it's meaningless. They want it completely gone, no families being earmarked with the historical titles. But he hated the royals most because the royals did receive those special privileges." He opened an encrypted file on the computer, entering his name and password to access it. "That grew into adulthood. At first, it was innocuous things such as taking to the press, and later social media, to speak out against the nobles, royals, and even the Church of Sweden. But now..." He turned the screen to face Brodie. "He's labeled a domestic terrorist, for obvious reasons."

Brodie leaned forward, reading the file full of death threats, bombings, and his attack against Gunnar. "Am I allowed to see this?"

"Most of it you can find in the papers. Except where I'm involved. And you've already seen those scars for yourself."

"What does he have against the Church of Sweden?"

Gunnar shook his head. "Calls it archaic, corrupt. Pretty much what he thinks about nobility, he thinks about the Church. Doesn't help, I guess, that the Royal Family still attends service regularly, despite the decline."

"Decline?" she asked as she scrolled through the file. Many of his bombings centered on historical sites tied to nobility, the medieval Swedish feudal system, the Church of Sweden, or the Catholic Church.

"The Church of Sweden has been losing about 1% of its members annually."

"Sounds like almost every other church in the world. Angry men like Anders can somehow sway people away from a faith they grew up in. It's a strange world we live in." She pushed the laptop back to Gunnar. "Do you belong to the Church?"

"I do."

She turned to him, stretching her legs across his lap. "What is it, like, denomination? I went to a rural Baptist church growing up, and you saw I attend a non-denominational one now. We don't have things like Church of America, or anything."

"Lutheran." He reached down and used his thumb to rub out the indentations the bar left on her knees.

"Oh of course!" She hit herself in the forehead. "Martin Luther. Reformation. That spread all over the area. Makes sense. Wow, that's a really long-standing Church to be declining."

"Times change, I guess."

She crossed her arms over her chest. "As I've said before, change isn't always good."

"And as you've said before, sometimes it is." He glanced up at her. "Like importing short, rock-loving, brunettes into Sweden. Or at least one."

Taking the job had been the question that kept her awake that night. Prayer after prayer was raised up, seeking God's guidance on the situation. The more she prayed and turned to her Bible, the more she felt this was the path He wished her to follow. "If I accept the job, I can't leave until my job at the school is finished, I've said my good-byes at the treatment center, and I've tied up loose ends like rent agreement, and such."

"Is that a yes?" He eyed her expectantly, continuing to massage her knees.

"That's a maybe, with stipulations, that leans more toward yes while you keep massaging."

"Hey, I can keep massaging. I'm Swedish." He rubbed her lower legs. "Have you ever had a Swedish massage?"

"I've never had a massage."

"That won't do!" He stood, lifting Brodie off of the stool. "Come on, lay on the couch. I'll massage you until you say yes."

"I'm not sure the yes counts if I'm half asleep and being bribed with a massage." She sunk into her couch, burying her head in the pillow she had given Gunnar to use for sleep.

"You were awake enough to read my Strand-file. I'm taking the yes anyway I can get it." He began rubbing her shoulders. "You know we have a lady on staff at Drottningholm that is a full-time masseuse."

"More bribery?" she asked, muffled in the pillow.

"Just facts." He dug his thumbs into her spine, causing her to grunt happily. Gunnar grinned. "Your back is nothing but knots. You are overdue for a massage. My skills only go so far."

"I can get a massage at any time?"

"Any time."

She paused, tapping her fingers on the edge of the pillow. "Okay. Yes. I'll take the job."

Gunnar clapped his hands. "Excellent."

Brodie rolled over to face the man with a smile on her face. "But remember what I said. Finish my job, say my goodbyes, and tie up loose ends. You have the answer though, so I guess that means you can go back to Sweden."

The smile left his face. "Why would I leave?"

She lifted herself onto her elbows to be face-to-face with the sitting Swede. "The queen said you were supposed to stay with me until you got my answer. You have it. You can go home to the family. Keep them safe from Strand." She put a pointed finger on his scar. "That's not just someone to ignore."

He stared at the pointing finger. "I can't leave you alone."

"Was that part of her orders? Like in Swedish?"

"Yes," he lied. The Queen had told him nothing of the sort, but surely, she would agree that Brodie's extension stipulations demanded that he stay to protect and escort her back to Sweden. He could not tell Brodie that it was because he

71

wanted to spend more time with her. In less than two days, she had completely intrigued him.

"Oh, then I'm so sorry. I was hoping you'd be able to return to your duties. I know that's worrying you." She sat up completely, patting his chest as an indication of his worry.

"Brodie..." He paused, awkwardly sitting on the floor, his face inches from hers.

"What is it?"

"I...um... what time do you leave to go to the school in the morning?"

She shook her head. "Right. School. Job. I usually get there at seven. I don't know how they'll feel about you following me in the classrooms."

"I will talk to your administrator. The royal children attend school, and we often stay in a teacher's workroom nearby." He stood, returning to his laptop.

"I do have my own desk in the workroom you can stay at while I work. Bring your laptop. Do your top-secret things." She abandoned the couch, returning to her bedroom door. "Maybe I'll bring you into a classroom if I have to scare a kid straight, especially about our cellphone policy."

"I will be at your disposal." He bowed his head.

Brodie smiled at his gesture and disappeared into her room.

Chapter Six

Brodie sang along with the internet radio as she toiled away at her kitchen bar which served as her desk. Her laptop, two textbooks, three yellow pads, and a stack of student folders sat on the bar. Gunnar worked in the kitchen, peeling and grating potatoes to make *raggmunk*, Swedish potato pancakes. He hummed a deep bass along with her.

"The tune is catchy," he observed. "But the words are depressing."

"Or romantic despite all the negative circumstances of their life."

He grinned. "Always the optimist."

"Not always, but I try." She flipped open a folder and began scanning its contents. "Like how I'm making these final reports for my students that have some issues. I'm being very thorough for the review they'll go through, and so their new teachers and counselors will be prepared. I can try to be optimistic, but I know the system too well. Most will ignore these reports and haphazardly proceed with their school year. Laziness causes just as many ripples as attentiveness does."

"The lazy man's ripples are not from him, but the approaching shark he ignores." Her teapot whistled, calling for his attention. Gunnar was amused at the wide-variety of teas Brodie store in her pantry.

Brodie beamed at Gunnar's statement. "I like that! Can I use that in my next blog piece?"

"Certainly. No credit please."

"You'll be referred to as 'my anonymous colleague'." She scratched a note on a post-it and placed it on the edge of the bar.

73

Gunnar eyed her. "If you know that it's pointless to do these reports, then why do you put so much effort into them?"

"It's the right thing to do." She stared at the folder. "And these kids deserve a chance. If someone doesn't give them one, they can self-destruct. I know; I was labeled an At-Risk kid in school. That's why all of their names are on my prayer board." Brodie referred to the bulletin board covered in index cards in her bedroom; Gunnar now understood its purpose. Her heart and faith was bigger than he had assumed.

"You were labeled an At-Risk kid?"

"You've done your background check by now, I'm sure." Gunnar remained silent as he cracked eggs over a bowl full of flour and milk. "I see you have. Then you know about my parents."

He found no point in hiding the truth with the woman, nor did he want to hide the truth from her. "They died when you were young, first your mother and then your father soon after. Their obituaries were short on details."

"My mother died when I was in the sixth grade, and my father did not take it well. We stopped attending our church because it reminded him too much of my mom. We moved from our house to a motel because the house reminded him of her. Looking at his two daughters reminded him of her, so he ignored us and stayed out at the bars and honky-tonks as long as possible. He let bitterness consume him." Brodie's face grew colder while she spoke. "I sat in my eighth-grade math class, wearing one of my few outfits and looking dirty, I'm sure, when they came for me: my school's principal, our guidance counselor, the county sheriff, and a lady from social services."

Gunnar slowly stirred the grated potatoes into the batter, unable to look at Brodie while she spoke.

74

"The children mocked me that I was in trouble while I left with the group. The teacher didn't even stop them, though any teacher with a brain would have made them stop. I was embarrassed, and afraid. The adults sat me down, glancing at one another, unsure who should speak. Finally, my guidance counselor broke the news. My father had been found dead in the motel room, and they were pulling me and my little sister from school.

"I remember crying, and asking what would happen to me. The lady from social services told me my aunt, my father's sister, was coming to retrieve my sister and I. They attempted to comfort me. I ignored them, asking how my father died. They refused to answer. I prodded the sheriff, and he broke. He told me it was the drink and sleeping pills.

"My aunt took my sister and I in. My sister adjusted better than I. Her young age at the time of our parents' death helped, probably why she didn't understand... still doesn't understand. I was old enough to be consumed with resentment. I acted out the entirety of eighth grade and would have continued into high school if one of my teachers hadn't stepped up and taken an interest in me. She cared too much possibly, but if she hadn't, I wouldn't be who I am today.

"So that's why I care. That's why I work so hard. Because I see myself in each one of these red folders."

Gunnar nodded. "I'm sorry for what has happened, but I am glad you have become the woman you are. You're stronger for overcoming your trials." He abandoned his *raggmunk* in order to walk to Brodie and offer her comfort. "I am no good at comforting words."

"I've already received the Greatest Comfort. But I do like hugs." He hugged her in response, and Brodie melted into his embrace. "You give as good of hugs as you do massages."

75

He stroked her hair, not wanting to let go.

"Seems so simple, finding out a child's interests and using them to encourage the kid. But that's all it took." She spoke into his torso. "I loved reading and cooking. She helped me sign up for our school's reading program, the community's reading program, and some home economics courses that had after-school programs tied to them. It kept me so busy that I was unable to find time to be angry, which is good, because my aunt blamed my father's death on me."

"How could that have been your fault?"

"People cope in different ways. Perhaps unhealthy and not right, but that was her coping mechanism. I understand that now. I don't hold a grudge. I only wish I could have understood that before she passed away a few years ago. We never had a chance to make amends. Maybe I should reach out to my sister for the same." She slipped out of his arms to return to her seat on the bar stool. "Holding grudges is what creates people like your Anders Strand."

"Evil creates people like Strand. But... I suppose that's what grudges are."

"I can agree with that." She flipped through the pages in the folder. "Think I'll change the music though. You may have been right about the depressing sentiment."

He laughed and returned to his meal preparation. "I'm not certain what to pair this with, since you don't eat meat and all that."

"Would you believe it? I once did eat meat."

"Should I ask what happened?" He scooped the batter into the largest skillet she owned. "And you need a griddle."

"I don't make a lot of pancakes. And I stopped eating meat in high school when we were fasting in prayer with my church youth group. I gave up meat as my fast, praying for a cure for cancer."

"And since there's no cure, you still don't eat?" He flipped the pancake then rummaged through the produce purchased the day before to search for berries. He recognized her high level of faith; it would truly take an act of God for him to give up meat –maybe an act of God in the form of a highly beautiful, highly intelligent, and highly gentle woman.

"Yes. Plus, I haven't felt like I've been released from my fast on meat, and, honestly, I'm not sure if I could go back to eating the stuff. After a while, I've lost the taste for it. I'm good with the vegetarian lifestyle."

"Know what I like about you? You are a vegetarian, but don't tell us meat-eaters how evil we are. I have seen some of those in my lifetime." He pulled out some strawberries and rinsed them in the sink.

"All I can do is lead by example," she acknowledged, "in all things."

"Well I'm not eating meat tonight, so you must do a good job of the leading by example. Now get your reports done, and I will have a delicious vegetarian-Swedish meal ready."

She smiled at him and turned her attention back to her work.

Gunnar drove from the school to the Main Street boutique; Brodie, lost in her work, did not notice the route he took until he turned off the ignition in a parking space.

"Why here?"

He laughed. "Sunday, you mentioned that you might need to shop for clothes if you accept the job. You've accepted the job. May as well shop for some new outfits that you think are acceptable for a royal nanny. I'm sure the Crown will approve a reasonable allotment for an appropriate wardrobe."

"What's a reasonable allotment?" she asked, closing her laptop.

"Sweetheart, at this thrift store, I doubt you will come close to that line." He turned off the ignition. "You have a little time to spare for clothes shopping, don't you?"

Brodie put away her laptop and student folders. "I thought you considered clothes shopping some sort of torture?" she teasingly asked.

"Some people are worth being tortured for." He stepped out of his car while Brodie sat stunned at his statement. "Coming?" he asked as he opened her car door.

"Of course."

They walked into the store. Brodie was greeted immediately by the woman behind the counter, and Brodie in-turn introduced Gunnar. "Everywhere you go, you have friends," he observed.

"They're not friends really, just the acquaintances I've made by frequenting the same places every day." She held up a black dress with buttons and a red collar with small, white polka dots. "That looks like a nanny dress." She glanced at the price tag. "Your queen is very well dressed, I noticed. Very, professional? Graceful? I don't know how to describe it. My dresses feel, childish, I guess. That one Saturday night? That's like the only dress I have that looks like a mature dress. Maybe it's the cut of the dress? Like this one I'm wearing is kind of loose, but this polka dot dress is more form-fitting. What do you think? Are sleeker dresses more professional?"

Gunnar, overwhelmed by the fashion talk, stared at her with glazed eyes. "I think you look good in whatever you decide to wear, and you should wear what makes you happy."

She rolled her eyes. "This is why I don't have a boyfriend."

"This is why I don't do clothes shopping," he responded, holding his hands up innocently. "Do I look like a man who knows fashion? I go to the tailor, I say 'make me look decent', and he does. Women's fashion is too complicated."

"I don't want to be out of place in Sweden or in the palace, or embarrass the family, or the children. I need to know if what I wear is okay."

"You should stand out a little." Gunnar paced around the racks of clothes with his hands in his pockets. "When the lurchers come, they should notice you. And they should notice you are different. That you are an American, and you are protecting the children. It would be a firm reminder for them."

She threw her hands up in the air. "I'm at a loss. I don't know what they wear in Sweden. I don't know what would send that message."

"Calm down." Gunnar held up a dress. "Why don't you try on dresses you like, and I will use my years of court-life experience to give you the thumbs up or thumbs down."

"After you admitted that you don't understand fashion?"

He grinned. "I don't understand fashion, but I understand politics. You pick the dresses; you do the fashion. I will merely let you know if they are politically savvy."

"Okay. Let's do this."

Gunnar sat in an armchair outside the single dressing room of the boutique. Brodie, with the assistance of the store clerk, rounded up a selection of dresses in her size and placed them in the fitting room. An hour passed as she tried on the various

79

outfits, posing for Gunnar who offered her thumbs up or thumbs down for each one. Those which received thumbs up were stacked on the table next to him. The clerk kindly lent him a newspaper as he waited on Brodie, and he amused himself with American current events as the future royal nanny lamented over her fashion choices.

Eventually, fifteen dresses made the cut, and Brodie began calculating the cost. Gunnar stopped her. "Don't worry. Like I said, you did not come close to the allotment line." He lifted the dresses and laid them on the counter. "Do you take credit?"

"Yes sir," she answered as she began typing the prices on the tags into her point-of-sale system. Gunnar watched Brodie slowly eye the shoes and purses lined against the brick wall of the store.

"Did you need shoes or accessories to go with these?" he asked her.

"Oh, I couldn't," she replied.

"We want these, and maybe a few more things," Gunnar whispered to the cashier.

"By all means," she responded, indicating the emptiness of the store. "I won't complain if you buy out the store."

Her honest statement caused Gunnar to chuckle. "I'll see what I can do for you." He walked over to Brodie. "Correct me if I'm wrong, but shoes are part of the outfit, right? You want the appropriate outfit, so you need the appropriate shoes."

She trailed her finger over a pair of beige pumps. "These are very professional," she confessed. "I don't know Gunnar. I feel like I'm taking advantage of the Queen's generosity, and I haven't even begun work. What if they invest in me, and I'm a complete disaster?   Maybe we should just forget about the clothes…"

"Nonsense."   He patted her back reassuringly.   "I'm insisting you do this, because I know the Queen would insist. And she would insist because she would want you to put your best foot forward. Press, lurchers, the public, all will see you at some point. She will want you to feel and look your best."

Brodie could feel her chest tighten at his comments. "I'm a simple girl, Gunnar. I don't think I'm prepared for this. You had this all your life. You were born for this. Me? No."

"I wasn't born for this. Roffe was not born for this. Jonna was not born for this. No one can be born and innately be prepared to be in the limelight. We're trained to be in the limelight. We're trained to be in the limelight over many, many years."

"You were trained?" she asked.   Fear caused her voice to tremble.

He stroked her hair. "Yes, I was trained. My father trained me, Roffe's father, The King, trained me, my teachers and instructors trained me, and even my mother trained me. Her training was the most important. She trained me to remain humble, to be kind, to protect fiercely and love whole-heartedly." He slightly laughed. "Maybe I am overdue for another training session from my mother."

"I think you're very kind and fiercely protective," Brodie whispered.

Gunnar placed a stray hair behind her ear. "And you are gentle, loving, smart, wise, beautiful… the list could go on. And while I have no doubt you were an adorable baby, you weren't born with those qualities. Good people existed in your life to help you develop those traits. And you know what? I will help train you to be in the limelight, and Queen Jonna will help train you to be in the limelight. Just as you will teach the royal children many fine qualities." He handed her the beige pumps. "So please, arm yourself with nice outfits."

She sighed. It was hard to imagine Gunnar as her fairy godmother, but at the moment, he certainly felt as such. "I want a copy of this receipt, and I want the amount deducted from my salary."

"That's between you and the Queen. I assure you: she is much more stubborn than I. But I can give you a copy of the receipt for your peace of mind."

He sat in another arm chair as Brodie began pairing pumps with her chosen outfits. As she did so, she educated Gunnar about the professionalism of pumps verses open-toed shoes or wedges. "Not that those aren't adorable shoes, but there is something to be said about a sharp-dressed businesswoman in pumps."

"They're all heels to me," Gunnar joked. He watched her try on a pair of navy blue pumps and admired the slenderness of her feet and ankles. They reminded him of the feet of the graceful ballerinas in her Degas print. "Did you ever dance? Ballet?"

"Not really. I used to have a tutu and dance around with my mother. She was the ballerina. Why do you ask?"

"Your feet. They look like you could be a dancer."

She wiggled her toes at Gunnar. "Foot fetish much?"

His nervous laugh and shake of the head could not mask the tint of red to his cheeks. The sight of Gunnar blushing caused Brodie to giggle. "No," he confirmed, "just observant." Squeaks left the antique arm chair as Gunnar shifted his position to avoid the sight of Brodie's feet.

"I guess I should get boxes too," she told Gunnar. "I think there's a box store down the highway a bit. Maybe they have those special boxes for dishes? I know they're not fancy china, but I really like them. First set of dishes I picked out for myself. Though I'm not quite sure what to do with everything. I mean, if I'm living in the palace, I don't need my dishes. But I don't want to get rid of them because they're my things, and I won't be in the palace for the rest of my life."

"We'll get you a storage unit for your things. Climate-controlled. Indoor. The whole works." He took his phone from his jacket to make some notes. "We can get the storage unit in Stockholm, so you have access to your things too."

"Mailing it then? I hope they don't break anything." She held up a pair of wool-lined boots; normally, such footwear would not pass her consideration due to the warm Texas climate. Sweden would most likely freeze her if she did not prepare. "The postal service has some bulls working in their china cabinet."

"Nope. We can take the boxes onto the plane with us."

"That's a lot of luggage to check."

He sniggered as he typed into his phone. "We're not checking luggage."

"I am confused now."

"We're taking State Flight out when we go."

"State Flight?"

"It's like what your country uses, Air Force One? It's the plane of His Majesty the King." He shifted again in the chair, still refusing to look at her feet. "The Royal Family insisted the use of it when I sent them word of your decision to take the job."

She gasped – she thought the shoes and clothing was too much. "I feel like Cinderella. Not that I'm becoming a princess, but you're like my fairy godmother granting me all these luxurious treats that I never could have imagined."

"Not just anyone can call me a fairy, or a godmother," Gunnar stood and stretched. His hand indicated the wall of shoes. "But if you find any glass slippers, I'll be happy to get them for you."

They shared a chuckle as Gunnar carried several boxes of shoes to the thrift store counter.

Chapter Seven

Gunnar sat quietly on a back pew of Brodie's church. The congregation was smaller on Wednesday night than on Sunday morning, but she had already informed him this would be the case. He held an abridged study pamphlet in his hand that the Wednesday night teacher had passed to everyone: *Overcoming Bitterness and Resentment.* He wondered if Kara, the night teacher, had coordinated with the Sunday morning pastor about their message. Did they know he would be in town, or did a higher power inform them this message was apt for their foreign visitor?

The class concentrated on the first part of the pamphlet, a section entitled "Focus on God". The Swede had no idea what that meant, despite his years attending services. For the last twenty years of attending sermons with the Royal Family, he never bothered listening to the words. Threats of imminent danger preoccupied his thoughts. It did not allow much room for understanding.

He thumbed through the pamphlet, browsing the contents and the bold subtitles throughout. "Stop Licking Wounds", "Fight Evil with Good", "Forgive Those Who Hurt You", and "Be Thankful for What You Have" were a few. He grunted at the notions. Forgiving those who hurt you was beyond comprehension, especially when that person took so much and still wanted to hurt you more. He felt an asterisk and subtext were warranted. "Forgive only if they ask for forgiveness, otherwise put a bullet in their head or throw them in jail." Prior to meeting Brodie, Gunnar half expected to die and reincarnate into a vengeful spirit. That was the future he not only expected, but wanted, if Anders Strand did not find justice beforehand.

"Are you okay?" Brodie whispered. She sat next to him, noting his white knuckles as he gripped the pamphlet hard.

He relaxed his hand. The glossy paper sat crumbled in his palm. "Yeah. I'm going to the restroom." He folded up the crumbled pamphlet and tucked it into his jacket pocket. With Brodie still staring at him in worry, he stood and left the sanctuary for the foyer. His mind whirled in turmoil, so much had happened in so short of a time. The queen's illness, the troubles the family now faced, and the feelings about Brodie which he could not decipher – all mixed together to form a concoction of confusion. Before this, life had been simple for him: Protect family. Hunt down terrorist. Be angry.

Now he felt less anger, less bitterness, less resentment. The answer why probably lay in the crushed leaflet which sat in his jacket pocket. When distracted by Brodie, thoughts of Anders Strand faded away, mostly. Until his whole heart felt engulfed by her alluring presence, and the image of her mangled corpse, like the woman long before her, consumed his mind. Then he would have to push Brodie away. He wanted to gauge her feelings for him, but to what end? Even if she had the slightest affections for him, which was a long-shot to be sure, he carried an anchor around his neck. And this anchor could get her killed.

Gunnar looked at his reflection in the bathroom's mirror. A criss-cross of wrinkles circled his blue eyes, indicating his age and worry. Even the blue of his irises no longer sparkled, appearing to be muddy water instead. Lines formed around his mouth: scowl lines. And his forehead was streaked with even more wrinkles. Where there were no wrinkles, there were scars: over his lips, his cheeks, and one eye. He looked like he felt. Old, ragged, tired, and bitter – the exact opposite of Brodie. Youthful, bright, happy, and loving, the Brodie of today would have been happy with the Gunnar of twenty years ago. The non-scarred, tight-skinned, blonde-haired, blue-eyed youth that laughed and loved despite being in the security business.

He threw water on his face in a futile attempt to turn back the clock. Wiping away the droplets, he squinted at the mirror again. All the wrinkles remained. "Forget it," he growled and returned to the sanctuary.

Brodie was not in her seat, though her Bible and purse remained. A momentary fear seized his heart before he noted her at the front of the sanctuary. Those in the congregation had gathered around her and now lifted the young woman in their prayers. He listened to the words of those who prayed aloud, asking God to guide her in safety and to use her to help others. Gunnar did not know what to think or what to do. Then he noticed it. She was crying, gently, into the tissues in her hands. Why was she crying? Did she not want to go to Sweden?

The prayer ended, and Brodie walked back to the pew, wiping away the remnants of tears. "What happened? Why are you crying?" he asked in concern.

"It's nothing Gunnar. I always cry when I pray." Her response made no sense to him. "I don't know how to explain it," she apologized. "It's just, I feel, overwhelmed by His presence. My sorrows leaves, and peace fills me. I guess the tears help the process, because it happens naturally." She finished wiping her tears away while Gunnar stared at her inquisitively. "Come on. Service is over. You promised me late night pho." She gathered her belongings and headed to the door.

"Brodie!" the pastor called out to her. "One moment, before you go, I feel like we should pray over your companion too. Gunnar, wasn't it?"

"Oh no," she responded quickly, "I'm not sure if he'd like –"

"Sure," Gunnar replied. He felt it could not hurt to have a blessing, even if this church went about it differently.

Shocked, Brodie set her belongings down at the end of the pew, and followed the two men back to the front of the church. Most of the congregation remained in the sanctuary, talking to one another in small groups. The pastor called their attention to Gunnar, and they gathered around the man in prayer as they had Brodie. She remained next to him, holding his arm as she prayed.

He kept his eyes closed and head bowed, respectfully, unsure how to act. Above the voices he could hear Brodie's whispered prayer next to him. Her voice was almost inaudible, but to him the words sounded as if she shouted them in his ear. She did not pray for safety and guidance. She prayed for him to receive healing and love. The words she uttered broke his heart; how could she have known? Tears stung the corners of his eyes. Swiftly, he wiped them away as the prayers ended.

The men behind Gunnar patted his back, and several of the women hugged him. Kara, the Wednesday night teacher, took his oversized hands in hers. Patting them, she whispered, "Gunnar, He wants you to find peace. 'Peace I leave with you, my peace I give to you: not as the world gives, do I give to you. Do not let your heart be troubled, nor let it be fearful.' He does not want to see you hurting, and just as He sends the Comforter to those who follow Him, He has sent someone to comfort you." The woman turned her almond eyes to Brodie who stood a few feet away, talking with one of the women who sung in the praise team. "But you cannot be comforted if you refuse to accept it."

His mouth hung open at Kara's words. He could not respond, and instead stared at the contrast between his leathery, tanned hands and her smooth, chocolate hands that held them.

"You don't have to speak, sugar," she chuckled. "I'm just the messenger. You know who to talk to." With a final pat of the hand, she departed to Brodie and the praise team member.

Gunnar slowly walked to the back of the church in deep thought. He did not know of the Comforter the woman had spoken of, but he did know the presence of Brodie comforted him. Before he reached the last row of pews, Brodie caught up with him, placing her arm around his. "Ready for pho?"

"Starved."

"I warn you. I'm absolutely messy when I eat pho. There's a place in another part of town called 'Pho is for Lovers' but I'm fairly certain pho is for friends. Broth goes everywhere. Good thing we're friends, right?"

Friends. He nodded a response and opened the sanctuary doors for her.

Chapter Eight

Half-packed boxes littered every available space of Brodie's miniscule apartment. Gunnar sat on her couch, carefully wrapping her sewing machine in bubble wrap. She sat nearby, cancelling utilities on her laptop. "One more task down, and so many more to go. Finish packing, pay rent, deal with the bank, set up forwarding addresses... I can do that right? Mail can go to the palace?"

"It can, but it can be delayed getting there. You can use my address if you'd like."

"Wait..." She placed her laptop on the coffee table. "You don't live in the palace? I thought you lived in the palace."

"I practically live there in my office, but I have my own house. Most of the staff have their own houses, only very few live in the palace. Personal attendants, like you will be, for example."

"Oh," she said, flatly.

"What's wrong kiddo?" He patted her on the knee, wishing to comfort her but remembering the word: 'friends'.

"I thought... I thought you would be at the palace. I thought I would have someone there."

"I'm always at the palace," he laughed, "sometimes many days straight without going home. But I happen to have a nice retreat. You can visit it anytime you like." He gently placed the protected sewing machine into a box. "Just give me time to clean it first. It's currently like a boxing gym." He snatched the nearby tape dispenser and closed the box. "Unless you enjoy the smell of sweat."

"Not generally, no."

"You didn't seem the type with your flowery dresses and girly perfume." He slid the box to the side. "Seriously, don't worry about being alone in the palace. I have no doubt you'll make friends easily in Drottningholm. It is likely I'll be alone, not you."

She walked to the kitchen. "I can't imagine you being alone. You're in charge of so many people, and then other people respect you…"

"Those on top are usually the loneliest." He followed her into the kitchen and liberated a water bottle from the refrigerator. "I spend my time immersed in work. The man you know here in America is not the one who left Sweden, and I doubt it will be the man who will exist in Sweden."

"Maybe this is a good vacation for you, to remind you of the man beneath the rough exterior." She loaded her cutting board with mushrooms, cherry tomatoes, onions, and bell peppers of multiple colors. "Plus, it's been nice having someone do the heavy lifting, like at the treatment center. I had no idea my two storage bins there were so heavy with props and puppets and crafts. Lucky for me, I had Mr. Muscles in tow."

"And Mr. Muscles is lucky that in Sweden I can assign other people to lift those bins to the playroom on the third floor." He grinned devilishly. "What's on the menu?"

"Pasta primavera." She patted his arm. "Did I mention it's been nice having someone to cook with?"

He gazed down at her, the devilish grin remaining. "What would you have me do, *chef*?"

"Rinse and slice." She slid her knife set to him and turned to her pasta containers. Her fingers tapped the sides of the canisters until she found the one labeled 'farfalle'.

"Will you miss cooking, once you have a professional cook preparing your meals?"

"Sometimes, I'm certain. When busy with work, I'm sure their preparation will be a time saver, and as a professional, I'm sure the food will taste better." She shrugged as she filled a pot with water. "But you have to admit, cooking can be fun."

"When not cooking alone." He smiled at her. "I hate cooking alone. I couldn't tell you the last time I cooked in my own kitchen. It's much more fun to have someone to talk to, or sing, or dance."

"I thought you don't dance."

He raised his hands innocently. "Who knows what can happen?" He commenced to slicing the vegetables.

Brodie grabbed her phone, turning on music. "Show me what can happen."

"What? I thought I was to rinse and slice."

She gently put a hand on his knife-wielding hand. "Come on Gunnar. This is your vacation away from yourself. Show off some moves."

His face turned red in embarrassment. "Brodie... come on." Her hand eased the knife from his. "I'm not sure this is a good idea."

She ignored his protests, moving to the music. They started to dance, awkwardly at first, but gradually finding a rhythm together to the music. "You're not too bad at this," she joked.

"Not too good either. Just know you'll meet a horrible fate if you tell anyone about this."

"What would you do to me?"

"Kidnap your rock Alfred and hold him hostage," he responded, matter-of-factly.

Brodie gasped. "How horrible!" She spun around, falling against Gunnar. He caught her, and they shared a laugh. For the briefest moment, both forgot about the cooking, enjoying the embrace. She wanted to say something to Gunnar. She wanted to confess she enjoyed the strength in his arms, and even the faintest scent of his cologne on his shirt. The way his robust hands rubbed at her back made her wonder if he felt interest in her as she did him. But the pot of water boiling over disrupted her train of thought, and she reluctantly returned to her cooking.

Brodie taped a box closed and scribbled 'books' on the side and top. Gunnar lifted the box and carried it to the growing stockpile in the living room. Any item she used for school or the treatment center had remained unpacked until Friday evening, and now the duo worked fluidly to finish packing for the next-day flight. Music filled the otherwise quiet atmosphere, and a delivery pizza supplied their dinner. Gunnar grabbed another box to assemble, eyeing the pizza and debating another bite.

The harsh sound of tape dragging across a box and a loud "Ouch!" distracted him from the thought of food.

"What happened?" he asked, rushing into her bedroom.

She threw the packing tape dispenser down and hurried to her bathroom sink. "I cut my finger on the jagged edge, and I think I packed up the first-aid kit like an idiot."

"I've got a little one in my bag." He went to his duffle bag which sat on the couch and returned with first-aid kit in hand. Brodie dried off her hand with the paper towels they now used in the restroom. She held a wad of the towels around her left pointer finger. "Here." He put the kit on the counter. "Let me fix it."

She turned toward him and held out her left hand. He grabbed her waist and lifted her onto the bathroom counter, causing a yelp of surprise to leave her mouth.

With precise movements, the Swede opened his kit and began disinfecting the cut. Brodie squeezed her eyes shut as the cut bubbled. "Wimp," he joked.

"It stings."

"Wimp," he repeated as he placed a bandage over the cut. "I'll do the tape from now on, and you can do the heavy lifting."

She shook her head. "Are you sure that's a smart idea? Look at these arms." She lifted her right arm and attempted to flex. Her baggy shirt simply hung loose and nothing appeared to move.

"Told you that you were a wimp. I'll have to train you in boxing when we get to Sweden. Toughen up these puny things." He took her right wrist and jostled her arm to prove its puniness. "Little noodle-arms."

"Noodle-arms?" she asked with a pout.

He grinned and lowered her arm, but continued to hold on to her hand. Brodie noted the fact. She enjoyed the touch. "Noodle-arms," he repeated. "I'll have to make you protein shakes to offset the lack of your meat-eating."

"You accept my vegetarian ways?"

"I accept it's between you and God, and it is part of your principles. I really like your principles. Probably should follow some of your principles myself, except for eating meat. I really like steak too much."

She smiled. "Explains why you look like a slab of beef." Her bandaged hand made a fist and lightly punched his chest.

"Feel like that boxer training with the beef, ya know? Pow, pow." She marked each 'pow' with another light punch.

Gunnar seized that hand and held it to his chest. "What now?"

Her eyes glanced to the ceiling as she struck a thought pose. "I can... head butt you."

"Not a good idea, it may hurt your money maker. I'm pretty hard-headed. I have steel bones in my forehead; it actually broke someone's jaw." His thumb traced the back of her hand, and he wondered if she could feel how fast his heart throbbed in his chest.

"I don't believe it." She offered a mock head-butt, but was met with Gunnar's lips on hers. Brodie froze, unsure what to do. Her feelings for Gunnar certainly existed, but it had only been a week since they first met. *A week in which we've spent almost every waking moment together,* she reminded herself. The thought caused her to relax and return his kiss. The constant proximity to the man had caused her affections to grow. She learned more about him, his trials and fears, his loyalty to those he protected, his humor and gentleness to those in need. Even the scent of his cologne was ingrained in her memory: its fresh, sporty top notes, citrus middle note, and woodsy, masculine base. The scent described him perfectly.

He lifted her hands to his shoulders, drawing her closer, deepening the kiss. Her lips tasted like mango from the lip balm she used. The subtle perfume she wore filled his nostrils: lychee, strawberry, lily, jasmine, and vanilla. The blend of spring berries and youthful florals became distinctly 'Brodie' in his mind. "Thank you," he whispered, tilting his head and allowing her a chance to catch her breath.

Brodie's cheeks flushed pink, and her eyes twinkled in delight from the kiss. "What for?"

"There was a fifty-fifty chance you would either return my kiss or slap me in the face." His massive hands trailed down her arms and back. "I didn't know how you felt, especially about some beaten-up old guy."

Her fingers played with a lock of his blonde hair that hung down to the nape of his neck. "I almost did slap you." She attempted to speak the words seriously, but could not hide the laugh on her lips.

"It's okay, I guess. Those puny things couldn't hurt me." He squeezed her upper arms tenderly. "Little noodle-arms."

Brodie pouted, but Gunnar kissed her once again. "I'm not noodle-armed," she protested between kisses.

"Mhm."

"I'm not."

He kissed her forehead and hugged her tightly. "I wish I had done this sooner." He sighed and rested his cheek on the top of her head. "Now it's too late. We leave tomorrow."

"But we leave for Sweden. We'll be together."

Gunnar remained quiet, enjoying the slight hint of bamboo in her hair and the feel of her in his arms. How could he explain the multiple reasons of why he could not be with her in Sweden? They both held duties to the Royal Family that would occupy their time. And always, always the Sword of Damocles over his head was the threat of Anders Strand. The psychopath had taken one love from him; how could Gunnar put Brodie, so full of love and innocence, in such a dangerous situation?

His silence at her question caused Brodie to push away from his embrace. "We'll be together, right?"

"I wish we could be." He walked to the door of the restroom, rubbing the back of his neck in quiet contemplation.

"There's complicated reasons why we can't be together when we reach Sweden."

Brodie could feel her heart sink. In one breath, she was able to recognize her affections for the man, and in the next breath she was forced to ignore them. "Why kiss me then?"

Her voice ached with confusion, anger, and heartache. Gunnar cringed. Her question was on-point; he was wondering the same thing. Sunday night after massaging her, he wanted to kiss her. Monday evening as he held her tight, he wanted to kiss her. And each day throughout the week the desire grew though the cause of the desire morphed as he learned more about her. His initial attraction based purely on her lithe frame and natural beauty grew into adoration of her kindness, courage, and faith. Qualities she could not recognize in herself.

"I couldn't hold back anymore." He leaned his forehead against the bathroom door frame. "It was stupid and selfish, but I couldn't... not. I shouldn't have. I'm sorry."

Staring at her nails, Brodie flicked at them absent-mindedly as she processed her emotions. She wanted to beat against his scarred-chest for placing her in such a mental whirlwind. Similarly, she wanted to wrap her arms around his neck and kiss him again. "What are the complicated reasons?" she finally broke the silence with her quiet question.

Gunnar toyed with the brass hinges of the door. "Duty. My assignment to the Crown is first, as will be yours. But mostly, your safety. Anders Strand wouldn't hesitate to abduct you in order to get to me, if he knew." He grunted, twisted his body to lean his back against the frame, and slid down to sit. "Anders is against the King, and everything I told you, but when he gave me these scars," he tapped his chest, "it was personal. I can't put you in the crosshairs of that madman."

"I won't be put in danger by you being my bodyguard?"

He shook his head. "Doesn't fit his M.O. It's an assignment, so you would not be in anymore danger than the standard threat of working for the crown." His hands fidgeted with his shirt. It felt as if the collar desired to choke him. "It wouldn't be personal. He wants personal pain."

The darkness and agony that crossed his eyes allowed Brodie to see a painful memory attempting to bubble to the surface. She slipped off the counter and sat on the floor next to Gunnar. Her hand rested on his arm, reassuringly. "I know there's more you're not telling me." He glanced at her, surprised, but not denying. "But that's okay. Come on. Help me finish packing. The sooner we're done..." She shrugged. "Maybe we can enjoy our time before Sweden."

Gunnar opened his arms and brought her into a hug. They sat in silence for several minutes, savoring the embrace and the intimacy of the proximity. He trailed his leathered hands over her smooth arms, wondering if the coarseness of his skin disturbed her. She made no motion to pull away from his touch. Rather, she appeared to lean into it. Were his doubts uncalled for? Were even his fears uncalled for? Anders Strand had been silent for several months now.

A horrific image of a mangled woman, a mangled Brodie, flashed before his eyes.

His body tensed at the sight, and Brodie lifted her hand to his cheek in response. "Are you okay?"

"We should pack, as you've said."

Silence followed as they returned to the boxes, placing the final few books and binders inside. She allowed Gunnar to tape the boxes closed while she labeled the contents with her permanent marker. The small apartment soon sat bare save for a stockpile of brown boxes in the living room near the door, a plastic-covered mattress leaning against metal rods that once formed a bedframe, packed-but-open suitcases, and the remaining few pieces of furniture that would be hauled away the next day. Brodie inspected the tiny living space, afraid to leave anything unpacked.

"I think that's it," she observed.

"Looks that way." He stacked the couch pillows on top of some nearby boxes. Taking a pillow and blanket from an open 'bedding' box, he started making a bed.

"Oh right." She glanced at her disassembled bed. "Forgot about sleeping. Guess I can throw the mattress on the floor and sleep on the plastic."

"Nonsense." He opened his laptop and sat it on the coffee table. "You can sleep on the couch. I've softened it up for you all week."

Brodie smiled. "What about you?"

He clicked an icon on his screen and a movie began playing. "I was just going to curl up at your feet. I think I'll fit." He laid back on the couch where he could watch the movie and threw the blanket over himself. "Care to join?" He indicated the empty space on the couch beside him. "Movie night."

"I like movies." She slipped under the blanket and turned to face the computer's screen. "Which one is it?"

"Some random action movie. You talk about them so much, I decided it must be your favorite genre."

She laughed and settled her head against his arm. "Of course it is."

"Next time I'll have a Regency-period romance handy. I was caught off-guard."

They settled against one another, offering a few occasional words about the actors in the movie or a plot-piece that caused Brodie confusion. "I'm not sure why she wouldn't try to send some message to the FBI agent," she told Gunnar as she toyed with his hand that set on her stomach. "All she can do is cry. That's not the time to cry when the terrorist has her on camera. Cry later. That's her time to be smart and use wordplay. Or blink out a message in Morse code."

"In my experience, the everyday civilian doesn't know Morse code," he declared.

Brodie rolled onto her back to face Gunnar. "I admit, I don't know Morse code. They should teach that in school, or... scouts? They teach knots in scouts, why not survival techniques?"

He smiled, letting his hand roam over her arm as she laid out the plan the kidnapped-victim in the movie should have followed. Despite the fictitious-nature of the movie, it slightly reassured Gunnar that Brodie thought on her feet. Then again, even the cleverest and most experienced persons seldom had the wherewithal to follow their brain in a panic-stricken situation such as kidnapping. He had first-hand experience in the matter. "You've thought this out."

"I watch a lot of cop shows, in the dark, while living alone. Sometimes, my imagination can take over." Her hand reached up and traced the scar on his cheek. "Maybe I'm just crazy."

"You're certainly not crazy. I'm glad to hear you're more alert than I first gave you credit for, back when you called me paranoid."

She laughed. "You're definitely paranoid. Why else would your gun be at arm's reach on top of the box behind me?"

"Safety first." He closed his eyes, savoring the gentle touch of her fingers over his face. "You should have just slapped me when I kissed you."

"Why would you say that?" Her hand now trailed to his neck and jaw, finding another scar there to trace.

"Because I don't want this to end. I don't want to land in Sweden and keep you at arm's length, but it's what must be done."

"Why? Can't you teach me some self-defense fighting or something?" She frowned, noting the movie playing behind her. That woman's fate is what he wanted to protect her from. It was understandable, but how could she ignore her feelings? She ran her fingers over his lips. "I like you. I want to go out with you, as my boyfriend, not my bodyguard."

He kissed her thumb. "I will make a promise to you. The moment that Anders Strand is taken care of, and cannot cause you any harm, that will happen."

"How long have you been hunting him?" Rain began to pour outside, marking the direction of the conversation.

His lips frowned, in response to both the weather and the memories of Strand. "Too long, but..." He sat up and reached for his leather pouch next to his gun, "I will work even harder to find him, with a stronger drive than I've ever had."

"You've had a pretty strong drive."

"Driven by anger and bitterness. Some emotions are stronger."

She tilted her head at him in curiosity. "Like what emotions?"

His cheeks blushed faintly, "Close your eyes."

"Why? What is it?"

101

"Just close your eyes," he commanded with a smile, placing his hand over her eyes. He placed the little robin's egg blue box in her hands. "Consider this a token of my promise." He pulled his hand away from her eyes.

Her laughing smile turned to a gasp upon seeing the box. "Oh, Gunnar... you shouldn't have. When? How?" She opened the box to reveal the matching blue pouch within.

"I have my ways, but it was on Tuesday."

Opening the pouch revealed the silver necklace she had eyed in the jeweler's window on Sunday. "Oh, Gunnar," she breathed. Her petite hand shook as she held the delicate silver chain in the air. "You, you really shouldn't have."

"I wanted to give you something that you deserve but would never give yourself." He took the chain and clasped the piece around her neck. "Something as beautiful, graceful, and faithful as you."

"It's so expensive," she whispered. "I can't imagine... I mean, every little girl dreams about the little blue box. But actually getting it? I don't know what to say."

"Don't say anything." He kissed her ear and massaged her shoulders.

She glanced over her shoulder at him and smiled. "Does this mean you liked me on Tuesday?"

"I told you I should have kissed you sooner, but I could not imagine someone like you returning my affections."

"Why wouldn't I?"

He chuckled. "Look at you. You're beautiful, inside and out Brodie. I'm old, worn-down, scarred-up..."

"That's not what I see at all," she interrupted him. She put her hand on his cheek. "I see a devoted, kind face. Scars? Sure. But scars are just symbols of your love."

"Love?" The word made him feel uneasy.

"Putting your life on the line like you do for the Royal Family, that's love."

He shook his head. "It's just a job."

"Would you take a bullet for the King?" Her hand traced up into his blonde hair, running her nails gently on his scalp.

"Of course," he kissed her wrist.

"That's love. 'Greater love hath no man that this: that a man lay down his life for his friends.' You certainly wouldn't take a bullet for someone you didn't like, or without being the most unselfish person on the planet. But I've only heard of one person walking this earth that had that level of love." She laid her head against his chest. "I'm happy with this person though."

He wrapped her into a hug and leaned back on the couch. "I think you're just happy that this person is going to be willing to go out in the rain to load boxes into a truck while you stay warm and dry up here."

"I don't want to look atrocious when we get to the palace," she joked. "Rain here, twelve hour flight…"

"No, *sötis*. You take what you want to change into on the plane. Dress and fix yourself up." He buried his nose into her hair. "It's a luxury plane, showers and sinks, whatever you need to freshen up."

"Wow," she giggled. "I may as well be becoming a princess. Fancy plane, living in a palace, little blue box… personal bodyguard." Her eyes closed and breathing slowed. "Let's stay like this for a while," she purred.

"Whatever you want." He closed his laptop with his foot and held her against him as she fell asleep. Gunnar remained awake for some time, enjoying the sound of the storm that fell in rhythm with the pounding of his heart. How would he be able to resist pulling her into his arms and savoring the happiness she gave him while in Sweden?

Brodie zipped up her garment bag that held her palace-arrival outfit. With one hand on her hip and another on Gunnar's gift hanging from her neck, she surveyed the room that had served as her cramped bedroom for the last few years. It was finally happening. She was leaving for Sweden. Her nerves nearly overwhelmed her, and she felt nauseous.

The apartment door opened, and Gunnar entered with one of his security agents. "Are you ready Brodie?" he called out.

"Yes!" she responded.

He opened her bedroom door, drenched in rainwater. Brodie smiled at his appearance; his wet hair matted to his face was ruggedly attractive. "I'm going to put these with my bag in the car," he stated, pointing at her remaining suitcases. "But first, I want you to meet one of my agents." Gunnar looked behind him and motioned a young agent forward. "Brodie Mayer, meet Loke Ostbërg, my youngest SÄPO agent protecting the crown."

The young agent, several inches shorter than Gunnar, stepped forward to shake her hand. "Honor to meet you, Miss Mayer." Her acceptance of his gesture was awarded with a wet hand. "My apologies."

"No, it's okay. I'm sure I'm about to be soaked, umbrella or not." She noted how Gunnar beamed at the young man and smiled. "Is everything ready?"

"Truck is packed and ready to go," Gunnar responded. "Are you?"

She glanced around. "I have to give my keys to the apartment office."

He nodded and turned toward Loke. "Take the truck to the plane. We will meet you there."

"Of course." The young man turned and left the apartment.

"I like that kid," Gunnar remarked after Loke left. "He's got a lot of potential."

"You were beaming at him like he was your son," she joked. She handed him one of her suitcases and grabbed the others for herself.

Gunnar took his duffle bag from the floor and wrapped the strap across his chest. Both surveyed the apartment as they spoke, ensuring nothing was left behind. "I trained him at the academy and in the field, so maybe the feeling is similar. At the very least, he is like a brother. I have an eye on him to be my replacement someday. Thinks sharp, far more tech savvy than I, and he's been a real asset on the Strand case." He shook his head. "I've made more progress with him on my team than the years before."

"Good!" she exclaimed. "If he can help you get Strand, then I really like him too." The two stopped at her front door at those words. "I guess, since he'll be on the plane, this is it?"

"I may have one trick up my sleeve before we land," Gunnar answered and lowered her suitcase to the floor. "But for the most part, this is it."

Brodie dropped her bags before leaping up to kiss him. He caught her leap, wrapping his arms tightly around her waist. Her feet dangled above the floor. The fierceness of the kiss threw Gunnar against her apartment wall, but he did not mind.

He wanted to guarantee it was a kiss to remember him by, uncertain when he would be able to give her another. Before he could pull back, she twirled her fingers in his hair and leaned in for a longer kiss. The action made Gunnar's heart leap with joy.

"I'll wear your necklace all the time," she whispered between kisses. "Think of you whenever I'm wearing it."

He kissed her cheek and jaw. "Don't for a moment believe that I'm not thinking of you."

She ran her fingers through his soaked hair, covering his face in kisses. "I don't know if I'll be able to concentrate and do my job. What if I couldn't do it anyway? I have a country on my shoulders. What if I can't save the heir to the throne from his own misery?"

"To heir is human," Gunnar joked. Her frown subsided for a brief moment at his pun. "Brodie, the queen knew you would be successful at this job in one meeting with you. I know you'll be successful because I've come to know you well. I have faith in you."

"I wish I could say that made everything better."

He kissed her deeply. "It will be okay. Ready to go to Sweden?"

"No, but time to do it anyway." They picked up the bags and headed downstairs to the apartment building's office. Brodie slowly handed the key to the building manager. That was it. She was no longer a resident of the United States.

Part Two: Sweden

Chapter Nine

Brodie spun a polished leather chair in the meeting room on the plane. Gunnar leaned over the oak table attempting to connect his laptop and the presentation monitor.

"Are we having movie night again?" she joked. She timed her landing into the spinning chair and giggled as the lush comfort whirled her about.

"I may have another movie on here, but it's another early-nineties-action-extravaganza."

She laughed and halted the chair's rotation. "I see a trend."

He focused intensely on the computer. "I'm a man of fine tastes in entertainment. What I was going to do was go through the staff in an overview for you, but I can't get this to work. Hold on, I'm going to get Loke in here." He stepped out of the room, calling to the young agent. He promptly appeared. "Can you connect my laptop to the monitor?"

"Of course." With ease, Loke worked on the laptop and turned to the screen. A click of the remote and Gunnar's desktop became visible on the monitor. "Can I do anything else for you?" Loke glimpsed at Brodie with a smile on his lips.

She politely returned his smile. "Where were you when I was trying to get my laptop speakers to work a few weeks ago?"

Loke shyly bowed his head. "Serving His Majesty, the King."

"Go figure," Brodie responded. "Thank you Loke."

Gunnar dismissed the young agent with a nod. He pulled up his slideshow and took a seat next to Brodie. The first slide was a picture of King Roffe with a bullet-point outline of information to the side. "You met him in the treatment center, King Roffe Victorrson. He married Jonna when he was 26, and took the throne at age 34 upon his father's untimely death." He cleared his threat. "It was labeled a heart attack, but I have never believed this."

"You think there was foul play?"

He shrugged his shoulders. "It's possible. Maybe I'm being paranoid; that's how I am, right? But there are plenty of ways to induce a heart attack." He rubbed the back of his neck. The short week together had taught Brodie he did this when shuffling through an assortment of rapid-fire thoughts. "Not that Roffe hasn't been a fine king, but he was heartbroken at the loss of his father. And now, he's losing his wife." His hand fell back to the table top. "It's been a sad existence for my friend in this past decade."

Without thought, Brodie placed a hand over his. She knew Roffe's existence was not the only one that had been sad.

Gunnar lifted his thumb over the back of her hand, gently rubbing her knuckles. A click of the remote, and the next slide of Queen Jonna appeared. "Jonna was only 21 when she married Roffe, but very mature for her age. She was attending university in England when Roffe and I visited. That is how they reunited."

"Reunited?"

"The two knew each other when we were all children. But she was five, and he was a crown prince of ten. Needless to say, he did not pay her much attention. That is, until she was older and more, developed."

"Development usually helps," she laughed.

"She was developed in more than just body. The king loves literature, philosophy, and ancient history. She did as well and held her own in conversation with him. It was her brains and gentle nature that attracted him to her." Gunnar smiled at Brodie. "It's like someone else I know."

"Perhaps I should take a course on Viking history," she stated seriously. "By the halls of Valhalla?"

Gunnar winced. "We will work on you." He pressed the button on the remote and a wedding picture of Roffe and Jonna popped up. "Even though the people clamored for a royal baby, they always do after a royal wedding, Roffe and Jonna agreed to finish their time at university. He began attending as soon as they met, you see. Taking courses on those subjects he loved... dragging his best friend and bodyguard into courses on literature, and," his face blanched, "philosophy."

Brodie arched her eyebrows in surprise. "Are you saying that you have a degree in the liberal arts?"

"Oh, the humanities," he lamented. "I have a Bachelor of Arts in Anglo-Saxon, Norse, and Celtic culture and history. There are worse liberal art degrees. Roffe wanted to study the Classics until I reminded him that our ancestors put those sheet-wearing Mediterraneans in their place." He winked. "Don't worry, we will get you enrolled in a course on Viking history."

"I know how Rome fell," she retorted happily. "We study them more than we do Anglo-Saxon, Celtic, or Norse history. American schools only care about British history after the Normans, I suppose."

"We barbarians are a bad influence," he facetiously agreed. "Roffe and Jonna ended up pregnant their final year of college though, but Jonna did not let the morning sickness keep her from graduating with honors. I was very proud of her, just as I am very proud of her now. She keeps her head high and eyes on target. She's a lady in every sense of the word." He pressed the remote again. "His Royal Highness, Niklas Victorsson, the

Crown Prince of Sweden. No, you do not have to call him that."

"Are you sure?"

"While he is a child, just call him Niklas. Not even Prince... especially not now. That is something his parents decided long ago because they feared it would make him entitled, as sadly so many affluent children become."

"I'm glad. I was hoping royal propriety would not interfere with my work on helping the children."

"No, that's not what will be the problem. I believe you already witnessed the problems with Niklas, or some of them. He attends the same private boarding school his father and I attended, though he arrived home early due to his mother's condition. He will be at Drottningholm for the summer." Gunnar shook his head. "I plan on assigning Loke to him. He's young, so Niklas may be less likely to object to the security detail. He can't stand being followed."

"He's going to love me then," Brodie lamented.

"You're young too, and pretty. He may not object." Gunnar scratched his chin pensively. "The boy has hit that age where he loves women and wants to party. Honestly, he's his father's son, but now I'm in charge of his safety, which means no sneaking out to the club."

"He may try to sneak out to the clubs more now that his mother is ill, or at least the desire will increase. I'll try my best."

"With you, me, and Loke, I'm hoping we can keep him out of trouble." Gunnar raised the remote, and continued to discuss family members, including Roffe's mother and Jonna's parents, siblings, and cousins. Then he went through the entire staff and security of the castle.

By the end of his presentation, Brodie sat wide-eyed with her hands in her hair.

"Did I break you?" Gunnar asked, leaning back in his chair.

"I feel broken. I cannot lie." She let her head fall onto the table. "I'm feeling quite overwhelmed."

"This was an overview. You'll learn everyone soon enough." He began rubbing her shoulders. "You can do it, *sötis*."

She sat up slowly. "I should probably start formulating my plan for the kids while we still have time before sleep." Her stomach growled. "But first, what do we have to eat on this plane?"

He smirked. "Fish. Lots of fish. We like fish in Sweden." He stood and helped her to her feet. "But luckily, I made plans for you. There's a restaurant in Stockholm that I'll take you to when we get a chance. It's dubbed 'veggie heaven' by my friend, and I had them cater especially for you."

"Veggie heaven? I like the sound of that."

Loke greeted them at the buffet. "I've never been to this place before," he confessed as he built a fajita with portabella mushrooms, "but it's not too bad for no-meat." His eyes fixated on Brodie.

"Fajitas!" Brodie excitedly clapped her hands. "Nice to know I won't be without my Tex-Mex while in Scandinavia."

Gunnar handed her a plate. "We've got everything you could want," he informed her. "Major metropolitan area just like anywhere else in the world – but with maybe fresher air, brighter sun, and beautiful canals."

Her eyes sparkled, imagining the pictures of Stockholm she had seen on the internet. "Think we can watch that movie while we eat?" she whispered to Gunnar.

He nodded, leading her back to the meeting room. Brodie settled in her chair. "Loke was staring. I can't eat while he's staring at me."

"I stare at you all the time when you eat," Gunnar teased. "Like Wednesday night when your pho was going everywhere?"

She playfully punched his arm. "Hey! That's not nice!"

"*Förlåt mig*," he apologized with a melodramatic bow.

"You know, you've never spoken to me in Swedish to woo me," she observed, picking up one of her fajitas. "Why is that?"

"I was not aware Swedish was considered a romantic language. Isn't that French? Or am I still ignorant of American women?"

"That's the usual, but I'm weird. Who knows what I would like?" The fajita was promptly stuffed in her mouth.

"If that's what you like, oh beautiful lady with face-full-of-fajita..." He leaned his head back in both hands and bounced his knee as he debated. Finally, he cleared his throat and began to recite:

Näcken, han spelar på böljan den blå,
Ljuft är att höra derpå!
Hafvets små elfvor i ringdans gå,
Och stjernorna tindra också.
Men Näcken, när han emot himlen ser,
Slår han sitt öga ner;
Ty bland de stjernor, som tindra der,
Freja ej mot honom ler.

Större än jordlifvets sorg är hans —
Bruden, han sökte, ej fans.

Slocknen, i stjernor, och döljen er glans!
I tärnor! Gån icke till dans!
Näcken, vid harpan, för berg och dal
Sjunger om kärleksqval,
Gömmer sig sedan i grönan sal,
Slutar så elfkungens bal.

Brodie's second fajita lay forgotten on her plate as she stared at Gunnar's recital of the poem. "That was actually quite lovely," she acknowledged. "I wasn't sure it would be, but it really is."

"Better than French?"

"Far better than French. What is it? What does it mean?"

"It's an old song about a water spirit playing his fiddle on the blue waves searching for his bride, but the goddess Freya does not give him her blessing. And without finding his bride, he continues on, his once joyous song now full of sorrow." Gunnar popped forward in the chair, turning his attention on the fajita. "Just something I had to memorize in grade school. Not a big deal."

"Not a big deal? I found it beautiful." She continued her dinner silently, smiling at the blushing bodyguard as he fumbled with the remote in order to start their movie and leave his poetry recital in the past.

Brodie double-checked her appearance in the mirror of the executive washroom. She opted to wear the 'nanny dress' for her first day of work, deeming its sleek cut and suit-like collar and sleeves would give the best first impression. Her hair was straightened and pulled back to match hairstyles she had seen women wear in business magazines. A deep inhale and a last run-through of her mental checklist satisfied her. She stepped out of the washroom with bags in hand.

Gunnar sat at a desk nearby, his back turned toward her and his head buried in a case file on his laptop. He was so engrossed in his work that he did not hear her. Brodie knew what that meant: Strand. Carefully, she set her bags next to the desk and peeked at the case file. It was about Roffe's father.

Until the plane ride, she did not realize his obsession with the terrorist. After the in-flight movie, they returned to the general cabin area where the chairs reclined and they could sleep. Surprisingly, Gunnar fell asleep before she had. She opted to lie there, facing the sleeping giant with her blanket pulled to her chin. Due to Loke's presence, they kept an empty seat between them, but at the time she wanted nothing more than to move next to him and hold him close. His face had contorted in his slumber; he slept in pain. It worried her, and her natural instinct was to comfort him. The few audible words he mumbled were "Strand" and "Brodie". She had debated waking him, lest speaking her name would give them away to Loke. During the debate, however, she too fell asleep.

He had been awake long before her, and she suspected he was already adjusting to the seven-hour time difference between Texas and Sweden. Unfortunately, Brodie had never left the central-time zone in her lifetime, and she could feel the difference while eating breakfast. Her mind told her it was supposed to be four in the morning, but her eyes told her another story.

"Do we land soon?" she finally asked, breaking her chain of thoughts.

Gunnar stirred from his trance at her voice. "We do. Best to put this away." He closed the computer and appraised her appearance. "The dress does look like a nanny's dress." He smiled.

She smoothed the front of it nervously. "Does everything look okay?"

"You look wonderful." He stood and gently put a hand to her cheek. "You are a wonder."

"I don't know how I'm going to do this Gunnar."

"I already said you'd be good at this job."

She covered his hand with hers, savoring the touch. "Not the job. Pretending I don't have feelings for you."

For a moment, Gunnar thought his heart would pound out of his chest. He cleared his throat and dropped his hand. "Maybe I should take you to my house. Once you witness how much of a pigsty it is, you'll get over me real fast."

"Only fair. You came over to my house, and I was afforded no opportunity to clean it first."

"Psh," he opened the door of the office for her. "Your apartment was nearly spotless when we arrived, except for the laundry hanging up to dry." He winked. "I'll never forget how red your face went when I saw your delicates."

"Gunnar!" she squeaked and hit him with her bag. "You swore to never speak of that."

He laughed like an impish boy of ten rather than a man of forty-four. "I'll never speak of it around others." They put away their belongings, bickering back and forth.

Loke watched with a smile, already buckled into his seat. "Seems you two are getting along famously."

"Miss Mayer is easily embarrassed," Gunnar remarked. "But on my honor as a gentleman, I cannot say why she is." He sat across from Loke and buckled into his seat. He eyed Brodie as she sat next to him. "It's a very... delicate... situation."

She narrowed her eyes at him and jerked the seat belt into position, causing him to laugh.

Chapter Ten

Gunnar stepped off the plane first and greeted the SÄPO agents that stood at the bottom of the airstairs with a wave. He yelled instructions at them in Swedish before turning to Brodie who waited nervously behind him. "They will get your luggage; come." He took her hand and helped her down the steps to the ground. "This is why I don't like heels," he pointed to the shoes that had caused her to be more cautious than normal in descent.

"I didn't want to be short in the land of Vikings," she responded. "Plus, they're cute."

"They're cute," he mocked her voice with a grin. He took an earpiece from one of the agents and prepared his gear for being back in his homeland. Brodie observed the airstrip. Several airline staff under agent supervision hurried about, retrieving their luggage and placing the suitcases into the trunk of a town car. Others unloaded her boxes into a truck for its shipment to the storage unit Gunnar had arranged for her. "Loke, oversee Miss Mayer's belongings that are going into her storage unit. Get that set up for her," Gunnar ordered.

"Thank you Loke," Brodie added on.

The silent agent bowed his head slightly at her then rushed to the truck.

Earwig in place, Gunnar made a gesture to the town car and asked one of his agents a question in Swedish.

"*Ja*," the man replied.

"The car's ready. Are you?" he asked, placing a hand on her back and leading her to the car.

"Doesn't matter. No turning back now."

They entered the car silently; Brodie could feel her stomach churn before the driver even moved the vehicle. She leaned back in the seat and watched the passing buildings and scenery of what would be her new home. Gunnar watched her. He remained as silent as she, afraid to let anything out of line be spoken over the earwig. She clutched her tote bag with nervous, fidgeting fingers. With a cautionary glimpse to the driver, Gunnar reached up to her hand and took it in his. He lowered their hands to the seat between them and massaged the back of her hand with his thumbs. She did not look at him. The smile on her previously frightened face spoke enough.

The treeline in Brodie's vision broke as the car turned onto a bridge. Across the water, she noted the vast pale-yellow palace and inhaled. "Is that it?" She turned to Gunnar, wide-eyed. "That huge thing?"

Her child-like excitement amused him. "That huge thing. The southern side, to your left, is where the family stays. The rest is open to the public for tours."

"Kind of like the White House. The President's family doesn't run around the whole thing like crazy people... that I know of."

"Now is the busy season. May to September it is open daily for tourists and groups, even the gardens. Makes my job a little harder."

"That must be hard, living in a tourist attraction."

"Being royalty is a tourist attraction."

As the car drove to the private entrance, tourists attempted to peer into the car, hoping to catch a glimpse of royalty. Gunnar eyed them all sharply, and Brodie suddenly understood the paranoia he had displayed early in his time with her. He pressed a hand over his earpiece and sent a few orders to his men.

"More tourists than normal," Gunnar informed her. "I'll need to have a quick word with some people when we get inside, and then I will give you a tour of the palace that those tourists do not get to touch."

They exited the car, and Brodie found the grounds breathtaking. She peered up at the three floors of windows, noting the intricate architectural designs along the roof. "I'm dumbfounded," she admitted.

"Put those in Miss Mayer's room," Gunnar pointed out her baggage to palace staff. He handed his lone duffle bag to one of the attendants. "You can put that in my office." He led Brodie inside, pointing out different features of the architecture and giving her a brief art history lesson about the property. She had to smile; her action movie hero was a cultured, liberal arts major.

Walking into the palace caused Brodie to stop and stare. The golden, high ceilings and intricate décor made her feel like she had stepped into Marie Antoinette's life, albeit in a colder climate. "This place is gorgeous, Gunnar. I can't imagine what it is like to grow up here."

"Well I never lived here..." he began.

"But you may as well have."

They paused as the king entered the entrance hall. Gunnar bowed, and Brodie attempted a curtsey.

"You do not have to curtsey, Miss Mayer," Roffe told her. "We do not expect that from non-Swedes." He placed a hand on Gunnar's shoulder. "I hardly expect it from this guy, and whenever he does bow, I feel like he's about to tell me bad news. There's no bad news I hope."

"No, Your Majesty," Gunnar replied. "I was going to meet with my team and see why there is a rush of tourists before giving Miss Mayer a tour."

"The news was announced about Jonna's condition," the king replied. "Ever since our return from America, they have come, leaving tokens of well-wishes for their queen. Pink ribbons, peonies, cards, handmade blankets, even those toy animals children play with." His eyes filled with sadness. "Jonna asks us to save all of them. Security inspects them, and then we set them up in her room. She told me that it makes her feel stronger to have such support."

"I'm glad people are doing that," Brodie commented. "Visual tokens of support are more beneficial than we give them credit for."

"I saw the report Gunnar made about you." Roffe smiled. "Your work on the grieving process is commendable. My wife suggested that in your time here, you should consider publishing papers on the subject. You would have our full support in academic pursuits."

"You did want to write a book," Gunnar reminded her.

She forced herself not to blush. Gunnar had been paying attention to her dreams.

"You may go meet with your team Gunnar," Roffe told him. "I can give Miss Mayer a tour of our home, and then show her to my wife's room. She is anxious to greet you." He offered his arm to Brodie.

She graciously accepted, and he led her through the ornate halls and rooms of the south-side of the palace. Gunnar watched them depart. Having been almost inseparable from Brodie for the past week made him realize how much he enjoyed her company. Only the faintest trace of lychee, strawberry, and vanilla remained in the air. He inhaled deeply before leaving for his office.

"My wife can no longer climb stairs without feeling faint," Roffe lamented to Brodie as they paused before a set of closed doors. "I had the staff create a new bedchamber for her on the first floor. We brought in a custom hospital bed to make her as comfortable as possible. But she misses the view she once had of the gardens. I try to take her for strolls, but, she's weak and it often gives her pain." He gestured to the door. "But your arrival is certain to make her happy."

He tapped on the door and poked his head in, whispering a few phrases in Swedish. After a pause, he opened the door wider and ushered Brodie into the room. Her heart broke upon seeing the queen lying on her bed. No longer did she wear her pristine wardrobe, but a long, baggy gown. Dark circles adorned her eyes, and her hair was mused from lying in bed.

"Welcome Miss Mayer... Brodie," she announced with a smile. "I was so pleased to hear from Gunnar that you accepted the job. I hope he treated you well and your travels were kind."

"He was, and it was, Your Majesty."

Jonna waved a hand. "No need for such formalities. Roffe and I have brought you in to be part of our family. Is that not correct, my love?"

The king walked to her side to hold her hand. "Of course. And we especially do not want you to call the children Royal Highness, Prince, Princess, or anything else that would make you subservient to them. You are in charge, not them. They need to understand this clearly."

"I understand."

"Currently, Niklas has returned to his school to finish his exams," Jonna informed her. "He will return on Wednesday for his summer vacation. Kjerstin and Mikkel are attending

122

their music lessons upstairs. Roffe has been taking care of the children," she smiled sweetly at her husband, "but he is the king, and cannot attend to them full-time. Despite how much he enjoys being a father."

"I always believed that I had shared the duties of parenting equally with my wife, but I have been proven wrong." His phone in his coat pocket buzzed, and he hurriedly attempted to silence it.

"Take your call Roffe. It will give us time to speak in private."

He nodded and slipped out of the room to answer the phone.

Jonna gestured to the chair beside her bed, and Brodie sat. "I do not know how you plan to proceed, nor do I want to interfere with your talent, but I do wish to be involved with my children until my last breath."

"I would not have it any other way."

"Gunnar told me I had chosen well. I think he is right."

Brodie blushed. "Thank you."

"I prepared files for you about my children. Allergies, medical histories, their lesson schedules, and anything more I could think of that would assist you. I had my staff take it to your room for you. I also would like you to come to my room before breakfast, to discuss daily plans and review the day before." Jonna took a haggard breath before proceeding. "I understand this is not a job with normal business hours, so we do wish to give you Saturdays completely free of the children. I would hate to see a... what's the phrase? 'Burn out'? You will also have evenings free from time-to-time as Roffe and I like to spend family time together."

"That is all acceptable, and gracious."

"I do not know all that will happen in these coming months, but I do know that every move by my family will be haunted by the paparazzi due to my illness. I know that there will be many affluent ladies making their presence known here in Drottningholm and at the Royal Palace in Stockholm." She tearfully cast her eyes down. "Royalty may not have any power in our democracy, but it's a symbolic position. Women can become very vile in order to get the title of 'Queen'. I want my husband and children safe."

"May I be forthright with you, Jonna?"

"Please do."

Brodie stood, pacing as she spoke. "I have seen the way the king looks at you. Should you pass, there is not going to be a Queen of Sweden until Niklas marries and takes the throne."

Jonna smiled. "You believe this?"

"With all my heart. My only concern is how the king will handle your death. Grief can be just as dangerous for him as the children, but he will be reminded of it every time women throw themselves at him, hoping to get the crown." She placed her hands behind her back as she stopped pacing. "Gunnar filled me in on some of the politics of the situation, but some are unwarranted. Roffe doesn't call you his queen because you wear a literal crown; he calls you that because you are his world."

The woman teared up upon hearing Brodie's declaration, reaching for a box of tissues on her nightstand. "Such chivalrous notions are considered outdated in Sweden, but I enjoy hearing that."

"I will help all that I can, both with the children, with you, and with your husband. The most important part is you overcoming your cancer. I know you think this battle is already lost, but it is not."

"Look at me Brodie. It has been a week since you have seen me last. I feel I am fading quickly. I wanted to see Christmas, but now I am hoping to see the end of summer."

Brodie took Jonna's hand in hers. "There once was an evil so great and terrible, an entire nation's army could not defeat it. The army called forth the strongest men and best weapons their country possessed in order to defeat that evil. But none of them could do it – they believed they lost the battle without ever fighting it. It took the simplest boy with the most antiquated, flimsiest weapon to defeat that evil. He didn't need to be strong in power; he just needed to be strong in faith."

Jonna looked at Brodie quizzically.

"When I was fourteen, my life was spiraling out of control. Both of my parents were dead, and I wanted to be dead too," Brodie confessed. "Then a teacher sat me down and told me what I just told you. It was a public school, so she couldn't tell me who the evil was, or the nation, or the simple boy, without threat of losing her job. But later I figured out who she was talking about. The evil was Goliath, the nation was Israel, and the simple boy was David. We always talk about 'David and Goliath' stories when the underdog beats the champion, but it's misleading. The story wasn't about David beating Goliath because he trained harder; it was about David beating Goliath because of his faith in God. He gave his battle to the Lord. He didn't try to do it on his own." She patted Jonna's hand. "And that's how you are going to defeat your Goliath."

The queen wiped tears from her eyes, but did not respond.

Brodie panicked, added, "I'm sorry if I offended. Gunnar told me the family attended the Church of Sweden, so I assumed…"

"No. You are right." Jonna hastily pushed hair from her face. "We have a chapel here at the palace that has high mass on the last Sunday of the month. We have been traveling for mass, but, I cannot anymore."

"Maybe the chapel can increase its activity? I'm certain they will be more than willing to make some changes for Her Majesty the Queen."

"I will ask Roffe his opinion."

"My opinion on what my dear?" he asked, returning to the room.

She waved her hand. "Nothing urgent. I'm sure Miss Mayer is exhausted from her travels, and has yet to greet the children. We will speak later, my king."

Roffe noted the weariness in his wife's voice. "Get some rest, and I will return shortly." He kissed his wife's forehead, and followed Brodie out of the room.

Gunnar walked slowly to the third floor, sipping coffee as he did. It felt good to be with his team again, going over updated security details and schedules with the increased tourist activity. But failing back into his old routine was easier said than done. His week with Brodie had changed him completely, and the hours dragged without her. A short meeting turned into a two-hour affair with an entire overhaul of shifts and appointments. Hundreds of emails and multiple mounds of paperwork had built up in a mere week. They arrived at the palace at noon. It was now nearly five (17.00) and tourists were leaving the palace as it closed for the day.

He reached the top floor and turned toward Brodie's new room. Now that tourists were vacating, he hoped to oblige her with a tour of the public area of Drottningholm. Before he could knock on her bedroom door, however, he heard singing from the music room down the hall.

Recognizing Brodie's singing voice, he walked down the hall to find her playing the piano and singing while Kjerstin and Mikkel danced. The children wore makeshift costumes of a fantasy princess and prince. Gunnar wondered if a princess and prince pretending to be a different princess and prince counted as "playing pretend". Kjerstin led her younger brother in choreography she made-up as they went, and Brodie performed a song from one of the animated musicals the children enjoyed.

"Dance with us Miss Brodie!" Kjerstin called out.

Brodie continued singing, but obliged Kjerstin by sliding off the piano bench to join their dancing. She reached the climax of the song, and twirled both children at the same time. The words spoke of love and dance. The children clapped for Brodie who spun quickly with a whip of hair hitting her face. Brodie noted Gunnar standing in the doorway, and her voice trailed off.

The children also spotted Gunnar and ran at him with cheers. "We missed you Gunnar!" Kjerstin informed him. The statement was emphasized with a tight hug.

Gunnar balanced the coffee cups in his hands carefully so as to not spill the hot contents on the children. "I missed you too little princess." He hugged Mikkel. "And you little prince."

"Did you hear Miss Brodie? She can sing the songs from Princess Snowdew!" Kjerstin ran back to Brodie and hugged her. "She is amazing!"

"That is quite the talent," Gunnar agreed. "Not just anyone can sing 'All the Pretty Lights' like a princess," Gunnar stated matter-of-factly. "It's after five," he told Brodie. "These two should probably be cleaning up for dinner."

Both children enthusiastically disagreed with his statement.

"Come on you two," she agreed. "We have all summer to play make-believe." She herded them out of the room. Gunnar handed her the second coffee cup, and Brodie smiled at the earthy aroma exuding from it. "Green tea? Who brewed this?" she asked with a sip. "It is spot on."

Gunnar shrugged his shoulders. "Someone instructed by the consumer."

She choked from a suppressed laugh. "You made tea, for me?"

"It felt wrong, like I was betraying my country by brewing tea instead of coffee. But, I thought you could use the caffeine boost. You know…" he gestured at the children behind their backs, "first day."

"Mmmm," Brodie took another taste of the tea, "caffeine."

"Miss Brodie," Kjerstin called out, back-tracking her steps to meet with the two adults who lagged behind. Her fists sat on her hips in a serious pose. "My mother normally picks out my outfits, but Father has been allowing me to do so this week. May I still?" The young princess flashed a hopeful smile at her new caretaker.

"We can do like a fashion show – you pick out three, show off your style, and I will pick from one of them."

Kjerstin gasped with a child's enthusiasm. "I want to be a fashion designer!" She clinched her fists happily. "I really, really do. I like your dress. I want to design pretty clothes like that!"

"Lucky for you," Gunnar told the young princess, "Miss Brodie knows how to sew, and she has an eye for fashion."

"WHAT?!" Kjerstin shouted with a jump and clap of her hands. "You really are amazing Miss Brodie! I will go make my outfits!" She ran to her room.

"I hope she starts with easy patterns," Brodie told Gunnar as they each held one of Mikkel's hands, swinging him as they walked. "You've seen my sewing limitations."

"I think you'll be fine." Mikkel clutched Gunnar's arm with both hands, and the bodyguard started lifting him like a weight. The boy giggled at the trick. "I missed our daily workouts little prince." He nodded at Brodie. "This guy keeps me in shape."

Brodie smiled, enjoying the sight of Gunnar playing with Mikkel. "Maybe you can help him get a quick bath while I set out his clothes."

"I think I can do that." Gunnar flexed his arm, letting the boy dangle from it, and walked into the prince's private restroom. He began the bath water as Mikkel took his shirt off. "What are these?" Gunnar exclaimed, pinching Mikkel's upper arms. "Have you been working out to get big like me?"

"*Jag… vikingar!*" He flexed his arms. "Rawr!" he yelled with intimidation.

From the front of the wardrobe, Brodie laughed at the two's antics. She set out a gray suit similar to the one Roffe had worn during her tour of the palace. "I'm going to check on Kjerstin," she informed Gunnar.

The man did not hear her over Mikkel's roars and splashes.

"Kjerstin?" Brodie asked with a knock of the door. "Do you have your outfits ready for me to pick from?"

The princess opened her door with a sour look. "I can't decide on shoes," the girl moaned.

"Shoes are always the hardest part," Brodie consoled her. "How about I help you, and let's see if we can do this together." The girl nodded approval and moved aside for Brodie to enter the room. The new nanny looked over the choices made by the princess. "These are really good choices, Kjerstin. You have a real future as a fashion designer."

Kjerstin beamed at the compliment.

"How about we go with this dress and jacket," Brodie picked up a gray and cream pinstriped dress and held the dress over a pair of shoes Kjerstin had chosen. "What do you think of these cream ones? It goes with the dress nicely."

"I like that!" The girl took the dress and stepped in front of her mirror. "Miss Brodie, can you braid my hair when I finish?"

"I can do that. Come get me when you're ready. I'll be in your brother's room." Brodie walked back to Mikkel's bedchamber. Already she regretted her decision to wear heels, but she did not want Gunnar to know. He leaned in the bathroom doorway, drinking his coffee while Mikkel crashed two longboats into one another.

"How did the fashion designer do?" the bodyguard asked.

"Really well. I think she's onto something with her career choice."

He grinned. "This one just wants to be a Viking. I admire that choice as well. I wanted to be a Viking too."

"Oh really? So, you could travel to a foreign land and take one of their women?" she whispered the joke. Instantly, she covered her mouth and checked his ear.

"I took it out before coming up," he reassured her. "And if I had attempted to take you in true Viking fashion, you would have slapped me."

130

She grinned. "There's a good chance of that."

He smirked, wanting nothing more than to pull her into a kiss. A splash of water reminded him of the presence of Mikkel, and he gestured to the boy. "Do you want to wash his hair, or should I?"

"You even do hair?" she asked in amazement. "Gunnar, do you secretly have children that I don't know about?"

"I feel like I have three of them, and he's the youngest." He handed Brodie his coffee and knelt next to the bathtub while rolling up his sleeves. "Alright, God of Thunder, time to wash your hair." Brodie happily watched the scene, and for the briefest moment, imagined it was their son he was bathing. She shook the thought from her mind. It was absurd to imagine kids with a man she had only met a week ago. She returned to Mikkel's suit, chiding herself as she did so.

Chapter Eleven

The first hint of pink touched the Monday morning sky as Gunnar crept up the three flights of stairs carrying a brown shipping box. It was early, and the palace was only beginning to spring to life. Unsure if Brodie would be awake, he paused outside her room. His desire to make the delivery prevailed, and he gently tapped the door with his foot.

"It's open," she called out.

He opened the door and slipped into the room. Half expecting her to still be in bed, he was surprised to see her at her vanity, combing her hair carefully. *"God morgon,"* he greeted her quietly. "You're up early."

"My body can't figure out what time of day it is still." She began pulling her hair back with clips. "What's in the box?"

"I brought your sewing machine from your storage unit." He placed the box on her bed. "Thought you should be armed since I opened my mouth to Kjerstin." He watched her fix her hair as he pulled his knife out of his pocket. The sight of the woman fixing her hair in the early moments of dawn caused him to smile. Knots filled his stomach, just as they had every time he heard her sing in the shower, or kneel down to comfort a child at the treatment center.

"How did it fare in travel? It's pretty old."

With his trance interrupted, he slid his knife across the tape. "So far, so good. I bubble-wrapped it with a whole roll, so that helps."

She giggled and playfully leapt to her feet. "You did not!" Brodie joined him in pulling the machine out and unwrapping it. The machine appeared intact.

"Where did you get this thing from?" he asked as he sat it on her desk.

"Thrift resale." She patted the machine and lifted her tote from the desk chair. "It's done me well. Care to get some coffee?"

"You're getting coffee?" he asked as he followed her to her door. "Who are you?"

"No, you're getting coffee," she corrected him, "and I'm getting tea." They walked down the stairs to the kitchens. "I save coffee for special occasions or when I need a mega-shot of caffeine and adrenaline."

"I hear it's safer than narcotics," he agreed. "And a bit more acceptable here in Sweden. Preferred, in fact."

She smirked. "I gathered that from the paperwork that came with my visa. Drugs bad. Coffee good."

They walked into the kitchen where Antonin, the family's cook, had begun to prepare breakfast. He ignored their presence as Gunnar poured himself a hefty cup of coffee and Brodie began brewing green tea.

"What's for breakfast, Antonin?" Gunnar casually asked.

The man grumbled before answering. *"Smörgås, gurka, nötkött,"* was the only response Gunnar received.

Brodie glanced at the food he was preparing, only recognizing the word 'smörgås' from 'smörgåsbord'. She spotted bread, butter, cheese, cucumbers, and sliced beef. "What is the queen having for breakfast?"

Annoyed, Antonin pointed with his knife at the food before him. *"Smörgås, gurka, nötkött,"* he repeated.

"Did the treatment center not send the food and meals list?" Brodie asked Gunnar. "Do you know?"

"I haven't heard about it, but I can find out. What's wrong?" Gunnar indicated the meal. "This is pretty common."

"There are foods that combat cancer," she stated as she rummaged about the kitchen for ingredients. Antonin attempted to shoo her away, but Gunnar stopped him. "Whole-wheats. Berries. Red grapes. Green tea. Garlic. Tomatoes. Broccoli. Spinach. That's just the tip of the iceberg. The treatment center has a whole list of foods, and they were even developing a cookbook for patients."

Gunnar calmed her down as she tore through the kitchen. "Antonin, serve the queen muesli and *filmjölk*. I will get this list for you to use." He handed Brodie her tea, and she poured two cups. "Off to see the queen?"

"She wishes for me to start the day with her, reviewing activities for the children." He held the kitchen door open for her. "I actually like the idea. She should be involved with every aspect of her children's lives as long as she's... cognitive."

They stopped outside the queen's room. "In that case, should you need me," he bowed, "I will be in my office, dealing with that, food investigation." He walked away to his office.

Brodie paused in order to watch him walk, hoping to suppress the flush on her cheeks. But his last-minute turn of the head and wink made the attempt fortuitous. She knocked on the door, and the maidservant, Tatiana, opened it. She greeted Brodie warmly and left her alone with the queen for private conversation.

"Good morning Brodie," Jonna whispered. Her voice sounded hoarse and dry.

"Good morning. I brought you some tea." Brodie handed the queen one of the cups. The woman inspected the tea while Brodie continued to speak. "It's green tea; it helps fight the spread and growth of cancer." Jonna took a sip. "I drink several cups a day. So much that Gunnar said I would not fit-in here, in Coffee Country." Brodie could not hide the joy in her voice at the mention of Gunnar's bantering. She cleared her throat. "Have you started your new diet yet?"

"I am uncertain. I do not feel as though my diet has changed."

Brodie sat in the chair next to the bed, taking a book and folio from her tote. "I was in the kitchen with Gunnar and Antonin a moment ago, and, I hope you do not find me presumptuous, but I – with Gunnar's aid – changed your breakfast to muesli. The whole grains and fruit are good for a cancer-fighting diet. And Gunnar is going to see that Antonin receives the diet from the treatment center."

"Your concern is admirable," Jonna replied. "And appreciated." Her worn skin tugged at the corners of her lips from an attempted smile.

The sight reminded Brodie of her own mother. "I suppose Gunnar told you about my parents in one of his reports?"

"He did."

"Once I reached high school, I embraced home economics. It had a fancy name – family and consumer sciences – or something like that. But it was a great class. On one hand, it taught me things my mother never had a chance to. On the other hand, it gave me an opportunity to research about nutrition and how to prepare meals that would prevent me from getting cancer. I was, and still am, terrified of this disease." Brodie inhaled deeply. "But there are survivors. And I think you are a fighter."

135

"I will be honest. I do not feel much like a fighter. When I saw the test results… all the dark spots… my only desire was to find someone to take care of my children." She tapped the side of the teacup. "Though surrender is unbecoming of the Queen of Sweden."

"Medieval Scandinavian women were as formidable in battle as their male counterparts," Brodie stated with a smile. "I imagine their descendants are the same."

Jonna chuckled at the sentiment. "I believe my king would not disagree with the statement, nor would he disagree with fighting this disease. If he had his way, we would have moved to America for the treatment center. Thankfully, Doctor Richards made contact with colleagues here and in Norway. I begin those treatments in a few days, when Niklas returns home, at Roffe's urging." She traced her finger around the edge of the cup. "I'm afraid of those treatments, Brodie. The hair loss, the sickness, the frailty – I don't want to wither away slowly while claiming that it is a fight."

"I can understand, and you are not alone. But this is not the old way of chemotherapy. They will be taking a holistic approach with you. That is going to help you stay strong, despite the radiation and chemicals." She lifted the book in her lap. "Speaking of which, I brought with me a devotional I have truly enjoyed. You commented yesterday about wanting more services in the chapel. I thought… perhaps… in the meantime… we could do a morning devotional before our daily meeting about the children."

The queen put a hand to her chest, and Brodie feared she had crossed a line. "I have never participated in a devotional. I am interested," she finally stated after a long pause.

Brodie nodded and opened to the first page. "Long before Zacchaeus couldn't see Jesus, the tree was already planted and nurtured to meet his need…"

Brodie led the children to the dining room for lunch when she noted Jarle, the king's personal butler, uncharacteristically running through the hall to the king's office. The sight caused Mikkel to giggle. "Shhh," Brodie told the young prince, scooting him into the doors of the dining room. "Look, Antonin has already sat out your lunch. Go eat, and we'll do some painting afterwards." The promise met zeal from the children, and they promptly began eating their meal. "Don't eat too fast!" Brodie warned them before exiting into the hallway.

The speed at which Jarle traveled made Brodie anxious. Was the queen okay? The butler had flown quite rapidly for a man of seventy years.

"They're here now?" Brodie could hear Roffe's voice carry down the hall. "Please go tell my queen. She will wish to be prepared to see them."

"Yes, Your Majesty."

Roffe hastily strode down the hall, pausing briefly to note Brodie's concerned face. "Are the children having lunch, Miss Mayer?"

"Yes, sir."

He smiled genuinely at the 'sir'. "It appears we have our first non-tourist visitors since news of my queen's illness was released. Would you care to join me? He's an old friend of Gunnar's and myself."

The words 'an old friend of Gunnar's' aroused curiosity in Brodie, and she promptly agreed. Accepting the king's arm, she walked forward to the private entrance of the palace's south-end. A gentleman in his mid-forties and a woman in her late-thirties stood there. Both wore designer fashion, and the woman complimented her expensive threads with even more expensive jewelry.

"My friends! Welcome!" Roffe exclaimed. He hugged the man and bowed to the woman. "I would like to introduce you to our new nanny, Miss Brodie Mayer of America. She has helped Jonna with the children tremendously. Miss Mayer, may I introduce Lord Carl Baltzar Horn af Rantizen and his sister, Lady Valanice de Geer af Kolyma."

"A pleasure to meet you." Reminding herself of the king's words the day before, she did not offer either a curtsey.

Lord Carl guffawed hardily and clapped a heavy hand on her back. "What part of America are you from? Must be a change in weather for you."

Brodie smiled at the man. He seemed genuinely amiable, and his beard made his appearance seem like the Swedish nobles of old. "I'm from Texas, and yes, I'm adjusting to the colder climates. Your summer temperatures are comparable to our winters."

Lady Valanice appraised Brodie with a cold, lifted eyebrow. Brodie assumed she must be one of the 'lurchers' Gunnar had warned her of. "Texas?" the woman stated haughtily. "Gun-wielding, brutish cowboys."

The comment made Brodie's Texas pride swell. "As opposed to axe-wielding, brutish Vikings?" she retorted. "But it would be unfair to judge a modern nation by its history. We learn from our past wrongs, do we not?"

Roffe grinned at Brodie's response, and the sentiment caused Valanice's face to flare in rage. Carl laughed again. "I like you, Miss Mayer! You would get along well with Nyström. Where is the old man?" Carl asked Roffe.

"Old man?" Brodie turned to see Gunnar approaching them with a smile on his face. "I look half your age, Horn." The two men hugged. "Pleasure to see you again, Lady Valanice." The quick glance he shot Brodie ensured her that was not the case.

The woman merely replied with a nod of her head.

"It's been too long!" Carl exclaimed. "When was our last hunting trip? September? We didn't even put the skis on."

"August. Start of the season. I thought of you while I was in Texas," Gunnar replied. "They were discussing boar hunting, and I thought 'Horn would love this'."

"We should take a trip then," the lord declared. "I've never been, and Miss Mayer could give us the tour."

Gunnar smirked at her. "I doubt Miss Mayer would wish to join us on a hunting trip. She's not a fan of the sport."

Brodie smiled. "I understand the need for boar hunting in Texas, but I am not one to partake."

"That is a positively splendid necklace," Valanice interjected into the conversation. Brodie noted she had been inching steadily closer to Roffe. Their arms were now only centimeters apart. "Wherever did you get it? Or, whomever gave it to you?" The woman's eyes darted at Roffe.

"It was a gift," Brodie responded. Her fingers protectively jumped to the necklace, and she was unsure how to answer. "A promise."

"Of course, a young, beautiful woman like yourself would have a suitor," Carl agreed. "I'm sure you dashed his young heart when you moved to Sweden."

Brodie laughed. "I wouldn't call his heart young, nor would I say it was dashed."

Gunnar cracked a smile but contained his laughter. She managed a joke at his expense, and only the two of them could enjoy it.

Valanice, on the other hand, stared at Roffe. "A promise necklace from an older gentleman in Sweden then? How interesting." She shuffled past the small party. "Is Jonna unable to receive visitors? How is the poor thing doing?"

Brodie, taking note of the woman's actions, pardoned herself. "I must, check on the children. They're at lunch; I promised them that we would do some art. Excuse me." She hurried away to the bewilderment of the three men.

Still sitting at the dining room table, Kjerstin and Mikkel vigorously colored their drawings while Brodie drew her own picture of a ballerina. She instructed Kjerstin to design her first outfit while Mikkel was to draw a Viking warrior – axe and all. The young boy occasionally roared in delight as he created a piece of armor in his imagination and rushed to apply the creation to paper. His sister practiced silence in her focus. Brodie found herself impressed at Kjerstin's sincerity in being a fashion designer. Most ten-year-old's changed occupational goals daily; Brodie herself wanted to be a ballerina, zoologist, astronaut, and folk singer throughout the fourth grade. Kjerstin proved to be the exception.

The princess held two colored pencils aloft, examining the slight difference in their shades of blue. Brodie's mind ran through a list of ideas to encourage the child's fashion pursuit: everything from shopping to meeting designers to fashion shows. As royalty, the world was truly this little girl's oyster.

"Where Gunnar?" Mikkel asked.

"Where IS Gunnar," his sister corrected him.

Brodie smiled at the young prince's love of the man. "He's working to put a bad man away, and to keep us safe," she told him.

"Is it the bad man who hurt him?" Kjerstin asked her. Brodie was caught off-guard. "My mother told me that Gunnar has scars on his face because a bad man hurt him."

Not expecting the children to know about such things, Brodie answered honestly, "Yes. It is the bad man who hurt him."

Kjerstin stopped coloring the skirt of her design. "I hope he catches the bad man because that man wants to hurt my father too."

Mikkel agreed with his sister in a mixture of Swedish and English.

"Don't worry; your father is safe. Gunnar will make sure of that," Brodie told the children, and she believed it. The worry on the children's faces hurt Brodie deeply. No child should worry about their parents' safety.

"Gunnar IS hero." Mikkel emphasized the 'is' with an added glare to his sister. He pointed at his Viking drawing. "Gunnar." The Viking had blonde hair, like Gunnar's, with a traditional helmet covering the eyes. The armor was a mix of metal and animal hides; vicious spikes covered the armor, daring anyone to come too close. Several axes circled the Viking, and Brodie was unsure if Mikkel could not pick a single weapon or intended his Viking to carry an entire armory.

Before Brodie could respond, Kjerstin sighed and placed her chin in the palm of her hand. "I wish I was a hero, like Princess Snowdew." She referred to the animated princess she played as the day before. "Princess Snowdew left her castle and fought bad guys and helped people. I am a princess. I should do that too."

"I'm not sure there are many yetis for you to shoot with magic arrows," Brodie replied, "but you can still be a hero."

"How?"

"You can..." Brodie thought quickly, "be a good example to others. Help others that are in need. Be kind. Make your mom and dad happy."

"We should find people in need." She slammed her colored pencils on the table defiantly. "Let's go!"

Brodie chuckled. "How about you finish your design, and I will talk to your mother about you becoming a hero."

Kjerstin tapped her fingers on the table, eyes dancing between her half-finished design and Brodie. "You promise to help me become a hero?"

"Consider me the Twinkleberry to your Princess Snowdew."

The answer pleased Kjerstin, and she returned to her design.

Chapter Twelve

Roffe and Niklas left the queen's room to greet the approaching Brodie, Kjerstin, and Mikkel. The younger siblings cheered in delight at the sight of their older brother, racing to hug him tightly. Roffe stood next to Brodie. "Miss Mayer, this is my son and heir, Niklas Herik Victorsson. Niklas, this is Miss Brodie Mayer. I believe you met before in the treatment center, where my son was, unfortunately, very rude to you. I apologize for his regretful behavior."

Brodie smiled. "It was a stressful time for everyone; there are no hard feelings."

Niklas gave her a slight bow, but did not respond.

His actions caused Roffe to frown, but Brodie observed more. The prince's eyes were slightly red, and he seemed uncharacteristically languid. More than that, a faint, acrid odor drifted around him. It took only a moment for her to recognize the scent. "I believe Kjerstin and Mikkel are wishing to give their mother pictures they created for her," she hastily told the king, hoping to be excused.

"Please, allow me," the king told her. "This will give you a chance to speak with Niklas, or should I say, a chance for Niklas to speak with you."

She took a calming breath. Her week had been a hard adjustment. Valanice had only been the first of several lurchers, though she had been the only one to imply that Roffe had given her the necklace. The next morning, Brodie had spoken to Jonna of her suspicions. In their conversation, she did not reveal who the true giver of the necklace was, bust she made it clear to Jonna that it was not Roffe.

Now she had a new challenge to face. "Let's speak in private then, Niklas."

"Whatever pleases you," he flatly responded.

They walked to a side hall devoid of personnel. Brodie turned to him, anger plastered on her face. "Your father, and even your mother, may not detect the odor that surrounds you, or the glaze of your eyes, but I am from America where marijuana use is very prevalent. But it is *not* okay, and, in fact, it is highly illegal in your country."

"Back off lady," he told her. He turned to walk away.

Despite Niklas being several inches taller than her, she stepped back in front of him, cornering him against a wall. "No, I will not back off. Your siblings do not need to be around drugs. Smoking dope ends today for you, do you understand me?"

"You are not my mother," he lashed out. "I do not care why they hired you. I do not care if you are sleeping with my father. That does not make you the boss of me."

Brodie's head jutted back in shock: first Valanice, and now the king's own son believed this. She barely spent any time around the king; how could such suggestions exist? "They hired me to keep you from acting stupid, which you apparently are doing a wonderful job of. I am not sleeping with your father. And if you will not answer to me, then maybe I should go get one of the many SÄPO agents stationed here to investigate the aura of pot that surrounds you."

"They will not do anything to me," he responded with a roll of his eyes.

She gave a mock laugh. "Oh, sure, Gunnar Nyström won't do anything about you committing a crime? The monarch is protected from prosecution, not his heir." His eyes widened at the mentioning of Gunnar, and Brodie knew she struck a nerve. She held out her hand. "Do you have any on you? Or maybe we should go through your bags together?"

He uttered a profanity in Swedish, reached into his pocket, and handed her the small bag with the drugs inside.

"Are there any in your bags?"

Another profanity uttered, and they marched to his room. She forced the rebellious prince to watch his entire stash of drugs swirl down the flushing toilet.

"The moment I detect you with marijuana again, I'm going to Gunnar and your father."

He scowled at her as she left his room.

Antonin chopped the head off a halibut as he prepared the family's evening meal. Gunnar stood nearby with a copy of the queen's new diet in his hand. *"You can continue to prepare what you wish for the family, but the doctors want the queen's meals to emphasize these ingredients. It can help make her better."*

"Are these doctors saying that my food made Her Majesty the Queen sick?" The irate cook shook his butcher's knife at Gunnar. "Because these doctors know nothing of my cooking!"

"They're not saying that. However, I will say, if you do not follow these instructions, then your foolish pride is going to make the queen sicker."

The cook turned his nose up at Gunnar, but snatched the diet out of his hands. "Bok choy? Edamame?" he read. "Where do you expect me to get these foods from? They want fresh ingredients. How are these things supposed to grow in Sweden? Do they know anything about Sweden?" The cook continued to rant, but he pinned the two pages of foods to his large bulletin board.

"I am certain you can find plenty on that list fresh enough. You can borrow Brodie. She likes shopping for fresh food, just not meat."

Antonin grumbled under his breath.

"Speaking of which, what do you have to eat? It is a nice evening; she and I may eat in the garden once everyone is gone."

"Helgeflundra." He continued to butcher the halibut.

Gunnar shook his head. "She is a vegetarian. She does not eat meat. Got anything else?" He began to peruse the produce.

"It is a fish. She does not eat fish?"

"Is a fish an animal?"

"No, it is a fish. Your älskling can eat fish."

"One, fish is an animal, so she can't eat it. Two," he frowned, *"she's not my* älskling." The term was a common term of endearment in Sweden, but it indicated love. Did he love Brodie? It did not matter; Antonin did not need to know about any level of affection he held for her.

The cook turned to him with a raised eyebrow. "Nej?"

Gunnar replied with a slow shake of his head.

"Would have fooled me," Antonin groused. He waved his hand at the produce. "Make her something yourself. Do not interfere with me. I already must make two meals."

Satisfied with the confirmation that Antonin was going to make the queen a special meal, Gunnar turned back to the produce before him. Using his limited knowledge of Brodie, he began to prepare a vegetarian meal for two.

Sooner than Gunnar expected, Brodie walked into the kitchen for a cup of tea. She noted him and smiled. He returned the smile. "How are the children?"

146

"Kjerstin is brilliant. She made her first design this week, and it looks really good. I'd wear it." She reached for the tea leaves. "Mikkel made a design too, of armor."

Gunnar laughed. "You may want a to-go cup," he stated, before she could grab a traditional teacup from the cupboard.

She responded with an arched eyebrow. "You sound like you're up to something."

"I'm up to our dinner." He lifted a cooler and blanket. "If you're game."

"Oh, I'm game," she beamed. Her eyes darted to Antonin who hummed as he prepared his food. She was thankful for the sour man's presence. It helped to keep her emotions in check. The kettle chirped, giving her another distraction. While completing her tea, she could smell citrus and wood and realized Gunnar stood behind her. "You don't seem the picnic sort," she stated quietly.

"You have been trapped indoors all week, as have I. The fresh air could do us good, and you can tell me how your first week went."

She tightened the lid on her mug. "I could use a nice walk."

"We will definitely have a walk." He glanced at her shoes. "And you're wearing flats for once. Good thing."

The property sat empty with the visitors departed, though the usually green baroque garden was littered with pink sentiments for the queen. Two staff members gathered these items. "It's nice to see people bringing these things for Queen Jonna."

Gunnar shrugged. "Perhaps. All I see is a field of security risks."

"Nice to see the paranoid Gunnar Nyström has returned."

"I thought you didn't like that Gunnar."

"Eh. I didn't like him too much in America, but I think he's what Sweden needs."

"Only here a week and you already see that?"

"When children are concerned about their father's safety, even while distracted by their mother's sickness, there is just cause for paranoia."

"Wait." He stopped walking in front of the ornate fountain that rested in the middle of the garden. "Kjerstin and Mikkel are worried about Roffe? They shouldn't be concerned about that. They're only children."

"I agree, but they are concerned. And concerned about you. Mikkel wants to practically be you. You're the Viking he drew." She noted a flash of pride on his face. "But Kjerstin mentioned the bad man who put the scars on your face, and how that bad man wants to hurt her dad."

He turned his head back to the palace, concern in his eyes. "You reassured her, right?"

"Of course. I told them they had nothing to fear as long as we have you." She walked past him to circumvent the fountain. "And I believe it."

"Do you?" He began walking again, following Brodie around the fountain.

"Why wouldn't I? I wouldn't have taken this job with a potential target on my back if I thought you were incapable of protecting me." She picked up a pink rose that floated on the edge of the water. "And if I believe you capable of protecting me, who you've only known a short time, then I certainly believe you will do whatever it takes to protect the man who is your life-long best friend."

"I am glad you have confidence in me, at least."

"I'm not the only one who has confidence in you, or you would not be in charge here."

Gunnar watched her twirl the thorn-less rose between her fingers as they walked in silence. The affirming words comforted him, but he chided himself for needing to hear them. He had spent the week cross-referencing known associates of Strand with recent activities, but found no trail leading to the man. Even Strand's cyber-voice sat silent. The SÄPO agent could not help but feel it was the calm before the storm.

They finally reached a copious tree near a pond where a myriad of ducks, geese, and swans swam about. He laid out the thick picnic blanket and knelt down with the cooler. Brodie joined him, staring at the waterfowl. "I've never seen swans in person. They really do glide beautifully along the water's surface. I thought that was merely poetic expression. Could do without the geese honking frantically though," she chuckled.

"Swans, romantic. Honk of a goose, mood killer. Unfair to the geese." He set out the food, and Brodie smiled as she noted the contents. "Cucumber and tomato sandwiches, zucchini rolls, fava bean salad, cherry tomatoes, and fruit salad for dessert."

"What did you bring for yourself?"

"The same thing. Honestly, I do not know how you survive off of this. This is why you have noodle-arms."

She pushed him playfully on his arm. "I don't have noodle-arms! Just tiny arms. They're... graceful." She pointed to the swans. "Like the neck of a swan."

"If that helps you sleep at night." He grabbed one of the sandwiches and started to eat. "So, Mikkel wants to be me, huh?"

"He wants to be the Viking version of you, at least. He drew a very interesting picture, and I've never seen so many different axes in my life."

"There is a museum in Stockholm we should take him to. It's ancient Stockholm, built around some archaeological dig. Don't think he has been yet."

Brodie blushed at the phrase 'we should take him', though she knew it was part of his duty to go with her and the children should they leave the palace walls. "That sounds fascinating, especially about the dig. I wouldn't mind seeing that either. There's probably a lot of great things here that I would never imagine seeing in my lifetime."

"Maybe I should take you sight-seeing tomorrow."

"I would actually like that." She picked up a zucchini roll. "You know, a palace garden, picnic, swans on a pond, all that's missing is classical music playing in the background and poetry reading and we've got a movie made for British television."

Gunnar smiled. "I sense a Regency-romance in the works. Think I know what I'm getting you for Christmas." He finished his sandwich thoughtfully before beginning:

Have you love for me,
Yours my love shall be,
While the days of life are flowing.
Short was summer's stay,
Grass now pales away,
With our play will come regrowing.

Take it not amiss!
Sang I of a kiss?
No, I surely never planned it.
Did you hear it, you?

150

Give no heed thereto,
Haste I make to countermand it.

Oh, good-night, good-night
Dreams enfold me bright
Of your eyes' persuasive mildness.
Many a silent word
From their corners heard, -
Breaking forth with gentle wildness.

He laughed at himself. "Bjørnstjerne Bjørnson, Norwegian, not that the memorization held up. I forgot half the verses or so."

Brodie stared at him, a cucumber sandwich frozen halfway to her mouth. "Wow," she eventually breathed. How could she resist her feelings for the man when he recited a love poem at a romantic picnic? She stuffed the sandwich completely in her mouth so she could not speak.

"There is my graceful beauty, stuffing her face once again with food," Gunnar joked. "Was the love poem too on the nose? Should I have gone with a war poem instead? I know quite a few of those, but I don't believe it would have worked in your Regency-romance scenario." He popped a grape in his mouth and bellowed a hardy laugh. "Unless it was the greatest Regency-romance movie ever made."

"Men are weird," she managed, her mouth still mostly full.

He stretched out on his side, propping his head up with one arm. "We are what God made us."

"Speaking of which, I started doing Bible devotions with Queen Jonna in the mornings." She plucked a handful of the cherry tomatoes. "I think she enjoys them."

"What have the devotionals been about?"

His question surprised Brodie, but she responded. "One was about how God knows the battles we will face, and he prepares aid for us long before our battle comes. It used the story of Zacchaeus, and how the tree first had to be planted before he could use it to see Jesus."

Gunnar nodded his head. "I never thought of the tree in that way. My mother used to tell me that Joseph had to be a shepherd and even a prisoner before he could be an advisor to the king; I suppose that works too. Everything Joseph went through, good and bad, prepared him to aid the king and save Egypt." He smirked and ate a slice of apple. "I think that story of my mom's always spoke to me, aid of the king and all."

Brodie found her mouth slightly open at the truth of Gunnar's statement. Had her own hardships in life been preparation to aid a queen and save a country?

"You look surprised to hear that I know about the Bible. I may not be the best member of the Church nowadays, but my mom did teach me a thing or two when I was younger and smart enough to listen to her."

"No, it's not that I'm surprised at you knowing..." She waved a hand in front of her face. "It just revealed something to me, personally. That's all."

A few of the braver ducks left the pond and slowly waddled in their direction. Gunnar took out a small loaf of bread and handed it to Brodie. "I thought this may happen, and knowing you, you'd want to feed the birds."

She grinned. "You already know me so well."

Gunnar watched her leap to her feet to meet the ducks with pieces of bread. He enjoyed watching her innocently run around with ducks, and now geese, following her. If every summer evening could be like this, he would find himself very happy.

Chapter Thirteen

Gingerly, Brodie brought the coffee cup to her lips and sipped. The bitter taste of the black coffee made her cough. Gunnar laughed. "I do not see how you drink that, at least without some creamer."

"Says the girl who drinks her tea straight."

She placed the coffee cup on their table, turning her attention to the Budapest roll they shared. "Tea is amazing and not bitter. But I guess the sweetness of this," she pointed her fork at the roll, "does counterbalance the coffee. Wow."

Gunnar watched the crowded coffee shop with an amused grin on his face. "Half of these people are looking at us like 'Poor guy; he's having to show the tourist the ropes'."

"Wait, are they really?" Brodie lifted her head and surveyed everyone. Young and old alike were gathered in close-knit groups, engrossed in their own conversations. "They are not. Everyone's having a good time."

"My mistake. It must have been me thinking that." She slapped his leg under the table, but he caught her hand in his. "Enjoying your tour of Stockholm so far?"

"Absolutely! It is so pretty! And I love seeing the blend of architecture from the 16th century all the way up to the ultra-modern spaces. But, mostly, I love seeing the older architecture. We do not have much in the way of five-centuries-old buildings in America."

"You like that huh?" His amused smirk indicated that he knew she enjoyed it. He nodded at the Budapest roll. "And appreciating your first official Swedish *fika*?"

"Drinking coffee and eating my daily calories in one ridiculously delicious roll? Absolutely." She took an enormous bite of the roll to emphasize her statement.

"I know a way to burn off those calories you're consuming." He squeezed her hand slightly, pulling it up to the bench they sat on.

"Aside from going outside and shivering because it is only in the sixties out there like my winter?"

"You will get used to it after some time, but no, I don't mean shivering off your calories." He played with her fingers. "I thought we could go to my place."

She turned toward him with a surprised expression, unsure how to respond.

"Of course, we would have to make a stop first. You need something to wear besides this dress. Not that I don't like the dress; it just wouldn't do."

Her mouth opened and closed, and her brow furrowed. "I'm sorry... what?" She yanked her hand back, protectively placing it across her chest.

Gunnar stared at her curiously, unaware at what had caused her outburst. "I didn't think you'd want to sweat in your nice dress."

"What are we doing at your house, Gunnar?" she asked gruffly.

"Training," he said nonchalantly, taking a long draught from his coffee. "You're the one who suggested self-defense," he added after swallowing the bitter liquid down.

"Oh!" Brodie giggled nervously. "Self-defense. Yes, that makes sense."

155

"What…" He started laughing. Realization dawned on him. "Brodie, I know that you are a lady. I would never."

Reassured, she dropped her hand back down to his. "You're right. I would need a few things first. I don't really have workout clothes." She noted his glance at her arms. "And yes, that is why I have noodle-arms."

"I knew you would see the truth of it."

"But first I'm eating this roll. What do they lace it with to be so freakishly delicious and addictive?" She took another large bite, and Gunnar laughed at her zeal about the dessert.

Gunnar opened the car door for Brodie. "Welcome to my home." Outside of the city and surrounded by trees, his house reminded Brodie of what would happen if a red barn and a cottage had an undeniably charming child. It sat upon a hill, with steps winding up to the main entrance and down to a side entrance. Both sets of steps were lined with wrought iron railings and wildflowers. Given the split-level nature of the house, she felt it was safe to consider the house four-stories: two downhill and two uphill.

"You didn't tell me you lived in a fairytale book," she responded. She viewed the red picket fence that lined his winding driveway. "This is really beautiful."

"Come see the inside." He was delighted that Brodie liked his house. They climbed the stairs and he allowed Brodie inside first. "What do you think of that view?"

From the front door, she could see the open-concept floorplan of the living room, dining room, and kitchen. However, it was the entire back of the house which caught her eye. Massive, floor-to-ceiling windows flooded the home with light, and the view was of the surrounding forest opening to the water of the nearby canal. She walked to the windows, noting that a few were actually sliding glass doors that led to his wooden deck. A set of steps led from the deck down to the water, where a pier extended out to a boat.

Gunnar watched as Brodie eyed the scenery with her jaw dropped. "The pier and the boat are mine too, if you ever want to go sailing, or fishing. I know how you love fish."

Her wide-eyes turned to him, dumbfounded by his beautiful retreat.

"Come, I'll give you the tour." He pointed out the kitchen. "I gave thought to hiring a designer, we have a lot of those here, but I never thought I would have anyone here, so..." he shrugged, "I built it myself and made it the way I would use it."

"You built the kitchen yourself?" she asked, further impressed by his long list of skills. She walked through the kitchen, gliding her hand over the butcher block island.

"I built the storage, the counters, and the island. It was a renovation of the layout before. This is an old home; I had to do a lot of renovations to it, like opening up the back wall with windows to capture the view. I bought the house for the view."

Brodie looked at a side wall of his kitchen that held empty shelves. "What were you planning here?"

"Herb wall. See the way the sunlight hits the wall? It would have been perfect, but I realized I'm not here enough to do the herb thing. I don't cook enough to do the herb thing. But I haven't thought of anything else to do with the space."

"I like that idea though. Fresh herbs are the best."

"Maybe. Some day."

She noted the stairs leading down to his office and gym. "And what's down here? A quarry?" Her hand patted the stone siding used on the descending staircase walls.

Gunnar shook his head and smiled. "That's more original to the house, and the stone was too lovely to remove. Downstairs on the bottom split level is my home office and gym. And sauna."

"You have a sauna in your house?" Brodie shook her head. "That is ridiculous and incredible."

He pointed upstairs. "The bedrooms are up there. I opened up the view in the master to overlook the water too." She rushed to the stairs in order to see the view. He followed her, pointing out an empty room as they walked. "I never have guests, so I saw no point in making this a guest bedroom. Left it empty."

She peeped inside, noting the windows looked over the treetops. "It's a nice-sized room though, with its own bathroom?"

"*Jah*." He opened his bedroom door. "This is where I come to unwind."

The view was nearly the same as the floor below, but the height difference allowed for more water and less trees. The room held a bed, nightstands, dresser, and fireplace; a modern-style bookshelf and cozy armchair sat next to the fireplace. A door sitting ajar led to the master bath, and Brodie could see the large soaking tub within. "I can see why." She walked to the window, looking down at the view once more. "And I can see why you bought the house for the view. It's very relaxing. And the water is so blue, and the trees so green. Everything seems so... pure."

Gunnar joined her at the window. "The house is not very lived-in, and very..." He struggled to find the words. "It's a bachelor's pad. But it's home."

She turned to him with a smile. "I really like it. I'm trying not to be jealous, but I'm jealous. I could never imagine in a thousand years owning something like this."

"I don't have many expenses, so I spent it on this, and the land. It keeps me from having neighbors too close."

Brodie reached up and pulled him down to a kiss. Taken by surprise, Gunnar nearly fell on top of her. "I'm sorry," she apologized. She stepped away from him, covering her face with her hands in distress. "I don't know what came over me. We were trying to play it cool, and I do this. I've stirred it all up again."

"You do that every time you look at me, Brodie." He gently pulled her into a hug. "I can't stop thinking about you, and I can't stand being away from you for long periods of time." He kissed the top of her head. "When Valanice upset you, it was the first time I considered knocking a woman to the floor."

She buried her head in his chest. "I considered knocking her to the floor too. She honestly tried to imply that I was having an affair with Roffe. And she's not the only one to do so."

"What? Who else?"

"I can't say."

He ran his fingers through her hair. "You can tell me anything. Just like... I can tell you anything." He sighed. "Brodie. I need to tell you about Katarina." He led her to the edge of his bed. "She was my fiancé, and she was murdered by Strand."

Her face paled, and she sat hard on the bed. "Your fiancé was murdered by him?"

His hand reached up to his right shoulder, massaging it as he spoke. "I met Katarina twelve years ago. She was from Italy, and we were very happy together. I proposed. She said yes. We were going to be married in this huge, elaborate ceremony, and she was so eager in her planning. One day she left to meet with the florist, but she never made it to the florist. I searched for her frantically. Then a video reached Bolstomtavägen. It was Strand. He offered an exchange: me for Katarina. I followed his instructions, went to Uppsala alone, and was taken by one of his men to where he kept Katarina." Gunnar sat on the bed next to Brodie. He ran his hands slowly over his face, and Brodie could tell he was holding back tears. She stroked his hair. "He had lied. Right when I thought he was going to release Katarina, when her tear stained face looked at me with a glimmer of hope, he shot her. I will never get the image..." he choked, unable to complete the sentence.

She hugged him tightly though she was at a loss for words.

"Roffe, the others, they all thought the cuts, the torture he put me through after that, before agents arrived... they all thought that the physical pain was the real torture. It wasn't. Nothing he could do to me could equal the pain of seeing her death over and over."

"I'm sorry Gunnar."

"It's taken me a very long time to recover from all that happened, a long time to stop wishing I had died instead. Honestly, I still wish I had died instead for the sake of justice. She was an innocent. You are an innocent." He wrapped his arms over hers. "That is what this monster is capable of. He reached right into my being and ripped my still-beating heart out, and I did not get it back until you. I do not want him to do that again. I want to keep you at a distance from me, to protect you. But it keeps me from giving you what I wish to give you, and he wins either way. But at least the second way, you live."

Brodie pressed her cheek against the top of his head. "Do you remember when we talked about the Americans and French refusing to let the terrorists change our way of life? We mourned, but we did not stop living."

"I understand what you are trying to say, but I care about you too much to put you in jeopardy."

"Gunnar..." she knelt in front of him and wiped the tears from his eyes. "I am not saying we announce to the world that we are together. But we can't ignore... I can't ignore how I feel about you."

He slid down to the floor to join her. *"Min vackraste,"* he whispered, kissing her forehead. "My private sanctuary can now be our private sanctuary, if you wish *käraste.* You're welcome here at any time."

"Maybe I'll plant those herbs for you." She settled back into his arms, setting her gaze upon the scenic view outside.

"Plant whatever you like." He attempted to point to part of his land from their seated position. "Over there, I thought of planting a garden after I built the toolshed. Toolshed's complete, and now it's just sitting in the middle of an empty patch of land. If you've got any ideas, I'm more than willing to hear them."

She rested her cheek against his. Her mind wandered with domestic ideas, and she had no desire to stop her daydreaming. "I wouldn't know what grows in this climate. But I can find out. I liked the flowers out front."

"They're wildflowers." He, too, found his mind drifting in a sea of domestic thoughts. The house was purchased by him after Katarina's death, and he used the renovations to take his mind away from the thought of her, of any woman. He had wanted nothing more than a hermit's retreat to wallow in his own misery. Now the house posed a new opportunity – with Brodie. *"Du är så vacker,"* he mumbled as he ran his fingers over her neck.

She peeked back at him. "I am... what?" she asked, hoping for a translation.

Gunnar's blue eyes sparkled, reflecting the subtle waves of the water outside. "You are so beautiful."

She blushed. "I really like you Gunnar."

"I really like you too Brodie." He tilted his head, regarding her intently. "I..." he paused. "I will do whatever you want me to do."

Her heart pounded as he leaned her back into a kiss.

Chapter Fourteen

Sunday morning, far before sunrise, found Brodie using the footboard of her bed to stretch. Her whole body felt as though it had been beaten, and she wished the palace masseuse worked on Sundays. Despite her petite frame, she was not in peak physical condition like Gunnar, a man who moved like a twenty-year-old. The man had trained her in basic self-defense. She believed their prior conversation about Katarina caused him to be tougher on her. After learning how to take down various attacks, regardless of strength- or size-advantage, he reproached her lack of strength-training and sent her to his weight machines.

Now her body cried out in pain.

But there was no time to be in pain. The queen wished to ride with the family for Sunday morning service, and Brodie would need to see to the children's preparation for such an outing. She opened the ornate armoire doors and perused the dresses purchased from the thrift store. She opted for a long-sleeved, black, conservative number. Although unsure about the formality of the church, she assumed that any place attended by a royal family warranted a solemn wardrobe choice.

While walking to her bathroom, a soft knock sounded on her bedroom door. She opened the door to find Mikkel standing there, clutching his teddy bear nervously. "What's wrong Mikkel?" she asked, kneeling down to speak on his level.

"Bad dream."

Brodie reached out to hug the boy. "It's okay. You can sleep in my bed. Will that make you feel better?"

He nodded silently and shuffled to her bed.

Before closing the door, she observed Gunnar headed down the hall, coffee in hand. He spotted her and strode to her door. "Good morning," he whispered, leaning in to kiss her.

She placed a hand on his chest and bobbed her head toward her bed. "Mikkel had a bad dream and is in my bed."

"Bad dream, huh?" He eyeballed the bed, seeing the young prince on his side, curled up with his bear. Brodie nicked the coffee cup from his hand and stole a sip. "Hey little thief, I didn't think you liked coffee."

"I needed the caffeine," she responded, choking down the liquid. "My body is sore."

Gunnar grinned with pride. "It should be. I worked you over pretty good."

"Gunnar?" Mikkel called out, hearing his buddy's voice.

"I'm here, *lille prinsen*." Gunnar walked over to the bed and sat next to him. "I heard you had a bad dream."

The boy nodded and leaned forward to whisper in the man's ear.

"That is a bad dream," Gunnar agreed. He patted the bed. "You lay back, and I'll tell you a story."

Brodie gathered her clothes and beauty supplies to take into the bathroom with her. She grinned at Gunnar relaying his tale in *svenska* to the lad.

"A long time ago, there was a mighty warrior named Einar. He fought many battles, and even faced a fierce dragon that held a maiden hostage. Einar became respected by the Vikingar for his fierceness in battle, and whenever trouble would strike, they would cry out, 'Einar, protect us.' And Einar would lift his axe and protect them.

"One day, a cruel ice-witch attacked Dagmar, the Queen of the Vikingar, and stole the queen's heart. The witch was jealous of the queen's beauty and grace, and thought if she took the queen's heart, the queen could no longer be beautiful or graceful. It caused the queen to become very ill, and she hid away in her castle. Her king, Gudbrand, mourned for her, and called for the witch to be hunted. Many young warriors of the Vikingar heeded their king's call, but others told the king, 'What of Einar? He has defeated the dragon! He can best the ice-witch!'

"Hearing this, the king called for Einar, and the mighty warrior obliged. He bowed before the king, and offered his services to his lord. The king told him of the ice-witch and the evil which she had done. He told Einar to travel west over the great ocean to find the man who knew how to defeat the witch. Einar obeyed the king's command, though he did so with great unease. For the king believed that Einar had, in fact, defeated a dragon, and thus could defeat the witch. But the truth was, the dragon had defeated Einar and merely fled the kingdom. Einar swore he would hunt the dragon and destroy the creature, but by the king's request, he was forced to journey west, away from the dragon.

"Einar crossed the treacherous ocean to the magic land of Gart, where the great wizard Havardr lived. The wizard was old, and had fought the ice-witch all his life. As the great wizard told Einar of his struggles with the witch, a beautiful elven maid entered the wizard's tower. Being an elf, she was far shorter than Einar, but her lean body was spry, allowing her to run unheard from her enemies. She apologized for interrupting the wizard and his guest, but Havardr beckoned her to him. 'This is the great warrior, Einar of the Vikingar, and he has been sent by his king to find a way to kill the ice witch.'

"The mentioning of the ice-witch angered the elf. The wizard explained to Einar, 'Alvilda's mother was killed by the ice-witch, and she seeks vengeance on the witch. You must take her with you in your quest.'

"Havardr's suggestion caused Einar to scoff. He was a mighty warrior, and needed no one to aid him, especially a small elf like Alvilda. The wizard held up a hand to the warrior to silence his protests. 'You will not be able to overcome this witch alone mighty warrior. You must take Alvilda, for her elven magic will be needed in your battles.' The wizard then gave Einar a ruby the size of his fist. 'This is an enchanted ruby that will help you track down the witch to her lair. Once there, you must work together to destroy her.'

"With the magic ruby in tow, mighty Einar and little Alvilda left the wizard's tower. He held the ruby aloft, and it guided them toward the witch's lair. Many enemies attacked Einar and Alvilda, but his great axe, and her magic arrows, struck down the creatures time and again."

Gunnar stopped speaking once he noticed Mikkel sleeping deeply. Carefully, he slid off the bed so as to not wake the child and crept to Brodie's bathroom door. A slight rap on the door signaled her to open, and she complied.

"Sounded like an interesting story. Maybe you can translate it for me some time," she whispered as she styled her damp hair.

He leaned against the closed door and shrugged his shoulders. "Maybe I could even finish the story. I'd like to know how it ended."

"You came up with that long story yourself?"

"About Einar the mighty Viking warrior, and Alvilda, his beautiful, short, elf companion?" Gunnar grinned at Brodie's blushing. "I think a higher power wrote that tale, and I'm merely imparting it a different way."

"Still… though… it's impressive. You can come up with a story like that to put a child to sleep."

He began massaging her back. "Like you weren't doing the same with those children at the treatment center. Or coming up with songs off the top of your head, or magic tricks, or puppet skits." He watched their reflection in the mirror. "I have to go see to the Royal Guard. See if they're ready for the procession," he whispered with a kiss on the cheek.

"Procession? Wait, is this going to be a big spectacle? Are people going to see me, or do I get to be in the background like you?"

He twirled her hair in his fingers. "You will most likely be seen. But just act normal." He noted the fear on her face. "*Hej,* they might not even see you. You're short, *jah?*"

She bit her lip in thought, and Gunnar reached down to kiss it. "I really must go to the Royal Guard."

"I will see you before we leave?"

"You'll see me when you get there. Just follow the king and queen. Loke and two other agents will be riding with the family and you. I have to see to the security of the church first."

"Okay." Brodie kissed him, not wanting him to leave her. She felt confident leaving the palace with him by her side, but, alone, she felt exposed to lurchers like Valanice, to critics, to paparazzi, and to Strand. She shivered, but Gunnar's gentle touch calmed her, for the moment.

167

Brodie stared at the cover of several Swedish tabloids. Her *svenska* was minimal, but enough English-language publications were amid the group to paint the picture: according to the world of the paparazzi, Brodie was the king's new mistress.

"Have you read the articles?" she asked Jonna. The two shared morning breakfast and tea before their devotional and agenda meeting. "I'd be afraid to."

"Rubbish journalism, if you can call it such. Hints of my eventual death, my husband's infidelity, and your involvement with it all – the whole scandal sounds like the work of Valanice and others who have insinuated as such during their time here this past week. Roffe did not warm to their advances, and now their vindictive natures have consumed them. But besmirching the Royal Family is old business to the tabloids, and those who embrace its gossip. We will merely counter it with a more reputable course of action."

The nanny held her hand to her head. She never had been the one for limelight. Even in her high school speech class, she fought the desire to flee. Performing in front of children was easy; being in the eyes of her peers was much, much harder. "I am so sorry that they even think I would... you know, with Roffe."

Queen Jonna smiled. "You have done nothing wrong. I know where your loyalties lie. You are my friend, Brodie. I even know where your heart lies."

Brodie's cheeks flushed.

"That secret is safe with me. You have both done well keeping it from others, but neither of you can hide it well when speaking with me about the other. The twinkle in your eyes gives it away."

"Does he know that you know?"

"Absolutely not, it would frighten him." The queen spread lingonberry preserves over her whole wheat toast. "I imagine the privacy is due to Strand?"

"It is."

"That is wise." The queen nodded to the tabloid. "I will speak with our publicist, and have her arrange interviews with various, *reputable* magazines. I am certain they will be interested in learning about the new royal nanny after this. Furthermore, go out and be seen with Mikkel and Kjerstin, but not Niklas. I do not need the horrid tabloids twisting the story from an affair with the king to an affair with the under-aged Crown Prince." Brodie blanched at the notion. "I agree. It is disturbing, but disturbing is what sells their papers. Niklas is old enough to see to himself, and his father wishes for him to remain in his office with him in order to teach my son his future fate."

The news was the best Brodie had heard all morning. She hoped Roffe's positive influence would help Niklas revert to his pre-drug behaviors.

"At the end of July is the king's birthday, and this year I wish to have a birthday ball for him at the royal palace. I will be bringing in an event planner that has worked the Nobel Banquet, and I may need your assistance in responding to her inquiries, should I be… indisposed."

While the queen's health no longer declined, she was not getting stronger. Frequently she rested, allowing the chemicals to fight the cancerous cells. "I understand," Brodie agreed.

"There will be many dignitaries. The Prime Minister, ambassadors, including your US ambassador, and a variety of nobles and prominent families of Sweden. That will include single, young, attractive, female nobles who will do their best to throw themselves at the king. Despite your previous statements, I still do not wish those, women," she said the word bitterly, "to come anywhere close to my king. And I suspect that with this tabloid piece, rumors will quickly spread among the small-minded. It is vital we use this time to establish that you are who you are.

"I have contacted a few tutors for you, as we spoke of last week. They will teach you *svenska*, dance, etiquette, and anything else we need to help you overcome this unfortunate event. Brodie, I do apologize. I never once believed such rumors would happen; it is not a circumstance I wished to put you through." The queen placed a frail hand upon her friend's and offered a sorrowful smile.

"It's okay. You aren't the one who caused this. It's the evil in their hearts that did so." Brodie patted her hand. "If anything, the injustice of it all only gives me more resilience to continue my work."

"That is good, because I imagine as each week passes by, I will rely on you more." Her eyes sparkled as if a sudden thought entered her mind. "I nearly forgot, in light of the king's birthday, I had Tatiana gather old photographs. Some may interest you." Brodie followed the queen's instructions to a decorative box full of photos. "Gunnar's birthday is only a few days before Roffe's; they have been as close as brothers since birth."

Brodie looked through the photographs. They revealed Gunnar as a baby, a young child, a teenager, and as a young adult in college. His skin was smooth without scars, his blonde hair stylishly teased in the late eighties/early nineties style, and there was a hint of mischievousness in his eyes. She blushed at the pictures.

"I am glad he has found love in you," Jonna told her. "He has been lonely far too long."

170

"Oh... I don't know about love..." Brodie hurriedly protested.

Jonna smiled. "But I do. I am happy for you both."

With her face turned away from the queen, Brodie blushed at the thought while looking over the pictures.

Gunnar stepped out of the royal family's official town car, checking the street for any threats. "Clear," he alerted the others on the security detail. He assisted Brodie out of the car and the two youngest royals. "Ready to see Vikings, little prince?"

"*Jah!*" roared Mikkel.

Gunnar grinned and closed the car door behind him.

"Take my hand Mikkel," Brodie instructed the young boy. He obliged, and with Kjerstin holding her other hand, the small group journeyed down the sidewalk to the museum entrance.

"Paparazzi have arrived," Gunnar whispered to her. "You are being seen out, just like the queen wanted."

Brodie smiled at him. "You take bullets shot from a gun for the family, and I take metaphorical bullets shot from a camera for them," she joked.

"I like your dress Miss Brodie," Kjerstin told her as she skipped over a crack in the sidewalk. Brodie wore a royal blue 1950s swing dress with a bulky yellow belt. "I am going to design one, except the top of the dress will be blue and the bottom will be yellow, and it will have a white belt. I will call it..." the girl paused with a whimsical smile, "Swedish Swing!"

Brodie smiled, picturing the dress Kjerstin described. "That sounds pretty cute, Kjerstin. I would buy it."

171

Gunnar opened the door to the museum, and with a fast glance, ushered them inside. "I, for one, am excited to finally come to this museum."

"What? You have not come to this museum?"

He shook his head and grinned. "Why do you think I suggested it for Mikkel? I wanted to see it too."

The museum's tour guide greeted them and began to lead them through the exhibits displaying centuries-old artifacts of medieval and ancient Sweden. Mikkel's eyes widened as he eyed a Viking longboat suspended from the ceiling, and Brodie noted that Gunnar's eyes did the same. The bodyguard knelt next to his young buddy, pointing out the different features of the boat. An image of the child-Gunnar from Jonna's pictures ventured into Brodie's mind, and she suppressed a giggle.

They were led away from the ship toward a medieval town set-up in the museum. Different tradesmen worked their various crafts, and the children were mesmerized by them. Mikkel could not be budged from the blacksmith's stall, and Kjerstin watched a weaver in amazement. They asked for an anvil and a loom, respectively.

"I'll put in a good word with the Tomten," Gunnar told them with a smile. He turned to Brodie to translate with a whisper, "Santa."

"Oh! Yes. I will leave a good word as well." She personally found herself mesmerized by the glassblower, and was in no hurry to depart until the man finished the bottle he was creating.

"May I have axe, Gunnar?" Mikkel asked him, pointing to the display on a nearby table.

The bodyguard eyed the weapons on the display table. "This one seems the right size." He held a hand-axe up to

172

Mikkel, and for the child it may have been a full-sized battleaxe. "What do you think?"

"We go kill *häxa* like Einar!"

Brodie and Gunnar exchanged a glance. "I believe that is a noble quest," she told the young boy and his Einar-counterpart.

Not to be outdone by her younger brother, Kjerstin found a small, handwoven tapestry to hang above her bed. Gunnar paid the tradesmen cash, with a generous tip for each. The three joined Brodie at the glassblower's stall.

"Isn't it fascinating?" she asked her bodyguard. "It starts out hot and wild. In time, it becomes a beautiful, functional piece if given the proper care..."

"... or a lump of dysfunctional shattered glass," Gunnar agreed. His eyes shifted to Brodie. "Very allegorical."

The edges of her lips smiled. "I hadn't thought of it that way. But very true." She eyed a piece already completed on his table. "Do you sell your goods as well?" she asked the man while he set his in-progress bottle to cool.

"I do. What piece do you like?"

Brodie pointed to a heart-shaped bottle, colored with deep reds and whites. "How much for the heart?"

"1200 SEK," he replied.

She attempted to evaluate the cost versus the beauty of the bottle and decided the price was worth it.

"I feel like I should get something," Gunnar joked as she handed the glassblower her money. "Everyone has a piece of history but me."

"I'm surprised you didn't get yourself an axe. Then you and Mikkel can play Viking."

"One does not play Viking. One is a Viking."

173

"Whatever you say, Einar." She winked at him and led the children to the awaiting tour guide.

Chapter Fifteen

Brodie leaned against Gunnar's car. He stared at her, questioning for the millionth time why she was with him. She wore an off-the-shoulder shift dress fashioned of bright-sixties-paisley material, and black go-go boots to match. The outfit, coupled with the scarf in her hair and oversized shades, made her carefree age more prominent. "I'm still adjusting to how narrow the streets are," she told him, motioning down the sidewalk she stood on. "But they're absolutely adorable. Look at these buildings. And look at all the pretty flowers, and the green bench. It's just... quaint. But not in a condescending way."

He knelt down, picking one of the flowers she pointed to. "Here you go, my flower-child, a *färgkulla.*"

"Where I come from, I think it's called chamomile, like the tea." She smiled and placed the golden flower behind her ear. "But it's pretty no matter what language the name is in."

He pointed to the yellow-bricked building across the street from his car. "Hungry?"

"I could ransack a garden like a crazed rabbit."

"Then you will love this place." He led her into the clatters of the busy restaurant. "This is an all-you-can-eat buffet... of nothing but vegetarian food."

"Are you serious?" she asked excitedly.

He bobbed his head 'yes' and waived at a waiter. The man motioned them over with wiry, tattooed arms. "Gunnar Nyström!" he greeted Gunnar with a hug. "I must say this is a place I thought you would never dine at." The waiter's British accent explained his choice of English over *svenska* to greet the couple.

"For the longest, I thought the same." Gunnar smiled at Brodie. "But for a good friend, I'm willing to make an exception. Brodie Mayer, this is Zavier Drummond, an old hippie from my London-days."

"Old hippie?" Zavier laughed. "I prefer to say, old friend. And any friend of my old pal Gunnar is a friend of mine." He shook her hand. "And I must say, I love this outfit."

Gunnar smirked. "Like I said, old hippie."

"Pleased to meet you Zavier, and thank you."

He waved for them to follow him. "I've saved you the best seat in the house."

Brodie followed the two men through the restaurant to its back patio. The view took her breath; the restaurant sat on a high hill overlooking the canal between Slussen and downtown Stockholm. Zavier led them to a private booth that faced the water. "The buffet is inside. Coffee for you, I take it?" he directed the question to Gunnar.

"Why even ask?"

The man's grin spread wide across his face. "And what can I get you m'lady?"

"What do you have in the way of tea?"

Brodie felt as though she had sung "God Save the Queen" due to his enthusiastic reaction. "Gunnar, where did you find such a beautifully charming lady with a love of tea?"

"Texas," he answered while attempting to remove a smudge from his aviator shades.

"Texas?' Zavier winked. "If I thought I had a chance, I'd ask you out on the spot."

Gunnar grunted.

"You flatter me," Brodie responded with a blush.

"It's not flattery my dear. So, our tea list..." He clasped his hands behind his back and began reciting the restaurant's long list of tea.

She gasped. "I could stay here, drink tea, and watch this view all day."

"Take as long as you want," Gunnar told her, finally satisfied with his smudge-less sunglasses. "We don't have anywhere to go until this evening."

Brodie glanced at Zavier. "I'm certain I can't stay here that long."

The Englishman lifted his hands innocently. "I'd have no complaints if you stayed."

She laughed. "Then I guess I'll take an oolong and see where the day goes." After Zavier left to fetch their drinks, she turned to Gunnar with a smile. "Where are we going this evening?"

"It's a surprise." He leaned back in the seat with his arms behind his head. "Racking up points while I can."

"Points for what?"

He grinned mischievously. "Whatever I think of."

Zavier returned with their drinks, and Brodie eagerly took her tea. "Thank you!" she beamed at the Englishman.

"Don't make me blush," he joked and walked away.

"Just think, you can be spending your Saturday with a guy like Zavier," Gunnar suggested.

Brodie put her tea down. "He's not a bad guy, just not my type."

"Not your type? He's like the older, male, British version of you – with tattoos."

"Gunnar..." she whispered. "If I wanted to date myself, I'd buy a mirror. You are my type."

He blushed, and the lines around his eyes wrinkled.

She pointed to a sailboat meandering down the canal and changed the subject. "Would you believe I've never been sailing?"

"I can believe that, and I can change it as well. Remember, I've got a pier and a lonely sailboat that hasn't been touched this year," he replied, putting down his coffee. "Come on; let's get you all that bunny food."

Brodie leaned back in their private booth with her feet propped up on the table. "So... much... food..." She poked her stomach. "I'm going to have a tea baby, look at this lump."

"Are you going to be able to walk?" Gunnar twirled a toothpick around his fingers. "Or will I have to carry you around for the rest of the day?"

Moaning, she attempted to lean forward. "I think I can... maybe..."

"You're doing a good job of it." He put the toothpick in his mouth. "I was thinking about my house and how it could use a little, personal touch. I told you about the garden, and the herb wall. But it's a little barren. Think you could give it the designer touch?"

"You want me to give a feminine touch to your home?"

"I want you to turn my house into a home. It's very... minimalist – doesn't look like anyone really lives there." He fidgeted with the toothpick. "I want it to be more inviting, for you." He stumbled over his words. "You're the only company I have, that is."

"It was pretty white: white furniture, white walls, white material." Brodie rubbed her full belly as she reflected on his house. "With that incredible view, though, would be nice to bring in some of the colors and textures."

He grunted an approving sound.

"You don't have any art, or throw pillows, or knick-knacks, or anything that says 'This is Gunnar's home', so that may be nice. And more warm blankets, for when I'm visiting." She attempted to sit up again. "Oh man, you're going to have to roll me out of here like I'm Violet Beauregarde."

"You're not a giant blueberry yet." He stood and stretched his back. "But I thought we could walk the neighboring shops and let you find those throw pillows and knick-knacks and whatever else you have planned."

"Shopping?" She slid her feet off of the booth's table, and stood. "That sounds like a wonderful plan."

"Magic words! 'Oh, I cannot walk'," he mimicked her. "Then, 'hey let's shop!', and suddenly, she's miraculously able to put her feet under her."

She playfully hit Gunnar in the shoulder and headed inside the restaurant.

"Leaving already?" Zavier called to them with a wave. "I thought you were staying all day."

"I told her I'd escort her shopping," Gunnar joked. "If she was out with the flu, it would have cured her." He handed Zavier a roll of krona. "Cover the bill and the tip?"

The waiter counted the money. "That's a very generous tip. When did you get so nice?"

Gunnar paused at the door of the restaurant. "Texas," he called over his shoulder.

Zavier responded with a thumbs-up and knowing wink.

"I was thinking about your herb garden wall, and I've seen where people have mini metal troughs. It will give the roots more wiggle room and bring in that earthy, rustic texture. And you can have matching metal containers out on the deck. Tie it all in."

They walked down the winding sidewalk to window-shop the stores. Brodie nearly skipped as she rattled on about gardening and decorating Gunnar's house. Gunnar strode steadily beside her with an amused grin on his face. "Mhmm," he agreed, enjoying listening to her plans for his house.

"And in the living room, you can bring in some blues and grays because the view of the water is absolutely stunning from the angle of the couch. Maybe you can find a nice piece by a local artist to go on the wall that's all sad and blank."

"My wall is sad?"

She looked up at Gunnar and pouted. "It's so sad, Gunnar. It's so sad!"

Running his fingers through his short blonde hair, the Swede chortled. "What if I painted that wall blue or gray?"

"That would be pretty." She peered into a store window. "This is fun, isn't it? Like... playing house." She quietened and turned back toward Gunnar. "Is that what we're doing?"

"I don't know." He watched a couple bicycle past them on the narrow Swedish road. "How would you feel about that, if we were?"

"It's a bit soon, but it's not like I'm living with you. I'm just decorating for you."

He nodded. "Right, just decorating."

"For you," Brodie added.

"Right." He turned his attention back to the toothpick. "Because it would be absurdly too soon to think of playing house."

"Absurdly." They walked along in silence until Brodie noted an organic produce stand and gardening shop. She dragged Gunnar inside for herb scouting.

Gunnar parked his car, full of supplies for his herb wall, outside a chic theatre in Slussen. A crowd of young adults shared coffee at the entrance, discussing art, music, and politics. Brodie inquisitively pressed her nose to his car window in order to watch the group. "What is this place?"

"Little two-floor theatre that has concerts for that indie folk music you like."

Her hair flew as she whipped her head to face him. "You're taking me to a concert for music you don't even like?"

"It's not that I don't like it." Brodie arched her eyebrow at his lie. He chuckled. "It's tea to my coffee, so to speak. That said," he took her hand in his, "I have no idea if the bands performing tonight are any good, because it all sounds like whiney women and men to me."

She pouted. "I sound whiney when I sing with my music?"

"You don't, but you don't sound like them."

"What do I sound like then?"

He lifted her petite hand to his lips. The action covered his blushing and inability to respond promptly.

181

"That bad, huh?" she joked.

Shaking his head, he kissed her fingers. "That good."

Brodie matched his blushing face. "Will… will they be singing in Swedish? Probably?"

"Actually, one of the bands performing is from America."

"Really?" she asked excitedly.

Leaning to the side with his head nearly resting on Brodie's shoulder, Gunnar pulled his phone out of his pocket. "Let me look who it was." His free hand quickly flew across the screen and retrieved the theatre's calendar. "Some group called Sweeter Peaches?"

A high-pitch squeal left her lips in response. "I love those guys!" She yanked the phone from his hand to look at the line-up. "They have an amazing harmonica player, and the lead singer has this gravel-vibe to his voice. And they have a banjo. Banjoes are what make this world a happy place."

"It's banjoes that do that?"

"Banjoes and puppies." She scrolled down the calendar. "Wow! Look at all the groups that come here! This place is amazing. Oh! In a month, Lake Eerie Band is coming! We have to go to that one. They're more rock, so you might actually enjoy yourself."

"I might enjoy myself tonight. Sweeter Peaches have a banjo after all."

She giggled and kissed his forehead. "Not just anyone can get away with sarcasm, but I like when you do it."

He offered a half grin and reached to open his car door. "We should stop before people get too close to the car. My tint job is only so good."

Too excited to wait for Gunnar, Brodie leapt out of the car and spun around. "Wow! A Sweeter Peaches concert. And that vegetarian restaurant! I really like this part of town."

"I had a feeling you might, Flower Child," he joked. "Should I get you a tea, or have you reached your tea threshold?"

"Threshold. I'm going to need to find a restroom in here. But I did almost try all of their teas!" she added cheerfully.

"The caffeine is showing." He handed their tickets to the doorman. *"Var är toaletten?"* Gunnar asked the man.

He pointed the way to the restrooms to the duo.

"I'll be near-ish by. I don't want to scare any women by standing too close."

"I think I'll be fine," she winked and disappeared into the restroom.

Gunnar leaned against a column, wishing he had another toothpick to pass the time with. Mass laughter announced the arrival of a group of college students entering the theatre. One young man, wearing a knit cap and thick-rimmed glasses pointed out Gunnar. *"When did they start hiring bouncers?"*

"There was a fight a few weeks ago. Maybe they want to take a precaution," one of the female students responded.

"Isn't he a little old to be a bouncer?" another attempted to whisper, but failed to do so.

The Sapö agent flared his nose at the comment.

"Hey, ready to get a good spot?" Brodie asked him. Pulling her hair back in a ponytail, she excitedly skipped to him. Her giddiness instantly faded the moment she saw the panged expression in his eyes. "What's wrong?"

"Nothing," he mumbled. He turned to leave the lobby and enter the theatre.

Observing the situation, and the glares cast by the students, Brodie placed a comforting hand on his arm. "They said something, didn't they?" she whispered to him.

"I'm too old to be a bouncer," he grumbled.

"You're not old."

"I was in *gymnasieskola* when you were born. Yes, I'm old." His words were bitter, and Brodie realized that the age difference ate away at him more than she imagined.

"Gunnar, I'll be thirty next year. It's not like I'm a college kid like them. Plus, you have a body of a twenty-year-old. I bet you could run laps around them."

He glared down at her with skepticism. "You don't have to lie to protect my feelings."

"I'm not lying." She put a hand on his chest to stop him from entering the theatre. "If I could get away with it, I'd kiss you here on the spot to shut those idiots up."

"It's not them. It's me too." He patted her hand. "We'll talk about it later. This is supposed to be fun for you. Sweeter Peaches have a banjo."

She smiled half-heartedly and entered the theatre. More pockets of youth greeted them inside, everyone sharing stories and coffee among themselves. "This does feel like moving to a new school and not knowing anyone," Brodie nervously joked. "Glad you're with me." She continued to scan the groupings before eagerly grabbing Gunnar's hand. "Look over there! It's Sweeter Peaches!"

"Why don't you go meet them?"

Brodie nervously hid behind him. "I don't want to bother them."

"They're meeting fans. You are probably more of a fan than anyone here." He pushed her toward them. "You'll be happier for doing it."

Sweeter Peaches consisted of four siblings, two brothers and two sisters, and a male cousin. The sister who played the banjo turned toward Brodie and Gunnar as they approached. "Hello!" she cheerily greeted them.

"She's too shy to say so, but she's a big fan," Gunnar announced, giving Brodie a final push. "Especially of the banjo."

"I'm a fan of the banjo too," the sister replied with a laugh. "Do you play?"

"I only play piano," Brodie responded; the slightest hints of nervousness traced her voice.

The other sister of the band, who played the bass, turned her attention to them. "Wait, I recognize you from somewhere."

"I've been to one of your shows before," Brodie replied. She shrugged. "But I never had someone literally push me to meet you."

"She's the royal nanny," the oldest brother with the gravel-voice told his sisters. "The news talked about her, remember? She's the American who moved to Sweden to be the nanny to the royal family."

Brodie stood in shock. American news channels were talking about her? One of her favorite bands recognized her? The phenomenon was surreal. "They talk about me?"

"It's the gossip news," the banjo-sister retorted dismissively. "I wouldn't pay attention to it."

"They say bad things about me, don't they?" Brodie could feel her heart plummet. It was bad enough to have Swedish tabloids talking ill about her, but America was her homeland.

"They say bad things about everyone. Really, don't worry about it."

She looked up to Gunnar, and he forced a smile on his face. "The Queen's plan will work, and everyone will get to know the real you. It will be okay Brodie."

"Are you her boyfriend?" bass-sister asked, reaching out to shake his hand.

"I'm the bodyguard," he replied casually. Hearing the question lifted his spirits. The members of the band seemed in their older-twenties, like Brodie, and if they believed he appeared young enough to date Brodie, then perhaps he was being too cynical.

"Wow, a bodyguard? That's pretty cool."

The band and duo mingled, chatting about music, America, and food. Brodie recommended them to the nearby vegetarian restaurant and to have Zavier as their waiter. Before the lights dimmed and the band returned to the backstage area, they all posed with Brodie for Gunnar to take their picture. Sweeter Peaches and Brodie were equally excited about having a picture of the 'other celebrity'.

"Can you believe that?" Brodie asked Gunnar while making their way to their seats. "They talk about me, peon me, on American gossip channels. Isn't that anti-American? I'm not there to defend myself. We're supposed to be able to face our accusers."

"I don't think your media, our media, or any media really plays by those standards."

Exacerbated, she threw her hands in the air. "Why would anyone want to be a celebrity?"

"I'm sure there are perks if you're a really, really big celebrity... maybe."

"Not worth it."

A local band took the stage first, singing completely in Swedish. Brodie, despite only understanding an occasional word, enjoyed the music. She danced in place often, and at other times, Gunnar surreptitiously placed his hands on her hips in order to lean in and whisper interpretations of the lyrics. Next, the Sweeter Peaches performed their set. Brodie happily sang along with every song, clapping a rhythm. The show reached the hour and a half mark, and a slight intermission was granted before the final two bands.

"I have to use the restroom again," she whispered to Gunnar. "I shouldn't have drunk so much tea."

"But Gunnar, tea is good for you," he mocked her voice, following her out of the theatre to the restrooms in the lobby.

"It *is* good for you. It's flushing all the impurities out of my body at rapid pace tonight."

The crowd proved thick in the lobby, and Gunnar walked ahead of her to clear a path. She held tightly onto the back of his shirt in order to not lose the man in the multitude.

"*Hej!*" A younger man pushed his way to Brodie. "*Ursäkta mig!*" His pushing broke her grasp on Gunnar's shirt, and the bodyguard felt the disconnect. "I know you!" he continued in English. The man had obviously been drinking alcohol rather than coffee.

"I'm sorry. I don't believe I've met you," Brodie declared, attempting to reach Gunnar.

187

"No, no. You're the American who's sleeping with the king!" His loud voice caused many to turn to the scene with interest.

"I'm not sleeping with the king." Fear rose within Brodie, and she wanted nothing more than to leave the theatre.

"That's enough pal," Gunnar told him. He pushed the man aside to place himself between the drunk and Brodie. "She is here to enjoy the music and have a good time like everyone else. You don't need to spoil it."

The drunk man attempted to reach past Gunnar to grab Brodie's arm. "Hey, I know I'm not royalty, but maybe you can do me a favor."

"Don't touch me," Brodie hissed at him.

Gunnar easily pushed the arm away. "Like I said, that's enough pal. Maybe you should return to your seat."

A woman began asking those around her if Brodie was truly sleeping with the king. Another confirmed the rumors because of the tabloids. Others mentioned how horrible a thing it was to do with the queen not even dead yet. The murmur spread through the crowd, and hands from behind Brodie grabbed her arms. She shrieked in terror at the touch, causing Gunnar to spin around. "Hands off!" he commanded.

The new drunken man holding Brodie responded with a fist thrown in Gunnar's direction. The bodyguard easily side-stepped the futile attack. Two more drunks leapt in to replace him. Gunnar dodged their punches as well, shuffling his feet to keep close to Brodie. Another man swung wide at Gunnar, hitting Brodie in the mouth instead. "Alright, you idiots asked for it," Gunnar announced.

He spun around, kicking Brodie's-hitter in the stomach. The man went flying into the crowd. This aroused more anger in the drunken crowd, and soon intoxicated men and women alike began brawling among themselves and with Gunnar and Brodie. Brodie did the best she could with the little self-defense Gunnar taught her, but found that despite the overwhelming chaos, she did not have to defend herself much. Gunnar, no longer attempting to be a peacekeeper, swept her into his graceful movements of high kicks and quick punches. His momentum allowed him to use his body as a shield for her while warding off attackers. It also carried them closer and closer to the door.

"Duck," he told Brodie. She immediately complied, and he sent a punch through a chair a man was about to use on her.

"Behind you," she told Gunnar from her crouching position.

He grabbed a piece of the shattering chair and swung it behind him, knocking the attacker down. "Come on," he leaned his body over Brodie and took her by the waist. Eluding the final throng of attackers, they reached the doors of the theatre as sirens sounded. "Run to my car," he told her, thrusting his keys into her hands. "Lock yourself inside. I'll be there shortly."

Brodie ran to the parking lot before the police arrived while Gunnar returned his attention to the hundred or so people who were out of control. The non-drinkers of the night attempted to flee the madness of the theatre, but found themselves trapped inside. Gunnar attempted to clear a path for them. In doing so, he found himself face-to-face with the college student in the knit cap and thick-rimmed glasses. The student, not a fighter in the slightest bit, shook with fear.

"*Tack*," he thanked Gunnar.

Gunnar wanted to retort about his age but merely waved them through the doors.

The yellow and blue *polisen* cars screeched to a halt outside the theatre. Gunnar calmly walked out to greet them, hands

189

held up with his badge displayed. Before he could call out, a chair cracked across his back. He stumbled momentarily before spinning and knocking the perpetrator to the ground with a right hook.

"You're Gunnar Nyström," one of the younger officers declared. *"You taught hand-to-hand combat at* Södertörn."

Gunnar wiped a trail of blood that ran down his cheek. A fresh cut sat below his eye. *"That's me."*

"What happened here?"

"A bunch of drunks started a fight at a concert," he answered nonchalantly.

"And why was that fight started?" a female officer asked suspiciously. "Why was Säkerhetspolisen here to be involved with it?"

Her colleague chided her. "He's not a regular agent; he's in charge of the royal family's protection." The man gasped. "One of the members of The Family isn't here, are they? Are they okay? Were they hurt?"

"I was here with the royal nanny. I'm assigned to her." He jerked his head at the original brawlers being led away in handcuffs. "Those idiots started to physically accost her, claiming she was sleeping with the king – which she's not – and it brought the drunken part of the crowd to anger."

"When did the angry mob turn violent?" the female officer asked.

"When they punched her in the face." Gunnar stood. "That's assault against someone under the Royal Family's protection." He pointed out the man who had hit Brodie. "I want to see that man in Bolstomtavägen."

The young officer diligently took notes as Gunnar spoke, giving them details about the initial confrontation. He refused to let them speak to Brodie and claimed he needed to tend to her medical treatment.

"And if that leaks to the press from the Polismyndigheten, *heads will roll,"* he gave a final threat and walked away to his car. Ambulances littered the available space, and paramedics walked through the calming crowd, offering first-aid to small injuries. Those with more serious injuries were loaded into the back of the yellow vehicles and rushed to the nearest hospital. He tapped on his passenger window and could hear a startled scream from within. "It's me Brodie," he called, soothingly.

The car door opened, revealing the crying young woman within. She held her face where she was punched, and her eyes were already red.

"Oh baby, don't cry," he whispered. He knelt down and hugged her. "Don't cry."

"This is entirely my fault. All those people are hurt and injured because I was there." She buried her face against Gunnar's neck. "I should never leave the palace."

"It's not your fault. They started this fight. That's what happens when you drink to excess." His words caused her to cry harder, and he realized she was probably reminded of her father. "Listen, you can't blame yourself for other people's choices. You hear me?"

She sobbed an 'uh-huh'.

"Let me see your mouth. Does anything feel broken? Your jaw okay?" He tenderly felt the swelling on her cheek.

"It hurts. I don't know how to tell if it's broken."

"Does it feel like your teeth have been turned inside-out?"

"No."

191

"That's good then. That's good." He wiped her tears away with his thumb. "He had a very weak punch, and that helps. You'll be a little sore and bruised."

She frowned, noticing the cuts on his face that bled. "You're bleeding."

"I'm taking us home, to my house. We need to get ice on your face and stop the swelling." He retrieved his keys from her. The parking lot filled with emergency personnel, theatre staff, concert attendees, and now with press. "Time to light the siren." He grabbed a small light and siren from a lockbox and placed it on his car dash. "Buckle up, lean your seat back, and close your eyes and ears. It'll be loud for a moment."

The siren blared, but did its job as Gunnar successfully managed to pull out of the parking lot. He kept the alarms going until he left Stockholm traffic behind for the quieter countryside he lived in.

"How do you not have a headache?" Brodie asked him once he turned it off. "That is so loud."

"What did you say?" he asked, slightly shouting. "I can't hear you." He turned to her with a grin. "I got used to it back in the day." His voice returned to a normal decibel. "But it does cause a little pain in my head."

He pulled into his long driveway, and Brodie felt herself getting sleepy. "I still need to use the restroom," she reminded him drowsily.

"Don't fall asleep," he quickly replied. "You can't fall asleep."

"But I'm sleepy."

He parked the car and helped her to the front door of his house. "You're sleepy because you have a concussion. You can't fall asleep for a little bit, okay? Go to the restroom, and I'll get your ice."

She stumbled to the main floor's nearby half-bath, barely able to close the door behind her.

"The queen is going to kill me," Gunnar mumbled as he grabbed an ice pack from his freezer and wrapped it in a towel.

"You shure I can't take jusht a quick, little nap?" Brodie asked while stumbling to his couch. He noted the slurring of her words. She attempted to unzip her boots but was unable to succeed. She threw herself down on the couch.

Gunnar sat on the floor, placing the icepack over her mouth. "I'm very sure. Stay awake for a few hours, and then I'll let you sleep. Okay?" She nodded while he slipped her boots off. "Stay sitting up. That'll help you stay awake. I'm going to go make my cuts stop bleeding." He entered the restroom and procured his first-aid kit from the medicine cabinet.

While rummaging in the kit, he dialed the queen's direct line. Jonna calmly listened to his recount of the incident, and his occasional grunt from the sting of medicine on his cuts. Upon completion she simply stated, *"You did all that you could do."*

"But, Your Majesty, I..."

"Gunnar, she cannot stay trapped inside the palace, and, with the gossip spread by Valanice and these journalists, something of this nature was bound to happen. That is why I wished for you to protect her."

"I failed at that. I think she has a concussion. She certainly is going to have a bruised face."

"She would have fared far worse without your presence."

"She is afraid of the children seeing her in this state."

193

"She can take time to heal. She should take some time if she has a concussion, anyway. We will be attending the service at the palace chapel. I believe we can manage the children."

"Yes, Your Majesty."

She wished him a goodnight, and he left the restroom to find Brodie staring at his ceiling. "I'm not shleeping," she whispered. "Jusht lying down. Makesh my head and fashe feel better."

He found a blanket and pillow and walked to his couch. "Come here sweetheart. You can use my lap as a pillow."

Brodie wrapped herself up in the thick blanket and laid her head on the pillow that sat in his lap. "That's comfy. I like thish blanket." She rolled on her side to face his stomach, and Gunnar's abs held her ice pack in place. "Feelsh like a giant shweater, but the shnuggly kind, not the itchy kind."

"I talked with Queen Jonna," he informed her. He rubbed her back while speaking. "She isn't upset and wants you to take tomorrow off to heal."

"But I can't go to the palashe. What will the kidsh think?"

"Stay here."

"I don't have anything here. Thish ish a conundoo-rum... conun-a-drum...conundrum."

Gunnar grinned at her drowsy speech. "You can borrow my clothes, and I can go get you something at ICA. Need to grab some food anyway. My pantry and refrigerator are empty, and I can't go catch you a fish for breakfast."

"If I ate fish, that would be a very woodshy thing to do," she agreed. "You're like a Shwedish Paul Bunyan, but without the blue cow. Or Daniel Boone? No, you're tall, sho probably Paul Bunyan." She raised her index finger, indicating she had a thought. "You think Paul Bunyan wash actually a Shwedish

194

immigrant and that ish why he wash sho tall?   Have I dishcovered the shecret of the shtory?"

"And the cow was blue due to frostbite?" Gunnar asked, unsure of the story she spoke of. However, he was willing to pursue any conversation to help her stay awake.

"That makesh shense. It'sh a Shwedish conshpirashy." She paused. "Gunnar, why do you care about your age? At the theatre, you were sho shad, but, I like your age. I like you. And I think your age hash helped make you who you are."

"Wrinkled?" he joked.

"Nooo," she retorted with the wave of her hand.   "A gentleman, and helpful. And really handshome. You're very handshome." She lifted her hand to stroke his face, attempting to be careful with his cuts, but her hand and arm did not respond as sharply as normal. "At firsht, I thought you were shcary, but then I realized the height and the mushles and the jawline were really handshome. Sho handshome. You think I'm handshome?"

"I think you're gorgeous." He kissed her roaming hand. "You know how I feel about you Brodie."

"Do I?"

He pulled her hand down to his chest, letting it rest against his heart. "You feel how fast my heart pounds? You're the reason for that. In a fight, I can steady the beat of my heart. When I shoot, I can time the squeeze of the trigger between my inhale and exhale. But around you, I lose all control. You drive me crazy, and all I want to do is be near you and hold you and make you happy."

Brodie stared up at him, her mouth open from the pain and pressed against the ice pack. Her hair was disheveled, and her makeup – what little remained – was streaked from her crying. "How can you shay that when I feel and look like poo?"

195

Gunnar smirked and kissed her hand. "Because I don't see poo, I see the beautiful woman I care about."

"If I could, I would kissh you, but I think moving might make me vomit."

"Yeah, we don't want that." He straightened her hair and pulled the ice pack away from her face. "Twenty on, twenty off." He checked his watch. "I can take you up to the bed and find something for you to wear." He lifted her easily in his arms as he stood and walked to the stairs.

"Now you know why you need a guesht bedroom," she told him as they passed by the empty room.

"I don't know. Think I'll leave it empty. The emptiness suggests possibilities."

"Posshibilities like turning it into a big library, or a mushic room," she leaned her head back over his arm, "or a nurshery."

Gunnar stopped walking at the word. "Nursery?"

"Yesh, you might have tiny man-giants shomeday." She giggled. "I shee the way you act with Mikkel. You shecretly want a tiny Gunnar."

He pushed against his bedroom door with his hip. "I never thought about it. Maybe I'm too old to start a family." He set Brodie down on his bed and remained leaning over her. "Do you want children?"

Her eyes slightly rolled back, and she placed her hands over her forehead. "Dizzy wave. Shorry. But yesh, I do. Someday." The slurring began to clear up while she spoke.

"I see." He walked to his dresser and slid open a drawer. "Would you want children with an agent whose very job puts him and his loved ones in danger?"

196

"I might," she whispered. She rested her hands on her stomach. "I might if that agent would learn he doesn't have to fight his demons alone."

He pulled a long shirt out of the drawer. "Maybe he does that so no one else gets hurt by them."

"Gunnar, come here." He did so, staring at the shirt and avoiding eye contact with Brodie. "I pray for you daily. I pray against the demonsh you fight. They already hurt me becaushe they hurt you." She gingerly set up and motioned for him to sit on the bed beside her. "But I think my prayers can only go sho far, if you don't pray too."

The Swede wrapped his arm around her bare shoulders. "How can I pray to someone who let Katarina die?" It felt good to have the question said aloud. For a decade, the question had festered within him. Why had God let Katarina die at the hands of that psycho?

"Because Strand killed Katarina, not God." Brodie took Gunnar's hand. "I asked these questions too, Gunnar. I asked, 'why would a loving God let my mother die? Why would a loving God let my father be taken from me shoon after?' I couldn't understand why He would allow sho much shuffering to enter my life, and I grew bitter."

He watched her hand caress his, but did not respond.

"Sho I understand. Why didn't God just heal my mother of cancer? Why did He let her get cancer to begin with? Why did He let Strand kill Katarina? Why is there even evil in the world?" Her words became clearer as she continued on. "There is evil because He gave us free choice. We have the choice to love or to hate, and the only way to defeat hate is to love. Katarina died because Strand chose long ago to give his life to hatred."

"That still doesn't explain why God didn't stop him."

197

"I can't answer that. There's a master plan that we see little of." She pointed to the mirror over his dresser. The reflection appeared blurred due to the darkness of the room. "For now we see in a mirror, dimly, but then face to face. Now I know in part, but then I shall know just as I also am known."

"That's what I don't like about this. I'm supposed to accept her death as part of a master plan?"

"Do you remember what you told me on our picnic? 'Joseph had to be a shepherd and prisoner before he could be an advisor to the king.' How do you think Joseph felt when his own brothers threw him in a pit to die, or sold him in slavery, or when he went to jail? He could have let bitterness destroy him like so many of us do, but he didn't. He had faith, and it was revealed to be a master plan."

He grunted, annoyed she had used his own words against him.

"Maybe you should pray. It's about relationship, not religion. If you were mad at me, wouldn't you talk to me about it instead of bottling it inside and letting it breed into a bitter hatred?"

"That would be the healthier option."

"This isn't any different." She exhaled deeply and took the shirt from his hands. "Think I'll need more ice."

He kissed her forehead. "You are pretty and wise, even with a concussion."

"I'm going to be pretty and asleep soon. I can't hold out much longer."

"I'll be back with the ice." Gunnar left the room and hurried down the stairs to grab a fresh ice pack. His mind replayed everything Brodie had said. It made sense, yet it did not make any sense. His anger at God was still as fresh as the moment he watched Strand pull the trigger at Katarina's head. Could he not have let the gun jam? He slammed his freezer shut at the thought and turned off the lights to his main floor. He easily could have let the gun jam.

A soft voice sounded in his mind. If Katarina had lived, then he would not have Brodie.

He paused on the bottom step of his stairs. "But if Katarina had lived, why would I have needed Brodie? I don't even have Brodie. It's dating. I was engaged to Katarina," he responded to himself and hurried up the stairs.

Brodie had managed to change into his shirt and crawl under his covers. She turned to face him with a weary smile.

"Here you go sweetheart." He placed the ice pack on her mouth gently. "You go to sleep, and I'll go to the store and grab some things for you."

Her hand covered his, holding him in place. "Gunnar, I'm glad you're with me. I thought I was happy doing what I was doing in America, but now I'm here... you're who I never knew I needed."

"You need me?" His question was quiet and slow.

Her eyes already closed, she responded with a nod and whisper, "I need you."

Gunnar leaned down and kissed her forehead. "*Jag älskar dig,*" he whispered, but she was already fast asleep. He shifted the ice pack on her so it would stay in place on its own. "If you let Strand take her from me like You did Katarina, I will never forgive You," he whispered. With a final kiss on her forehead, he left for his home office and gym.

The sun landed on Brodie's face and her eyes fluttered open. With a grunt, she turned her head away from the bright light which sent sharp pains through her head. Her aches felt duller than the night before, and she uttered a prayer of thanks. "Gunnar?" she whispered. The pillows and blankets had the faintest trace of his cologne, and she buried her nose in the pillow, enjoying the comforting scent. The scent and the soft mattress relaxed her.

From the hallway traveled Gunnar's voice speaking his native tongue rapidly. The tone of his voice indicated he spoke about official business. Attempting to climb from the bed, she succeeded to slip a leg out from under the blanket as the Swede entered his bedroom. She smiled at him and pushed her hair out of her face.

The sight of her caused him to smile, and his tone softened. "*God dag*," he spoke into the phone before turning it off and dropping it in his pocket. "*God förmiddag*," he told Brodie. "I thought you were going to sleep all day. How's your head?"

"It feels better, but the sun is a little bright."

"I can fix that." He walked to the window and pressed a button on the side. A wide shade slowly descended to mute the blazing sun.

"That's fancy, Nyström."

"Main floor has it too." He sat at the foot of his bed and took her free foot in his hand. "Feeling hungry?"

She giggled as he slightly tickled the bottom of her foot. "Depends on what you're serving." She pressed her foot against his chest to protect from his tickling.

"I had *filmjölk* and berries while you slept." He ran his hands over her lower leg and massaged her calf muscle.

"That sounds good." She made to stand, but Gunnar used his hold on her leg to keep her in bed.

"I will bring you some." He left the room to retrieve her meal.

Brodie grinned at the thought of breakfast in bed. She propped the pillows against the headboard and sat up. He returned with the yogurt-like substance, berries, and two cups of coffee on a tray. The tray also held a yellow flower that caused Brodie to smile.

"Reminded me of that flower song your band sung last night," he mumbled, taking his cup of coffee and walking to his shaded window.

"You're a softie." She mixed her berries into the thick, sour milk slowly. "Thank you. I don't remember much of last night, but I remember you took care of me."

"So, you don't remember that magical kiss and how you were going to start eating meat again?" Gunnar shook his head. "That's a shame."

"Almost had me with the magical kiss, but not that meat thing." She took a bite of the *filmjölk* and winced. "I promise I'll get used to the taste sooner than later."

He indicated a few shopping bags on top of his dresser. "I picked up some things for you while you slept. I have no idea if they'll fit, but I'm sure it'll be better than trying to fit in my clothes."

"I don't know what I would do without you," she admitted. She pushed around a lingonberry with her spoon. "That scared me last night. Hearing their anger and feeling their hands on me." She frowned. "Imagine if you weren't there."

"I don't want to imagine that."

"And it made me think about Niklas. He thinks the same as the angry crowd did. I knew we started off rough…"

Gunnar stopped her. "Niklas thinks you're sleeping with his father?"

"He is going through some things, which, I can't really talk about, but he needs help. He's the one I came to help the most, and he's the one I'm helping the least."

"Why can't you talk about it?" He sat on the bed next to Brodie. "You can tell me anything."

She shook her head. "I can't… for now. If things get out of hand…" Her face contorted, and Gunnar stroked her hair.

"Don't worry about it. I'm sure you'll be fine. You're wiser than you know. You spoke some sense to me and you were on the verge of passing out."

"I can't imagine I made sense at all last night. It's such a blur. I almost didn't realize where I was when I woke up."

Gunnar moved the tray to a nightstand. "Even if you can't remember, I can. And I'm the one who needed to hear it."

"Glad I could help then." She wrapped her arms around his waist and rested her head on his chest. "I don't want to leave your arms."

"I'm happy with that." He kissed her forehead and closed his eyes. The night before had been a restless one for Gunnar: a trip to the supermarket, a lengthy phone call with headquarters about the fight, an anger-riddled workout in his personal gym, and fishing from his pier. His attempt to sleep on the couch was met with tossing and turning.

His breathing began to slow, matching Brodie's slow breaths, and soon they were dozing in each other's arms.

Chapter Sixteen

Brodie sat in the Drottningholm palace's meeting room with Queen Jonna, the royal family's publicist, and Gunnar. The king paced frantically behind his wife. "How could people possibly believe that I would have an affair?" he yelled. All remained silent as he ranted. "How little do they think of their king? How little do they think of their queen? And to resort to violence over the situation? That is unacceptable! We brought Miss Mayer here to heal wounds and make life easier. This is not healing."

The American felt like a failure.

Jonna spoke. "Miss Mayer is not at fault for the press and malicious women like Valanice de Geer af Kolyma spreading abhorrent rumors about you or her. There are those who rely on falsehoods and the most contemptable stories possible in order to achieve their agendas. It is unfortunate that so many have chosen to listen, believe, repeat, and respond with violent outbursts. We will simply meet these rumors head-on. Is that not correct, Agnetha?" She eyed the publicist who nodded her head.

"Indeed, Your Majesty, we will use Miss Mayer's unforeseen celebrity status to project a positive message about her, the royal family, and the new initiative Her Majesty the Queen wishes to begin for the cancer society."

Red-faced with anger, Roffe asked, "Are you assured this will work, or will it only escalate the problem?"

"Your Majesty, the reason they say 'there is no such thing as bad publicity' is because an effective publicist can make any horrid incident into gold for their client. I reassure you; I can cast Miss Mayer in the positive light she deserves."

"My love, trust me," Jonna calmly stated, reaching a hand out to her husband, "this too shall pass."

He kissed her hand. *"Mitt hjärta, mitt liv,"* he whispered to her.

The sentiment caused Brodie to smile and cast a glance at Gunnar. Her Swedish bodyguard already had his gaze upon her and offered the subtlest of winks when their eyes met.

"Do not trouble yourself with this further, Roffe," Jonna told her husband. "We shall oversee Miss Mayer's publicity, and she shall continue to help with the children. Now we have your birthday to plan."

Brodie marveled at the tactful way the queen had told her husband, 'I love you, but get out.'

"I understand." He kissed her hand once more and walked to the doors. "Gunnar!" he called out. Gunnar stood to his feet and followed the king out of the room.

The event planner entered shortly after their departure, complete with a portfolio holding her presentation. Brodie helped the woman and her assistant set-up the various boards. The level of detail amazed Brodie.

"You recall our conversation about Miss Mayer's dress," Jonna reminded the event planner. "This is the young lady."

"Of course, Your Majesty." She nodded her head at Brodie with a snap to her assistant. "Pictures and measurements." The assistant pulled out his phone and measuring tape to comply. "We will have something made for her before the ball. I'll bring in hair and makeup as well."

"Nothing too heavy in makeup," Jonna responded. "Brodie's greatest physical feature is her natural beauty."

Brodie blushed at the queen's compliment.

"As you wish, Your Majesty." The planner made a few notes on her tablet before turning to her meal board. "You requested a light, summer-time menu with some traditional Swedish flavors, and we hope you enjoy our selection." She handed everyone a menu. "I also strived to keep the color-theme within the food selection as best as possible."

The king had only one request for his birthday ball: he wanted the color to be pink in honor of his wife's fight with breast cancer. Ladies were expected to wear pink, and gentlemen were expected to wear pink boutonnieres with their tuxedos. Brodie's stomach flipped in anticipation over the ball.

"Drink selections will include fresh-squeezed pink lemonade, blackberry limeade, watermelon coolers, peach mojitos, strawberry bellinis and margaritas, and pink sangria."

Brodie found herself thirsty after such a list. Despite that half of the drinks were alcoholic, they still represented the delicious fruit drinks available in the summer.

"Hors d'oeuvres will include tomato flatbread with goat cheese, fresh corn blinis with smoked salmon and chive cream, mini lobster rolls, peach and pepper kebabs, and grilled shrimp salad in radicchio cups."

"And that is two vegetarian options?"

"Yes, Your Majesty. We consulted your diet plan to formulate this menu."

Queen Jonna, pleased with the response, nodded.

"For the birthday cake, we have hired Chef Sévère Alban LeClerc to create a strawberry layer cake. Here is his design." She indicated a beautiful, multi-tiered cake with the Royal Family Crest drawn on the middle tier. Intricate flowers flowed down the layers, coupled with the variety of red berries that grew fresh in the Swedish summer. "In addition to His

Majesty the King's cake, we will also serve a rhubarb sorbet for a cold-pairing."

"This sounds delicious," the queen approved.

The event planner smiled with a sigh of relief. "Next, we have our decorations." The planner went through every minute detail of the ball, seeking the queen's approval on each.

Queen Jonna obliged her with consistent approvals, but when discussing musicians, she turned to Brodie. "Miss Mayer, do you dance?"

"I..." she stuttered. "No, Your Majesty." Brodie could dance her own funky American moves, but no proper dances for a royal ball.

"We will need a dance instructor sent to the palace for Miss Mayer and to give my son, Prince Niklas, a refresher course."

The planner made another note on her tablet.

"I also expect a few representatives from the cancer society momentarily. I plan on doing an initiative in conjunction with the society to raise funds for cancer research. I will announce this initiative to the press this week in the baroque garden, and then have a silent auction at the ball to launch these funds."

"Do you know what you will be auctioning?"

The queen shook her head, and turned to the others. "I am open to suggestions."

Everyone remained silent. Brodie stared at her hands in deep thought. "Kjerstin." She smiled. "Kjerstin's clothes. She has her sketches ready to be created as doll clothes. We can have the dolls as models, and people can bid on the princess's first designer set. Most of the designs are pink; it will work perfectly."

"And my daughter will finally feel like a hero," Jonna agreed. "I like this idea greatly."

"I will set aside a place for the auction," the planner agreed.

Agnetha moved her seat to sit beside Brodie. She showed her tablet screen to the young woman. "Her Majesty the Queen asked for me to set up a few official social media accounts for you to use, and for me to train you in how to use them."

Brodie skimmed the page. "And this will work?"

The publicist smiled. "I am the royal family's publicist for a reason, Miss Mayer. Trust me."

Chef Antonin served lunch for the planning committee upon the arrival of the cancer society's representatives. Another hour passed as plans were made, and Brodie excused herself to retrieve Mikkel and Kjerstin from their summer tutor. Taking the stairs too quickly, she nearly collided with Loke around a blind corner. "Oh, I am so sorry Loke."

The young agent helped to steady her. "It was my fault completely, Miss Mayer."

"Please, call me Brodie."

"Of course, Brodie." He bowed his head, watching her continue down the hall. "By the way, Brodie," he called out, jotting after her, "I was wondering, if maybe…"

He faltered on his word choice, and Brodie knew what was coming.

"I was hoping, to ask if you, needed…" he stammered over his words. "Could I have the honor of accompanying you to the King's Ball?"

Gunnar returned to the hallway, removing his earbud as he walked. He paused as he watched Brodie and Loke.

Panic consumed Brodie. "I… I'm sorry Loke. I'm already attending with someone else."

"Someone else?" Loke asked in surprise. "You have already met someone here in Sweden?"

"Yes, his name is…" Brodie bit her lip. "Zavier. His name is Zavier. He's British."

The name drop surprised Gunnar.

Loke's surprised face was forced into a smile. "Of course, Brodie. You're very attractive and kind; I should not be surprised that another has already approached you. Please, excuse me." He walked away in a huff.

"You're attending the King's Ball with Zavier?" Gunnar asked.

His voice startled Brodie, and she spun around to face him. "I guess I am now." Her hands went to her temples. "I was panicked, and I just blurted out the first name I could think of that wasn't yours." Gunnar laughed. The action further frustrated Brodie. "This isn't funny."

"It's going to be hilarious to see Zavier at a ball. I can't wait until we tell him."

"We tell him?"

He affectionately patted her back. "I'll always have your back, Brodie. Let's go round up those children." They continued up the stairs, discussing the intricacies of a ball.

"I am sleepy Miss Brodie," Mikkel told her. He yawned to prove his point.

"Sleepy? What were you doing in your lessons?" Brodie inquired.

"He was running around mostly," Kjerstin giggled.

"Were you supposed to be running around?" Gunnar asked him.

"I was moon!" he answered happily. "I was spinning fast!"

"The moon?" Brodie asked with a smile thrown to Gunnar.

"I will show you Miss Brodie," Kjerstin told her. "You stand there like the sun. And I will be the earth, and I walk around you in a circle." Kjerstin walked around Brodie in a circle and began spinning. "Then I rotate while I walk around you. Then the moon starts..."

"Moon!" Mikkel shouted and jumped in, spinning around as he circled his sister who circled Brodie. "Moon is fun!"

Brodie laughed. "Alright Mr. Moon. You can take a very short nap." Gunnar grabbed him and lifted him into a spinning hug at Brodie's statement. "Can you get him to bed, and I will check on you both shortly to make sure he's actually sleeping and not playing Einar?"

Gunnar grinned. "I cannot make promises." He headed to Mikkel's room, still spinning the boy around.

"Kjerstin, your mother thought of a way for you to be a hero."

The little girl bounced up and down. "She did? She did! Oh! I knew she would! My mother is the greatest!"

Brodie smiled. "She really is. Your mother is going to begin a project to help others who are sick like her. And she would like for you to help her."

"How can I help?" The princess's eyes lit up with sincerity, but her hands were held out innocently, feeling she had nothing to offer.

"You know the pink dress designs you've drawn?" The girl acknowledged with a bob of the head. "What if I help you sew

210

those this week for some dolls, and we put on a fashion show of your designs. Then, at your father's birthday ball, we sell the dolls and your clothes."

"And the money will go to help the sick people?"

"That's right."

Kjerstin's smile reached from ear to ear. "Yes! I love this! And my mother thought of it? Isn't she wonderful? I will give her extra kisses today."

Brodie patted the girl on the head. "I think she would really like that. Let's go gather your designs and bring them to my room where my sewing machine is."

The princess took off at full speed down the hall to her room. Brodie slowly walked after her, pausing at Mikkel's opened bedroom door.

"Sleep," she whispered to Gunnar who held a plastic shield to deflect blows from the prince's plastic battle axe. His mock innocence cause Brodie to laugh – if only she could attend the ball with him.

Chapter Seventeen

Gunnar stood with Niklas at a makeshift shooting range in the English garden of the palace. Visitors had already left for the day, and Loke stood nearby to ensure no one disturbed the target practice.

"Have they taught you shooting at school?" Gunnar asked, raising his bore rifle.

"They have not," Niklas responded. He examined his unloaded rifle.

"How are we supposed to have young Olympic biathlon winners if it's all skiing and no shooting?" He aimed at the target fifty meters away and shot.

"Perhaps you should enter the Olympics," Niklas suggested in response to the perfect shot.

Gunnar laughed. "That's a young man's sport." He lowered his rifle and turned to Niklas. "Training to be a competitor, and Olympian, that's a good pursuit for a young man, even a prince."

"Did my father put you up to this Gunnar? He wished to be an Olympian in his youth."

"No, your father did not put me up to this." Gunnar walked over to the teenager and helped him with his standing position stance. "I wanted to make sure you were okay. We haven't spent much time together since you have become a young man."

Niklas lowered his gun. "I see. That nanny, Miss Mayer, told you about the drugs. That's why you're putting on this elaborate Olympian façade."

Gunnar's immediate frown and crossed arms let Niklas know he had miscalculated. "Miss Mayer only stated that she was having difficulties helping you. She never mentioned anything about drugs. What have you become involved with, Niklas?"

"*Forget about it.*" He attempted to walk away, but Gunnar grabbed his arm.

"I'm in charge of your safety. You can tell me about it, or we go to the king. Those are your only options."

The boy ran his fingers through his hair. "I was having a hard time calming down at school when mom got sick. Another of the guys offered me a cigarette. I thought it was a cigarette. But it was marijuana. And it worked Gunnar. I was able to sleep for the first time in days."

"I understand stress and anger induced insomnia. Drugs are not the way to handle the problem."

"Hey, you handle your problems however you want to handle them, and I'll handle my problems my way." Niklas jerked his arm away from the large man's grasp. "I don't need morality lessons from any of you. You just let that Mayer woman into my home so she can do what? Hurt my mother more by sleeping with my father?"

"How little respect do you have for your father to believe such rumors?" Gunnar asked angrily. "You spend more time with him than anyone else in the palace so you know he has not been with her. And do you actually believe he would cheat on your mother?"

Niklas tightened his jaw and looked away.

"I don't care what tabloids say, or what your friends say, or what women who seek to backstab your mother do, or anything else that is festering in your head. You know the truth, and the truth is your father loves your mother to the moon and back. He would rather die than betray his love for her. And it was your mother's idea to bring Brodie to Sweden to help you and your little brother and sister to reach acceptance with her disease."

"She's done a poor job of that," retorted Niklas.

"She's done a poor job with you because you're too busy getting high to give her the time of day, and because you're the Crown Prince, she's letting you get away with it. Meanwhile, your siblings are doing much better, and even your mother has developed a close friendship with the woman. And together they pray for you. What do you do? Spit on them by believing these stupid stories about adultery."

The Crown Prince dropped his bore rifle and walked away.

"I will be bringing a dog to the palace, and I better not find any drugs," called after him.

"*How can you? Your precious* Brodie *flushed all of mine down the toilet!*" Niklas yelled back. He veered angrily and disappeared behind the hedge entrance of the baroque garden.

Gunnar, upset that the afternoon had not gone as planned, kicked at the grass and shot haphazardly at the target. Another perfect shot.

Kjerstin stuck her tongue out in deep-concentration while creating the finite details of her designer doll dress. "What do you think Miss Brodie?" she asked, giving the final tug to the eighteen-inch doll's head scarf. The princess had insisted for all of the dolls to be shaven bald or hair cut short in honor of her own mother losing her hair. She wished to show that even women without hair could be fashionable and beautiful.

"I think she is gorgeous, Kjerstin." Brodie lifted the final dress off of her sewing machine. The use of tulle was extensive on the design, and the nervous Kjerstin did not have the gentle touch required to the sew the material. "And here is the final number for Model Camilla."

"Thank you." Kjerstin took the dress and began adding the tiny embellishments she had created. "Do you think this will really help people?"

"I believe it will. I spoke with Miss Agnetha about your designs, and she is going to make them public for anyone to bid on online, not just those attending. She's taking it to the media. This is your big fashion debut."

Kjerstin stopped with her embellishments and walked to her stack of drawing. "What if I give my drawings away with the doll and dress? I can sign my name to them like the big designers do."

Brodie flexed her sore fingers with a smile. "I think that would be nice. I can make copies of your drawings though, and you can sign the copies to give away. I think you'll want to keep the originals for now. But we can frame the copies so they look very nice."

The young princess considered the plan. "Yes, let us do that."

"Is Model Camilla ready for the fashion show?"

"Wait, wait. She needs her hat!" Kjerstin ran to her doll to place the hat and scarf upon her head. "Now she is ready!"

They used a plastic bin to carry the ten dolls and walked downstairs. Brodie checked the time. Family and friends should be gathered in the meeting room. "Wait right here," she told Kjerstin outside the door. Slowly opening the door, Brodie peeked inside and found everyone ready. The king and queen appeared especially proud of their daughter. A red

215

cloth was laid out on the table to serve as the dolls' catwalk. Everyone sat on the far side of the room so the princess could walk her dolls down the table. "Is everyone ready for the debut of *Rosa* by Kjerstin Sofia?" Brodie asked the small audience.

Cheering and whistles were the response.

She opened the doors and ushered Kjerstin inside. The young designer bowed to her family and the palace staff, and then placed her doll bin on a stool at the head of the table. "I wish to thank everyone for coming to my show this Friday night," Kjerstin announced, giving a dramatic flair like a true designer. "The theme of this show is *Rosa* in honor of my mother." She bowed at the applause, adjusting her extra-large sunglasses and scarf while doing so.

Gunnar, who sat at Roffe's right hand, laughed at the little girl's antics as she signaled Brodie to begin the model and outfit introductions. He held his phone aloft and began filming the two.

"Move aside Cinderella, model Camilla will \ be the life of the ball with this tulle gown..."

Kjerstin spun her doll around, allowing the tulle to rise slightly.

Agnetha took close pictures of the dolls on their runway, and at the end of the show had Kjerstin pose with all of her 'models' for a picture. Brodie informed her of Kjerstin's desire to include an autograph copy of each design print with the matching model. The publicist smiled at the idea. "A brilliant idea. I will update the website information."

The princess ran to Brodie holding three of her models. "Selfies!" she called out.

Brodie laughed as she pulled out her phone. "You're too young to want selfies all of the time." They posed together with giant smiles, and Brodie took the picture.

"But Miss Agnetha has you posting pictures online. You can post that one and help my dolls sell for mother."

"You're right. I can do that." She turned toward the publicist. "What are the hashtags you're using for this again?"

Kjerstin hurried to her mother and hugged her. "Did you like it mother?"

The queen wiped tears away from her eyes with her husband's handkerchief. "I loved it Kjerstin. It was very beautiful."

Roffe, holding Mikkel in his lap, patted his daughter's back gently. "You are very talented, *mina älsklingar.*"

"Did you remove the hair from the dolls?" Jonna asked her daughter.

The princess nodded. "I wanted people who lost their hair like you to know they are still beautiful. You are still beautiful mother." She hugged her mother's neck tightly, and the queen returned the hug with tears.

Chapter Eighteen

The mid-morning sun illuminated the herb wall in Gunnar's kitchen, and Brodie placed the last metal trough on one of the shelves. Mini-chalkboard signs on the troughs indicated the names of the herbs.

"Hey, that looks good," Gunnar declared as he entered the kitchen from his deck. He washed his hands in the sink while examining the wall. "I couldn't understand the chalkboards until now."

"Yeah? You like it? This country-chic style is pretty popular back in South Hills." She cleaned up her mess of potting soil and various plastic wrappers. "They make it seem a little like home."

"Then I really like it." He knelt down to help her clean the gardening supplies. "And guess what I found while I was outside?"

"A troll, from Norway," she answered matter-of-factly. "He claimed he is lost, but, suspiciously it looks like he was eating a goat."

Gunnar laughed. "I'm not a sure a troll could eat a goat. Goats don't seem to like them."

"That's why the troll was eating one. It was either him or the goat."

"You're a goof." Gunnar threw away the garbage. "And actually, it was a wild strawberry bush I found on the north side of my property. The birds haven't gotten to it yet."

"Really?" Brodie asked excitedly.

"Yes. Want to go pick some?"

"Absolutely." She struggled with the bag of potting soil, trying not to spill any on the now-clean floor or her white, tulle dress.

He took the bag from her. "I'll put this in the shed if you find a bowl for the strawberries."

"Thank you handsome." She kissed his cheek before he lifted the heavy bag and opened the sliding door for him.

"And thank you *sötis*," he kissed the top of her head and walked outside.

Brodie grinned and returned to the kitchen. She watched Gunnar walk to the red barn-style shed where he hoped to plant a garden. "Where we plan on planting a garden," she reminded herself. Idyllic daydreams of their future together in the house paraded through her mind. "Maybe even build a little greenhouse for anything that needs warmer temperatures." She found a hefty, earthen bowl. Slipping on her sandals, she ran outside to meet Gunnar. "I was thinking you could do a little orchard on this side of the garden," she pointed out the empty land that ran between the shed to the tree-line, "and put up a fence to keep elk out. Then over here you could do the cold-weather crops like lettuce and carrots. Then in this space you could build a greenhouse off of the shed, if you wanted any warmer climate vegetables or fruits. What do you think?"

He surveyed the areas while she explained the various ideas that her daydream provided. "You've been giving this a lot of thought."

"My mind can wander. But imagine how nice some apple trees would be. Fresh apples you pick yourself?"

"I suppose if I'm planting trees, I'll need to do that sooner than later." He stroked his chin in quiet contemplation. "You're giving me a lot of work to do in the summer."

She noted his perspiration and giggled. "This is wonderfully cool. I could probably use a jacket."

He hugged her tightly. "Oh sweetheart, you are going to freeze when the winter comes."

"I'm not stepping foot outside when the winter comes." They walked down the narrow path he carved earlier through the trees on the north half of his property. "I'll wear a thousand layers of clothes if I do."

"Maybe Kjerstin can design a line of clothing for you," he joked.

"She probably could. She's impressive, and so excited about the auction at the ball. The fashion show already has her talking non-stop about new designs." She wrapped her arm around Gunnar's waist as they walked.

"I had to film the show. I can't believe how mature she's getting. She's definitely going to go far."

They continued in silence, enjoying the sound of the different bird calls and the rustle of the wind in the leaves. Brodie sighed happily. To Brodie, Gunnar's house was paradise. After a five-minute walk, they reached the bush Gunnar spoke of. It brimmed with lush strawberries.

"Oh wow," she exclaimed. "I think my mouth is watering." She began picking the ripe berries vigorously. "Think of everything we can make with these. Maybe a nice fresca to cool you down."

"We can take some and make jam for the winter. My mother always did that when I was younger."

She shook her head. "You know I don't know how to make jam."

Gunnar arched his eyebrows. "I thought I could invite my mom over, and she could teach us."

Brodie froze with her hand full of berries. "You want me to meet your mother?"

"If you would like. She knows about you."

"You told your mother about me?" Brodie suddenly felt very shy. "What did you tell her?"

"The truth: what you did in America, why the queen hired you, and that I was assigned to you. And that you're smart, beautiful, charming, funny, kind, and I adore you."

Brodie blushed. "Adore me?"

Gunnar placed his armful of strawberries into the bowl and placed the vessel on the ground. "Adore you." He took her hands in his. "Brodie Mayer, I have known you for almost two months now, and I am overwhelmed with how much I adore you. If this is what two months is like with you, then I wonder what six months will be like, or a year, or... more." He could not manage to say the word 'lifetime' though so much of him wanted to. "We Swedes are often very slow when it comes to affection, but with you, I cannot help myself."

Her blushing intensified and Brodie could feel her entire face heat-up at this sentiment. "I'm not Swedish, but, I feel the same. I never thought I would feel like this, so attached to someone, and in such a short time."

He ran a hand through her long hair. "It helps that we spend so much time together, or at least in the same building."

She laughed. "That does help."

"Brodie Mayer," he inhaled deeply and spoke the words slowly, "*jag älskar dig* – I love you." He could feel his stomach tighten as he awaited her response.

She threw her arms around his neck. "I love you too." She kissed him deeply, happy to hear the words from him. "I love you so much."

He lifted her in his arms, returning her kiss. "What would you think about finishing up these berries, taking them home, making a picnic, and going out on the water for lunch?"

"I think that sounds lovely."

"And this afternoon, let's head to Stockholm."

"Where to?"

He nuzzled her ear with his nose. "I have a little surprise for you, and I promise this one is private. No drunken crowds to interfere."

"You're always giving me surprises and special treats." She stroked his cheeks with a twinkle in her eye. "I feel spoiled."

"That's what you do when you love someone." He returned her feet to the ground. "And I do love you." He leaned in slowly, running his fingers over her neck. *"Du är min renaste tröst, du är mitt fastaste skydd..."* he whispered. "You are my purest comfort, you are my steadfast shelter. It is a Karin Boye poem, and when I look at you, I hear the words of the poem. I never knew the meaning of the poem, how her comfort could hurt like fire and ice, but I understand now. When I look into your eyes, I feel so much..." Gunnar's brow furrowed, and he found himself stumbling over his own words. "I feel as though saying 'I love you' isn't even enough."

Brodie wrapped her hands behind his neck and answered his stumbling words with a deep kiss. When her lips parted from his, she grinned. "You're sweet."

"That's the strawberries," he whispered and gently brushed her bottom lip with his. He whispered Swedish words of affection in her ear while holding her waist. Together, entwined in the embrace, they accomplished filling the strawberry bowl and departed for the house.

Brodie still glowed from their lunchtime cruise in Gunnar's sailboat. The crystal blue water, rocky crags, and coniferous forests provided beautiful scenery, and she enjoyed watching Gunnar in his white linen chinos and blue polo. His nautical attire only enhanced his appearance as an experienced sailor. She eyed him now driving to downtown Stockholm. A smile lingered on his lips from their excursion on the waves.

"I really liked sailing." Her eyes darted between the buildings outside and Gunnar. "South Hills is between two lakes, but I've never been out on the water. Plus, I think the canals up here have much better scenery."

"I've always loved sailing," Gunnar agreed. "I don't do it often because sailing alone isn't as enjoyable, but I especially enjoyed sailing with you." He shot her a smile. "The wind blowing through your hair, and that pretty white dress, you could be a model in a sailor's dream."

"Oh Gunnar," she giggled. "You could be a model sailor. You could even be a... a model Swede. If in my mind I imagined how a Swedish man should look, you'd be him." She laughed and kissed his cheek.

"You're still a goof." His smiled broadened at her compliment.

She eyed the building Gunnar parked near. It overlooked water, as so many places in Stockholm did, and its architecture spoke of an official building several centuries old. "What is this?"

"The National Museum." He cut the ignition and turned to her with a smile. "It's technically closed for renovations, but since most of the collection technically belongs to the king, I was able to pull some strings and get us a private tour."

She smiled. "Truly?"

"Yes. Since they are doing renovations, I had to be selective about the tour, but I think you'll enjoy it." He walked around to her door, "It's not the Louvre or anything, but we do have a worthy collection, if I may be so bold to say so."

"It's a very lovely building."

He led her to a side door where a curator greeted them. "I apologize for the mess," she told them as they weaved through construction areas. "Renovations are plaguing us at the moment, and we've had to move some of our pieces to nearby museum and galleries. Unfortunately, most of the collection has remained here in a safe storage area – though I suppose that is lucky for you!" They followed her down a flight of stairs into a renovation-free, quiet hallway. "Your private showing is through these doors here."

"One moment." Gunnar put his hands over Brodie's eyes. "Okay, let us in."

The curator opened the door with a keycard. She helped Gunnar lead the blinded Brodie into the room, and then unobtrusively departed, allowing the two to be alone.

"I hope you enjoy this as much as I enjoy time with you. I love you, Brodie Mayer."

He uncovered her eyes, and she gasped. The room was filled with paintings of ballerinas and dancers, sculptures, and drawings – a private exhibit of Edgar Degas. Her hands covered her mouth to keep from squeaking in delight. "Oh my... oh wow..." She bounced to a nearby painting of ballerinas, their arms lifted in dance. "Aren't they so graceful? Look how he captured it so brilliantly... I..." She began to cry. "I've only seen these in books and on the internet. I never thought I would see such things in person."

"I know how much Degas means to you, and the ballet, because of your mother." He handed her his handkerchief.

"And in addition to this private showing, we are going to take the children to the Royal Ballet performing at the theatre next week."

"Oh Gunnar." She threw her arms around his neck. "You are so incredible, and wonderful... thank you so much."

"*Sötis*, you have given me so much; I want to give you these magic moments in return."

"I've given you so much?" Brodie arched her eyebrows in confusion. "Gunnar... you're the one who's done all the romantic gestures, protected me in that fight, restore my confidence when I beat myself up..."

He put a finger to her lips. "And you are the one who helped me see the light again. You know I was in a dark place since Katarina's death, and I still struggle with it, but if you hadn't reached out with your love..." He shook his head with a grin. "If you had never reached out to me, or been a part of my life, I don't know if I ever would have talked things out with God."

"I'm sure he would have brought someone else into your life. Don't you remember the parable of the lost sheep? The shepherd had one-hundred sheep, but one went astray. He left the ninety-nine that had not gone astray to recover the one he lost. And when the lost sheep was brought back to the flock, he rejoiced far more at that, than at the ninety-nine who were never lost. Gunnar, you're that little lost lamb."

"I've never been compared to a lamb before," he chuckled. "I thought I could get by on my own strength and experience out there by myself, but I have to admit the happiness and peace I feel is not something I could ever create." Gunnar kissed the top of her head. "I'm not perfect. I'll never be perfect. And I know I'm going to screw up at times, but that

225

doesn't mean I don't love you. That doesn't mean I won't try to be a better man."

"Was that to me or the Lord?"

His eyes turned skyward. "I guess both."

She laughed and kissed Gunnar, happy that he was now on the road to peace. His past would never disappear, but for now, he no longer lingered in the misery as before. All that remained was the present, and the future – and the threat of Strand still lingering over their heads.

Gunnar and Brodie left the vegetarian restaurant with Zavier. He locked the door while laughing. "I can't believe you dropped my name like that," he amused. "But then again, maybe I can. Maybe my special charm is too much for you to bear."

"I'm certain that's it," Gunnar jested.

Zavier leaned against the restaurant's brick wall. "Laugh it up all you want, but your woman is going with me to a royal ball." He slicked his black hair back and grinned. "I may sweep her off her feet."

"Or the paparazzi may sweep you off your feet," Gunnar shot back. "They tend to swoop."

"Ah yes, swooping is bad." He scratched his chin. "But I suppose for a friend, I can face the madness." He blinked at Brodie. "Especially now that you're seen in a more positive light."

She laughed. "Not by all, but I don't think there's a fear of a riot breaking out. Security will be everywhere."

The Swede patted the Englishman's shoulder. "But to be clear, if I have to choose between saving you or saving Brodie... well, we'll come visit you in the hospital."

"That's horrible, Gunnar," Brodie laughed.

Zavier walked between them, his arm wrapped around both shoulders. "It's bloody-well nice to have a friend like Gunnar, isn't it?"

"Indubitably," Brodie agreed. "How did you two become friends anyway? You don't seem like you would have run in the same circles." She leaned against Gunnar's car, watching the two laugh. Zavier only stood an inch shorter than Gunnar, and, when not standing next to the large Swede, his wiry frame caused him to appear even taller.

"I was a bartender at the pub he frequented in his college days. This man could put away his drink."

Brodie frowned at Gunnar; one part of her attraction to him was he never drank alcohol.

"I put away my drink back then," Gunnar agreed. "A little too much. Taught me a lesson."

"Yes, this man can put away his drink, but he certainly cannot function with it in his system. Roffe and Jonna sat with Gunnar at the pub, and this bloke starts to lay-in to Roffe. Your bodyguard-boyfriend was hard with several pints in him and thought he could take on this footballer."

"It was a good idea."

"You were barmy."

They shared a laugh. "Needless to say, Brodie," Gunnar told her, "I lost my first fight, and it taught me to never drink again."

She smiled. "I'm glad you learned your lesson."

"I am too." Zavier elbowed Gunnar. "One of the greatest pub fights I had ever seen, or been in."

"It's where we became friends," Gunnar agreed. "Despite my idiotic behavior, this guy helped me out that night. Don't let his boney-arms fool you; he can pack a punch if need be."

"It's been a bit since I've thrown a punch," Zavier admitted. "I devote my life to peace now." Zavier leaned against the car next to her. "And how have you recovered since your run-in with violence?"

She placed a hand to her jaw in memory of the event. "It doesn't hurt so much now unless I sleep on it funny. Luckily, nothing was broken."

Gunnar's phone rang, and he excused himself from Brodie and Zavier's conversation. "Nyström," he answered gruffly. In a matter of seconds, he began roaring into the phone in Swedish.

"What's that about?" Brodie asked Zavier. She hoped his grasp on the Swedish language was better than hers.

"Pass," he responded with the shake of a head. "My Swedish isn't blooming good enough to translate that tirade."

"We have to go," Gunnar told them, hanging up his phone.

"What's happening?" she said. She hugged Zavier and hurried to her side of the car.

"Niklas is at a club, and surprise, he needs help." He briskly shook Zavier's hand before diving into the driver's seat.

"What is he doing at a club?" Brodie shrieked. The engine roared to life.

"Who knows? Scoring more drugs?" They waved at Zavier and sent the car peeling downhill to the highway connecting Slussen and downtown Stockholm.

"I thought Loke was his bodyguard. Where is he at?"

"Good question. I'd like to find that out myself."

Dodging traffic expertly, Gunnar hastily arrived at the downtown club the Crown Prince called from. The agent flashed his badge and charged past the bouncer. The bouncer attempted to stop Brodie, and Gunnar turned around, pulling her inside with him.

"*She's with me,*" he growled.

They scouted the club for Niklas, but it did not take long to find the crowd gathered around the boy. He sat on a couch trying to hide his face. A member of the paparazzi stood in the crowd, taking pictures with his camera. Gunnar pushed through the throng and tossed his coat over Niklas to protect the boy from phone cameras.

The paparazzi man attempted to run at the sight of Gunnar, but Brodie bumped into him, knocking the camera to ground. "*Jag är ledsen!*" she managed to shout in her rudimentary-Swedish over the electronica music. She knelt down to pick up his camera, but deftly and swiftly removed the SIM card before he noticed her. He took his camera and gruffly ran away.

Gunnar lifted Niklas to his feet, ensuring no camera phones could capture his face.

Brodie noticed one girl with her phone out but not attempting to take pictures of the prince. "One second, Gunnar," Brodie told the man. She walked over to the girl and jerked the phone from her hand.

"*Lägg av!*" the girl shouted at Brodie.

The nanny ignored the club-goer's command as she scanned through the phone's pictures. Several were taken of her and Niklas, including drinking and making out. Brodie commenced to deleting the pictures. "She bought him drinks,"

Brodie informed Gunnar, nodding to the girl, "and took pictures of them together."

"That's my phone," the girl growled, attempting to take her phone back from Brodie.

"And this is the Crown Prince, which you knew, and you bought him drinks, even though he's four years younger than the legal drinking age," Brodie responded.

"*Jag mår dåligt,*" Niklas moaned to Gunnar.

"What did you put in his drink?" Brodie asked the girl. She leaned forward, putting Niklas's face in her hand. "What drug did you give him?"

"I didn't give him anything," she protested. The girl visibly wanted to leave, but her eyes remained locked on her phone.

"I can take him to the hospital, and we can do a tox-screen, in which case I will arrest you for attempted assassination of His Royal Highness."

"Assassination?" she squeaked. "All I did was give him a little rohypnol in his drink!"

"You roofied him?" Brodie shouted. "How much did you give him?"

"Only a little in his drink."

"Gunnar, we need to take him to the hospital. Roofies in alcohol can lead to an overdose."

The girl's eyes widened in fear. "Overdose? No! It was only a little bit!"

Gunnar hurried out of the club with Niklas. Brodie faced the girl. "We're keeping your phone to track you. Heaven help you if something happens to that boy." She pushed her way through the horde to crawl into the backseat with the prince. "It'll be okay Niklas," she reassured the boy as he began to fall out of consciousness.

"I'm going to take him to my doctor," Gunnar told Brodie. "If we go to the hospital, it'll hit the press."

"Are you sure? We can't play around with this. He's losing consciousness."

"This guy can take care of him." Gunnar pulled down a dark street, parking in front of neo-mod house. He knocked on the door while Brodie attempted to help Niklas to his feet. The door of the house cracked open, and Gunnar exchanged hushed, rapid words in Swedish with a dark figure. "Baby, stay in the car," Gunnar whispered as he took Niklas from her.

She gave him a nervous glance, but he reassuringly placed a hand on her cheek.

"We'll be right back. Everything will be okay." He put his car keys in her hand and walked into the house.

Brodie bit her nails while curled up in Gunnar's coat. The dark street was cold and scared her, but the shady nature of the man in the house worried her more. She lost track of time as she shivered. Common sense told her to start the car and turn on the heat. Common sense also told her to stay quiet and invisible outside the stranger's house. Finally, a light caught her attention, and she pressed her face against the car window. Gunnar stepped out of the house, carrying Niklas in his arms.

She opened the door for him, and he slipped the teenager into the backseat. "His stomach has been pumped," Gunnar whispered. "He needs to rest."

"He'll be okay?" she asked.

"Yeah. Let's take him back to my place." He closed the door and noticed Brodie shivering. "It'll be okay," he whispered, hugging her tightly. "Stay the night, and we will all go to the palace in the morning."

"You really need a guest room," Brodie stated.

He kissed the top of her head. "I don't know. I was thinking of making that a nursery." He winked and helped her into her seat.

The drive back to Gunnar's house was silent, and he placed a hand on her leg when not using the gearshift. She smiled and enjoyed the momentary peace. The trees lining his long-drive greeted her as though she were truly returning home. "I'll get the door," she whispered to Gunnar. She hurried up the wildflower-trimmed steps to his front door.

Gunnar followed and carried the half-asleep prince to his couch. Brodie knelt next to the boy, stroking his hair.

"Thank you," Niklas whispered to her.

"You're welcome."

"Wish that paparazzi hadn't gotten away," Gunnar said, examining the club-girl's cellphone. "I'll have to call Agnetha and warn her."

"The paparazzi got away, but his SIM card didn't." Brodie reached into her purse and pulled out the SIM card. "You might need this for your investigation." She tossed the card to him.

He grinned. "How did you manage this?"

"I accidentally knocked his camera down with my purse, and I may have taken the card out before giving it back to him. One too many action movies with you gave me the idea."

Gunnar smiled. "That's only a little attractive."

"Are you going to tell my father?" Niklas asked Brodie. He reached for her hand, and she detected tears in her eyes.

Gently, she took his hand. "You have to tell your father. You have to tell him about the marijuana, the partying, the drinking, everything."

"I can't," he cried. "He won't want anything to do with me."

"Of course he will."

"No, I'm a disappointment. My grades were horrible, and he yelled at me. He hated me."

"He didn't hate you, and he won't hate you for this."

"How do you know?" Soft sobs tumbled from the prince's lips.

Brodie regarded Gunnar. He sat back in his armchair, ankle over knee, no longer checking the phone. He watched her intently. "I know because you're not the first wayward son to think he won't be welcomed home." She readjusted her legs to a more comfortable position before continuing. "There was a father that had two sons, and he gave his younger son his inheritance. The younger son took that wealth and went to live in the city. He partied, drank, did drugs, everything you have done and more, and he wasted all of his money. He began to go hungry, and soon found himself eating out of the garbage. Once he realized how low his life's circumstances had gotten, he decided he would either starve to death or return to his father."

"He returned to his father?" Niklas asked.

"He did. He returned to his father, threw himself at his feet, and cried out, 'I dishonored you. I am no longer worthy to be called your son.' But the father hugged him, kissed him, and called for the best clothes to be put on his son and a feast to be held in his honor.

"The father told everyone, 'We must celebrate because my son was dead and is alive again; he was lost and is found.' You see, that father's love was so much, he didn't care about the negative his son did as much as he cared about his son returning to him, and becoming a better man than he was before he left."

"So, the father forgave his son just because his son returned?"

"The father forgave his son because he returned and admitted he was wrong. The son asked forgiveness. That's what you'll have to do with your father. And your father will be happy to have you home, safe and sound."

Niklas smiled despite his tears. "Will you be there with me?"

"I will be with you, but you must do all the talking."

The teenager closed his eyes, and Brodie could see peace finally upon his face. She located a blanket and wrapped it around him. Gunnar was nowhere to be seen. She soundlessly walked to his office, suspecting he would be researching the girl who had drugged Niklas. Instead, he sat in his office chair, crying and praying.

"Lord, for too long I have been running from you. I thought I could do it all on my own, but You've made it clear to me that I can't. You sent a messenger. I understand. It's not about being a better man. I can say I will be one, but I can't be one without Your aid. I'm a sinner, and I receive Your salvation. I trust You as my Savior to see me through all my trials. Thank You, Lord."

As silently as she approached the room, Brodie walked away from the office door and made her way to the upstairs bedroom.

The night continued on, and Brodie tossed with every passing minute. She had been smart enough to leave the supplies Gunnar purchased for her concussion-stay in his restroom and to bring an extra set of emergency clothes. But these supplies did not offer her the comfort she hoped for. Niklas's life-threatening situation, though past, still scared her. She was happy that it brought a change of character, but she was responsible for him. She had kept his drug use from everyone – even the queen.

Soft creaks and footsteps signaled the approach of Gunnar, and she rolled on her side to face the door. It opened slowly; the giant Swede attempted to not wake her. "It's okay Gunnar. I'm awake."

He entered normally with her declaration. "Unable to sleep?"

"Too much thinking."

"I understand that." He lumbered to his dresser. "Finding clothes to change into. I'll go sleep in my office, if I manage sleep."

"Who was that man, doctor, friend of yours?" Brodie sat up, pulling a pillow in her lap to hold.

Gunnar threw a shirt and pajama pants over his shoulder. "You know that spy movie we watched, and he had a guy to fix up his bullet wound? That was my version of that."

"Really? You need a clandestine surgeon guy?"

235

"Sometimes. Sometimes it's better to not publicly go to the hospital." He walked into his bathroom and closed the door. Within a moment, he opened the door. Grinning, he remarked, "First my pillows smell like lychee and jasmine, and now my bathroom?"

She laughed and dropped to her stomach on the bed. "I had to get the gross club smell off of me. It was a mix of alcohol, sweat, vomit, and cheap perfume."

"You're right. I have to shower now," he stated, smelling his shirt. "Combat the floral barrage with my woodsy-man-soap." He closed the door again, and Brodie could hear the flow of water in the pipes surge before it erupted out of his shower. She squeezed the pillow to pass the time while he clattered and clanged into his shower. Then she froze, hearing a sound she never expected: Gunnar singing a Sweeter Peaches song.

The sound of his deep, very off-key and flat singing caused her to laugh. She buried her face in the pillow so as to not wake Niklas downstairs. She remained in the position until Gunnar left the bathroom, still drying his hair. Knowing she laughed at his expense, the Swede rolled his towel and swatted it at her bottom. "Ouch!" she squeaked, but the hint of a giggle remained in her voice.

"I thought you said my singing was alright."

She flipped onto her back so he could no longer swat her. "But you were really getting into that flower song."

He smiled sheepishly. "I really like that song, okay? I confess." Tossing the towel into the open doorway of the bathroom, he sat on the edge of his bed. "You've done a horrible thing to me. Do I look like a guy that should like such a song?"

Brodie leapt forward, throwing her arms around his neck. "Certainly. Maybe grow some pigtails," she teased, playing with the hair above his ears. "And little freckles on your cheeks and nose." She ran a finger across his face to exaggerate her statement.

"Should I change my name to Longstockings as well?" He reached behind him, clasping his fingers together behind her back. "Gunnar Longstockings – Klas Gunnar Longstockings. Has a horrible ring to it."

"Klas?" She rested her chin on the top of his head. "Klas? Who is Klas?"

"I am Klas, but only my mother calls me Klas. It was her father's name."

With a giggle, she pinched his cheek. "Oh, little Klas, you are such a mama's boy. It's adorable."

He leaned back and attempted to squish her with his body. "Nothing wrong with loving my mother."

"Nope, there's not Klas." Her laughter intensified as he turned and began tickling. "Stop it – hehe – stop or you'll wake Niklas!"

Gunnar stopped tickling her and opted instead to stroke her face. "Funny thing: lying here with you, I forgot about the rest of the world."

She smiled. "How am I even supposed to respond to something as beautiful as that?"

"Gunnar Nyström, you're the strongest, smartest, and sexiest man alive," he answered, parodying a feminine voice.

"So strong, smart, and sexy," she mockingly agreed.

"Music to my ears," he approved with a kiss. "Think I could steal one of these Brodie-scented pillows for the office?"

"I don't know," she responded and extended her arms across the pillows on his bed.

He pouted. "Even your rock Alfred has a pillow to sleep on. Shouldn't your boyfriend get one?"

"Yes, but Alfred's pillow is a very tiny pillow."

"Alfred is a very tiny rock." He ran his hands slowly over her extended arms, teasing her skin with the tips of his fingers. "I'm a little bit bigger." He kissed her fingers. "I may need a bit more cushion." He kissed up her arm to the curve of her neck. "If you were the kind lady I know you are, you'll relinquish a pillow to me."

Brodie exhaled a deep breath. She felt as though she had inhaled the entire time he kissed her. "Take your pillow, you alluring imp."

He winked and stole the pillow from behind her head.

Chapter Nineteen

The king's office hummed in silence. Niklas stood before the grand oak desk of his father, head bowed and hands covering his tearful face. Brodie sat in an armchair in the corner of the office, hoping to remain ignored in the exchange while fulfilling her promise to the Crown Prince.

Roffe stood and clasped his hands behind his back. Overwhelmed with all of the information, he turned to his window to view the tourist boat that sailed over the peaceful water. The tourists, awed by the beauty of the royal residence, had no idea of the tension within.

"I am sorry father. I don't deserve to be your son; I will leave," Niklas managed to choke before turning to the door.

"Nothing you can do would change the love I have for you, son," Roffe's response was stained with tears. He strode to the door in order to stop his son's departure. "What upsets me most is that I almost lost you, and I knew nothing of the situation. I could be seeing you in a morgue this morning, and that is a pain I could not bear. I love you Niklas." The king grabbed his son by the shoulders and pulled him into a tight hug.

The teenager cried into his father's chest, hugging him tightly. "I love you too," he whispered between his sobs. "I will stop hurting our family. I don't want to go back to that school or see those guys again."

"We will send you to a new school," the king agreed.

Tears filled Brodie's eyes at the touching scene. Her basic grasp on the Swedish language did not help her understanding so much as the body language between father and son. Unobtrusively she rose from her chair and slinked to the door, seeing herself out. Before closing the door, the king made eye contact with her, and nodded his thanks. She smiled and returned the silent nod.

The quiet, loving moment was ruined as she heard Gunnar's boisterous yelling from his office. "Oh dear," she mumbled. The yelling intensified closer to the office. "He's found Loke." Without knocking, she entered the office to find her boyfriend red-faced and shouting at the young man he once called a brother. "Gunnar..." she started.

"Not now Brodie. This man must answer for his lack of responsibility."

Loke's pleading eyes landed on Brodie. "Gunnar, the king has forgiven Niklas. Perhaps you can find it in your heart to forgive Loke?"

"Forgiveness between a father and son is nothing like this. Loke's stupidity could have gotten Niklas killed. Why wasn't I informed of the situation Loke? Where were you?"

Brodie sat on Gunnar's desk, eyeing the pale-faced Loke. "You were sick, weren't you? You still look ill."

"I... yes..." Loke confessed. "My stomach upset me, and when I went to the restroom, Niklas fled."

"I wouldn't be surprised if Niklas spiked Loke's food," she told Gunnar. "You can't ignore the call to the bathroom as a valid reason, Gunnar. That's the one thing that takes anyone out." Her Swede grumbled and sat roughly down in his office chair. She could sense his anger ebbed, and Loke would retain his position. "And given Niklas's new found attitude on life, I doubt Loke will have to repeat the experience. Everyone has learned from this, including you and I. So, give Loke another chance."

Gunnar tapped his fingers on his desk, staring at the young man he once trained. "Loke, you're on administrative leave until you get over your stomach-bug. Then come back, on probation." He looked at Brodie. "Does that sound fair?"

"Paid administrative leave?"

"Paid administrative leave. And you better thank Brodie for saving your job... after you're well again." Loke thanked both of them before running away to find a nearby restroom. "You're too kind, you know that?" Gunnar asked Brodie.

She shut the door to his office. "Am I? Maybe that's my problem. I'm too kind." Her eyes drifted to a stack of magazines on the corner of his desk. She was on the cover of a few. "Heavy reading?"

"I'm keeping them for posterity. And because there's a gorgeous woman on the cover. And look at this one," he picked up the magazine on top and turned to multiple pictures of Brodie in different outfits serving as centerfold, "many pictures of my *älskling* in this one."

"The one that talked about my fashion and nothing of substance? Really?"

"I know you have substance; I don't have to read it."

"I think after the children return to school, I'm going to buckle down and do research. Publish some papers. Less of the media circus, and more of the science."

He stood from his chair and wrapped his arms around Brodie. "Fashionista and scientist. I'm a very blessed man."

"What if I also said, I'm thinking about taking a few courses toward a graduate degree?"

"Fashionista, scientist, and college girl... college girl..." Gunnar grinned. "That sounds nice."

"Perv," she laughed, kissing his cheek playfully.

241

"Seriously, I'm glad you are pursuing your graduate degree. You're a smart woman, and I'm in awe of your brain. I hope you go on to get a doctorate."

"You do?"

"Absolutely. I'll do whatever you need me to do to help you get there." He kissed her ear. "Not to mention I can tell my mom I'm with a doctor."

"We would be introduced as Mr. and Dr. Nyström." She glanced at him to read his reaction to her statement, but she was merely met with a smile. "That will look amazing on Christmas cards."

Gunnar laughed.

"Maybe we can go up to Lapland and take our picture with the Aurora borealis in the background for one of the cards. I mean, I may freeze to death, but imagine all my friends receiving that card! They'll be so jealous! Oh, and I can make the card play that Princess Snowdew song about the pretty lights to really rub it in." She started humming the song.

"No, no, no!" He covered his ears. "I refuse to let that song get stuck in my head. Once it gets there, it never leaves."

"I imagine it's hard to feel like a Viking warrior with a little animated princess singing in your head." She winked and wiggled out of his arms to his office door. "The lights in the sky are like the love in my heart," she sang before darting out of the room. He growled a response.

"Special delivery for Brodie Mayer," Gunnar announced. He carried a shipping box into his kitchen where Brodie stirred a bowl of batter. "Order something special for your first ball?"

"Nope. It's something special for you. Open it up!"

He grunted but followed her orders regardless. "You bought me records?" he asked, retrieving several classic rock records from the top of the box. "These are some of my favorites, but *sötis*, I don't have anything to play them on."

"Keep going!" she called out. The batter emptied into two cake pans, and Brodie placed them in his oven.

Gunnar unearthed a portable record player at the bottom of the box. "This is like what Roffe and I used to have at Sigtuna." He laughed. "How did you... why...?"

Throwing her apron on its hook, she giggled. "You're not the only one with connections, you know."

The feel of vinyl in his hands excited Gunnar, even causing him to feel younger. "This smells like a scheme with the Queen."

"And the King." She wrapped her arms around him. "Happy birthday!"

"Oh, *älskling*, you shouldn't have." He returned her hug. "I didn't know you were aware of my birthday."

"Connections," she joked. Her hand ran over his stomach. "Just like I talked with your mom, found out your favorite meals, and I'm going to make those for you today."

"I'm warming up to this scheme of yours." His face flushed while he kissed the top of her head. "Records, food, any other surprises I should be aware of?"

"Now, now, you have to take them as they happen." She patted his stomach. "But the theme of the day is for you to relax and do whatever makes you happy."

He lowered his kisses to her ear. "Don't tease me Brodie. I'd spend all day on my deck with you."

"I'm sure we can find some time for that, after I finish in the kitchen." She offered him a quick peck on the lips before turning back to the recipes on the counter.

"You're going to make meatballs?" he asked. He gathered his birthday present and began to setup the record player in his living room. "I don't think I've ever seen you touch meat."

"The things I do for love," she responded. "Lucky for me, your mom was very understanding about my meat-cooking ignorance. Walked me through the whole thing, and I took notes."

Gunnar put a record on and laid down on his couch. "I remember playing air-guitar to this on the top of my bed in the dorm. I got so into the music that I jumped up, and my head put a hole through the ceiling."

Brodie giggled. "I'm not surprised."

She listened to Gunnar recount a variety of nostalgic boarding school tales that the albums brought to mind. "There used to be this girl, Annika, I think her name was. She must have been in love with Roffe; always was hanging out around us. Never really talked with us though. She was a metal head; I remember that. Wonder what happened to her? I should ask Roffe if he ever asked her out..."

After several tracks, his stories turned to snores, and Brodie shook her head with a smile. The break in storytelling allowed her to follow his mother's cooking instructions, and she hoped by the time Gunnar awoke from his nap, his lunch and birthday cake would be ready. Bouncing from oven, to stovetop, to herb wall, Brodie used her years of culinary experience in an attempt to beat the end of the record. "How can he sleep to this music?" she asked herself during a guitar solo. "Metal doesn't seem like lullaby music."

As expected, the end of the record woke Gunnar from his nap, and he slid off the couch to his feet.

"Enjoy your nap?" Brodie asked from the dining room. Candles lit the intimate *smorgasbord* of Gunnar's favorite foods.

"Wow," he breathed. "How long was I asleep?"

"Not terribly long, but I've trained my whole life for this," she jested. "I used to do culinary competitions in home economics. It's all about the timing." She patted the chair she leaned upon. "Come sit, eat. I've got meatballs and lingonberry jam, your mom's *kroppkakor, gravad lax...*"

Gunnar's kiss stopped her rambling. "It smells wonderful. It looks beautiful. You are amazing *gumman*."

"That's easy to say when you haven't eaten anything. Please, sit, eat. I have to go finish your birthday cake." She pushed him down in the chair and patted his head. "I didn't have any elk. Your mom said you love it, but I was fresh out."

"Out for now. A few more months and hunting season starts." He began loading his plate with the various dishes. "I'll probably head out with Roffe and Horn, and if we're lucky, Niklas. He's old enough to join a club."

"Uh-huh," Brodie agreed. "I'm surprised he's not already." Carefully, she placed strawberries on top of the cake. "When you hunt, you take care of the meat and everything. I don't have to deal with a dead carcass, and elk eyes staring at me, right?"

"Don't worry. I'll take care of any dead animal: elk, boar, or fish."

"That's a relief. I'll cook it, but not if it has eyes." Satisfied with the cake, she sat at the table beside Gunnar. "Even when I used to eat meat, that was a line I couldn't cross."

245

He patted her leg. "You didn't make anything for yourself?" Most of the dishes she had prepared were meat-based.

"I plan on filling-up on potatoes and birthday cake." Her eyes sparkled in the candlelight. "Plus, I've been snacking while cooking."

They enjoyed the meal in near-silence, preferring to savor the other's company in the intimate setting. After two platefuls, Gunnar finally lowered his cutlery and inhaled deeply. "I don't know if I room for birthday cake," he confessed.

"Even if it's my very first *sockerkaka* that I made with strawberries we picked when we first said 'I love you'?" Her statement was accompanied with a pouty lip and blinking eyes.

"You've convinced me." He stood and helped Brodie to her feet. "But I'm putting all the food up and washing all the dishes."

"Not on your birthday... wait, why am I arguing this point?" He laughed and tapped her nose with his finger. "I looked up the Swedish birthday song to sing to you, but I can't remember the words."

"That's okay, this is more than I expected." He indicated the cake. "And this is gorgeous. Fashionista, scientist, college girl, cook, and baker? You're the only birthday present I needed." He lifted her in his arms and kissed her neck. "How about we eat this cake out on the deck locked in each other's arms?"

"I'm suddenly not very hungry," she whispered.

"Neither I am," he returned her whisper and kissed her once more.

Chapter Twenty

Pink covered every inch of the ballroom for the king's birthday. Traditionally, Swedish blue and gold would be used for the décor, but the king's insistence on the color reflecting his wife's battle defied convention. Even the multi-tiered birthday cake was adorned in pink fondant with marzipan carnations and bright berries. The carnation became the queen's flower of choice for her charity-pursuits, and all gentlemen in attendance wore a carnation-boutonniere in Her Majesty's honor.

"I've never been to a ball before, let alone a royal ball," Zavier told Brodie. They walked with arms linked, observing the decorations and ignoring murmurs among gossipers. "I guess royalty go all out. Hate to see what it's like back home, where the titles carry weight."

"British royalty and nobility were the only kind I knew about before Queen Jonna approached me. I mean, I knew other countries had royalty, but America's media loves the British monarchy."

"You blokes merely thought you escaped our Crown," he joked.

"Yeah, ironic. Fight a war to free ourselves from a British king simply to be obsessed with a British queen and her family." Brodie pointed to a lighted display case. "Let's go look at Kjerstin's dolls. I have blisters on my fingers from sewing these."

They reviewed the ten dolls rotating on pedestals within the case. A chic sign in the center of the case read 'Rosa by Kjerstin Sofia'. "These are impressive. She came up with these all by herself?"

"A full summer of drawing, coloring, going to fashion shows, reading books, and shopping at fabric stores has culminated in these ten dolls. All I did was sew the more complicated pieces, and teach her to sew the basics."

"I feel like I should place a bid on one of these." Zavier checked the silent auction bids listed. "But they are far out of my price range. Looks like the Queen's charity initiative is going well."

Brodie peeped at the numbers. "Oh, sweet Lord, that's wonderful news for the Queen and for Kjerstin! When the children arrive, I'll have to show her."

"Here's your chance," he told her with a nod of the head to the stairs.

The three children stood at the top of the stairs; Niklas held his younger siblings' hands. "His Royal Highness, Crown Prince Niklas the Second, Duke of Västergötland," the herald announced. All idle conversation ceased at the announcement of the royal children. "Her Royal Highness, Princess Kjerstin Sofia, Duchess of Värmland, and His Royal Highness, Prince Mikkel Johan, Duke of Hälsingland and Gästrikland." Niklas nervously shifted under the eyes of so many, but his sister pointed at Brodie and the display case of her dolls. He nodded and followed her lead.

"Miss Brodie!" Kjerstin shouted happily, hugging her. "You are beautiful!"

"As are you." Brodie straightened the princess's hair affectionately before turning to Niklas and Mikkel. "And you are such handsome princes." She hugged Mikkel and adjusted Niklas's seraphim blue Sash of the Order. "You look like you're ready for the throne."

He smiled and bowed his head. "Thank you, Miss Brodie. I fear it will take far more than looks to prepare me for the job."

"You have an excellent teacher in your father."

"How are my dolls doing?" Kjerstin squeaked as she jumped to see her dolls. Zavier helped her view the dolls while Brodie read the current bids to her. "Mom is going to be excited, isn't she?"

"Definitely," Brodie agreed.

Kungssången, the Swedish royal anthem, began playing, marking the arrival of the king and queen. Niklas straightened his stance at the sound. Ever since his prodigal son return, the Crown Prince ensured the upmost propriety around his father. Roffe appeared with his wife in her wheelchair as the four-part choir concluded the first stanza of the song. The herald announced Their Majesties and the king's forty-fifth birthday. Everyone applauded.

"Thank you for your kind birthday wishes and for attending this wonderful event hosted by my exquisite wife." Roffe acknowledged the applause. "This has been a trying year for my family, but with the help of God Almighty, and our family and friends like you, we have become closer than ever before." Roffe took Jonna by the hand. She gingerly squeezed it and shakily stood to her feet. Gunnar, who hid in the shadows of the royals, stepped forward, offering an arm to Her Majesty.

Jonna steadied herself with Roffe and Gunnar's aid before speaking. "We wish to thank all who have visited us this summer, and all who have contributed to the cancer society."

"Please be sure to visit the display of our daughter's first fashion line. She is helping her mother raise funds and awareness for breast cancer research by auctioning ten dolls." Roffe thanked everyone once more before assisting Jonna down the steps of the hall.

Gunnar hastily carried the Queen's wheelchair down the stairs. Her short trip down the stairs winded Jonna, and she gratefully sat in the chair. Kjerstin bolted forward to be at her mother's side. The queen hugged her daughter tightly, holding a whispered conservation. The royal group made their way through the crowd to the display case.

"Kjerstin told me how well the auction is going," Jonna directed her comment to Brodie, "and she could not contain her enthusiasm."

"She's right; the auctions are doing very well." Brodie bowed her head to Roffe. "Happy birthday, Your Majesty."

"Thank you, Miss Mayer." He noted Zavier on her arm and briefly glanced at Gunnar in surprise. "Zavier Drummond, it has been many years since I have last had the pleasure of your company."

Zavier nodded his head. "It has, Your Majesty. Miss Brodie invited me as her friend so I could wish you a happy birthday." The two men shook hands. "And it's a lovely ball, Your Majesty," he added to Jonna with a kiss on her hand.

"Thank you, Mister Drummond. I am pleased to see you are enjoying yourself."

While everyone exchanged pleasantries, Gunnar's eyes drifted to Brodie. She wore a pink-pastel Grecian chiffon evening gown and carnations in her hair, and he felt entranced by her exquisiteness. Her sparkling eyes caught his, and she blushed. They stepped to the side in order to speak privately. "You look gorgeous," he whispered in her ear.

Brodie shyly straightened her dress. "You look dashing too."

He chuckled. "This is the black suit I always wear on duty."

"But with a carnation. It's a very nice touch."

"*Grattis på födelsedagen!*" Horn greeted his friend with birthday wishes. He clapped him hardily on the back. "And

251

you are as graceful as ever, my queen." The stout man bowed to Jonna.

Valanice eyed the queen though her gaze quickly drifted to Brodie and Gunnar. "The hall is charming, Your Majesty, but you do surround yourself in interesting company."

The audible venom in her voice caused Brodie to return to Zavier's side lest the noblewoman's scorn be directed to her friend.

"Whatever do you mean, Valanice?" Jonna politely responded.

"I find it odd that the *au pair* has been invited to His Majesty's birthday celebration. Do you not, Your Majesty?"

"I certainly do not, for I am the one who invited Miss Mayer to attend. The children are here, so she should be here to see to their needs. Furthermore, Miss Mayer is a dear friend of mine and invited accordingly."

Zavier snickered at the queen's poignant reply.

"And who are you?" Valanice asked him haughtily.

He bowed with a mocking smile. "Lord Zavier Drummond, Duke of Wellington, third cousin of Her Majesty, the Queen of England."

Valanice's face blanched. "I beg your Lordship's pardon." She curtsied and hurried away.

"And off she goes to fact-check my story, no doubt," Zavier laughed. "Imagine me, a duke."

Horn and the others joined his laughter. "My sister has always been eccentric, God love her. My apologies, Your Majesty."

"My dear friend, you have no reason to apologize," Jonna smiled warmly at the man.

"And you my friend," Horn turned his attention to Roffe, "I do believe it is time to begin planning a hunting trip for next month, with Gunnar of course."

Gunnar laid his hand on Niklas's shoulder. "I may or may not be able to attend a hunting trip due to the job, but I believe Niklas would be more than willing to attend such a trip."

The Crown Prince's eyes eagerly met his father's smiling face.

"That is an excellent idea," Roffe agreed. Niklas's excitement could be felt by all. "You are overdue to join the club as it is."

"Thank you, father."

Roffe hugged his son. "I failed to see you were becoming a young man, and all young men need a healthy pastime."

"Are you going to dance, Miss Brodie?" Kjerstin pointed to several couples waltzing. "You've been practicing all summer."

"All summer?" Zavier mused. "I think I can dust off a waltz if you're game." Gunnar cleared his throat. "And I'll be a perfect gentleman."

Brodie smiled. "If you promise to be a gentleman." She followed him to the center of the hall and into a basic box-waltz. Embellishments were added to the dance as the two found their comfort in the rhythm.

Gunnar watched the duo, eager for the day when he could be the one to accompany Brodie to a ball. "Are you Mister Nyström?"

A gentleman Gunnar somewhat recognized approached him. "I am. How may I be of service?"

"Sheldon Briggs, United States Ambassador to Sweden," the man held out his hand.

"A pleasure," Gunnar stated with a firm handshake.

"I believe you are the assigned bodyguard to our Miss Brodie Mayer?"

"I am."

"Excellent. I wished to introduce myself to our star American in the Swedish royal court. It's only a shame we have not been formally introduced before."

"A shame, indeed." Gunnar surreptitiously rolled his eyes. He could not tolerate the politics of his own country, let alone the politics of other countries. "Miss Mayer has mentioned the embassy on a few occasions; however, between the children's needs, the queen's illness, and the media circus surrounding her, she has had no time to visit. I am certain you understand."

"Of course." Ambassador Briggs nodded his head solemnly. "The media circus was heart-breaking with such vicious rumors. I am genuinely happy to see that has passed."

"She is as well." Gunnar eyed Brodie as she laughed and twirled in Zavier's arms. "This is honestly the first time I have seen her laugh, carefree, in the public eye since her arrival."

"Understandable, given the small riot at the theatre. I do wonder though, why the US embassy was not contacted about the event? I have heard she was injured; yet, nothing crossed my desk. Not even a courtesy phone call."

"Ambassador... I am not one for politics..." Gunnar began.

"This is not political, Officer Nyström. That is why I am discussing this with you. You are the security detail for an American citizen working for the Swedish Royal Family. By her citizenship alone, I am accountable for her safety and well-

254

being. Next time something happens to Miss Mayer, I wish to be informed. Is that perfectly understood?"

Gunnar felt his jaw tighten. "Perfectly."

The waltz ended, and the two dancers returned to Gunnar. "Did you see this beanpole dance?" Zavier laughed.

"A graceful waltz by all accounts," Brodie returned the joke. She stopped short at the serious look on Gunnar's face and the gentleman by his side. "Is everything okay?"

Before Gunnar could introduce the ambassador, the man extended his hand to Brodie. "Sheldon Briggs, the U.S. Ambassador to Sweden. It is a pleasure to finally meet you, Miss Mayer."

"Oh! Ambassador! A pleasure to meet you; I have been wanting to see the embassy, but you would not believe the chaos that comes with this job."

He grinned. "We have seen the headlines Miss Mayer. You have certainly taken Scandinavia by storm. The Royal family is notoriously secluded, and for them to hire an American au pair… it is truly a historical event."

Brodie arched her eyebrows. "Historical? Oh, I didn't know I was doing anything historical."

"We are watching your success, Miss Mayer. All of America is behind you." He bowed. "I must take my leave. I see my wife from across the room is beckoning for an all-too-rare dance. Pardon me."

The three watched the ambassador disappear into the crowd. "If all of America is behind me, why haven't I heard from my sister?" she asked Gunnar. Her shoulders slumped. "That guy knows how to kill a party."

Zavier clapped Brodie and Gunnar on the shoulders. "I saw a balcony. Fresh air would do everyone a bit of good." He led Brodie away, and Gunnar followed in a stoic bodyguard role.

"You look lovely tonight, Miss Brodie."

She paused Zavier's long strides in order to acknowledge the call out. Loke stood alone in a hallway alcove. "Thank you, Loke."

His smile widened. "Perhaps, if Mister Drummond does not mind, you can save a dance for me?"

"We shall see, Loke. Thank you again."

The three continued down the hallway to a balcony, and Gunnar let out a deep sigh. "Have you even breathed since the Ambassador left?" Zavier asked his friend.

Brodie giggled at the accusation. "I think he was inhaling the whole time. What did the ambassador say to you before we came over?"

Gunnar's eyes examined the curiosity in her eyes and smiled. "Nothing but petty politics that you do not need to worry about." Alone with only Zavier on the balcony, he reached his arm around her waist and pulled her in close to kiss her forehead. "His concern was null and void because nothing will ever happen to you again."

Their British ally stepped away to look over the railing to the city lights and canals in an attempt to bequeath them privacy. Acknowledging his gesture, Brodie wrapped her hand around Gunnar's neck and tilted him down to her lips.

From the hallway, Loke stopped his progression forward at the sight of the kiss. Heartbroken, the young agent slowly sauntered away, unnoticed by all.

Part Three: Advent

Chapter Twenty-one

Gunnar and Brodie walked through the woods on his property. She wore a knit wool cap and a calf-length, thick coat, hugging herself from the late-November temperatures. He carried an axe over one shoulder and whistled a Christmas tune. Brodie found him to be more Paul-Bunyan-like in his Buffalo-plaid shirt, red cap, and axe, and she wondered if her shivering body qualified as Babe the blue-ox. "What do you think of that one?" he asked and pointed out a fir tree that stood roughly seven-feet-tall.

"I don't know. I mean, it's pretty, but I've always had artificial Christmas trees." She walked to the tree. "I'm out of my element on this."

He leaned his axe against a thicker tree. "Looks sturdy and healthy," he stated while examining the fir. "Smell that, you can't get that smell from a fake tree, *älksling*."

"It does smell nice." She ran her gloved fingers over the branches. "We can put it in that floor space between the living area and the dining room, unless you put your tree somewhere else."

"I haven't had a tree since I've had this house. Never felt like celebrating the holiday." He hefted his axe into his hands. "Stand back."

Brodie hopped backwards to give the man room to chop down the young tree.

"But I think that spot will be nice. I don't have much in the way of decorations either; we'll have to go get some."

"Or make some. That would be special. Wish I knew how to make those straw farm animals you Swedes have. Maybe I can call your mother and ask?"

He laughed. "She bought our Christmas decorations so I don't believe she can help you." The tree fell over, and Brodie jumped at the crash. "Got the twine?"

From her coat pocket she produced a ball of twine and tossed it to Gunnar. He caught it and began preparing the tree to be transported to his home. "This is a pretty big tree. It's going to need a lot of decorations."

"I can already hear the gears in your head turning. They're saying: 'shopping' and 'craft store' and... what's that? Gingersnaps? Aww, you spoil me."

"Gingersnaps? I certainly wasn't thinking that," she laughed. She picked the axe up from the ground and shook it in a faux-menacing stance. "You best behave, Klas Gunnar Nyström."

Gunnar began walking to the house with the tree in tow. "Oh no, you first-named me."

"I did. Plus, your mom hasn't shared her gingersnaps recipe with me yet. You'll have to rely on my American-Christmas treats."

"I'm still recovering from your American-Thanksgiving-tofu-turkey treat." He patted his chest to suggest indigestion. "Next American-Thanksgiving, I vote a little hen on the side for me."

"I guess I can agree to that. What about my Christmas-tofu-ham?"

"No, absolutely not. We're having dead pig and fish, and you can have some weird tofu on the side. And to win my point, I'm going to invite my mother over for Christmas Eve dinner, so that's two versus one for real ham."

"Alright, alright. I'm outnumbered." She trotted to the shed to put the axe away, sparing a glimpse to the finished greenhouse built over the fall. The feat caused her to swell with pride, even if most of the hard work was accomplished by Gunnar. "Won't there be a big meal at the palace on Christmas Day too?"

"There will be, and I've always eaten there before, but..." His face contorted as he lifted the giant tree up the steps of his deck, "...I wanted to start our own Christmas traditions."

"That's really sweet of you." They left the tree on the deck in order to prepare the space for its placement. "I think a nice tradition we should start is putting mistletoe over this backdoor."

"I don't need mistletoe when I've already got this stunning face luring me in for a kiss every second of the day." He wrapped his arm around her and pulled her into a kiss. "Your lips are freezing."

"The weather is freezing." She slumped her shoulders. "I don't know if I'll ever adjust to how cold it gets up here."

"And you wanted to go see the Aurora borealis in Lapland," he laughed. "You'd become a human icicle."

"Not if I had my love to keep me warm." She poked his chest. "And fifty layers of thermal underwear."

"Fifty layers? I guess I can roll you around." He kissed her forehead. "But I think you'll adjust, and, when you're more comfortable with the cold, we'll go see the lights."

"That sounds nice. Hey, why don't I make some coffee and *kanelbulle*, you put on some Christmas music, and we set up the space for the tree?"

"*Kanelbulle*? I love how Swedish you're becoming." He pecked her lips and departed to his growing record collection.

"My love for cinnamon rolls predates my Swedish adventures," she protested. Despite the remonstration, she smiled. Her six months in Sweden proved to be the greatest time in her life. The early rumors and animosity toward her in the summer was far outweighed by the healing she witnessed in the Royal Family. Paparazzi, while still present, hounded her less and discovered new quasi-scandals to attack. The King's Ball and Brodie's public friendship with the queen during charity events provided the Swedish people reassurance that no improprieties took place in the Royal residence.

The fall had also afforded Brodie opportunities she had only dared to dream of. Gunnar and Jonna equally pushed for her to attend courses at university to pursue her graduate degree in psychology, and she published a paper about the effects terminal illnesses had on adolescent behavior. The publication was met with general enthusiasm. Already, she worked on an outline for a book on the subject.

Christmas music trickled out of Gunnar's record player with the accompanying pops of vinyl. He hummed and sang along. "Next week's the last ballet of the year at the theatre," Gunnar announced while walking into the kitchen. His hands held a bundle of mail. "Such a shame that the daytime performance will be when the children are in school."

"Is that so?" Brodie sprinkled brown sugar over the rolled-out dough. "What will it be?"

"The Nutcracker."

"I do love the adventures of Clara and her Nutcracker Prince."

After turning on his coffeemaker, he thumbed through the mail. "I suppose we should go then. The ballet troupe is from New York." He snorted surprise at the mail. "Letter from your sister."

"My sister?" Her hand held tightly to a container of cardamom. "She hasn't spoken to me in years. I've reached out and reached out, only to get nothing in reply. What is it? Did she hear I'm working for royalty and wants to create ties again with my pseudo-celebrity status?"

Gunnar pried the cardamom from her hand. "You heard the ambassador: everyone in America has your back. Read the letter and find out what she wants."

Hesitant, Brodie stared at the green envelope in his hand.

"Don't you want reconciliation?"

"I... do," she sighed. She snatched the envelope and strode to the dining room table to read in private. Gunnar quietly deposited the remaining mail in his kitchen counter basket in order to finish the cinnamon buns. Silence filled the house until soft sobs began tumbling out of Brodie's lips. "My baby sister wants me to visit her, the next chance I get for vacation."

"Then we should go."

"We?"

"I'll always be your bodyguard, Brodie."

She wiped tears from her eyes with the brim of her apron. "You're so sweet. And she, she's had some things happen recently that opened her eyes to the importance of family. Family, it really is important, isn't it? I was so focused on mending the Royal family, that I neglected my own."

"Glad that you get this opportunity." He slid the tray of buns into the oven. "Christmas miracle?"

Brodie laughed and joined him in the kitchen. "I think we've had a few miracles this year. Don't you?"

"And to think... the year isn't over yet." They shared a gentle kiss. "Now about this tree..."

"Right. A tree. Decorations." She glanced at the tree sitting on the deck. "Our tree. Our decorations."

He nodded. "For our... home."

"Our home?"

Gunnar took her hands in his. "Ours. Look around." He twirled her about to see the herb wall, the decorations in the kitchen, dining room, and living room, and to the outside where the orchard, garden, and greenhouse stood. "Those are all because a woman named Brodie entered my life and turned this shell of a house into a real home. And I wouldn't want to consider it anything other than ours."

She smiled and leaned back against him. "It truly is ours, isn't it? I can say I've worked this land with my bare hands."

He rubbed her hands with his thumb in response to her statement. "Yes, you have." He glanced at her left hand and the empty ring finger. "Maybe it's time to reward your hands for all that work."

"What did you have in mind?"

"Brown sugar, molasses, ginger, cinnamon, cloves, flour..."

"Are you listing the ingredients for gingersnaps?"

"I certainly am." He laughed as she playfully tickled him and chased him out of the kitchen to prepare the space for the tree.

Chapter Twenty-two

Eyes alert for anything suspicious, Gunnar walked down the aisles of the empty cathedral. It was the last Sunday of November and the first Sunday of Advent. The arrival of the Royal Family to the cathedral on such a holy day increased the terrorist alert within his agency. Satisfied with his surveillance, he knelt at the altar.

"Dear Lord, I am sorry for having been so stubborn these last few years. If anyone knows what it is like to lose someone, You would know. But I pushed You away, like You were the least likely to understand, like it was all Your fault. I know You have forgiven me, but I feel so unworthy to come to You, asking for something after only coming back to You. Brodie mentioned on Friday that we've had a few miracles this year, and I know that's Your hand at play in it all. You have given me so much, and I should not ask for more. But Jonna is still not better, Lord. She loves You, with all her heart. Please, don't let her suffer. Heal her body, and help her continue to help others, showing Your love. And...and... Lord, please give me the ability to track down Anders Strand and put him behind bars. I know it's selfish. I know I ask that so I can have my happily-ever-after with Brodie, but he is a monster that needs to be caught and helped. The silence has gone too long, and I'm afraid many people are going to be hurt needlessly by him. Please Lord, help guide me. Let Your will be done, through me."

He stood and placed his hand to his forehead. Making the Sign of the Cross, he finished his prayer aloud, "In the name of the Father, and of the Son, and of the Holy Spirit, amen."

"I never thought you the religious type."

Recognizing the voice immediately, Gunnar grabbed his gun. He aimed it at the man who calmly stood in the middle of the aisle with his hands clasped behind his back. He wore a black suit and sunglasses, but Gunnar had no doubts. Anders Strand stood before him. *"I was praying that you would be delivered to me, and here you are, an early Christmas present."*

Anders lifted his hands. "I respect holy ground Klas, and on Advent no less. Are you going to be the one to taint this sacred ground and day with bloodshed?"

"If it comes to bloodshed, I think God will understand."

"If God approves of the murder of an innocent in the middle of his church, then maybe I have been justified in my campaign against him."

"I believe we have a different idea of what innocent means."

Anders calmly removed his sunglasses and offered a wicked smile to his nemesis. His eyes no longer appeared natural. The irises were solid black.

"What did you do to your eyes?" Gunnar asked with a slight cringe.

"Oh this? This is symbolic of the power I now possess, Klas dear. Power over life and death, power over your mind, power over your fears." He checked his watch. "For example, you examined this whole cathedral yourself, Officer Nyström? You, the man all the little boys and girls training to be agents and police wish to be."

Finger on the trigger, Gunnar fought with himself about taking the shot. The man's words made him pause. *"What have you done?"* He reached to his ear and pressed a button on his earpiece. *"What have you done to the cathedral?"*

"I have done nothing, yet. But, being the benevolent man that I am, I thought perhaps you wished to see your sweet Katarina."

The mention of her name on Anders' lips caused Gunnar to tense. His fellow agents could be heard over his earpiece, assessing the situation they now heard.

"You remember her, don't you Klas? She was beautiful. Italian, right? She smelled like orchids, as I recall. Orchids. I like orchids. Maybe I'll put an orchid on your grave to honor all these good times we have had." Anders laughed at the pain on Gunnar's face. "Are you a fan of music, Gunnar? Of course you are. You had that record player when we were boys in school. Rock and metal, that's what you were a fan of. It made you so popular with the ladies. With my lady. I prefer classical myself. Maybe that was what made me an outcast – too much culture for the likes of you. Shall we have a concert? You and me, surely by now your people are hearing our little chat. They can evacuate the building all they want, but this sanctuary is for us. They come in, everyone dies."

"They won't come in," Gunnar assured him. The voices over the earwig reaffirmed his order.

"Fantastic. I wouldn't want our reunion interrupted with unwelcomed visitors. Though I'm certain it's a reunion far delayed. I have been watching you, months now. You arrived at the palace with that American woman at the beginning of June. She's gorgeous, and you know, she reminded me a bit of Katarina."

The mention of Brodie froze Gunnar in terror. His fear had been realized.

"I read the news about her being the king's mistress, and I laughed. Roffe has a type. We both know that. Jonna is his type, and he's a sickening sentimentalist who would not cheat on his poor, dying wife. She will die, by the way, Klas. No medicine on earth can cure her. But, that American, what is her name? Brodie? An ugly name for a beautiful woman, and she is your woman, isn't she Klas? Don't look so surprised, I guessed it the moment she stepped off the plane."

"If you even attempt to harm her, I will rip your arms, legs, and head off with my bare hands."

"Does she get excited with your Viking charm? Spread her legs when you threaten men with mutilation?"

Gunnar could feel anger and hatred bubble to the surface of his emotions while Strand spoke of Brodie, but the final statement was too much to bear. He squeezed the trigger, and Anders fell to the ground. In the briefest of moments, time froze. Burdens lifted from Gunnar's shoulders: he was free.

A horrendous laugh rose from the body of Anders. "You truly have no sense of honor, Klas. Killing a man on holy ground. But I told you, I have power over life and death. You cannot kill me." He sat up slowly and raised his hands in mockery of the Crucifix. "I am more powerful than your Messiah."

Loud explosions erupted at his statement, and the entire cathedral shook.

"You want to desecrate holy ground with bloodshed?" Anders shouted over another explosion. "Then so be it. This ground will bury you. Enjoy the concert!"

Collapsing stone surrounded Anders as classical music began playing. Stained glass rained down from an exploding window, and Gunnar lifted his arm protectively. Clutching his gun in his left hand, he dodged collapsing debris forward to the location Anders stood. But the terrorist was nowhere to be seen.

"Strand *sighted!*" he yelled over his earpiece. He hoped the message could be heard over the crashing of cymbals and exploding stone and glass. *"Pull the Royal Family back!"* Agents began shouting over their communication units, indicating the message was received.

Leaping away from a falling pillar, Gunnar's gun was knocked from his hand by a tumbling chunk of medieval stone. He could hear the bones of his hand and arm break before he felt the pain. The cathedral was imploding on him. Every crash of the cymbal indicated another explosion. He could not escape. With a final burst of energy, Gunnar dove under a stone pew and blacked out.

Brodie ran out of the royal family's town car and into the hospital, forsaking the temporary agent assigned to her. She reached the front desk of the emergency room in a panic. "Gunnar Nyström, Klas Gunnar Nyström, where is he?" she wailed.

The woman behind the counter merely looked at her and blinked.

"Where is he?" Brodie shouted, slamming her hand down on the counter.

"We cannot give that information away," the woman finally responded.

Roffe entered the room with his accompanying agents. "Please tell us where the man is," the king asked the woman kindly.

Recognizing her king immediately, the woman began typing. "Yes, Your Majesty. He's on the fifth floor, A-wing,

Room 122. Go down this hall and take the elevators at the end. It will take you right to the A-wing."

Placing a hand on Brodie's back, he guided her down the hall. Neither spoke but feared the worst for their loved one.

The elevator felt slow, and Brodie's stomach tensed as the doors opened to the fifth floor. She bolted forward, finding Room 122 with ease. The view from the room's large glass window caused her to cry out. Gunnar lay still and his left arm was covered in a cast from shoulder to fingertip. The rest of his body was a mixture of bandages, burns, and bruises.

King Roffe stood behind her. Slowly he ran his hand over his face, distressed at the sight. "How bad is it?" he asked one of the officers guarding the door.

"Your Majesty," the man bowed. "His left hand and arm were broken in multiple places and will take over a month to heal. Lacerations cover his body from the debris hitting him, and he suffered burns from the explosions." The agent shook his head. "I went through the rubble. A miracle saved this guy."

"A big cross fell on the pew he was under. The angle it leaned at created a cave around him. It was a miracle," the other officer agreed.

Brodie put a hand up against the window. "Thank you, Jesus," she whispered. "Thank you."

"Was Strand in the rubble?" Roffe asked the officers. "Did they find his body?"

"No, Your Majesty," they responded. "No trace of the man, but everyone is looking for him."

She attempted to tune out the rest of the conversation in order to watch Gunnar through the glass. They spoke of the death toll, minimal due to Gunnar's quick thought to send an alert on his earpiece. One altar boy, in a restroom, who would never reach graduation, and, in his office, a young priest who had only begun the ministry, had been taken by the fiend. She wept at the destruction caused. For once, Brodie wished they spoke in Swedish rather than English. A doctor joined them, telling the king the medical woes of Gunnar.

"He's resting now, and needs plenty of rest. His body suffered much for a man his age. Broken bones, burns, smoke inhalation..."

'A man his age' made Brodie cringe. Gunnar was in better shape than most teenagers in America; he would recover.

The healing man barely turned his head toward the glass window. One eye remained swollen shut and another opened only halfway, but he spotted Brodie. Calling her name only produced a hoarse growl.

"Let me in," Brodie told the doctor and officers.

"He's still recovering..." the doctor began to protest.

"Please."

The king nodded to the officers who allowed her entrance to the room. She held her hands to her chest at the sight of the IVs, tubes, and monitors surrounding him. Her memory flooded with the image of her mother who had just as many monitors as she faded away in a hospital bed. Attempting to not choke on her tears, she reached down to Gunnar's right hand and held it.

"Brodie," he whispered. His lips were heavily chapped around his previous scar, but tiny cuts from flying debris also left their mark.

"I'm here baby; I'm here." She wanted to stroke his face but was afraid to cause him pain. "I won't leave your side."

"Did they find him? Was his body uncovered?" Gunnar's voice slightly cleared with every word, but remained raspy nonetheless. No doubt his throat suffered from the smoke inhalation.

"No, they didn't. There were two others though... they... they didn't make it."

Gunnar closed his eyes and cursed under his breath. "He wore a vest; should have shot him in the head." His hand weakly squeezed hers. "He knows about you. He threatened you."

Brodie felt sick. If Strand could do this to Gunnar, then what could he do to her?

"I'm going to double the protection on you. He won't touch you, *älskling*. Maybe this is a good time to visit your sister and get away from here."

She pulled a chair up to the bed. "I'm staying with you. If he wants you or if he wants me, he'll have to take us down together."

The man smiled with his eye closing drowsily. "You're stubborn, my beautiful angel." He drifted asleep, clutching her hand.

"I don't want a transfer," Gunnar growled to his nurse. A half day had passed, and with the doctor's consent, the hospital wished to transfer the man from ICU to a regular room. "I want out of here. There is a terrorist out there who wants us dead."

The nurse sighed and turned to Brodie. "Maybe you can reason with him."

"You need to rest sweetie," she attempted. "If we transfer to the new room, it'll be more spacious, and I can bring in your laptop for you to work on."

"I need to talk with my task force; I need to go through the timeline... He said things that made me... I need to be involved Brodie."

She patted his hand. "How much longer will he be in the hospital?"

"His burns are not as deep as the doctor first assumed, but she does want to make sure the burns don't become infected – that can be a day or two."

Gunnar grumbled at the number.

"And if your burns become infected, you'll be here longer," Brodie chided him. "Let's take the transfer to the nice room with the private bathroom so I can shower." His frown made her add, "You can always face-time with headquarters until you're released."

"There will be internet?" Gunnar asked the nurse. "And a place for Brodie to sleep?"

She nodded 'yes'.

"Transfer me," he growled with a wave of his hand. "And get me some decent food for when I arrive."

"You are still on a liquid diet," Brodie reminded him. "Broth for you."

"Broth," Gunnar muttered. "A man can starve at the hospital."

"If you tell me what you would like, I can have an order put in for them to prepare while we move you to your new room."

"I would like a steak," his sarcastic response was cut short by a coughing spasm.

Brodie frowned to see him in pain. He had always been the strong one; now it was her role. "He likes the beef consommé but needs two bowls. And apple juice and coffee." She stepped back so the nurse could unhook and change different wires and tubes. "He also likes the orange ice pops."

"There will be a workstation near your room with a refrigerator full of ice pops, ice cream, sherbet, chilled fruit cups, and gelatin, so he doesn't starve," the nurse informed her. "There's also a coffee machine, hot water dispenser, and tea bags."

"Tea bags? They must have known you were coming." Gunnar beamed up at Brodie, and it reassured her to see him with a sense of humor returning. "You should order some food for yourself. You haven't eaten since you've arrived."

"I'll be okay. I can go down to the café and pick something up."

"Not without armed escorts."

Brodie sighed. "Is that possible? I can order room service too?"

"Of course. There's a full menu on my stand, along with an extra copy of his liquid diet menu. You can even order your food, if you'd like, while I fix his tubes. The room you will be moving to is C-714."

"Thank you." Brodie perused the menu. "You would think a hospital served more vegetarian options."

Gunnar snorted. "We're in Stockholm, not... San Francisco."

"Hmph, maybe I'll call Zavier and order delivery. He'll want to know you're alive anyway." She picked up the room phone and placed Gunnar's food order for his new room. When she attempted to order a side salad for herself, she met

274

resistance from the kitchen who claimed that their system only permitted them to provide the room with liquid diet meals. Brodie relayed this information to Gunnar's nurse, who, with an annoyed sigh, took over the phone conversation.

"I don't know what the kitchen staff think sometimes," the nurses apologized after hanging up. "They must not realize some people have guests that get hungry too." She called out the door for a fellow nurse to assist her in transferring Gunnar to his new room.

Brodie and two agents followed them as they traversed down the halls and elevators with his hospital bed. "So, is this bed mine to keep? It follows me from room to room?"

"It stays with you the entire time you're here," his nurse answered.

"And when I leave?"

"It stays with us." They began attaching his cords and wires in his new room.

"What if I bought it? It's pretty comfortable, and I think this slight incline does wonders with my snoring."

"It did make his snores less, boisterous," Brodie agreed jovially. "Maybe we should find you a mechanized bed that can incline after you are released."

"Certainly. After I'm released, and after I catch Strand, we will hop over to IKEA and start shopping." His utterance of Strand's name ceased the frivolity in the air. "Brodie, can you call Loke to bring my laptop?"

"Of course." She sat on the couch-slash-bed and dialed Loke's number. While speaking with the young agent, she eyed Gunnar. His emotional struggle was apparent on his face. How would he be able to defeat Strand in such a physical and mental condition? There was no doubt this was only Strand's first of many attempts. "Dear God, please be with him," she prayed.

Brodie led Gunnar to his bed. "I should be going to my office, not to my bedroom," he attempted to argue with her.

"You were on your phone with headquarters the whole ride from the hospital to here. Before that, you were on your laptop for six hours…"

"He mentioned 'his lady' at the cathedral. Who was his lady? Why bring that up? And what did he do to his eyes? Contacts just to look more grotesque? Hyphema?" he began rambling.

"The doctor said you needed rest."

"Hospital doctors…" he grumbled. "This is why I have my guy. No paperwork or overhead…"

She pulled the covers down on the bed, ignoring his grumblings. "If you don't rest, then you won't heal. If you don't heal, then you can't catch Strand."

"And you…" Gunnar's protest stopped short when Brodie turned to him with her arms crossed. "You are right," he acquiesced.

She stepped up to him and began unbuttoning his shirt. "I will try to be as gentle as the nurse was."

Gunnar lifted his right hand to Brodie's hair. "I would rather you undress me than the nurse – anytime."

A rose-tint colored her cheeks. "Not how I imagined this would happen." He adjusted his right arm to help her pull the first shirt sleeve off. "Would be easier if you didn't have such

276

bulky arm muscles," she jested while sliding the second sleeve off his injured left arm.

"I suppose this would be easier if I had noodle-arms like yours."

"Hey, not fair. I have a little muscle now." She flexed. "See?"

"Oh, would you look at that," he laughed and poked the faintest bump of a bicep. "It's only taken six months of working out."

"And after six months of your tutelage, I think I can finally disarm a bad guy and open a pickle jar." She tossed his shirt onto his armchair. "What would you like to wear to sleep?"

He reached out to stop Brodie from walking to his dresser. "You don't have to do this Brodie. I have two working feet and one working arm."

"So, you would have been able to get your shirt off yourself?" she asked with an arched eyebrow.

"Okay, the shirt would have given me problems. But pants, shoes, turning my covers down..." he rubbed her arm affectionately. "You don't have to take care of me."

"Yes. I do." She marched over to his dresser and pulled out a pair of his pajama pants. "Gunnar, I was in the car with the Royal Family. I heard the shouts about you and Strand. Then I heard it. I heard the explosions, and in the distance, I saw the cathedral crash in on itself." Her tears fell onto the flannel pants. "Two hours, Gunnar. For two hours, I thought you were dead."

He paused unbuckling his belt. "Two hours?"

"I cried until I began to heave. Then I heaved... When they told the king you were alive, he immediately informed me and took me to the hospital to see you. I swore that I would be the strong one now. So – just let me take care of you."

Gunnar took the pajamas from her hands and set them on top of his dresser. "I need help with my belt," he whispered.

Brodie quickly wiped her tears away and loosed the belt from his pants. "Thank you."

"I'm not used to needing help. Or letting someone help me."

"I know. You're strong. Stubborn. And you're always the one in charge." She helped him change into the pajamas.

"Clearly, I've met my match in those departments." He smiled and brushed hair out of Brodie's face. "And I'm happy with that."

She smiled and ran her hands gently over his chest. "A whole new set of scars," she sighed and checked a few of the bandages to ensure they did not need to be changed before he slept. "At least nothing was infected."

"Do I have the okay for bed, Nurse Brodie?"

She nodded. "Come along Officer Nyström. I will tuck you in."

He hugged her tight while walking to the bed. "Thank you, Brodie."

"Promise not to die on me again." She helped him to gently slide into the bed.

"I promise." Before she could walk away, he tugged her arm with his right hand and pulled her down to the pillows next to him. "Stay with me."

"I was going to sleep on the couch…"

He smiled. "Just stay for a moment… give me, two hours? I owe you two hours."

"Two hours," she agreed and curled up by his side.

Gunnar wrapped his healthy arm around Brodie and kissed the top of her head. He wanted to cry and apologize for letting this all happen – for causing her fear. She certainly would not have faced terror had she remained safely in South Hills. But he knew better. Brodie would reprimand him for these thoughts. She loved him and the life they were building together.

"Do you believe in guardian angels?" he whispered.

"Of course I do. The Bible says we're protected by angels."

He played with her hair while remaining silent. Finally, he stated, "I think I saw mine. Under that pew. I saw an explosion, and the world falling in on me. Then, a bright light. There was someone, with dark hair but who shined – brilliantly – holding that steel cross. That's all I saw, the last thing I saw, before waking in the hospital." Gunnar took a deep breath. "Am I crazy?"

"You're not crazy, darling." Brodie ran her hand over his chest reassuringly. "The spiritual world is all around us. You saw a glimpse of it." She toyed with a button his pajamas. "My mother, in her final days, said she could hear a choir singing. That gave me comfort. One day I'll find her again in heaven."

Gunnar kissed the top of her head. He did not mean to cause her thoughts of her mother. "Dog or cat?" he blurted out.

"What?" she laughed.

"Dog or cat?"

"Both." She smiled. "Big family. Lots of pets."

"Oh? Big family? Lots of pets? When did we decide this?"

"Just now. And I want one of those Norwegian Elkhounds. I always thought they were adorable, but Texas is far too hot to have one. They'd melt. This weather is perfect."

"I could use a good hunting dog when I go get elk," he agreed.

"Hey! You can't take my fluffy baby hunting! He could get hurt."

Gunnar laughed as Brodie started listing all of the different pets she wanted. "I hope Alfred doesn't get jealous."

"Oh no. He will always have his place next to my bedside."

"Then maybe I'm a little jealous of Alfred."

Brodie giggled and stretched up to kiss him. "You have nothing to be jealous of."

Gunnar grinned and returned her kisses.

Chapter Twenty-three

A heavily-bandaged Gunnar walked down the halls of Drottningholm with Roffe. His left arm's cast hung in a blue sling, and he absent-mindedly fidgeted with a bandage on his right ear. "Do you honestly plan to hold the Nobel Banquet with Strand actively on the loose?" Gunnar's voice was still coarse from the smoke inhalation and tubes used by the hospital.

"We have hosted the Nobel Banquet for one-hundred and fifteen years. I will not allow Strand to take this away from us."

"But..." Gunnar's face contorted. "I can't guarantee it will be safe. I checked the cathedral, Roffe, with my own eyes. That is on me. The death of that boy and priest are on me."

Roffe stopped walking and put a strong hand on his friend's shoulder. "No, that is on the evil which consumes Anders Strand. You cannot blame yourself. You've read the investigation reports; there is no way you would have found the explosives."

Gunnar frowned. "I should have sent in a K-9 unit. They could have detected it..."

"You know they may not have. It was a new explosives formula." Roffe patted his shoulder. "You will learn from this attack to provide proper security at the Noble Banquet."

"Of course." Gunnar felt somewhat reassured at the king's words. They continued to Roffe's office in silence, turning on a television to local news. "Who leaked that information?" Gunnar asked. The journalist reported the only two deaths in the attack. "I had hoped to make Strand think I died."

"Do you think there's another mole?"

Gunnar shook his head. "I don't know. Too many involved in the aftermath. Foolish hope to keep my survival hidden."

"Change your strategy. No hiding. Face him head on." Roffe sat at his desk and picked up a pen. "Another reason to hold the banquet."

His lifelong confidant sat in a leather armchair. "How are you playing the speech?"

"Since the prime minister and I agreed that no matter what I say, I cannot affect my election status," the king smirked, "I have decided to be forthwith, brave, unwavering in the face of danger, and a call to prayer and love."

"Call to prayer? You're playing with fire."

"What are they going to do? Elect a new king?" Roffe chuckled. "A call for prayer and love is exactly what is needed in the aftermath of a crisis. And you know Strand better than I – how upset would he become if I responded with that rather than anger? Makes me exuberant imagining it."

"Don't be too kumbaya with this speech," Gunnar grumbled. "I appreciate the sentiment, but people still want to be reassured that they are safe. And that cathedral was a loved landmark – they are going to want revenge."

"Revenge is not what we should seek. We seek justice to be served."

"That's why you're the king, and I'm just a security guard."

Roffe tugged stationary toward him. "I would say you are more than a security guard, and that is why I value your words of wisdom."

"My word of wisdom is," Gunnar stood, "I would have hired a speech writer long ago."

"That's not my way. I prefer to stare at paper nervously until the words are gifted to me: the way my father taught me."

Nodding, Gunnar opened the door. "I have my own miraculous writing to do for Bolstomtavägen. I don't know which is harder: writing a speech for the whole country or writing a report explaining how the cross saved me."

"There's a sermon in your speech. May be good for others to hear."

Gunnar grunted. "Or they may have me dismissed as insane." He departed for his own office, allowing Roffe the opportunity to meditate on his speech writing.

Jonna shuffled through paperwork in a file on her lap. Brodie sat in an armchair nearby; she attempted to focus on the teacher's letter before her but found concentration difficult since the cathedral attack.

"Are you feeling alright?"

The queen's gentle question forced Brodie to look up. "I… I could lie and say yes."

Jonna smiled. "You do not have to lie with me, Brodie. I was there too. I know the fear that seized you." She shook her head. "Had it been Roffe – you are handling this far better than I would have, in your place."

"I must be putting on a strong appearance, but Jonna – when that cathedral collapsed, I felt everything within me die. I don't know how to explain it. The thought that he was gone – I lost who I was."

"When you love someone, they become a part of you. Their suffering is your suffering. Their happiness is your happiness.

283

Two have become one flesh. It is no wonder that so often when one spouse passes on, the other follows soon." Jonna glanced at a bedside picture of her wedding day and worried if Roffe would behave the same.

Brodie thought of her father after her mother's death. Was his love so deep for her mother that it destroyed him to lose her? "I'm terrified to think I am like that. I've been so afraid of developing cancer like my mother that I never thought I could be developing traits like my father."

"Yes, I understand how that would alarm you. Brodie, when you give your heart away," Jonna inhaled deeply, "you take a risk. It is a gamble. It can be the greatest experience or the greatest sorrow. But look back on your time with Gunnar. Was that time, those memories and emotions, far superior to that momentary feeling of loss?"

"Of course." Brodie's hands darted to her eyes to ensure tears did not escape. "But what if next time it's not a momentary feeling of loss? What if Strand wins?"

"Strand will not win." Jonna stated this matter-of-factly. "Evil does not triumph over good. As I recall, a young woman once told me a story of a shepherd boy named David who defeated a giant evil named Goliath. She was restoring my faith, and she spent this summer building up my defense against fear."

Hearing Jonna use her own words against her caused Brodie to let her tears run free. She could not argue with what the queen said.

"Oh Brodie, do come here." Jonna reached her arms up. Brodie complied and sat on the edge of the bed where the queen could hug her. "You have been so focused on serving others and tending to our needs, that you've not taken the time to build your own faith. Faith is fuel. You must refill so you do not run dry."

"Yes. You are right." Brodie wiped her eyes. "Gunnar told me that he saw an angel in the explosions who protected him. Of course, God is protecting him. I pray every night for his protection. Maybe it's become routine. Why would I pray for that protection then fear he's going to be taken from me?"

"We have all done such." Jonna patted her back. "Brodie, you are a woman of remarkable faith. All of our faith is tested – mine was. I did not believe I would see Christmas. Yet it is only a few weeks away."

"And I believe you will see many more Christmases, Jonna," Brodie affirmed.

"I do feel stronger now than I did in the summer," the queen agreed. "Brodie, I love you as if you were my own sister. We will pray, together, over you and Gunnar, as we have prayed over me."

The sentiment made Brodie hug Jonna, and, together, they prayed.

"How are you feeling, Gunnar?" Niklas, home from his new boarding school due to the terrorist threat, sat across from the man in his office.

Gunnar raised Niklas' bore rifle with his right arm. The long weapon in his non-prominent hand felt bulky and heavier than normal. *"I'm adjusting."* He placed the rifle back on his desk to inspect a broken mechanism. *"How has your aim gotten?"*

"Better, but I am not you."

Gunnar snorted. *"I am not me anymore."*

The prince frowned. "I am sorry Gunnar. I wish..." He fidgeted with his words. "I wish I had not been such a distraction for you, and for Loke, this summer. Maybe you would have had progress on capturing Strand." He stood and walked to Gunnar's side. "I know Loke was searching for Strand while on my security detail. He mentioned him frequently on the phone." Niklas shrugged. "When I was not trying to escape his presence, that is."

The older man slipped his glasses on in order to better see the delicate mechanism that required his attention. "Yes. Loke has played a prominent role in the hunt for Strand. I did not realize he was working on the assignment so much though. I should commend him for it." With one-hand and a tiny screwdriver, he tightened a loose screw.

"After the school year, I am going to try-out for a qualifying race."

"Qualifying?" Gunnar smiled. "For the Olympics?"

Niklas beamed and nodded his head.

"I am proud of you, Crown Prince." Gunnar handed him the rifle and tussled his hair. "Go test that. It should fix your problem. I have to see your mother."

"Thank you, Gunnar." The two left the office; Niklas headed to his makeshift shooting range, and Gunnar toward Queen Jonna's chamber.

Tatiana opened the door to allow Gunnar entry. *"It is Lord Nyström,"* the maidservant announced. She laughed at Gunnar's blanched face at the announcement. *"I must do something to bring humor around here,"* she joked.

Gunnar smiled and hugged the older lady. *"I would have it no other way, Tat-tee."* She nodded and closed the door behind her, allowing Gunnar a private word with the queen. *"How are you feeling, Your Majesty?"* He pulled an empty armchair up to her side in order to take her hand in his.

"I could ask you the same," the queen replied. "You have certainly looked better."

He grinned roguishly. *"I have also looked worse."*

She offered a slight laugh. "Good to see your sense of humor returning."

"Brodie would call it my 'coping mechanism'. The joys of dating a psychology student." He patted Jonna's hand and leaned back in the chair. "Have you seen her today? Is she okay?"

The queen smiled. *"She will be."*

"That is what I was afraid of. I could tell at the hospital and at home – she should not have to deal with this. I tried to keep everything hidden. I tried to keep her safe. How did he know?" He shook his head and leaned it against his right hand. "I do not know what to do."

"Do about what? You still love her, do you not?"

"Of course, I do." He sighed. "But do I move forward like normal? I thought about... well, if Strand knows, no point in being a secret relationship. Right?" He shifted in the chair. "I can take her out, and hold her hand, and..." His eyes met Jonna's eyes, and he smiled. "Jonna, I want to ask her to marry me."

Jonna smiled and clapped her hands together. *"That is wonderful to hear. Do you have the ring? When will you ask her? Where?"* The mention of a proposal turned the usually regal Jonna into an excited young lady. *"I know she will say yes, Gunnar."*

287

"I have the ring." He took a small box from his pocket and handed it to Jonna. "I was going to propose after we returned home from the cathedral on Sunday, but... that clearly did not happen. Now, I do not know. Maybe on Christmas? That seems so far away. Time is short. I thought, I could take her to the Nobel Ball. If Roffe insists on having it still, then, I can be there. And I believe Brodie will love the ball."

Jonna nodded. "I will make sure you have everything you need. Two seats, a car, and a dress for Brodie."

Gunnar stood and kissed Jonna's forehead. *"Thank you, fairy godmother."*

The baroque garden was overrun with reporters, cameras, and security in anticipation of the king's speech. Brodie and Gunnar watched from the television in his office. Due to his injuries Gunnar had been forbidden by the king to attend the speech with the other security personnel.

"We anxiously await to hear what King Roffe of Sweden has to say after Sunday's attack that left two dead, several injured, and a historic cathedral in shambles," a British reporter announced. They had found a British news channel in order for Brodie to benefit from her native language both in commentary and in translated subtitles.

"My project is complete," Gunnar announced with a click of the mouse. "Bolstomtavägen will have to accept that Strand is insane and a miracle occurred."

"True on both accounts," Brodie took his hand. "I'm very thankful for the miracle... not so much for Strand."

His thumb rubbed the back of her hand. "This whole year has been full of miracles, and you're the one I'm thankful for most of all."

"Oh Gunnar," she blushed.

"I'm serious Brodie." He sighed deeply. "The cat is out of the bag about us, at least with the one person we wanted to keep it from, so, um..." He faltered over his words. "No reason to hide anymore. I guess, what I mean to say is, we need a change of strategy."

"You are so adorable when the Scandanavian-shyness puts you at a loss for words."

Gunnar frowned. He, for one, hated the shyness.

"I'm sorry. I'm sorry." Brodie patted his hand, knowing he wished to appear confident, not shy. "Change of strategy?"

"Approach our relationship head on. Be public about it if we want – if you want."

"Are you sure? We won't be poking a hornet's nest will we?"

"Brodie – I think the hornet's nest has already been shaken, thrown at the wall, cut in half, and mauled by a bear." He gestured to his various injuries. "I don't believe going out to *fika* and holding your hand will be disastrous."

"Going out to *fika* is always disastrous, on my waistline."

He shook his head. "You're imagining that, *sötis*. In fact, I think you have lost weight."

"Puh-leeze," she exaggerated. "I don't think I could fit into the gown I wore at the King's Ball that was cut to exact measurements."

"Sounds like a reason to have a new gown made."

"Why would I have a new gown made?" she laughed. "That isn't really daily-wear."

"You'll need something to wear to the Noble Banquet and Ball."

"Aside from Niklas, I don't believe the children are attending, so I won't be attending. I probably will have St. Lucia preparation to do with Kjerstin." She stopped rambling upon noticing his arched eyebrows. "Am I missing something?"

"I am going to the ball – with you."

Her jaw dropped. "You're going to the ball... with me? But you don't do balls. You don't dance... You... what?"

He laughed, rather hoarsely, at his girlfriend. "I don't do balls because, one, I'm always on security, which, thanks to Strand, won't be the case. And, two, I have never had anyone to attend a ball with on the rare few times when I was not on security detail."

"But the dancing?"

"It is the year of miracles." He lured her down into a gentle hug. "And after seeing you dance with Zavier at the King's Ball, I'll admit, I don't want to see you attend any more balls with anyone other than me."

"Awww, you were jealous of Zavier," she jested.

His face flushed, but a need for response was cut short by the announcement of the king's arrival on the television. Unlike more jovial times, *Kungssången* was not played. A stern frown and wrinkled brow adorned Roffe's weary face. "He must have been awake all night," Gunnar mumbled. "He needs a speech writer."

"That would lose a personal touch, don't you believe?"

He grunted. After all this time, Brodie understood the different interpretations of Gunnar's grunts. This particular grunt meant, 'You are correct, but I do not wish to admit such.'

Roffe unfolded a stack of papers and cleared his throat.

"My dear compatriots,

"This Sunday, a terrorist attack shook Stockholm at its very core when numerous explosions destroyed an iconic cathedral that has withstood five centuries of reformation, violence, war, and destructive forces of nature. Two of our own, two who have devoted their lives to serving God and their community, were brutally murdered in these attacks. For these crimes, we seek justice to be served. Already, our law enforcement agencies are collaborating to locate the perpetrator of these attacks so that no future acts of terror come forth from his hands. My primary concern has, and always will be, the safety of the Swedish people and all those we call welcomed and cherished guests in our country.

"There are many servants of evil in this world, whether a terrorist destroying a house of worship or the cancer attacking my wife's body. We see it in the eyes of a starving child and in the wars plaguing our world. These servants seek to spread more evil: anger, fear, hatred, greed, pride – but that is exactly what we must not let happen. We cannot let evil win by consuming us with these detrimental traits. Instead, let us turn to good. In Romans 12:21, the Apostle Paul says, 'Do not be overcome by evil, but overcome evil with good.' This is what I call for today: that we shall overcome the evil in our world not by force, but by good. Let us aspire to love our neighbors, to care for one another, to speak in kindness, and to pray.

"I have been advised against calling our nation to prayer, but it is my hope that the transformation prayer has brought forth in my family may be brought forth in your own families, your own communities, in our country, and in our world. Pray

291

for transformation and that hearts will be softened for love to shine. This is the only true path to peace and prosperity.

"My family and I shall pray for the families and loved ones for those lost in the attacks. We will pray for those injured, that they may be healed. We will pray for all of you whose hearts are filled with fear, that you may be comforted. We shall pray, and we shall act. I hope that you will do the same.

"God bless you, and God bless Sweden." Roffe bowed his head and retreated into the palace.

"An unorthodox speech from King Roffe of Sweden today at the Drottningholm Palace's baroque gardens," the journalist concluded. "Calling for love, kindness, and, most shockingly, prayer in the wake of Sunday's terrorist attacks."

"Psh," Brodie responded to the commentator. "A man calls for prayer after a tragedy, and, suddenly, it's unorthodox and shocking. Prayer has been a part of cultures all over the planet for all of human history, but, no, now it's taboo."

"Strange times we live in," Gunnar agreed. "No matter what the journalists say, I think that was a good speech. It is what we needed."

She ran her fingers through his hair. "Prayer, love, kindness, and maybe... an act of God dealing with Strand?"

Amused, Gunnar arched his eyebrows at Brodie. "That's unlike you."

"I suppose seeing you in the hospital has changed me. So, don't let it happen again." She sternly wagged a finger at him.

"I promise," his eyes narrowed, "the next time I am face-to-face with Anders Strand, he will be brought to justice."

The tone of his voice assured Brodie that his words were true.

Chapter Twenty-four

Orchestral Christmas melodies drifted from Brodie's phone. She nervously examined herself in the full-length mirror of her room. Unlike the King's Ball, she had no children to fuss over or to use as a shield from the surveying eyes of vicious scrutiny. These eyes would belong to not only the elite of Sweden, but to the elite minds of the world – Nobel Laureates. Yet the eyes which mattered most to her would be the eyes of her date. Finally, her fairytale would come true: Cinderella attending the ball with her Prince Charming.

A soft tap on the door of the room forced her to tear away from the mirror and her daydreaming. "Who is it?" she called.

"It's me," Gunnar's voice rumbled.

She opened the door and smiled. "You look dashing." He wore a tuxedo rather than his normal suit, and Brodie reached up to straighten his bowtie. "How's your arm? Did it hurt getting the shirt and jacket on?"

A long pause followed her question before Gunnar shook his head. "I'm sorry, what?"

"Are you okay?" she laughed. "I asked about your arm."

"Yeah, it's fine. Jarle helped me," he referred to the king's butler. With a deep exhale, he gingerly moved a loose strand of hair behind her ear. "My God, you are gorgeous."

"You like the dress?" She glanced down at the dark blue chiffon gown. It was strapless, with golden beading and embroidery around the neckline that resembled the seventeenth-century floral designs found in the décor of her room. Pleats of chiffon flowed from her waistline, giving it a subtle ballgown quality. "I thought the blue and gold made it very Swedish."

"It's nearly as breath-taking as you." He reached behind her neck and unclasped the necklace he gave her six months before.

Her hand leapt to hold the charm against her collarbone. "What are you doing?"

"I know you love this necklace, and, trust me, it makes me very happy that you still wear it, but I have something special for tonight." He took a square, flat case from the inside pocket of his tuxedo coat and placed it on her dresser. Away from her view, he slipped her necklace into the case, and then lifted another necklace to reveal to her.

Brodie gasped at the new piece. It was gold with intricate lace work roughly one-inch wide around the whole necklace. The center of the necklace extended further and was coupled with small gemstones to create the illusion of two peacocks resting upon a heart. An upside-down crescent moon sat above the two peacocks.

"Oh Gunnar, it's beautiful. Are the peacocks glass? They're very pretty."

Chuckling, he walked behind Brodie and positioned the necklace around her neck with his good hand. "No, my love, that's not glass. Those are sapphires, emeralds, amethysts, and diamonds."

"What?" she gulped. Her hands shook as she assisted Gunnar in clasping the necklace. "This has to be worth a fortune!"

"I'm certain it is. I should probably get it reappraised for insurance." He kissed the back of her neck. "It's a family heirloom."

She nervously kept her hand over the necklace. "What if something happens to it? What if it falls off?"

"It will be fine. Besides, my mother insisted you wear it for tonight's event." He gestured to the mirror. "See for yourself."

Tentatively, she peered into the mirror. Her jaw dropped at the image before her. A year ago, she was wearing cheap, thrift store clothing and eating Chinese take-out for Christmas. Now she wore a designer-made, one-of-a-kind dress and an heirloom necklace that appeared to belong to royalty. "I feel like a princess," she whispered. "Like when Clara kills the Rat-King and enters the land of the Snow Queen to find herself transformed along with the handsome Nutcracker Prince at her side."

Gunnar took her hand in his. "I'm no prince, and the Rat-King is at large, but for tonight and forever, you are my princess." He kissed her hand, and she felt like crying. "And on that note, can you assist me with the final piece of my outfit?"

"I suppose I could, but you look pretty completed to me."

"If only." He nodded at the flat case. "I need help with everything inside. Not putting them on would offend someone I'm sure." He lifted a chain of gold that held a gold and diamond medal. "His Majesty the King's Medal."

"Geez, Gunnar, aren't these big deals?" She looped the chain around his head.

"Just a fancy way of saying I do my job. I can't – not - wear it to a formal occasion, and that's why I have to wear these too." Several ribbons and medals filled the box.

"There's so many!" she gasped. "I had no idea you were a superstar. What's this one for?" She lifted a random medal from the stack.

"I believe the official claim is 'heroic deeds in Norway'."

"Wow, an international superstar! And this one?"

"Remember my scar from being shot in Helsinki?" he chortled. "These all go in a certain order across my chest and such. Let me arrange them, and I'll tell you about each one." Gunnar sorted the commendations; some bequeathed by royalty of other European nations, and others awarded by the Swedish military and police. After arranging them on the dresser, he guided Brodie to the correct place to pin them. "Maybe I should invent a counterbalance to affix to my back to offset the weight of all these. Makes me feel front heavy."

Her eyes sparkled at the sight of Gunnar wearing his full honors. "You say you're not a prince, but look at you. You may as well be, or a full-fledged king."

"A title I would never want." He smiled and bowed slightly. "M'lady, are you ready to attend the banquet?"

She giggled. "M'lord, I believe I am." Linking arms, the duo descended down the halls of the palace to an awaiting town car. "Imagine, when this palace was built, we would be taking a horse-drawn carriage to the banquet and ball. How romantic."

"I've considered a sleigh for when it snows, but no point in a sleigh for only one. I'm not Santa. I just ski around the property."

"How far does your property go to need a sleigh?" Brodie inquired. She knew the driveway from the highway to his house wound through trees for a mile and a half, but she did not know how much further into the woods his property line extended, save for what they had walked.

"All the way until you reach the national reserve, and then down the highway to where the canal gets close to the road. And that's the property I bought from some businessman with no heirs. All that land around my mother's house is mine in joint ownership with her. And I own some hunting property up north that I inherited from my father."

Brodie stared at him blankly.

"We're an old family," he mumbled. "I'm certain we owned more than that, but I haven't really looked at any records."

"Wait... Gunnar, was your family nobility?" Brodie could only assume that an 'old family' which owned large amounts of land had been nobles.

He offered her a half grin. "Yeah, about that, I should tell you. I did inherit a title from my father. But it's really meaningless like any other title that's not royalty." The car joined the line in front of the Stockholm City Hall.

"What is your title?"

"I'm *Greve av Kuressare*, like a count. At a very formal occasion, they would call me Lord Nyström." He snorted. "Me, a Lord."

They followed the crowd of people into the Blue Hall where cameramen were strategically placed for the live coverage of the event on Swedish television. Gunnar eyed the security detail, attempting to ignore the urge to be in control. "The flowers are lovely," Brodie said in order to distract him.

"They're from Italy," Gunnar responded sadly. "Sanremo. That's how I met Katarina. Her family was in charge of bringing the flowers here."

"I'm... I'm so sorry Gunnar. If I had known," Brodie frowned, "I wouldn't have said anything."

He smiled at her. "Don't worry my dear. You didn't know, and the past is in the past." They rounded the long banquet table in the middle of the hall, politely acknowledging those present. "I'm sorry I couldn't get us two seats at the big table," he joked. "I didn't win a prize, and too many dignitaries this year for us to squeeze in."

She giggled. "That's okay. This is so eloquent; I can't imagine I'm even here. Am I dreaming?"

"You're not dreaming." Gunnar pointed out their seats at a side table. The side tables were equally as elegant as the main dignitary table with white table cloths, floral centerpieces and candlelight, and fine china and silverware. Brodie noted the King's Ball had been a more casual affair with emphasis on hors d'oeuvres and mobile socializing, whereas the Noble Ball emphasized placement and fine, multi-course, dining.

They chatted with those around them before trumpeters heralded the entrance of the royals and the laureates. All in attendance stood in respect for the procession. Queen Jonna, relying heavily on her son and husband, managed to traverse the staircase, much to the approval of all.

Brodie felt Gunnar's arm around her waist, and she smiled in sweet contentment.

"Oh, my – goodness," Brodie breathed to Gunnar. She practically bounced on the tip of her toes while following Gunnar into the Gold Hall where attendees of the banquet already danced to the jazzy sounds of a big band. "That dessert parade, a literal parade of desserts while a choir is singing. Who does that? Do you think they do that at the White House? Is that what the President gets to do all the time? I should have gone into politics."

"I think you would have done poorly in politics," Gunnar laughed. "You're too nice."

"That's true," she laughed. "But oh, that meal; it was so rich. I wanted to stop eating, afraid I was going to rip my dress at the waist. But I couldn't stop eating because I've never had food so delicious. No offense to you. Or to Antonine." She breathed deeply. "I'm glad they have a dance afterward. Burn off that food." She started swaying to the beat. "We should find Roffe and Jonna first though, don't you think?"

"I'm certain there will be a crowd around them, but I could probably break a path through."

At the end of the hall, the royal family was surrounded by dignitaries, celebrities, scientists, and authors. Jonna noted the duo, however, and waved them over. "You look absolutely lovely," she told Brodie. "And a beautiful piece of the House of Nyström's history around your neck." The queen eyed Gunnar with a smile. "Does this mean more celebrations are in store?"

He cleared his throat nervously. *"That remains to be seen,"* he answered in their native tongue. The nervous glance toward Brodie indicated to Jonna to remain silent on the subject.

"It has been some time since I have seen you in full regale," Roffe cheerily proclaimed, patting his friend on his right shoulder. "The look is more becoming than the black-on-black suit, shades, and earpiece. And you, Miss Mayer, look absolutely wonderful." He offered both a quick hug. "I hope, for the night, you have put recent events aside and enjoyed yourselves."

"I know I've enjoyed myself," Gunnar agreed. Brodie's eyes met his, and the sparkle of happiness was unmistakable. "And I believe Brodie doesn't want the night to end."

"You've got that right," she agreed.

The band began playing a new song, and Gunnar took her hand in his. "May I have this dance?"

"Yes sir!" she cheerfully responded.

Her enthusiasm carried through dance after dance. Gunnar began stiffly at first, but each song loosened his movements. They enjoyed laughing and talking with those around them. Brodie twirled about the floor as her one-armed dancing companion led her through a variety of spins. "You dance like a ballerina," he whispered as she returned to his arms.

"Maybe I'm still inspired by that Nutcracker show we attended – you know, before all the things." She smiled and lifted her hands to his neck. Without the use of his left arm to guide her, Gunnar allowed Brodie to do most of the leading. It was hard for him to imagine that she had no dance lessons before this summer because she possessed natural talent.

"I think you're a natural. And I think your mother is smiling down from heaven at her little ballerina at the ball." He kissed her smiling cheek. Thirty minutes and a high-energy rumba later, he paused. "Let's go somewhere to cool down and catch our breath?"

Believing his injuries were catching up to him, Brodie acquiesced and followed him out of the Gold Hall to the balcony overlooking the Blue Hall. Staff bustled about, clearing the banquet tables to prepare the room for tourist arrival. "This is absolutely amazing Gunnar. I was amazed by the King's Ball, but this is just, astounding."

"I'm glad you're enjoying yourself." He leaned against the marble railing. "And I'm glad you're at ease at an event such as this, but equally as content at my home picking strawberries or on the canal in my boat. I'm glad we can go to the ballet together, or to concerts of bands you like. I am glad we can go on hikes on my property or at the reserve. I am glad you love my mother and learn her recipes and how to make jam and that you make your own clothes and plant your vegetables in my garden. I want to take you on trips across Europe, around

301

the world. Those bucket list cities you told me: Paris, London, Rome, and Venice. I want to go with you back to Texas with you and to see your sister. I want to be there when you get your masters and your doctorate. I want to be there for your first book signing and your first lecture on adolescent behavior in the grieving process."

Brodie could feel her stomach tighten during Gunnar's speech. Butterflies slowly erupted.

"And I don't want to do those things as your bodyguard. I want to do those things as your best friend, your other half... your... husband." He dropped to one knee and extracted a ring box from his jacket. "Brodie Helsa Mayer, would you do me the honor, of marrying me and becoming Lady Nyström, *Grevinna av Kuressare?*"

She threw her hand over her mouth to keep from crying out. Did she want to marry Gunnar? Certainly. Now she merely needed to compose her emotions long enough to respond. His thumb opened the ring box. The solitary princess-cut diamond sparkled in the glow emanating from the Gold Hall. The stone was larger than any Brodie had seen in person, and she assumed it was at least two carats.

Before any words could escape her lips, Loke ran forward, calling for Gunnar. Gunnar, in turn, grumbled under his breath while returning to his feet. "I don't care what it is, Loke. Go away."

The young agent stopped short on the staircase, clinging to the rail. "But sir, it's Strand. They've sighted him in the tower."

Gunnar's face contorted in ambivalence. He had just taken an important step in his relationship with Brodie, and did not wish to leave her side. But, it was his duty to catch Strand.

"Go!" Brodie told him.

His eyes widened at her response. "Are you sure?"

"Catch him so we don't live in fear of him anymore."

Understanding her concern, Gunnar closed the ring box and slipped it into his casted arm's sling. "Give me your back-up," he ordered Loke.

The younger agent complied and relinquished his back-up service weapon to his commanding officer.

"I love you Brodie," Gunnar offered her before sending a silent prayer to God that this would not be the final time he would see her. "Get her to safety," he told Loke. "Make sure the team leads the family out and evacuate the guests."

"Yes sir." Loke withdrew his service weapon and placed a guiding hand on Brodie's arm.

Her eyes followed Gunnar who raced down the stairway to the City Hall's Tower Museum. "He's only one-handed, and it's his right arm. Will he have support Loke?"

"There are other agents at the Tower," he assured her. "He'll be fine."

Gunnar stormed through the door of the Tower Museum's lower level. The museum had been closed during the Nobel events, and the lights were off. He felt the hair on the back of his neck prick up; something was very wrong. Where were the other agents? Why were the banquet guests not being evacuated? He wished he had an earwig to ascertain the situation. Gun at the ready, he slid around a statue and listened for any out-of-place nuance. The tower was silent. Strand was not in the Tower Museum.

Had he escaped before Gunnar reached the location? If that was the case, where were the other agents of the security detail? Would they have not been outside in the *Borgargården* patrolling for his whereabouts?

He cracked open the museum's doorway and peered at the empty piazza. Nothing out of the ordinary met his eyes. Everything felt absolutely wrong, and that meant Loke lied about Strand's appearance. He purposely wanted Gunnar away from Brodie.

The realization caused Gunnar to rush into the piazza toward the doors of the Blue Hall. His footsteps echoed against the stone floor of the courtyard. Why did Loke want Brodie? Was this tied to Loke's timid affections for her? Or was this more sinister? Was Loke a mole working for Strand?

A scuffle in his peripheral vision caught his eye. In *Stadshusparken,* the sculpture-adorned park between City Hall and the water, the silhouette of Loke led Brodie to the gap in the fence. A boat with two shadowed figures awaited them at the quasi-dock.

"Brodie!" Gunnar yelled in a deep rumble. He conjured all of his strength to rush out onto the green lawn of the park.

The appearance of Gunnar urged Loke to hurry, and he shoved Brodie into the boat. Her scream spurred Gunnar in his sprint.

"Let her go Loke!" Gunnar called out. He pointed his weapon at the man. Despite using his non-dominant hand, his aim was rocksteady. "Don't make me shoot."

Loke raised his hands cockily. *"Shoot me then,"* he taunted in Swedish.

"What did Brodie do to you?" Gunnar pointed the gun at the ground and shot. Nothing happened. Loke had known that Gunnar would request his back-up service weapon and sabotaged the gun. "Why are you doing this?"

"I know you're distracting me because you've discovered the gun doesn't work." Loke drew his weapon. "Stand down or be put down. Those are your only options." Brodie, afraid at the situation Gunnar faced, screamed again and attempted to strike one of her captors. "Keep her quiet."

Gunnar used the distraction as an opportunity to rush Loke and knock the gun from his hand. Reeling from the hit, the younger agent stumbled back a few steps. He quickly regained composure and sent a barrage of kicks to Gunnar. Due to his injury and inability to use his left arm, Gunnar was forced to jump back. The retreat angered the senior agent who lashed back with a shin kick. The more powerful kick caused Loke to falter, and Gunnar believed he had the advantage in the scuffle.

Hurrying forward to the struggling Brodie, Gunnar was knocked off his feet by a leg sweep from the fallen Loke. The injured combatant landed on his broken arm. The King's Medal hit the stone pavers with a sickening thud. Pain swept through Gunnar's body. Nerves flared, and he found himself unable to move. Loke relentlessly kicked the immobilized man in his stomach and sides. Blood began to trickle from the corner of Gunnar's mouth. His medals worked against him, extra weight that shook and pierced into him with every well-placed kick.

"Stop it! You'll kill him!" Brodie shouted. It took both of the hooded men to hold her in place in the boat. "I'll go with you willingly Loke, if you stop hurting him!"

The bargain caused Loke to end his tirade and return to the boat. He shouted orders to the two other men in Swedish before gently taking Brodie by the arm. Tears filled her eyes. She refused to cry in front of Loke, but fear for Gunnar's life clutched her stomach. He managed to lift his head to meet her eyes. For the first time since she met him, Brodie saw fear in her love's eyes. As the boat sped down the canal, Brodie could see security agents rush to Gunnar's fallen body, and she prayed that they were not too late.

"Brodie," Gunnar called out. He coughed up blood. "Brodie."

The voices of his comrades blurred while calling out his name. Tears stung his eyes and blurred his vision of the retreating boat. When she needed him most, he had failed her. His desire for revenge against Strand blinded him to the treachery in his pupil's heart.

"Nyström! Gunnar!" A member of the security detail knelt next to him, checking his vitals. She called out for an ambulance. "Was it Strand, sir?"

"Loke Ostbërg."

"Loke Ostbërg? But he's…"

"…a traitor." He attempted to sit-up, but the pain rushing through his body caused him to be sluggish.

"Sir… you shouldn't move! Wait for the ambulance!"

"I'm tired of ambulances. Get me everything we have on Loke. Interview, interrogate, everyone who knows him. Friends, the team, family, even the woman who pours his coffee at *fika*. I want his bank statements. I want his *Grundskola* diary. Go!"

The agents around him hurried away to perform their new assignments and escort the family from the Gold Hall. The party was over.

Chapter Twenty-five

The boat docked in Västerås, and Loke used his *Säkerhetspolisen* credentials to avoid suspicion. In a post-terrorist-attack-world, who would question the very men and women meant to protect civilians from terror? Brodie remained silent, now uncertain of Loke's mental stability and the eager bloodlust of his two hired goons. She was certain if any well-intentioned person attempted to help her, their life would be forfeit. Thus, she quietly prayed and bided her time until she could attempt to escape.

Upon arrival at the Västerås Airport, Loke regretted not being able to purchase her more suitable attire to combat the cold and offered her his suit jacket. The cold biting at her skin forced her to oblige. "When we reach Kiruna, I will find us something." He tenderly touched her hair, and she flinched. "I don't want you hurt."

"You don't want me hurt, but you kidnap me?"

"No, no, you misunderstand," Loke rebutted in genuine belief of his noble intentions. "I saved you from Nyström. I liberated you. Bad things happen to those he loves. With me, you'll be safe."

She fought the urge to slap Loke across his face.

"I will make you happier than he has ever made you, Brodie." He helped her into a seat on the private jet reserved for their voyage. "I have powerful allies, and, with their aid, you will be more glamorous, more comfortable, than the queen. You won't have to work for the Royals anymore."

"I like my job."

Her retort caught him off-guard. Loke sat in silence, staring at her for the entirety of the flight.

"Are you okay my friend?" Roffe asked Gunnar. The king stared at his friend who laid on Brodie's bed. "Can I get you anything?"

"Retirement papers."

Roffe shook his head. "You still have many good years ahead of you."

"Do I? Because at the top of my game, I would have noticed the signs pointing to Loke's treachery. I wouldn't have let Strand get away. I wouldn't have let him destroy the cathedral and kill those two people. I'm washed up." He lifted Brodie's necklace, letting the lamplight twinkle off of its silver. "Wanted to marry Brodie and live a quiet life. Now it's all happening again."

"You don't know that." Roffe sat on the edge of the bed. "It is Loke, who has done this for his own twisted-notion of love, not Strand, who does this out of hate."

"How do I know Loke is not working with Strand?" Gunnar slapped a hand to his face. "He was on the task force, and he profiled Strand better than anyone. How could I be so stupid as to not see the connection?" He felt like crying. How could he have failed Brodie in such a way? He had promised her. He had spoken to God countless times about her safety. "My gut told me to keep her at arm's length, to not fall in love. I knew this could happen... that this would happen. But I couldn't control my emotions, could I? No. I kissed her. I loved her like I've never loved before, and now she's gone."

"She's gone, but she's not lost." The king shook his finger at Gunnar. "Blaming yourself will not help you find your love. She needs Gunnar Nyström, the man who doesn't feel sorry for himself or dwell on past regrets, but rather the warrior who will stop at nothing to see his companion safe."

The statement caused Gunnar to remember his story of Einar, the mighty Viking warrior, and Alvilda, his lovely elf companion. He always fancied himself to be like the mighty Viking warriors of old, and yet, his friend's words convicted him. Would Einar crawl into a cave and bemoan the abduction of Alvilda, or would he find the abductor and cause him to pay? The answer was obvious.

Roffe patted his friend's leg. "I came to tell you, the American ambassador has contacted Washington, and their FBI is on the way to help find their abducted citizen." The news was met with a scowl by Gunnar; he knew better than to involve the US embassy. "I shall leave you to your planning."

The royal left the room, and Gunnar turned to the small box and pillow Brodie jokingly used as a bed for her pet rock. "Well Alfred, what would Einar do?" The necklace in his hand made him smile. He sat up and placed the band around his neck. "The better question is, what would Alvilda do? And she would pray for guidance rather than mope around. Then she would tell me that I need to accept the fact that I'm one-armed, not as young as I once was, and going crazy because I'm talking to a rock." Standing to his feet, Gunnar slipped the necklace under his shirt. "Time to hit the shooting range and regain my focus."

As he left the bedroom, he noted the bulletin board hung on the wall. Despite being an ocean away from South Hills, Brodie had kept her prayer wall up for her former students. He noted new additions to the board and leaned in for a closer look. All the members of the royal family were on the board, members of Gunnar's team, including Loke, and even those like Valanice, who had done wrong by her. He inhaled deeply.

If Brodie did not give up on those who could even be considered her enemy, then Gunnar could not give up on her.

He stormed out of the room.

The clerk in the Kiruna sportswear store tallied up the cost of the fur-lined boats and heavy down coat piled on the counter. "You brought me here," Brodie told Loke, emphasizing the word 'brought', "so you can pay the lady." Loke silently, and grudgingly, complied. With the long, warm coat enveloping her, she felt safer from the roaming eyes of her captors.

Despite Loke's mental instability, it was his two hired hands she feared more. One viewed her lustfully, like a piece of flesh he wanted to use to satiate his carnal desires. The other viewed the golden collar around her neck, and there was no way she would allow him to take Gunnar's family heirloom from her.

"Have you ridden a dog sled before?" Loke asked her.

She shook her head. "No." Her eyes drifted to the red wood of the iconic Kiruna Church. It was one of many Swedish sites she and Gunnar had planned on visiting.

"Then today is your lucky day." He barked orders in Swedish to the two men. They hopped on their snowmobiles and sped away, leaving Loke and Brodie alone. "He wanted me to arrive as soon as possible to the base, but dogsled is far more romantic and appropriate for my future bride."

Her eyebrows arched at the words 'future bride'. "Who is he?"

"You will see soon. Come." He took her by the elbow and led her through the snow-covered streets. She hugged her heels tightly to her chest, and the motion gave her a brief moment to smile despite her circumstances. Gunnar was right. She should not have worn the heels; she had been unable to run in them. Shortly, she heard the sound of dogs barking, and the sound turned her nervous smile to a frown. Would this be her last chance to escape?

The snow grew thicker and the wind sharper as the dog sled journeyed further north to Loke's mysterious destination. Brodie narrowed her eyes, wishing to close them against the assaulting flurries, but refusing to be blindly led to any destination with her captor.

"Look there, my bride," Loke stated. He pointed at the night sky, and despite the snowstorm, Brodie could make out the shimmering greens and blues of the northern lights. Her stomach cringed; she wanted to first witness the Aurora Borealis with Gunnar. "I told you the dog sled would be romantic. The lights, the way the snowflakes adorn your hair…" The young man reached out to Brodie's hair that had become loose and wild in the Lapland winds.

Her head instinctually jerked away from him, and the action momentarily unbalanced the sled. Loke quickly adjusted his own weight to keep the sled upright.

"You will learn to love me as I love you," he chided her. "We are nearly there."

Amid the whites and grays of the sky and land, Brodie noted dark beams jutting from the earth. She forced her eyes to open, despite the burning the wind caused. Every detail of the location had to be observed. She needed to find a means of escape, or a way to send a message to Gunnar. Her life depended on it.

The dogs turned into a small alcove, and one of Loke's minions from before took the reins. "He is down below and wants to see you and the girl."

Reality hit Brodie in the stomach. It had to be Strand that Loke worked with. "He is going to kill me Loke. Is that what you want?"

Loke helped her to her feet. "He will not kill you. You are my reward for reporting on Nyström to him."

"He will use me to lure Gunnar out here. And he will kill me like he killed Katarina before. And he will kill you as well Loke. The man is psychotic." She attempted to step away but the cold in her legs caused her to falter. She landed against a stone wall; her hand hit a metal numeric marker that fell in the deep snow next to her. Her eyes landed on the marker, and she resisted crying. Her fate felt as hopeless as the abandoned sign in the snow.

"Psychotic? That is a rather strong word to describe someone you have not met, my dear."

The new voice caused Brodie's eyes to lift from the sign. A man a few inches taller than her walked forward from a tunnel leading down into what appeared to be an abandoned mine. His half-grin and black eyes left no doubt in Brodie's mind: this was Anders Strand, the man who nearly killed her beloved. "I watched a cathedral crumble upon itself with people left inside," she replied flatly. "There is only one word to describe that."

He held his hands up innocently. "I gave your Gunnar Nyström a choice: to respect holy ground or to desecrate it. He made the decision when he pulled the trigger. Or did he tell you that? Did he tell you that he shot at me, unarmed as I was, in a church?"

"Yes." Brodie frowned. "And that he should have aimed for your head. I couldn't agree more."

Anders laughed. The menacing sound made Brodie cringe. "You are bold. Bolder than his last fiancé. You remind me of someone dear to my heart. Come, Loke. Bring her." He turned away, and Loke led a reluctant Brodie after him.

"You had someone dear to your heart?" Brodie asked. She recalled Gunnar's rambling about his encounter with Strand in the cathedral. He had mentioned his lady, yet Gunnar knew of no one. Given their long history, Brodie found it odd that Gunnar knew nothing of Strand's prior romances.

"Are you trying to understand me, Brodie Mayer? Hoping to find a compassionate side to me, something to play off of, thinking you can change my heart from black to gold?" He stopped in front of a larger, rusted drill. "This is not one of your animated princess movies. This is reality. This is fulfilling a promise. Taking a stand for what is right."

"How is killing innocent people 'taking a stand for right'? And what barbaric person makes you promise to kill people?"

In an instant, the back of Anders' hand smacked Brodie's cheek. She stumbled into Loke who wrapped his arms around her. Before he could protest the treatment of his reward, Anders pointed at Brodie. "Annika was not barbaric. Do not speak of things you do not know." He glared at Loke. "Gag your woman's mouth before my hospitality runs thin." The terrorist stormed down a hallway, alone.

Gunnar entered the control room where his team gathered with information on Loke's association with Strand. The results were minimal, judging by the empty whiteboard at the

313

end of the room. Loke had been trained well; Gunnar chided himself for it.

"The FBI agents are here," one of his agents whispered.

He noted the black and white suits in the corner of the room, reviewing a file on the case. With a heavy sigh, Gunnar approached the small team. "Gunnar Nyström. I'm in charge of the Royal Family's protection team."

"Jacob Berg, this is my team." The man indicated the three behind him. "Reginald Hines, profiler; Geri Reynolds, forensic analysis; Robert Krenshaw, our tech guy." Terse handshakes of formality were exchanged. "We read your account of the kidnapping. You are assigned to Brodie Mayer?"

Gunnar nodded, awaiting the forthcoming scrutiny. "Per His Majesty the King's request. She is under the same protection as the royal family."

"And yet... it was our American who was kidnapped."

The Swede nodded knowingly. The scrutiny was to the point. "She was singled out."

"For being American?" the profiler, Hines, asked.

"For being my fiancé."

The matter-of-fact announcement made his team stop working to stare in surprise at Gunnar. It was one thing to read it in his report of the incident; it was another for their boss to announce it aloud. He had been completely silent of his personal life after Katarina.

"Your report states that this... Loke Ostbërg, has been obsessed with our victim for several months now..."

"Yes. She's a beautiful woman, and his puppy-eyed-feelings for her became obsession." Gunnar's voice tensed. "But he's only a tool of the man named Anders Strand."

Gunnar whistled, and a member of his team brought a box full of reports on Strand. "It's obvious he's manipulated Loke's desire for Brodie to kidnap her."

"Your evidence for this?"

He narrowed his eyes before. "Because that's Strand's way. *Motis operandi.* He has done it before." Gunnar said nothing more as he walked to the white board, reading the reports his team had found. Several photos found in Loke's apartment were of Gunnar and Brodie at his house. Sitting on his deck, sailing on his boat, and working in the garden and orchard. The pixilation of the pictures indicated a long-scope camera. "So... this is how Strand knew. Mats, were these all the pictures?"

"Whole box of them." The agent named Mats grabbed a box full of developed pictures and handed them to Gunnar. Everywhere they had gone, Loke had seemed to follow them.

"No wonder he was never there for his detail on Niklas." Gunnar had questioned the boy more about his assigned agent, and Niklas admitted that he was hardly around. The absences were never reported due to the Crown Prince's attempts at freedom. Any other assignment, and Loke would have been noticed missing.

Gunnar again chided himself and wondered if the 'Strand' that Niklas mentioned Loke spoke of on the phone was the agent talking directly to the terrorist. He turned to have one of his tech team search for the phone Loke used. It was most likely a burner phone, or several, that had since been destroyed.

Mats continued, "He also took pictures of different cathedrals, monuments... including the latest."

"Let me see those," the FBI agent Berg called out.

Upon an approving head-nod from Gunnar, the young agent complied.

"Loke was playing errand boy for Anders this whole time," Gunnar stated. "No wonder there was no chatter... that Loke could profile him so easily..."

"Perhaps it is best if my team takes the lead on this," Berg suggested. "You're emotionally attached to the parties involved, it could compromise..."

"No."

"This is an American civilian's life on the line."

"It's my fiancé. Taken by the agent I trained. Taken for the psycho who has tortured me for decades. This is my case. Want to help? Stay out of my way." Gunnar walked to the exit only to be met by his reporting officer, the head of the Department of Security Measures. "Sir," he stopped to acknowledge the man.

"Nyström, we've received a video... you and our American friends will want to watch this." The graveness in the man's voice made Gunnar's stomach tighten. He followed his superior to the table and turned toward the large screen. An image flashed up, and it made him nearly vomit.

Brodie was tied to a chair with a gag around her mouth. She still wore her outfit from the banquet, and Gunnar hoped that meant it had never come off for any nefarious reason. She shivered uncontrollably. Still unadjusted to the cold, coupled with fear – he imagined her body must be in pain simply from the shivering. Streaks in her makeup indicated her tears, and she repeatedly blinked, holding back more. Gunnar could barely watch.

"Klas Gunnar Nyström, *god dag*." Anders Strand appeared in front of the camera, blocking Brodie from view. "I have learned that lovely Miss Mayer here doesn't speak our native

316

tongue, so out of courtesy, I will use her language." He walked over to Brodie and stroked her hair. "Not the smell of orchids… no, I get a bit of strawberry from this one. Something else mixed in with it, but I'm not well-versed in today's fragrances." He lifted her hair to his nose and continued to smell it. "But it is a nice scent. Klas, I don't know if I want to offer to let this one back to you. She might prove fun. It has been some time."

Brodie refused to cry out at the indication. She stared straight ahead at the camera. Blinking, but remaining calm considering the circumstances. Despite the situation, Gunnar swelled in pride at his beloved's resolve.

"Any last words for your lover my dear?" Anders began to untie the gag around her mouth. "You see Klas, despite my statement, I have promised her to dear Loke for his faithful service. I suppose that's one you never would have guessed. You called him, what, your star pupil? A brother to you?" The man offered a repulsive smile to the camera. "Your fiancé, your star pupil, and now this girl. Perhaps you're not as good as you think you are." He took the gag off of Brodie's mouth and knelt beside her. "Come now Miss, tell the man who failed you goodbye before Loke takes you as his bride."

She inhaled deeply, no longer blinking. "Take care of Alfred for me; put him to bed every night." With a breath, she added: "The lights in the sky are like the love in my heart. I'm sorry we couldn't have our wedding at the wood shrine."

"Now, now, enough sentiment." Anders placed the gag around her mouth. "You'll have a lovely wedding with Loke, I'm certain." He walked forward to the camera. His black eyes narrowed, and he whispered: "Should they live to see it. Clock is ticking Nystrom. Same time, different place?"

The video feed ended.

All eyes turned to Gunnar. His strong jawline went ridged as his mind weighed all that had been said. "Send me that video Mats."

"Let our team help Nyström," Berg offered. "We can analyze the video. Maybe something in the background can help."

"Give them whatever they need Mats. I need to rewatch the video." Gunnar left the room as the video began replaying on the screen.

Lights off in his house, Gunnar sat at his home office desk watching the video on repeat. Anders was never clever with his words. He was giving Gunnar the same amount of time to reach him as he did with Katarina. However, this time, no directions on where he was located. That meant Anders planned on killing Loke and Brodie. No games. Only a scheduled execution.

He had to arrive first.

And he felt the key to that arrival was in Brodie's strange words. 'Put Alfred to bed'. Alfred, a pet rock. Why would she mention this? He jotted the phrase on a notepad. Next he put the phrase 'song about the pretty lights'. She quoted lyrics from a song she knew he hated; one of the Princess Snowdew songs about the aurora borealis. Was this what she meant? Was it a clue to her location? She had to be somewhere far enough north to see the lights.

Checking the date, he calculated the latitudes from which the lights could be seen. It could somewhat narrow his search, assuming Strand remained in Sweden. And there was a high probability of that. The man refused to live or work out of anywhere other than his homeland.

Gunnar typed in the coordinates on his computer, and a map colored-in the possible area. Lapland. It was a lot of land to search. Which led to his last clue. 'Wedding at the wooden shrine.' They had never discussed where their wedding would be. They had never discussed a wedding. But Gunnar knew she would be traditional – she would want a wedding in a church. Yet what church was a wooden shrine? He eyed the map on his computer and concentrated on various city names, hoping one would spur a memory or idea.

After some time, the city of Kiruna leapt out at him. He drank a lengthy gulp from his coffee. The iconic Church of Kiruna was one of the largest wooden buildings in Sweden, and was commonly considered 'the Shrine of the Nomads'. He and Brodie planned a trip to see the famous building, and then north to see the northern lights– once she had adjusted to the cold.

On his map, he circled Kiruna. The path to the northwest led through several towns and eventually Abisko National Park, a main tourist attraction this time of year for those wishing to see the northern lights. Gunnar imagined Strand would shy away from areas with high levels of traffic, especially if he did not want to be found. Furthermore, Brodie would not have referenced Kiruna. It had to have been the last settlement she saw before Strand's hideout.

He tapped his pencil over the phrase 'put Alfred to bed'. An exasperated sigh left Gunnar. "What does putting a rock to bed have to do with anything?" he asked aloud. He stood and stretched, hoping the physical activity would help his mental activity. A brisk walk up the stairs to his kitchen for a refill of coffee made him pause. The stone walls of the staircase made him recall Brodie's first venture to his house. "Wait... a rock bed. A quarry." He started typing furiously on search engines available to the *Säkerhetspolisen*. "After the granite boom died, a lot of quarries were abandoned. Some became music venues, others are still having their fate discussed. But those out in the middle of Lapland where there's little population... no one is discussing them." His search brought up several quarries far north of Kiruna. "Still too many."

He put the video on repeat, wondering if there was anything left to indicate where she was. Perhaps the Americans had been able to find additional information with their video analysis. His finger flirted with his cellphone. Should he call Berg?

The thought paused as his mind drifted to happy memories with Brodie: their first kiss; the first night curled up on the couch and watching a movie. It was so innocent in the first week. They were learning about each other. No danger. Only the two of them, in a dark room as he was, sitting in front of his laptop.

Gunnar snapped his fingers. The movie they had watched had an abducted girl in it, and Brodie laid out the plan she would use. She had done it. Giving a message to the captor while on video. And blinking a code. Once more he watched the video, noting her constant blinking. It was rhythmic. He knew she had not learned Morse code, despite her statement during the movie. But a pattern and message certainly existed. Two blinks. A pause. One blink. A pause. Four blinks. A pause. Then the pattern began again. Her code was 2-1-4.

He cross-referenced the number with his other information and found an abandoned quarry numbered 214A9. The only quarry with the numbers '214' that existed north of Kiruna. Gunnar grabbed his service weapon and a bag of equipment and hurried out of his lower-level door.

Another vehicle parked in his driveway made him stop. Despite the heavy gearbag slung over his right shoulder, Gunnar managed to calmly raise his service weapon at the unfamiliar vehicle.

The door of the all-range vehicle slowly opened and Agent Berg stepped out, hands raised. "Nyström, you can lower your weapon."

Gunnar did so slowly, untrusting of anyone after the treachery of Loke. "What are you doing here Berg?"

"I came to let you know we had a lead, and to make sure you did not leave on your own when you heard it." He indicated Gunnar's weapon and gear. "You obviously don't need that lead. You found where Brodie Mayer is located. Did Strand send you another message?"

The Swede edged to his car. "No. Brodie sent me a message when she spoke. What lead did you discover?"

"Our analyst was able to tell a rough location of the video. The lighting indicated reflections of the northern lights coming through open parts of the room's ceiling. Background indicated an abandoned mine..."

"Wrong." Gunnar threw his bag in his backseat. "She's in a quarry. And I know which one."

Berg grabbed a bag out of the backseat of his SUV. "You're not going alone."

"I don't know you. I don't want you."

The two men stood eyeing each other across Gunnar's car. The tension could be cut with a knife. "Ambassador Briggs especially requested me. He considers Brodie Mayer a friend, and wants to make sure America protects its own." The statement caused Gunnar to shake his head. "I'm here to do my job." He pointed at Gunnar's left hand in its cast sleeve. "And you are going to need an extra hand."

Gunnar frowned. The American was right. He was not physically fit to do the job on his own. "Grab your gear and get in. We're going to catch a flight."

"To where?"

"Kiruna."

The abandoned quarry whistled as subarctic winds howled through its neglected machinery. Brodie shivered at the sound. Despite the heavy coat and boots Loke supplied her with, her body had not adjusted to the below-freezing winter climate of Lapland. Her teeth chattered, and the movement only increased the severity of her headache. But as much as she wanted to close her eyes and seek a moment's rest, she could not turn her eyes away from the brooding figure of Anders Strand.

He hunched over a thick text with brittle pages. A pistol sat at his fingertips. Brodie noted that his lips slightly moved as his black eyes scanned the contents of the pages; she wondered if he mouthed incantations. Nothing about her captor surprised her anymore. Her spirit could sense the darkness surrounding him. He had completely allowed his hatred of the royal family, Gunnar, and the Church to consume him, and, in doing so, opened himself up to any path or power who promised him vengeance. She half-expected a goat to be chained somewhere, awaiting its end in a Satanic-sacrifice.

"You're still cold," Loke tenderly whispered as he knelt next to the shivering woman.

Her eyes narrowed. "Naturally I am. It's fifty degrees colder here than the winters I'm used to, and even the winter I enjoyed in Stockholm – in the palace."

The emphasis on the phrase 'in the palace' caused Strand to stop his reading in order to glare at her. "Must be nice in the palace with all those servants to pamper you while they make barely enough to feed their families."

"How little you know," Brodie retorted. "I am one of those servants, and the Royal Family is most gracious with their salaries."

"I am certain they are when you are lying with their beloved Nyström."

She snickered. "Again, you claim things which you know nothing of. I do not *lay* with Gunnar."

Anders grinned, and Brodie suddenly worried she had spoken too haughtily. Perhaps it was best that Anders did not know about her chaste relationship with Gunnar.

"But all that time at his house... and you never...?" Loke asked. His excitement was all too apparent in his question.

Before she could respond, Anders started laughing. His cruel laughter made Brodie cringe, and she turned her face away from the man. "Loke! What fortune for you!" He closed the book shut with a loud thud. "You get a virgin bride!" He strode over to Brodie and knelt beside her. "That is what you are, isn't it? A virgin bride?" When Brodie refused to meet his gaze, he forcefully grabbed her chin and turned her face to his. "Answer me. Are you a virgin bride?"

"Virgin? Yes. Bride?" She paused and glanced at Loke. "Not his."

Hurt flashed across Loke's face, but Brodie did not care.

"Just because you promised Loke a bride, does not mean he will have one. Just as someone promised you vengeance... you will not have it."

Angrily, Anders pushed her back against the stone wall she rested on. Pain shot through her head, but she fought against it. "You know nothing of me," he yelled. "How dare you speak to me as if you do. Don't you realize what you are? You are nothing. You are a nobody." He grabbed his pistol and turned toward her. "You are pretty bait, nothing more."

Loke stepped between Anders and Brodie. "You promised me her... don't..."

The terrorist let out an exasperated sigh. "Nyström called you his star pupil, and yet you don't even see it, do you?"

"Loke," Brodie stated. She was aware of Strand's intention, and, despite her anger at Loke, did not want to see the man killed. "Please, just sit by my side..."

The young man turned to Brodie. His eyes were wide in earnest admiration; finally, Brodie consisted to his presence and wanted an intimate moment with him. Anders and his gun were completely forgotten. "You... want me?"

Anders feigned gagging noises. "Leave, Loke."

"But..."

The barrel of the gun was pressed to Loke's head. "Leave Loke, while you have the chance. Check on my men out front." The man nodded and left. Brodie sat on the ground, alone with Anders. "He used to be smarter, more useful. His infatuation with you made him daft. And showing his hand to Nyström makes him useless as my mole." Anders knelt next to Brodie, running the pistol's barrel over her jawline. The proximity of the weapon made her respond by pulling her head as far back as she could. Anders snickered. "Don't worry about this. The safety is on. For now."

She wanted to divert her eyes away from the horrific blackness of his eyes, but she refused to cower.

The gun traced down from her jaws to her neckline and over her necklace. "What's this?" Her refusal to answer made his face contort into an evil grin. "I bet this is a bit of pretty jewelry from the coffers of House Nyström. Sign of nobility and all things I hate." He reached to take it off but she jerked away. The movement lowered his gun to the top of her dress, and he momentarily forgot the necklace. "You were good bait for Loke. You are good bait for Nyström. I could even use you to award some of my other men. It gets lonely in Lapland." His eyes drifted down as he ran the gun across the top of her dress, pulling the material lower. "But I might personally find use for you before this is over. I have always been attracted to bold women."

Brodie's face contorted in disgust. "I would rather die."

He pressed the gun to her jaw and took the safety off. "I can arrange that."

She refused to cry or panic, and resorted to silently praying. The gun beneath her began to shake. Finally, Anders pulled it away.

With a huff, he walked back to his thick book. "Hard to enjoy a corpse with no face," he muttered.

The implication of his statement made Brodie feel ill. She shifted her body further from Anders and continued to pray.

Far from the location of the quarry, Gunnar and Berg stopped their snowmobiles behind a snow-covered mound of stone. "It should be north of our location," Gunnar told Berg. He pulled a pair of military-grade binoculars from his pack. Despite the whirling snowstorm that brewed around them, the binoculars allowed him to zoom in on the quarry's entrance. Two sentries sat outside. The blurry reds and oranges of their heat signatures paced in bored circles, and one lit a cigarette judging by the burst of heat in front of his face. Neither seemed alert to their duties.

Gunnar passed Berg the binoculars. "Only two out front."

"Anders cannot hear us enter, or Brodie's life is forfeit." Gunnar refused to allow Strand another opportunity to bring him before his love and shoot her before his eyes. He refused to once again allow him to slip away while the authorities entered the hideout. He took a silencer out of his case and began attaching it to his service pistol. "I have a long-range, but I'm not a good enough marksman to take them out in this snowstorm with one hand."

Berg lowered the binoculars. "What model?"

"You a sniper?" Gunnar asked as he pulled out his case.

Berg nodded. "Marine Corps. Three tours."

"Afghanistan?"

"Desert Storm."

The answer satisfied Gunnar and he slid the case to Berg. "Give me time to get closer; be easy to do in this weather. You take them out, meet me inside. I'm going straight to Brodie." The two shared a handshake before Gunnar hurried into the blinding snow. Once he was lost to Berg's regular vision, the FBI agent put on the binoculars and set-up his gun.

Loke sat next to Brodie, stroking her hands gently to keep them warm. "And once we are married, I have a nice cabin in the woods we can move to. I know how much you've enjoyed picking berries, and planting a garden... I can give you all of that. And then, when you're tired of the simple life, I've got a loft in the city we can come back to."

Lack of sleep and food began to catch up with Brodie. She felt light-headed, and she could barely make out all that Loke

326

was saying. She knew what it was about though: their future together. It was all he could talk about. Her auto-response became 'uh huh'. But now she found it took too much of her energy to even offer that.

Her faith began to falter.

Anders walked into the room, checking his watch. "It's time Loke. I now pronounce you husband and wife. Kiss the beautiful bride."

Eagerly, Loke did as he was told. "Your lips are so cold..." he whispered. Before he could finish his statement, a shot rang out from Anders' gun. Loke fell over.

The unexpectedness of the murder shook Brodie out of her state of mind, and she cried out. Loke's blood covered the coat he had purchased for her, and he laid before her in shock from the heavily bleeding wound in his side.

"Let it never be said I do not keep my promises. Loke got his bride."

Brodie rushed to Loke's side, attempting to use the coat to stop his bleeding. "You're a monster."

Anders grinned and waived his hand in a grandiose fashion. "Consider it my wedding present. Nothing brings newly-weds together like a fatal wound. See how you fret over your captor's loss of life?"

"That's because most normal humans react that way when someone has been murdered in front of them. We don't harbor hatred and let it twist us into whatever pathetic creature you've become."

"Pathetic?" Anders grabbed Brodie's hair and pulled her up. "I hold your life, your very existence, in my hands, and you think me pathetic?" He pressed her against the wall, gun at her head. "Tell me I am pathetic again, and you take a bullet to the brain. I do not even care what your corpse will look like."

She locked eyes with him. "We all have to die sometime. You don't control my fate – only God does."

Fuming, Anders pressed the gun harder against her. "If there is a God, he doesn't stop death. He has no power over death or life. If he did, good people would not die."

"Good people die because of bad people like you," Brodie responded.

"When a car wraps around a tree, no one causes that."

"Is that what happened to Annika?" Brodie saying the name caused Anders to stiffen. "She loved Roffe, but he didn't love her. Made you promise to kill him out of revenge because you were smitten with her. She used you, even after her death. You're not going after royalty or nobility because of some higher self-righteousness. You're doing it for a girl who used you like a pawn." Brodie narrowed her eyes to meet Anders' own narrowed eyes. She could tell by his tense jawline she had hit the nail on the head. The clues had added up: between Gunnar's occasional mentioning of the girl that followed he and Rolfe at their boarding school where Anders also attended, and Anders reactions about the same girl. Even as he read his book, he would occasionally mutter her name. "It is like one of my animated princess movies after all."

He shook her head with his grasp of her hair. "You believe yourself to be clever..."

"Let her go, Anders."

Brodie felt her body fill with renewed energy. It was Gunnar's voice.

"You are late Nyström." Any psychological shake that Brodie's assessment had given him faded with the arrival of his nemesis. "Loke has already left the party." Anders turned to face Gunnar, the gun still pointed at Brodie's head. A cruel smile stretched on his lips. "And his bride is about to join him."

"No, I'm not," Brodie seethed. With the moves Gunnar had trained her on over the summer, she smashed Anders hand to the wall. The gun fell, discharging harmlessly into stone.

Anders returned her attack with a slap to the face, knocking Brodie to the ground. Her head hit a snow-covered stone. Before Anders could reach for his gun, Gunnar was upon him. With one-hand, he threw the smaller man across the room, and away from any weapon access. "You okay love?" Gunnar asked Brodie. He knelt next to her, quickly assessing her health.

The reunion was short lived as Anders grabbed a wooden chair and hit Gunnar across the back with it. Gunnar rolled away from Brodie and attempted to retrieve his service weapon that flew to a gap in the wall. He crawled to the fissure only to find that the gun had fallen into the chasm below. It sat stuck on one of the many metal rods that jutted from the quarry's stone walls.

"Your sentiment blinds you," Anders stated. He had retrieved his own gun and walked toward Gunnar. "Checking on the girl before you finish me off. Foolish." He lifted his gun. "I have finally won. You will die by my hand. My promise to Annika will be fulfilled."

"Annika?" Gunnar asked. Confusion flooded his face. "The girl from school that liked Roffe?"

"Roffe?" Anders stepped closer, his gun aimed at Gunnar's forehead. "She never cared about Roffe. It was you. You were all she could talk about, but whose father was it that put her father in jail? Yours. She loved you, yet you betrayed her."

"I never betrayed her. I barely knew her."

"You were always blind. But now your blindness will be your end. You will die. The Royal family will die. We will see the end to all nobility; we will see the end to all those with privilege across the world. And it will all start with your death. You will die. Brodie will be mine... oh yes. I can think of no better use for her. Any last words, Nyström?"

Gunnar's eyes drifted from his gun in the chasm to the man standing above him. "I may be blinded by sentiment, but you are blinded by arrogance."

Perplexity covered Anders face, but he did not receive a chance to question the statement. Gunnar kicked out at Anders' hand, causing the gun to fly out of it. Reaching forward for the weapon, Anders faulted and tripped over Gunnar's other leg. He tumbled to the void below.

Berg rushed forward, service-weapon at the ready, and noted the gruesome scene. "You okay Nyström?" he asked Gunnar, helping him to his feet.

"Better than him." Gunnar did not even offer Strand a second glance, but hurried back to Brodie's side. "Brodie..." he whispered.

"Is it over?" She reached out for him, and he scooped her into his one arm. The side of her head was bruised from hitting the stone, but the packed snow helped prevent a fatal fall.

"It's over."

From his arm, she looked at the sky above the open-aired quarry room. "They are pretty lights, aren't they?"

Berg walked over to the book that Strand had been reading. He slowly turned the pages as the couple spoke.

Gunnar grinned. "The lights in the sky are like the love in my heart." He kissed the top of her head. "You were very clever, my love. You did exactly what you would said you would do."

"We finally got to see the lights. Like we wanted." She shivered in his arm. "Gunnar... yes."

He frowned, trying to understand what she meant. "Yes? Yes to what *sötis*?"

She smiled. "My answer to your question: yes."

Understanding her finally, his face lit up, and he smiled. "I love you Brodie." He bent down and kissed her. "I will always love you."

She smiled and her eyes rolled back in her head. "Brodie, stay with me." He lifted her with Berg's help. "She's in shock, hypothermia, wouldn't be surprised if she has a concussion and God knows what else. Need to get her out of here stat."

"My team is already on their way." Berg took Brodie from Gunnar, giving him the book. "You will need to take a look at this Nyström. It involves you, the king, and I don't believe Strand was alone."

Gunnar frowned and glanced down at the book. "Let's get her to safety first."

The two men headed out of the quarry.

Epilogue

Brodie sat on the floor in front of the Christmas tree in Gunnar's house along with Kjerstin and Mikkel. The three worked on handmade ornaments for the large tree, and Kjerstin insisted on the heavy-use of glitter. Nearby, Jonna sat on Gunnar's couch, happily watching her children in deep, creative thought. In her lap sat the newest member of the Nyström home: an elkhound puppy named Berg. The puppy pulled at the blanket in her lap eager to jump down to the ground and join the children.

"You've really made this a lovely home," Jonna told Brodie. "Last I was here, it was rather austere. Much like the man who built it."

"I heard that," Gunnar's voice boomed from the kitchen where he and Niklas hung garland.

Niklas laughed. "My mother called you austere."

"Keep it up." Gunnar smirked at the young man. "My father put me in charge of your Olympic training, when he's unable to see to it personally."

The prince attempted a mock frown, but acquiesced to a smile. "I couldn't ask for better trainers."

Gunnar returned the smile and ruffled the young man's hair.

"After you and Gunnar get married, are you going to have a baby?" Kjerstin asked Brodie as she held up her glittery ball.

"Kjerstin!" Jonna chided her daughter for the prying question.

The young girl put a hand on her hip. "But mother, that's what married people do."

Brodie, blushing, glanced up at Gunnar who walked into the living room. "I'm not sure Kjerstin…"

"Well," Gunnar smiled, "I have a room upstairs that I was thinking about turning into a nursery since someone wants a big family with lots of pets."

Brodie returned his smile.

"Wouldn't that be fantastic?" Kjerstin shouted. "I could help take care of the babies." She bounded over to her mother to show her the ornament in closer detail. While her mother enjoyed the ornament, Kjerstin covered the puppy in kisses.

Mikkel, not to be outdone by his sister, rushed to Gunnar to show his popsicle-stick snowflake. Brodie, still recovering from her captivity-spawned health issues, slowly stood to her feet. To Jonna's delight, Niklas rushed to her side to help her. "Do you need help Miss Brodie?" he offered.

"You can help me set the table before Gunnar's mother gets here." She walked with Niklas past the tree into the kitchen and dining area. "It's more nerve-racking with her coming, now that she's my future mother-in-law, officially."

The young prince shook his head. "Too much responsibility. I'm never getting married."

She handed Niklas the special Christmas dishware that she and Gunnar chose on her first shopping trip after the days she spent at the hospital. "You have already doomed yourself. We have a saying in America: 'never say never'. Once you do, it's bound to happen."

Before Niklas could respond, the front door received a loud knock, and swung open. "Knock! Knock!" Zavier shouted. "Look at this! A full house!" He assisted Gunnar's mother into the house. "Careful Lady Nyström, this abode looks to be full of royal vagrants."

333

The elder woman chuckled as she hugged her son. "It's been many years since I've seen these royal vagrants." She patted Mikkel on the head. "You were just a baby last I saw you." She looked around at everyone. "And where is my future daughter?"

Brodie stepped forward, blushing at the sentiment. "I'm here."

They shared a hug, and Gunnar smiled at the sight.

"The food is ready!" Roffe called from the kitchen. He had been happy to get away from the palace for a Christmas Eve's meal with his best friend, and even insisted on cooking – a former hobby that he intended on venturing into again. "I must warn you though, it has been some time since I donned an apron. And, Miss Mayer, I have never attempted tofu in my life."

"Oh dear, what have you done to it?" Zavier laughed while poking the tofu with a spoon. "Brodie and I are going to starve now." He helped Roffe bring the food to the table.

"When do you plan on going back to visit your sister?" Jonna asked Brodie as she assisted her to a dining room chair.

"The week after Christmas, and before the New Year. Then Gunnar and I plan on spending New Year's Eve in New York City. I've always wanted to do that."

"You didn't have enough fun already?" Zavier asked her with a smirk.

Brodie sat next to Jonna. "I can't help it. Every day with Gunnar is an adventure." Her statement caused her Swede to wink in return.

"Speaking of the states," Zavier mentioned. "I'm thinking of moving there myself. Start my own restaurant. There's a place for sell in the town you moved here from."

"South Hills?" Brodie asked.

"Right-o. It was a good place to start my search. With that cancer treatment center there, would be a good place to start a vegetarian-friendly restaurant. And you say the town is growing, I might as well prosper with it." Zavier shrugged his shoulders and sat next to Roffe. "Though it may be a step down, rubbing shoulders with royalty to a small business owner in Texas."

"I would not call it a step down," Roffe responded. "Just a step in a different direction."

Gunnar ensured his mother was settled in her chair before taking his own seat. "Maybe you can come with us when we go visit Brodie's sister."

"I believe the word for that is 'imposing'," Zavier joked.

"It wouldn't be imposing at all, Zavier," Brodie smiled. "I want to see this place you're looking to buy in South Hills. My curiosity is peaked."

"Plus, she knows all the hipsters in town. You can have a truly grand opening." Gunnar held up his hands. "Let's bless the food." Everyone joined hands, and Gunnar began to pray:

"Dear Father, thank you for giving us a day where our family can come together. Despite a year of tragedies, You have given us a year of miracles, and we thank You for each and every one of them. Thank You for our health, our safety, and our love. Please bless this food, and bless us in all of our future endeavors. In Your name, we give thanks. Amen."

And the table in agreement concluded: "Amen."

Works Cited

Bjørnson, Bjørnstjerne. "Love Song". The Bjørnstjerne
    Bjørnson Megapack, edited by Wildside Press, LLC,
    2014. p. 2313.

Boye, Karin. "Du är min renaste tröste", 1996. Translated by
    Jenny Nunn in "To a friend", 1997.
    www.karinboye.se/verk/dikter/du-ar-min-renaste-
    trost.shtml.

"Necken, han spelar på böljan den blå" from Ny Visbok af BC,
    1893, which indicates that it sang to an Italian melody.
    Re-published in Visbok, 1923 and Lennart Kjellgren,
    Visor frän farfars tid, LT pocket, 1973. Author
    unknown.
    http://sv.wikisource.org/wiki/Näcken_han_spelar.

Glossary

Älskling – 'darling', indicates love

Bolstomtavägen – the headquarters for the Säkerhetspolisen (SÄPO)

Borgargården – courtyard, in context specifically the courtyard of the City Hall

Chef- boss

Du är min renaste tröst, du är mitt fastaste skydd - you are my purest comfort, you are my steadfast shelter (an excerpt from a Karin Boye poem that begins the same)

Du är så vacker- you are so beautiful

Färgkulla – literal: 'Color Ball', the Swedish name for *Anthemis tinctorial*, commonly known as the yellow chamomile

Fika – literal: 'coffee' or 'to have coffee'; a social gathering centered on drinking coffee

Fikabröd – cakes or pastries eaten with coffee

Filmjölk – literal: 'sour milk'; a popular fermented milk product with consistency of buttermilk and often eaten with breakfast foods such as cereal or muesli

Förlåt mig- forgive me

God dag – good day

God förmiddag – good morning

God morgon – good morning

Grattis på födelsedagen – happy birthday

Gravad lax – dill-cured salmon

Greve – count

Grevinna - countess

Grundskola – elementary school/grade school/grammar school

Gumman – 'old woman', a term of endearment

Gurka - cucumber

Gymnasieskola – senior high school/upper secondary school

Häxa - witch

Hej – hey/hi/hello

Helgeflundra- halibut

Ja/Jah- yes

Jag älskar dig – I love you

Jag är ledsen- I'm sorry

Jag mår dåligt – I feel bad

Kanelbulle – cinnamon bun

Käraste - Dearest

Kroppkakor – potato dumplings

Låt inte gräset gro under fötterna – Don't let the grass grow underneath your feet

Lägg av – Stop it

Lille Prinsen – Little Prince

Min vackraste – My most beautiful

Mina älsklingar – My darlings

Mitt hjärta, mitt liv – My heart, my life

Nötkött - beef

Nej - no

Polisen - police

Polismyndigheten – literal: "The Policy Authority", the official Swedish state authority that oversees the police

Raggmunk- potato pancake

Rosa - pink

Säkerhetspolisen -literal: 'Security Service', the Swedish Security Service; it is a government agency responsible for counter-espionage, counter-terrorism, and the protection of dignitaries

Smörgås - sandwich

Sockerkaka – sponge cake

Sötis – cutie or sweetheart, a term of endearment

Stadshusparken – literal: city hall park; a park that runs between the Stockholm City Hall and adjacent canal

Svenska – Swedish

Tack - thanks

Tomten – sometimes called 'Nisse', they are house gnomes that serve a similar role to Swedish children as Santa Claus does for others

Ursäkta mig- excuse me

Var är toaletten – where is the bathroom

Vikingar - Vikings

Acknowledgements

Thank you to my family, friends, and educators who have prepared me along my journey. Thank you to God who fed me words when there were no words to write, and who inspired pastors to present certain sermons that were needed for my characters to learn from (Bro. Dennis preached the message of Joseph that Gunnar speaks of, and never was a message so much needed for myself and my book). Thank you to my parents who continue to be my biggest support in all of my writing. Thank you to my beta-readers for this book: my mom (who loves the genre), Traci, and Joci. To Alyssa, Brittany, and the rest of my church family who has prayed over me: thank you – your faith keeps me going even when mine has dried up. And to the guy who said from the start of our relationship that he wanted me to fulfill my dreams of being a writer, I love you. Your love helped seal the love I speak of in this book. You sacrificed many evenings together so that I could work on this book, and I am well aware of it.

Finally, to the actual Royal Family of Sweden, who is absolutely nothing like the fictitious Royal Family I have portrayed, you are a truly inspirational family. I learned so much of your family and country during my research, and I have completely fell in love with all of it. Thank you for all that you do for your people and for your international community. *Tack så mycket!*

About the Author

Ashley Maureena is a resident of the 'best US city to live in' Frisco, Texas, where she enjoys the excitement of city life, Friday night lights, and sprawling ranch land all within twenty minutes of home. When not processing paper in a cubicle, she explores her native Texas and caters to her cat's every wish. Ashley holds a degree in History and Education from the University of Texas at Dallas and served in the public-school system and non-profit sector. Please feel free to follow her on social media or drop a line.

www.ingramcontent.com/pod-product-compliance
Lightning Source LLC
Chambersburg PA
CBHW020214260626
47156CB00002B/379